Julia,

The Single Black Mom,

Raising Sons

Sheilah Y. Kimble

Scripture quotations taken from the King James Version Bible, the New King James Version Bible, the NIV Life Application Bible all © 1960, 1962, 1963, 1968, 1971, 1972, 1973, 1975, 1977, 1978, 1984, 1995; New Strong's Concise Concordance & Vine's Concise Dictionary of the Bible © 1997, 1999 by Thomas Nelson, Inc.

Printed in the United States of America.

Table of Contents

Dedication

First of all, I would like to dedicate this book to God for providing me with the vision and dream to write this book. I give Him the honor and glory while also having an attitude of gratitude as He is the part of my life that has given me the strength to persevere. I would also like to thank my pastor as well as the pastors in my family and those pastors who have inspired me over the years to keep my eyes on the prize by trusting in God and keeping the faith.

To my grandparents (may they rest in peace) and parents who molded me to be the strong woman that I am today. To all of the Black mothers, single or married raising children, especially Black males in America, our tasks are difficult but not impossible, because God gives us the strength to persevere as we are survivors. We have survived because we have gone through the storms and battle tests of slavery beginning in 1619, and we will go through the storms of pseudo slavery in the future. This book is also dedicated to my daughter Ardys S. Duncantell, who is a strong young Black woman raising two girls, Zaniyah and Xyeiir who will also grow up to be strong Black women and mothers.

I wish to dedicate this book to my son Marcus D. Perry, and his son Isaiah as well as Isaiah's mom, it is also in dedication to the memory of my late son, Arthur Lee

Duncantell II, and his sons King Arthur and Saint Demetrius Duncantell, to all of my male cousins, nephews, uncles, male friends and all of the males of color in the world who were raised by strong women, especially Black women.

Mother To Son
Langston Hughes

"Well son, I'll tell you;
Life for me ain't been no crystal stair.
It's had tacks in it,
And splinters,
And boards torn up,
And places with no carpet on the floor—
Bare.
But all the time
I'se been a-climbin' on,
And reachin' landin's,
And turnin' corners,
And sometimes goin' in the dark,
Where there ain't been no light.
So boy, don't you turn back.
Don't you set down on the steps
"Cause you finds it's kinder hard.
Don't you fall now—
For I'se sill goin,' honey,
I'se still climbin,'
And life for me ain't been no crystal stair."

Society says that the Black woman smothers her boys, disallowing them to grow up to be men. Society does not realize that as a mother, especially a Black mother, we want to keep our children close and our sons closer because just like that slave mother, we never know when our sons will be torn from our loins and gone forever. Such poems as "The Slave Mother," and "Bury Me In a Free Land," by Frances Ellen Watkins Harper, are just a few reasons why many mothers feel the need to coddle their children throughout life, especially their sons. Death by design is because of the color of our skin which causes the Black male to be doomed before his life begins.

A Death of Innocence That's Labeled Before Birth

Chapter 1

"The real man smiles in trouble, gathers strength from distress, and grows brave by reflection." Thomas Paine

Today, just as the yester-year of 1619 Black males have faced enormous challenges and continue to do so today. Many Black males who are raised by single Black women often experience adversities such as poverty, mental health issues, absent fathers, violence within their communities, and the backlash of their social environment on a daily basis which can be more than stressful. Additionally, the fact that many Black males make risky decisions, they do so based on what they have experienced, and how they relate to the single mothers who are contributors to their stability or instability in their lives.[1] When I hear songs such as "Dear Mama," by Tupac Shakur, and other songs such as it, I often think about some of the experiences that Black males endure,

---

[1] Bowman, S.W. (2011). Multigenerational interaction in Black middle-class wealth and asset decision making. *Journal of Family & Economic Issues, 32*(1), 15-26.

especially those raised by single mothers despite her success or lack thereof. If you listen to the words in Shakur's songs and not just the music, he speaks of some of his life experiences. He speaks about the inner-city crimes and violence, the hardships, racism, relationships, and social issues.

Despite many Black males growing up in poverty, there are those who grow up with confidence and a sense of strong self-worth knowing where they came from, who they are and where they want to be. For those of you in mainstream society who do not know what it is like to be in poverty and then having been catapulted into poverty can create a scary experience. Then there are those of you who would find themselves in desperate situation and even commit suicide because poverty carries an array of physical and mental health concerns. And when I say commit suicide, I do not necessarily mean by their own hands but by the life that they live or by the environment in which they are surrounded.

Then there are those Black males who constantly display a sense of anger, bitterness, and frustration, because they do not know exactly how to express themselves. Their anger and frustrations may not always have been demonstrated outwardly but through their gifts and talents such as the way Tupac and so many others have demonstrated. The reason for their anger and frustration is usually because they are misunderstood by mainstream society and many around them. It is also because of the way they may have been treated.

However, in any case, when you have grown up in poverty and have been granted the opportunity of success, having been in poverty for some can also bring a sense of confidence and gratitude. I will often say, sometimes going from rags to riches can also cause you to be a little humbler, while having an attitude of gratitude.

9

A death of innocence that is labeled before birth is the myth of the Black male and the stereotypical, discriminating, racist, hateful, inhumane, uneducated (about culture), and ignorant stigma that is bestowed upon him. Why is it that the Black male has been metaphorically personified as the negative forces of social constructs in American history? It is the Black male who was told that he possessed animalistic or savaged ways while being treated as equal to or less than an animal; yet, it was he who was enslaved and considered as chattel and a second-class citizen. Why is it that Black males are considered as being the carriers of a contagious disease or terminal illness that is, and always has been festering as part of America's problems as she, America, deals with a deeply rooted hate and jealousy that has lasted more than 400 years?[2]

For the single Black mother, she wants all that God has in store for her to give her sons as well as her daughters. It is a struggle for her to provide for her son and try to raise him to be not only a man but a gentleman in a society that loathes him. Yet, we as mothers must also teach our sons not to give up on their dreams despite what the world may think or say, we must teach them not to procrastinate in achieving their goals, letting them know that with God, nothing is impossible. Remember, the longer your son takes to try to achieve his goals the less of a desire he will have in making those dreams come true and time does not stand still for no one. Oftentimes that is part of the risk taking decisions that he makes as he decides what it is that he wants in life when there is limited to no parental support.

A mother (most, anyway) has a love for her child unlike no other, and because she wants what is best for her son which is to thrive, not just struggle to survive, she

---

[2] Jones, D. Marvin. (2005), "Race, Sex, and Suspicion: The Myth of the Black Male." Greenwood Press; Westport, CT.

must also help him to recognize that there is a cultural difference that her son should be aware of. The uniqueness in the number of households that are led by single Black mothers, does not always identify the characteristics of those single Black mothers who have raised successful Black men to those in mainstream society. It is also something that mainstream society does not want to talk about. Mainstream does not want to speak about those single Black mothers who raise their sons to be successful because it does not depict the negative images of who and what Blacks in society are supposed to be according to their standards.

Black female-headed households are often identified as a woman raising gangbanging thugs who turns out to be drug dealing pimps or convicted criminals, and because of this stereotypical ignorance, it cannot be synonymous with successful Black males who are productive citizens not only in their communities but in society as a whole. Now, ask yourselves, why has such information been obsolete or limited from our current literature? Why has so much information concerning Black cultural history not been introduced to all cultures in mainstream?

Black males are often depicted as negative images through the media which are most often glamorized, demonstrating that Black males have the highest statistical rates as being victims of homicide more than their male counterparts from any other group of males in society. So, does most movies that are shown personifies many Black males as pimps, con men, convicts, and pandering drug dealers who are absentee fathers that indulge in a life of crime? Even though Blacks as a whole have knocked down many of the barriers that have hindered them in the past, they still have many more barriers to knock down and eliminate.

The theme of such scenarios is that there are many Black males who do not want to get stuck on a road that is leading to nowhere becoming an unsuspecting failure. He wants to be able to succeed while living out his American Dream and having a piece of the pie. He has to survive for his future and the future of his future, he must understand that a death of innocence that is labeled before birth is to "set you down in a ghetto in which, in fact, it intended for you to perish."[3] James Baldwin says, "The only way [the White man] can be released from the Negro's tyrannical power over him is to consent, in effect, to become Black himself, to become a part of that suffering and dancing country that he now watches wistfully from the heights of his lonely power and, armed with spiritual traveler's checks, which visits surreptitiously after dark."[4]

It is though many Whites cannot love because they fear what they do not understand, and for those who are included in this category, to be a part of an abject ignorance is "to be judged by those who are not White. Because Blacks are stereotyped to be 'uncivilized,' savages, it is those groups of Whites who have the 'private fears' to be projected onto the Negro.[5]" Baldwin's writings where projected 35 years ago which have proven to be validated even today; fear is the ignorance that promotes racism and the labyrinth of attitudes.[6]

The ignorance of such atrocities are continually perpetuated today as they were during the period of 1619, atrocities that many in mainstream society allows to fall upon

[3] Baldwin, James (1963) "The Fire Next Time." Originally published in hardcover by Dial Press. New York. Published in the United States by Vintage Books.
[4] Baldwin, James (1963) The Fire Next Time: "Down at the Cross," p. 110." Originally published in hardcover by Dial Press. New York. Published in the United States by Vintage Books.
[5] Baldwin, James (1963) "The Fire Next Time, (page 96)." Originally published in hardcover by Dial Press. New York. Published in the United States by Vintage Books.
[6] Baldwin, James (1963) "The Fire Next Time." Originally published in hardcover by Dial Press. New York. Published in the United States by Vintage Books.

deaf ears, which means that the atrocities of oppression, hate, wickedness and evil will never be resolved because there are those Whites who refuses to give up their power and yet will call themselves Christians and display their inappropriate behaviors in the name of God. How, if God made us all in His image? Not everyone is perfect in any race, so why is there a need to feel as though one group is more superior or exalted higher than another? How does one hate another because of the color of their skin having such a bitter taste of hate in their mouths and yet you say that you love God? According to 1st John 4:20, "If a man says, 'I love God, and hates his brother, then he is a liar; for he that does not love his brother whom he sees every day, how can he love God whom he cannot see?"

The Black race has been resilient, so much so that they have withstood the test of time since 1619. There are those who have tried to eradicate an entire race and yet, that race still stands. The definition of resilient is the power or ability to return to the original form, position, etc., after being bent, compressed, or stretched; elasticity. For the single Black mom, she is resilient because she has had to overcome her own adversities. Her resiliency is one that is created through the lens of the author, who has also raised her children as a single Black mother, and which the research for this book has been collected.

Such research has been collected because of the way in which the single Black mother and Black males are viewed, which has a common theme which is deeply rooted in the lives of the single Black mother who have raised successful sons. Her resiliency has given her the ability to be strong, persevere and overcome despite her adversities, yet for the Black male, her son, he continues to survive in a society where he is only tolerated because many classify him as being invisible.

How many of you have read Ralph Ellison's "The Invisible Man," or Richard Wright's "Native Son?" I suggest that you purchase copies of these book and read them regardless of race or ethnicity. I use excerpts from Ralph Ellison's book, "The Invisible Man," because the Invisible Man is a story about a young Black man who is college-educated and struggling to survive and succeed in a society that racially divided. A society who is refusing to see him and those like him as human beings. "I am an invisible man. No, I am not a spook like those who haunt Edgar Allan Poe; nor am I one of your Hollywood-movie ectoplasms. I am a man of substance, of flesh and bone, fiber and liquids. I am invisible, understand, simply because people refuse to see me. Like the bodiless heads you see sometimes in circus sideshows, it is as though I have been surrounded by mirrors of hard, distorting glass. When they approach me, they see only my surroundings, themselves, or figments of their imagination - indeed, everything and anything except me."[7] "In fact, the African American male is a number of things, which are invisible and overinterpreted among them."[8]

Societal attitudes concerning their views about the Black male has not changed much from the time of slavery, to the writings of Ralph Ellison's "The Invisible Man," or even today. "In our society, it is not unusual for a Negro to experience a sensation that he does not exist in the real world at all. He seems rather to exist in the nightmarish fantasy of the White American mind as a phantom that the White mind seeks unceasingly, by means both crude and subtle, to slay." ("An American Dilemma: A Review," *Shadow and Act*"). This was a quote that was from Ralph Ellison's review of a Swedish sociologist by the name of Gunnar Myrdal who wrote a book titled "*An*

---

[7] Ellison, Ralph. (1952) "The Invisible Man" Random House Publishing: New York.
[8] Mercer, Kobena. "The Endangered Species: Danny Isdale and Keith Piper."

American Dilemma" (which explores the roots of prejudice and racism in the U.S.) which anticipates the premise of *Invisible Man*: Racism is a devastating force, possessing the power to render Black Americans virtually invisible. By describing one man's lifelong struggle to establish a sense of identity as a Black man in White America, Ellison illustrates the powerful social and political forces that conspire to keep Black Americans "in their place," denying them the "inalienable right to life, liberty, and the pursuit of happiness" guaranteed to all Americans. (As numerous historians have pointed out, the U.S. Constitution explicitly excludes Black Americans, who, until 1865, were perceived not as men, but as property).[9]

Even though the Invisible Man was set during the pre-Civil Rights Era in the United States, when the segregation laws barred African Americans from enjoying the same human qualities of life as their White counterparts, society must continue to understand that today, it is the same game, just different players.[10] Not much has changed since then. The difference is that this is the year 2018, not 1930 and Black males are still being discriminated against, beat, lynched, and shot down like wild animals in the streets by many in law enforcement as well as those in society, just because of one's deeply rooted hate against another because of the color of one's skin. Richard Wright's "Native Son," was about the urgency for Blacks in America to wake up during the 1940s from its self-induced slumber to the realities of racism. This theme was also set during the pre-Civil Rights era. Why is the African American minority so despised from an unjust perspective? Blacks have been catapulted out of legal clutches of slavery only to be catapulted into the clutches of a pseudo-slavery.

---

[9] Washington, Durthy A. *CliffsNotes on Invisible Man.* 24 Jun 2018 </literature/i/invisible-man/book-summary>.
[10] Ellison, Ralph. (1952) "The Invisible Man" Random House Publishing: New York.

In Richard Wright's "Native Son," Bigger Thomas, is the main character who is falsely accused of raping Mary Dalton, a White woman, and a crime that is actually worse than murder in the minds of many individuals of European decent in mainstream America, a crime that so many Black males have been falsely accused of causing them to lose their lives. Irving Howe summed it up quite well. "The day 'Native Son' appeared, American culture changed forever. It made impossible a repetition of the old lies, (and) brought into the open, as no one ever has before, the hatred, fear and violence that have crippled and may have yet destroyed our culture."[11]

A death of innocence that is labeled before birth is George Junius Stinney Jr. who was a part of that pre-Civil Rights Era, who was one of those Invisible Men and Bigger Thomas's." Stinney Jr. was the extension of fear, violence and hatred that has continued to cripple a culture, a culture that has never made America great. On June 16, 1944, Stinney Jr., was wrongfully convicted of a murder that he did not commit in his home town of Alcolu, South Carolina. During this time period, Blacks were often falsely accused of crimes that they had not committed by an unjust justice system. He is one of the youngest persons in the history of the United States in the 20th-century to be sentenced to death and to be executed, only being 14 years old at the time of his execution.[12]

The jury trial did not last long as all as Stinney was convicted in less than 10 minutes, during a one-day trial, by an all-white jury[13] with the charge of murder in the

[11] Wright, Richard (1998) [1940]. *Native Son.* New York: Original 1940 edition by Harper & Brothers, 1998 version by HarperPerennial.
[12] Banner, Stuart (March 5, 2005). "When Killing a Juvenile Was Routine". The New York Times. Archived from the original on April 12, 2016.
[13] Bever, Lindsey (December 18, 2014). "It took 10 minutes to convict 14-year-old George Stinney Jr. It took 70 years after his execution to exonerate him". Washington Post.

first degree of two White girls, Betty June Binnicker age 11, and Mary Emma Thames, age 7. After his arrest, it is said that Stinney confessed to the murder.[14] Being Black and scared, Stinney, was obviously coerced into confessing to the crime.[15] There was no written record of his confession apart from notes provided by an investigating deputy,[16] and no transcript was recorded of the brief trial. He was denied appeal and executed by electric chair. Since the wrongful conviction and execution of Stinney, there is now a question of his guilt, the validity of his reported confession, and the judicial process that led to his execution which should have been extensively criticized.[17]

In the recent years, there has been a group of lawyers and activists who have investigated the Stinney case on behalf of his family. In 2013 the family petitioned for a new trial. On the 17th of December 2014, Stinney's conviction was posthumously vacated 70 years after his execution, because the circuit court judge ruled that he, Stinney had not been given a fair trial;[18] nor had he been given an effective defense in addition to having his Sixth Amendment rights violated.[19] The judgment noted that while Stinney may in fact have committed the crime, the prosecution and trial were fundamentally flawed.[20] Judge Mullen ruled that his confession was likely coerced and thus

---

[14] "State Prison Protects Negro after Slaying". St. Petersburg Times. INS. March 25, 1944. Retrieved October 18, 2015.
[15] "Youth Admits Killing Girls". The Milwaukee Journal. AP. March 25, 1944. Retrieved October 18, 2015.
[16] McVeigh, Karen (March 22, 2014). "George Stinney was executed at 14. Can his family now clear his name?". The Observer. Archived from the original on March 19, 2016.
[17] Collins, Jeffrey (January 18, 2010). "SC crusaders look to right Jim Crow justice wrongs". Spartanburg Herald-Journal. AP. Archived from the original on May 29, 2016.
[18] Turnage, Jeremy (December 17, 2014). "George Stinney, 14-year-old convicted of '44 murder, exonerated". WIS. Archived from the original on March 3, 2016.
[19] McCloud, Harriet (December 17, 2014). "South Carolina judge tosses conviction of black teen executed in 1944". Reuters. Archived from the original on December 22, 2015.
[20] McVeigh, Karen (March 22, 2014). "George Stinney was executed at 14. Can his family now clear his name?". The Observer. Archived from the original on March 19, 2016.

inadmissible. She also found that the execution of a 14-year-old constituted cruel and unusual punishment."[21]

"The ruling was a rare use of the legal remedy of *coram nobis*. Judge Carmen Mullen ruled that Stinney's confession was likely coerced and thus inadmissible. She also found that the execution of a 14-year-old constituted 'cruel and unusual punishment,' and that his attorney 'failed to call exculpating witnesses or to preserve his right of appeal.'[22] Mullen confined her judgment to the process of the prosecution, noting that Stinney "may well have committed this crime." With reference to the legal process Mullen wrote "No one can justify a 14-year-old child charged, tried, convicted and executed in some 80 days," concluding that "In essence, not much was done for this child when his life lay in the balance."[23]

Then eleven years after the wrongful execution of Stinney, Emmett Till was another part of that pre-Civil Rights Era, who was one of those Invisible Men and Bigger Thomas's." Till was another extension of that fear, violence and hatred that has crippled a culture, a culture that has never made America great. On the 20th of August 1955, Emmett Till, was a 14-year-old, African-American male from Chicago. He left his home for the summer to visit with some of his relatives in Money, Mississippi. This was a tiny cotton gin town which was located on the eastern edge of the Mississippi Delta. His badly mutilated corpse would be returned to his hometown of Chicago in a coffin less than two weeks after his arrival to Mississippi. Till was not a civil rights activist, nor was

---

[21] Barbato, Lauren (December 17, 2014). "The Youngest Person Executed In America, George Stinney Jr., Almost Certainly Wasn't Guilty". *Bustle.com*.
[22] Barbato, Lauren (December 17, 2014). "The Youngest Person Executed In America, George Stinney Jr., Almost Certainly Wasn't Guilty". *Bustle.com*.
[23] McVeigh, Karen (March 22, 2014). "George Stinney was executed at 14. Can his family now clear his name?" *The Observer*. Archived from the original on March 19, 2016.

he politically active, nor had he gone to Mississippi to change the Jim Crow culture; however, the national media focused its attention on the circumstances that surrounded his death, the trial and acquittal of his alleged killers that would have an everlasting impact on our society, even today, which is one that no one could have ever imagined. The Emmett Till case had become one of the key incidents of 1955, the explosive year that launched the modern Civil Rights Movement.[24]

A death of innocence that is labeled before birth are the injustices endured that have been repeated time and time again against Black males with no means to an end by White Americans, those who hatefully commit the crimes, and those who do nothing to stop the crimes such as what was done to Emmett Till and so many other countless Black males, known and unknown.

More than 60 years after the brutal murder of Till, Carolyn Bryant Donham, the woman who accused Till of making an inappropriate pass towards her, recanted her story in 2017 who was then 82 years old. She said that the allegations that she had made against Till were false. In her interview with author and Duke University scholar Timothy B. Tyson in 2007 for his new book, *"The Blood of Emmett Till,"* and according to *Vanity Fair* and the *"Austin American-Statesman"* which was published for the first time, Bryant Donham indicates that she accused Till of physically and verbally harassing her. And according to *Vanity Fair* she said, "That part's not true.[25]"

[24] Crowe, Chris. (2001) "The Lynching of Emmett Till." Phyllis Fogelman Books, Summer 2003.
[25] Kimble, Lindsey. People Crime "Emmett Till's Accuser Recants Part of Her Story — 60 Years After His Beating Death Stoked Civil Rights Movement." people.com/crime/emmett-till-carolyn-bryant-interview (Article written January 27, 2017).

At the age of 82, Bryant Donham also wrote her own memoir, *More Than a Wolf Whistle,* which is kept with Tyson's research materials at the University of North Carolina, according to school officials. But, at Tyson's request, the manuscript will not be available until 2036 or until Donham death.[26] Another innocent Black male accused of a crime that he did not commit, murdered because of a lie and the color of his skin. This sounds like a scene from the movie "Rosewood," a scene that plays consistently in the lives of the Black male and from so many different perspectives.

Then there is the post-Civil Rights Era and that same scene from the movie "Rosewood," that is being played out in American society where Black males such as Abner Louima has fallen victim to the hate that is entrenched in our society, just from a different perspective. Louima born in Haiti later moving to Brooklyn where in 1997 he was viciously kicked and beaten with fists, nightsticks, and handheld radios by officers with the NYPD. Once Louima arrived at the station, the beatings continued as he is cuffed. He was then sexually assaulted by a Brooklyn police officer inside of a bathroom at the station with a broomstick.

Later there was 23-year-old Amadou Diallo, an unarmed immigrant from Guinea who was shot 41 times killed by officers from the New York Police Department because they thought that he was a rape suspect from the previous year.

James Byrd Jr. was an unarmed African-American man who was murdered by three White supremacists, in Jasper, Texas, on June 7, 1998. Shawn Berry, Lawrence

---

[26] Kimble, Lindsey. People Crime "Emmett Till's Accuser Recants Part of Her Story — 60 Years After His Beating Death Stoked Civil Rights Movement." people.com/crime/emmett-till-carolyn-bryant-interview (Article written January 27, 2017).

Russell Brewer, and John King willingly dragged Byrd for three miles behind their pick-up truck along an asphalt road. Byrd, who remained conscious throughout most of his horrific ordeal, was killed when his body hit the edge of a culvert, severing his right arm and head. The murderers drove on for another mile before dumping his torso in front of an African-American cemetery in Jasper. Byrd's lynching-by-dragging gave others the incentive to the passage of a Texas hate crimes law. It later led to the federal Matthew Shepard and James Byrd Jr. Hate Crimes Prevention Act, commonly known as the Matthew Shepard Act, which passed on October 22, 2009, and signed into law on October 28, 2009 by President Barack Obama.

To fast forward, "a death of innocence that is labeled before birth," is another post-Civil Rights Era and that same scene from the movie "Rosewood," that is being played out in American society where Black males are being executed due to hate, jealousy, fear and ignorance. There is Trayvon Martin, an unarmed 17-year-old African American male from Miami Gardens, Florida, who was fatally shot in Sanford, Florida by George Zimmerman, a neighborhood watch volunteer. Martin had gone with his father on a visit to his father's fiancée at her townhouse at The Retreat at Twin Lakes in Sanford. On the evening of February 26, Martin was walking back alone to the fiancée's house after purchasing a bag of Skittles and an Arizona iced tea at a nearby convenience store. The neighborhood had suffered several robberies that year. Zimmerman, a member of the community watch, saw Martin and reported him to the Sanford Police as being suspicious. Moments later, an altercation between the two individuals took place and Zimmerman, a 28-year-old man, fatally shot 17-year-old Martin in the chest.

Michael Brown, an unarmed 18-year-old African American male, was a suspect in the "strong-arm" robbery of a convenience store. Brown was fatally shot by Darren

Wilson, a 28-year-old White police officer in an encounter that took place a short distance away from the convenience store, several minutes after Officer Wilson received a radio alert which included a description of a suspect. Brown was accompanied by his friend Dorian Johnson who was 22. Wilson said that an altercation ensued when Brown attacked Wilson in his police vehicle for control of Wilson's gun until it was fired. Brown and Johnson then fled, with Wilson in pursuit of Brown. Wilson stated that Brown stopped and charged him after a short pursuit. In the entire altercation, Wilson fired a total of twelve bullets, including twice during the struggle in the car; the last was probably the fatal shot. Brown was hit a total of 6 times from the front.

On April 12, 2015 Freddie Gray Jr., an unarmed 25-year-old African American man, was arrested by the Baltimore Police Department for possessing what the police alleged was an illegal knife under Baltimore law. While being transported in a police van, Gray fell into a coma and was taken to a trauma center. Gray died on April 19, 2015; his death was ascribed to injuries to his spinal cord. On April 21, 2015, pending an investigation of the incident, six Baltimore police officers were suspended with pay. Walter Scott, shot on April 4, 2015, in North Charleston, South Carolina, following a daytime traffic stop for a non-functioning brake light. Scott, an unarmed Black man, was fatally shot by Michael Slager, a White North Charleston police officer. Slager was charged with murder after a video surfaced which showed him shooting Scott from behind while Scott was fleeing, and which contradicted his police report. The race difference led many to believe that the shooting was racially motivated, generating a widespread controversy.

On July 6, 2016, Philando Castile, a 32-year-old Black American who was licensed to carry a gun, was shot and killed by Jeronimo Yanez, a St. Anthony,

Minnesota police officer, after being pulled over in Falcon Heights, a suburb of Saint Paul. Castile because he looked like an armed robbery suspect, was in a car with his girlfriend, Diamond Reynolds, and her four-year-old daughter when he was pulled over by Yanez and another officer.

On 18 April 2018, the mutilated bodies of two young African-American men, Alize Ramon Smith and Jarron Keonte Moreland, were found in a pond near Moore, Oklahoma, where they had had been reported missing by relatives a few days earlier. Smith and Moreland were the victims of a "modern lynching" that has gone largely unreported in the mainstream media.

On May 29, 2018, 31-year-old Sherell Lewis, an African American man was hit by a pickup truck and killed while being a Good Samaritan for trying to remove dangerous debris from a roadway in Leesville. It was his birthday, and he was a barber who was well known in the community for his generosity with local youth. His death was devastating. His accused killer, Matthew Martin, an 18-year-old from Hineston, was the driver of the 2003 Chevy truck that hit Lewis, according to the Louisiana State Police. Martin bragged and boasted on social media how he had killed some nigger. Then there are those such as Alton Sterling, Eric Gardner, Terrence Crutcher, Tamir Rice, Keith Scott, Sean Bell, Oscar Grant, Laquan McDonald, and countless others known and unknown which also includes Black females. A death of innocence that is labeled before birth is the racism and discrimination that is thrusted upon our Black males which is more than just a 'Wolfe Whistle,' it is a means to control and oppress what you fear because of your ignorance.

A death of innocence that is labeled before birth is the racism and discrimination within our justice system that has become a pervasive subject demonstrating that there is an overrepresentation of Blacks being arrested more than Whites. In 1999, the UK did a publication called the Macpherson report which reported in February of that year as being a defining moment in British history concerning race relations. The report, done by Sir William Macpherson, was followed by an inquiry into the Metropolitan police's investigation of the murder of a Black teenager named Stephen Lawrence. This investigation concerning Lawrence focused on 'institutional racism' through 'unwitting prejudice' towards minorities which oftentimes causes them to be at a disadvantage contributing to the racial discrimination towards Black people and minorities throughout not only the United States but the United Kingdom as well.[27] Because of institutional racism this has caused serious problems within the criminal justice system, in a variety of ways.[28]

A death of innocence that is labeled before birth is the mainstream media who is like the instigator who stirs up trouble and encourages then glamorizes the negative and destructive behaviors within the Black community perpetuating the cycle of violence. This is something that they dare not disclose concerning similar incidents within a White impoverished community. With the worlds observation of the constant violence within the Black community, such destruction leads to more police brutality which is then aimed towards Blacks, especially the Black male.

Why does mainstream society's criminal justice system heavily and systematically incarcerate our Black males while also policing the bowels of the ghetto? It seems as though the deeply rooted hate that festers within the bowels of the American justice

---

[27] Lea, J. 2003. "The MacPherson Report and the question of institutional racism". *Howard Journal*, 39(3): 219–233.
[28] Lea, J. 2003. "The MacPherson Report and the question of institutional racism". *Howard Journal*, 39(3): 219–233.

system is also entrenched within the bowels of American society. Such entrenchment is the cancerous disease of ignorance that infects our society and always has. Racism against the Black male is something that the Black male has to deal with daily regardless of his status or educational background. And because the Black male has to endure the vile hatred of evils and racial disparities of racism, such experiences can also be deadly. Black males are the targets of social control, violence and societal injustices. Racism against the Black male is not a deviant behavior that is directed against them it is a deviant behavior that has become a normal occurrence. It is the abuse that is being bestowed against the Black male that has become so well rationalized that it is to be invisible and justifiable.[29]

Racism and how others view Blacks also plays a role in a jury's verdict and a judge's sentencing. It is often stated that Blacks commit crimes because they are Black. This is why it is a death innocence that is labeled before birth, and that is because the Black male has already been labeled and discriminated against before he is even born. The invisible Black male and the Bigger Thomas's are continually imprisoned not only in the minds of themselves because of how many in society view them, but because in the minds of a society, they choose not to acknowledge his existence when it is not beneficial for them.

Could it be that the violent behaviors that many Black males possess stem from slavery, and the way that they have been treated down the years in addition to how many of European decent view Black males? If this is the case, then this should be part of the assumption. Once Europeans kidnapped Africans from Africa forcing them into

---

[29] Jones, D. Marvin. (2005), "Race, Sex, and Suspicion: The Myth of the Black Male." Greenwood Press; Westport, CT.

slavery, they began treating Blacks as subhuman savages because of their differences or because of the Europeans refusal to accept the Africans ways of living. So, by treating the African as an animal the African male did only what he knew how and that was to survive, defending himself and those who came from the same country which he had come from regardless of what tribe he was from. All he knew was that the White man was a threat to all who were Black like him. For the Black male, the identification of being a Black male is like being in a cultural prison segregated in isolation from mainstream society. As D. Marvin Jones so noted, "the meaning of being a Black male is that one can never fully cross a line that separates civilization and the savage."[30]

A death of innocence, labeled before birth is the Black male being guilty before he is even born. He has become a victim to a heartless and cruel society even before conception.

Exactly why was slavery created? Was it because Whites were actually the lazy ones using slavery to benefit from and gain wealth off of the backs, of those who bled, sweated and died for the sake of hate and jealousy? Is it because the Black male is so hated that his mere existence reminds the White male of what the Black male can be capable of when he thinks of those such as Nat Turner, David Walker, Denmark Vessy and so many others? Or is it the fear and guilt of how another human being is capable of treating another so inhumane?

Black males are not uncivilized savaged animals, nor are they endangered species, they are human beings with a mind. As stated earlier by Ralph Ellison, "The Black male is an invisible man. No, he is not a spook like those who haunt Edgar Allan

---

[30] Jones, D. Marvin. (2005), "Race, Sex, and Suspicion: The Myth of the Black Male." Greenwood Press; Westport, CT.

Poe; nor is he one of your Hollywood-movie ectoplasms. He is a man of substance, of flesh and bone, fiber and liquids. He is invisible, understand, simply because people such as those who are so imbittered by their own ignorance and hate refuses to see him. Like the bodiless heads that mainstream sees sometimes in circus sideshows, it is as though the Black male has been surrounded by mirrors of hard, distorting glass, trying to figure out the image of who he is and that the White man who hates him so views him by. When they (society) approaches the Black male, they see only his surroundings, or the surroundings that they encase him in, themselves, or figments of their imagination - indeed, everything and anything except the Black male."[31] A death of innocence that is labeled before death can also remind one of the book by Harper Lee, "To Kill A Mockingbird," where the mockingbird is a symbol of innocence, just like those such as Emmett Till and Tamir Rice. Another must read book.

In the story, "To Kill A Mockingbird," Atticus, played by Gregory Peck, who is a well-known and prominent attorney living in the racist town of Maycomb, Alabama during the Great Depression tries to teach his children to view certain aspects of life from a different perspective without being judgmental. In the movie version, Brock G. Peters plays Tom Robinson, a Black man who has been accused of raping a White woman. When Atticus decides to defend Robinson, his children are subjected to abuse by other children because of what they have been taught because of their parent's ignorance, fear and hate. Because of what the Finch children are enduring, their Black cook Calpurnia, takes them with her to the local Black church where the children are

---

[31] Ellison, Ralph. (1952) "The Invisible Man" Random House Publishing: New York.

greeted with warmth, kindness and understanding by a close-knit community that demonstrated how color-blessed they can be.[32]

In a town so full of a deeply rooted hate, jealousy and racism, there is a lynch mob that tries to lynch Robinson the night before the trial but they're unsuccessful. During the trial, the Finch children sit in the "colored only balcony" with the towns Black citizens as Atticus proves that Mayella and her father are not being truthful. Just like the case of Emmett Till, despite the significant evidence proving Robinson's innocence, an all-White jury convicts him. In the case of Till, despite the evidence proving that his accused killers murdered him, an all-White jury acquitted his White accusers. Eventually knowing how inevitable his fate was even though he is innocent, Robinson tries to escape and is shot to death. Jem Finch not only loses faith in the justice system but goes into a depression having a sense of distrust.[33]

The likelihood of any Black male getting a fair trial during the 1930s, before or after was not likely. Harper Lee, a White woman, helped to bring about the awareness that Ralph Ellison and Richard Wright so eloquently displayed. She also made America stare prejudice and injustice in the face as she was one of many who began to wake up to the ignorance of fear and that unknown hate. Just like Jem Finch observing the injustices that were bestowed upon an innocent Black man and losing faith in the justice system, Lee allowed other to understand what Atticus meant when he taught his

---

[32] SparkNotes Editors. (2002). SparkNote on To Kill a Mockingbird. Retrieved June 15, 2018, from http://www.sparknotes.com/lit/mocking/
[33] SparkNotes Editors. (2002). SparkNote on To Kill a Mockingbird. Retrieved June 15, 2018, from http://www.sparknotes.com/lit/mocking/

children to view certain aspects of life from a different perspective without being judgmental.[34]

Because Scout Finch learns firsthand how important it is to understand that many perish because of ignorance, she obtains "some valuable life lessons from her father." She sees that doing the moral thing, may not always be an easy, or popular, or safe thing to do, but it's the right thing to do. She also learns that everybody deserves to be treated with dignity and to receive justice, no matter what their skin color is. Scout embraces her father's advice to practice sympathy and understanding and demonstrates that her experiences with hatred and prejudice will not corrupt her faith in human goodness.[35]

Now even though Harper Lee's book, "To Kill A Mockingbird," was based on fiction, Lee wanted to bring to life the rape trial of Tom Robinson which was at the center of the plot that was actually based on several of real life trials of Black men who were being accused of violent crimes that had taken place during the years before Lee had written her book. For Lee, it is impossible for her to exaggerate her personal account concerning racism. If anything, she has attempted to downplays her account making it seem more subtle, unlike many Black defendants from that particular time period, Robinson was blessed to have obtained a competent defense lawyer who had faith in him and believed in his innocence. Even though Robinson is able to escape

[34] SparkNotes Editors. (2002). SparkNote on To Kill a Mockingbird. Retrieved June 15, 2018, from http://www.sparknotes.com/lit/mocking/
[35] SparkNotes Editors. (2002). SparkNote on To Kill a Mockingbird. Retrieved June 15, 2018, from http://www.sparknotes.com/lit/mocking/

lynching by a mob, he is unable to escape the inevitable which is the deeply rooted hate of racism thus still leading to his death.[36]

There was "one lesser-known trial that was likely a contributing factor to Lee's novel, which was a murder case in which Harper Lee's father, an attorney named A.C. Lee, had participated in. A.C. Lee defended Frank and Brown Ezell, a Black father and son who had been accused of murder.[37] Like so many other Blacks, especially Black males, regardless to whether or not the evidence proves otherwise, there is a great chance that they will be found guilty, as Ezell and his son were, both found guilty and executed by hanging. Because of the outcome of the Ezell case, A.C. Lee never tried another criminal case, which led to the speculation that inspired Lee's novel which was influenced by her father's experience with the racism of the judicial system, which for a person of color is often unjust.[38] Institutional racism has always been an intrigue factor in America which has always been part of America's dark secrets, which are actually not so secret.

The Book *"To Kill a Mockingbird"* is also a reflection of the infamous Scottsboro Boys trial, which is one of the best-known cases of the 1930s. The incidents that lead of to the case happened in 1931, when a group of White teenagers began a fight with several Black teens and boys on a train. When the trained arrived at its destination and both groups were getting off the train, the White teens told the sheriff that they had been attacked. In such an instance, they dare not tell the sheriff that they were the

---

[36] SparkNotes Editors. "SparkNote on To Kill a Mockingbird." SparkNotes LLC. 2002. http://www.sparknotes.com/lit/mocking/ (accessed June 23, 2018).
[37] SparkNotes Editors. "SparkNote on To Kill a Mockingbird." SparkNotes LLC. 2002. http://www.sparknotes.com/lit/mocking/ (accessed June 23, 2018).
[38] SparkNotes Editors. "SparkNote on To Kill a Mockingbird." SparkNotes LLC. 2002. http://www.sparknotes.com/lit/mocking/ (accessed June 23, 2018).

instigators that initiated the fight and obviously lost. With such being said, there were also two White women claiming that they had been raped by these young Black men.

The classic innocent poor and delicate White damsel in distress cries out when things do not go her way. Now because of the supposed assault on the White teens and the alleged rape of two White women, there were a total of nine Black teens who were arrested for the rape. Some of the defendants in this case were as young as twelve years old. This group of defendants became known as the "Scottsboro Boys," for the town in Alabama where the first trial was held.[39]

The initial trials were very expeditious, with as little as a day for each trial. The lawyer defending the teens had not practiced law in many years and was assisted by a real-estate lawyer from Tennessee who was unfamiliar with both the case and Alabama state law. The defense offered no closing arguments and did not address the prosecution's request that the defendants be sentenced to death by the electric chair for their alleged crime. As usual, there was an all-White jury. This jury deliberated the first case, involving two of the defendants, for less than two hours before finding the defendants guilty.[40]

Once the initial trials were completed, the all-White jury found all but one of the defendants guilty, the case was appealed several times. The appeals claimed that the all-White jury was biased. However, because of history consistently repeating itself and having those who are in denial of being hateful racist, and not wanting to be labeled as such, it is a known fact that this all-White jury was anything but biased. In the defense

---

[39] SparkNotes Editors. "SparkNote on To Kill a Mockingbird." SparkNotes LLC. 2002. http://www.sparknotes.com/lit/mocking/ (accessed June 23, 2018).
[40] SparkNotes Editors. "SparkNote on To Kill a Mockingbird." SparkNotes LLC. 2002. http://www.sparknotes.com/lit/mocking/ (accessed June 23, 2018).

of their clients, the Scottsboro Boys, their lawyers were ineffective in proving that the jury was in fact not biased, showing that the boys' sentences were unfair and lost their appeals.[41]

When the new trials were held, one accuser admitted that she had invented the allegations of rape. Again, this is a repeat of history, "Rosewood," Emmett Till, and the countless others. In 1932, the case reached the Alabama Supreme Court, which affirmed seven out of the eight death sentences. After several more appeals the case went before the US Supreme Court, where charges against four of the defendants were dropped. The rest of the defendants either eventually escaped or were released from jail.[42]

One of the defendants who had received the death penalty in the final trial eventually violated his parole and went into hiding. He later wrote a book about his experiences and horrific ordeals after being pardoned by the governor. In 2013, the remaining three defendants whose convictions hadn't been overturned and who hadn't yet been pardoned received posthumous pardons. The Scottsboro case has become a leading example of the injustice of all-White juries, and has been adapted in many books, plays, and movies. Scottsboro is now home to the Scottsboro Boys Museum and Cultural Center.[43]

A death of innocence that is labeled before birth is a demonstration of how many parallels there are between the Scottsboro cases and *To Kill a Mockingbird,* and how there have been so many Black lives that have been destroyed because of hate and

[41] SparkNotes Editors. "SparkNote on To Kill a Mockingbird." SparkNotes LLC. 2002. http://www.sparknotes.com/lit/mocking/ (accessed June 23, 2018).
[42] SparkNotes Editors. "SparkNote on To Kill a Mockingbird." SparkNotes LLC. 2002. http://www.sparknotes.com/lit/mocking/ (accessed June 23, 2018).
[43] SparkNotes Editors. "SparkNote on To Kill a Mockingbird." SparkNotes LLC. 2002. http://www.sparknotes.com/lit/mocking/ (accessed June 23, 2018).

racism. There are the select few that ask why Black lives matter, shouldn't all lives matter? Yes, all lives matter, but why is it that Black lives are so insignificant? As in the Scottsboro case, *"To Kill A Mockingbird,"* it focuses on the concerns and allegations that a White woman can cry rape and how a Black man done so, and even if he is found innocent, in the majority of instances he is, his life is worthless because of the deeply rooted hate that has infested a country that people think is great.[44]

A Black man's crime, the color of his skin. His punishment, death. This is what the Scottsboro Boys faced as they were accused of raping White women, a crime that was punishable by the death penalty in Alabama at the time. Also, as in Scottsboro, one major problem in Tom Robinson's trial is that the jury is racially biased. An all-White jury. Because racism is a learned behavior that is infested by generations of a deeply rooted hate, the jury in "To Kill A Mockingbird," before he can face a fair trial. While the defendants in the Scottsboro case were being held in jail a lynch mob demanded the teens be turned over to them; the sheriff called the Alabama National Guard to protect the jail and moved the teens to a new location. Throughout the twentieth century, black men were frequently lynched on the basis of someone's unfounded accusation, sometimes for violations as small as allegedly winking at or catcalling a white woman. The lynchers usually went unpunished for the murder.[45]

Beginning with the deeply rooted infestation of racism that has manifested itself throughout American history, is something that both Jem and Scout understood after their dad tried teaching them about being judgmental, especially in the south. Because

[44] SparkNotes Editors. "SparkNote on To Kill a Mockingbird." SparkNotes LLC. 2002. http://www.sparknotes.com/lit/mocking/ (accessed June 23, 2018).
[45] SparkNotes Editors. "SparkNote on To Kill a Mockingbird." SparkNotes LLC. 2002. http://www.sparknotes.com/lit/mocking/ (accessed June 23, 2018).

of circumstances that occurs even today, it is of the utmost importance that the single Black mother also teaches her children about Black history as well as cultural history and what has and may occur in her son's life. Black males as well as Blacks as a whole have endured "in the exhausting daily humiliations of terrifying lynch mobs,"[46] whether it was the past types of lynch mobs or modern-day lynch mobs, which is a never-ending story that cannot be stress enough. Lynch mobs for their justice and the injustices of Blacks.

For the single Black mother, not only has she become aware of what her son faces, but she must make sure that her son becomes "aware of both the fragility and the strength of their community"[47] and how the experiences that they face have a commonality as many have had as they too have had to face such evil and wicked atrocities.[48] The single Black mother knows that her son will "endure several of appalling incidents throughout his life that will teach him about the insidious nature of racism."[49]

Just as recent as 40 years ago, there were those White teachers and professors who would explain to the Black and Brown students, especially the Black students and the males that they "are expected to become only athletes or servants."[50] In many cases,

---

[46] SparkNotes Editors. (2002). SparkNote on I Know Why the Caged Bird Sings. Retrieved June 15, 2018, from http://www.sparknotes.com/lit/cagedbird/

[47] SparkNotes Editors. (2002). SparkNote on I Know Why the Caged Bird Sings. Retrieved June 15, 2018, from http://www.sparknotes.com/lit/cagedbird/

[48] SparkNotes Editors. (2002). SparkNote on I Know Why the Caged Bird Sings. Retrieved June 15, 2018, from http://www.sparknotes.com/lit/cagedbird/

[49] SparkNotes Editors. (2002). SparkNote on I Know Why the Caged Bird Sings. Retrieved June 15, 2018, from http://www.sparknotes.com/lit/cagedbird/

[50] SparkNotes Editors. (2002). SparkNote on I Know Why the Caged Bird Sings. Retrieved June 15, 2018, from http://www.sparknotes.com/lit/cagedbird/

the single Black mother "begins to fear for her children's well-being"[51] because now his confidence to excel has been shattered, especially with her sons, not only because of the harsh realities of racism but because of the history that Blacks have endured over the centuries. Let him know about all of those successful Black males who have accomplished many positive endeavors in life.

Black males have made great contributions to society and savor such achievements and accomplishments. Remember, Africa was the first continent to be created and the first to build a university, Timbuktu. African American's have extraordinary and intellectual males such as P.B.S. Pinchback, (Pinckney Benton Stewart Pinchback), raised predominantly by his mother, was the first Black Senator elected to a full six-year term in the U.S. Senate in 1873, by White politicians during a ten-year period known as Black Reconstruction (1867-1877).[52]

His parents, placing great emphasis on education, Supreme Court Justice Thurgood Marshall always cared about his fellow man. When he practiced law in Baltimore, Maryland, he represented many clients without getting paid. Marshall graduated with honors from Howard University Law School. In 1940, he was named chief counsel for the National Association for the Advancement of Colored People (NAACP). During his years with the NAACP, Marshall and his staff won 29 out of 32 Supreme Court cases. His most famous victory came in the 1954 *Brown vs. Board of Education of Topeka, Kansas case*. The historic decision overturned the "separate but equal" doctrine that had justified segregation since 1869.

---

[51] SparkNotes Editors. (2002). SparkNote on I Know Why the Caged Bird Sings. Retrieved June 15, 2018, from http://www.sparknotes.com/lit/cagedbird/

[52] Salley, Columbus. (1993). "The Black 100: A Ranking of the Most Influential African Americans, Past and Present." Carol Publishing Group. Secaucus, N.J.

In 1965, Marshall was appointed solicitor general of the United States. When a vacancy occurred on the Supreme Court, President Lyndon B. Johnson nominated him for the seat. In 1967, this great jurist became the first Black justice of the United States Supreme Court. Marshall had dedicated his life to protecting the rights of all Americans, and even though Marshall came from a two parent middle class household and the descendants of slaves, his mother being an educator herself instilled educational values concerning the importance of the United States Constitution.[53] Marshall once noted, that he "first learned how to debate from his father, who took Marshall and his brother to watch court cases; they would later debate what they had seen. The family also debated current events after dinner. Marshall said that although his father never told him to become a lawyer, he "turned me into one. He did it by teaching me to argue, by challenging my logic on every point, by making me prove every statement I made."[54]

Then there are those such as Dr. James Derham,[55] born a slave and owned by several doctors. Born in 1762,[56] he worked as a nurse which allowed him to save up enough money and purchase his freedom in 1786"[57] and then opening up his own practice in New Orleans.[58] In the electric and revolutionary atmosphere of the 1770s, Blacks discovery two ways to obtain their freedom. They could join the British Army on the one had or, for a while they could join the Continental forces. In the midst of all of

[53] Salley, Columbus. (1993). "The Black 100: A Ranking of the Most Influential African Americans, Past and Present." Carol Publishing Group. Secaucus, N.J.
[54] Ball, Howard (1998). A Defiant Life: Thurgood Marshall & the Persistence of Racism in America. Crown. p. 17. ISBN 0-517-59931-7.
[55] "James Derham". Journal of the National Medical Association. 4 (1): 50.1912. PMC 2621656, PMID 20891259.
[56] "James Durnham, A pioneering Physician and a Skilled Healer". African American Registry. African American Registry. Retrieved 10 May 2018
[57] Charles E. Wynes (July 1979). "Dr. James Durham, Mysterious Eighteenth-Century Black Physician: Man or Myth?" The Pennsylvania Magazine of History and Biography. 103 (No. 3): 325–333.
[58] Morais, Herbert Montfort (1968). The history of the negro in medicine. New York: Publishers Co., under the auspices of The Association for the Study of Negro Life and History. p. 9. Retrieved 10 May 2018.

this, James Derham was just another Black teenage male—a piece of property belonging to a Philadelphia medical practitioner. He was eager and alert, but too young to enlist. When the good doctor was arrested for treason, James was sold to another doctor. As a matter of fact, his next two owners were medics.

By the time George Washington was inaugurated as the first President of the United Stated, young Derham was the country's first Black doctor. And like most of the 3500 medical men at work in the country at the time, he was apprentice-trained. He had learned his art while assisting his owners.[59] In every field of endeavor there are Blacks who overcame the inevitable obstacles. Once trained, however, hostility and prejudice often forced them to develop separate or parallel institutions. Even today, the National Medical Association (NMA) is the Black equivalent of the American Medical Association (AMA). There are the analogous law groups, banker's groups and others that you can rest assured exist—and for good cause.

Dr. Daniel Williams, the Black pioneer in heart surgery, is also responsible for the first nursing school for Black women in America.[60] Dr. Daniel Hale Williams was an African-American general surgeon, who in 1893 performed the first documented, successful pericardium surgery in the United States to repair a wound. He founded Chicago's Provident Hospital, the first non-segregated hospital in the United States, and also founded an associated nursing school for African Americans.[61] Williams mother also became a single mother once his father passed away.

---

[59] Butler, Rufus. (1978). "Black Energy: A Coloring Book for All Ages." Bhang Production; Los Angeles, CA
[60] Butler, Rufus. (1978). "Black Energy: A Coloring Book for All Ages." Bhang Production; Los Angeles, CA
[61] Organ, Claude. *A Century of Black Surgeons, The U.S.A. Experience,* Chapter 8, p. 311 *Daniel Hale Williams, MD*; Transcript Press, Norman OK, 1987 ISBN 0-9617380-0-6

Then there is the first Black filmmaker, Oscar Micheaux who was the quintessential self-made man. Oscar Devereaux Micheaux was an African-American author, film director and independent producer of more than 44 films. Although the short-lived Lincoln Motion Picture Company was the first movie company owned and controlled by Black filmmakers, Micheaux is regarded as the first major African-American feature filmmaker, a prominent producer of race film, and has been described as "the most successful African-American filmmaker of the first half of the 20th century." He produced both silent films and sound films when the industry changed to incorporate speaking actors.[62]

Novelist, film-maker and relentless self-promoter, Micheaux was born on a farm near Murphysboro, Illinois. He worked briefly as a Pullman porter and then in 1904 homesteaded nearly 500 acres of land near the Rosebud Sioux Indian Reservation in South Dakota. Micheaux published novels in Nebraska and New York and made movies in Chicago, Illinois and Los Angeles, California. Micheaux left "autobiographical" records in his first three novels, *The Conquest* (1913), *The Forged Note* (1915) and *The Homesteader* (1917), in which his protagonists play out a young Black man's life in rural, White South Dakota. Micheaux began his career with door-to-door sales of his early writings to neighboring farmers. Encouraged by the modest success from his first novel, Micheaux gave up farming to write six other novels about this period and region.[63]

---

[62] Pearl Bowser and Louise Spence, *Writing Himself Into History: Oscar Micheaux, His Silent Films and His Audiences* (Piscataway, N.J.: Rutgers University Press, 2000); Betty Carol Van Epps-Taylor, *Oscar Micheaux: Dakota Homesteader, Author, Pioneer Film Maker* (Rapid City: Dakota West Books, 1999).
[63] Pearl Bowser and Louise Spence, *Writing Himself Into History: Oscar Micheaux, His Silent Films and His Audiences* (Piscataway, N.J.: Rutgers University Press, 2000); Betty Carol Van Epps-Taylor, *Oscar Micheaux: Dakota Homesteader, Author, Pioneer Film Maker* (Rapid City: Dakota West Books, 1999).

D.W. Griffith's powerful and vitriolically anti-Black movie *The Birth of a Nation* ironically impressed upon Michaeux the ability of a filmmaker to tell a complex, multi-character story every bit as compelling as a novel. Oscar Micheaux soon got the opportunity to test his theory in 1918 when he was contacted by the Black-owned Lincoln Film Company in Nebraska to adapt his third novel, *The Homesteader,* to film. Michaeux rejected the offer and instead moved to Chicago where he made his own movie version of his novel. *The Homesteader* was the first full-length feature film written, produced and directed by an African American. It was also a commercial success when it grossed over $5,000.[64]

Oscar Micheaux's desire to control the production and distribution of his films would be the hallmark of his career. He would persuade the best Black actors of his time to work in forty-four mostly low-budget films he produced between 1919 and 1948 that appealed to the rapidly growing Black urban audiences of the post-World War I period. Most of Micheaux's films were detective stories, quickly written, filmed, edited and released. His African American audiences rarely complained since they were starved to see people on the Silver Screen who looked like they did.[65]

Micheaux on occasion tackled more complex subjects in his films. *Within Our Gates*, his fifth film, specifically attacked the racism portrayed in *The Birth of a Nation*. He also took on controversial subjects in the Black community including interracial romance, skin color hypocrisy and corrupt clergymen. As importantly, his

---

[64] Pearl Bowser and Louise Spence, *Writing Himself Into History: Oscar Micheaux, His Silent Films and His Audiences* (Piscataway, N.J.: Rutgers University Press, 2000); Betty Carol Van Epps-Taylor, *Oscar Micheaux: Dakota Homesteader, Author, Pioneer Film Maker* (Rapid City: Dakota West Books, 1999).
[65] Pearl Bowser and Louise Spence, *Writing Himself Into History: Oscar Micheaux, His Silent Films and His Audiences* (Piscataway, N.J.: Rutgers University Press, 2000); Betty Carol Van Epps-Taylor, *Oscar Micheaux: Dakota Homesteader, Author, Pioneer Film Maker* (Rapid City: Dakota West Books, 1999).

films in the 1920s and 1930s contrasted sharply with the Hollywood image of Blacks as lazy, ignorant and sexually aggressive. Many White critics belittled Micheaux's amateur movie-making skills, yet his audiences devoured his product, making him the most successful Black writer, producer and director in the United States until his death in Charlotte, North Carolina in 1951.[66]

A death of innocence that is labeled before birth says that the Black male is not supposed to succeed, especially if he is the product of a single mother. Because the single Black mother has to endure so much, there is a special love that she has for her child that no other parent outside of her culture could understand. She is a mother that knows the negative encounters that her son may face as he deals with the cruelties of this world by being a Black male.

Each one of the Black males described and even more too numerous to name, encompasses the myth that Black males cannot succeed. These are all Black males who were raised by a Black mother, and often she was single. Her son should understand that he should respect his mother because he himself understands that she struggles to fight and keep her son safe while trying to show him how to survive in the world without a father or a male role model. With this being said, a single mother can raise sons of greatness, especially the single Black mother.

At one point, being a single mother was frowned upon and limited to poor and minorities women. Being a single mother was also synonymous with welfare. However, single motherhood is now becoming the new "norm." "This prevalence is due in part to

---

[66] Pearl Bowser and Louise Spence, *Writing Himself Into History: Oscar Micheaux, His Silent Films and His Audiences* (Piscataway, N.J.: Rutgers University Press, 2000); Betty Carol Van Epps-Taylor, *Oscar Micheaux: Dakota Homesteader, Author, Pioneer Film Maker* (Rapid City: Dakota West Books, 1999).

the growing trend of children born outside marriage — a societal trend that was virtually unheard-of decades ago. Decades ago there were approximately 4 out 10 children who were born to unwed mothers."[67] Nearly two-thirds of those children were born to mothers under the age of 30.[68] Today 1 in 4 children are born to mothers under the age of 18 — a total of about 17.2 million — who are being raised without a father.[69] With all of the single-parent families in the U.S., it is the households with single mothers who make up the majority. According to the 2017 U.S. Census Bureau,[70] out of about 12 million single parent families with children under the age of 18, more than 80% were headed by single mothers.[71]

Societal attitudes are, "if sons are not raised with a male in the home, whether it is a father figure or a male role model then his life is automatically doomed, especially if he is a Black male. There is always that stigma that a single mom raising sons are failures because of the extra baggage that society has to take on. This is a myth that must be dispelled because as you can see, there are several Black males who have become successful, those such as, Jean Baptiste Point du Sable, Norbert Rilleaux, Martin Delany, William H. Carney, Elijah McCoy, George Washington Buckner, George Washington Carver, W.EB. DuBois, Booker T. Washington, Scott Joplin, James Weldon Johnson, W.C. Handy, Arthur W. Mitchell, Oscar Charleston, Oliver Law, Edward Brooke III, and so many others.

---

[67] Lee, Dawn. (2018). Single Mothers Statistics. "*Child Trends, Births to Unmarried Women*" January 10, 2018
[68] CDC, Births: Preliminary Data for 2015, Table 4
[69] U.S. Census Bureau – Table C2. Household Relationship and Living Arrangements of Children Under 18 Years, by Age and Sex: 2016.
[70] U.S. Census Bureau – Table FG10. Family Groups: 2017
[71] Households led by a female householder with no spouse present with own children under 18 years living in the household.

A death of innocence that is labeled before death means that the Black male comes from a broken household. According to the Merriam-Webster dictionary, to be broken means to be violently separated into parts; to be damaged or altered by or as if by breaking; having undergone or been subjected to fracture. Dysfunctional means that something is not working properly; it is marked by impairments or abnormal functioning. Again, societal attitudes are that if single mothers raise sons then they are poor or minority. So, if this is the case, then those males tend to be broken or dysfunctional which means that they come from broken homes or dysfunctional families. So, by coming from broken homes or dysfunctional family then this means that they are being raised where there is no male role model within the household.

According to a Pew Research Center Survey, "nearly half of two-parent households in the U.S. today, have children who are raised by parents who both work full time. Yet most Americans say that children with two parents are better off when one of them stays home to tend to the family."[72] Unfortunately, we do not live in a time such as June Cleaver in "Leave It to Beaver." When speaking about a mother being single, it does not necessarily mean that she is unmarried, her husband could be in the military, she could be separated, divorced, widowed or her husband incarcerated. Psalms 146:9, "The LORD watches over the foreigner and sustains the fatherless and the widow, but he frustrates the ways of the wicked." Psalms 68:5, "A father to the fatherless, a defender of widows, is God in his holy dwelling."

There are many in society who try to dissuade single mothers in living out their dreams and achieving their goals which is some of the adversities that she faces as she

---

[72] Graf, Nikki. (October 10, 2016) "*Most Americans say children are better off with a parent at home.*" Pew Research Center, Survey Conducted June 5-July 7, 2016.

struggles to make it on her own with limited assistance. Proverbs 27:17, "As iron sharpens irons, so one man sharpens another." For every single mother who shares her testimony on how she persevered as a single mother, she reaches and teaches other mothers how she too can persevere and aim for the stars achieving her goals. For me, Christ was the center of my life that helped me to hold it together. Sometimes I know I let my faith waiver, but it was always my elders, whether from church, school, close family friends or family in itself, they encouraged me to never give up or give in but to keep the faith as they helped me to stay on course.

Raising my children as a single mother I often referred to Philippines 3:13-15, "Brethren, I count not myself to have apprehended: but this one thing I do, forgetting those things which are behind, and reaching forth unto those things which are before, I press toward the mark for the prize of the high calling of God in Christ Jesus. Let us therefore, as many as be perfect, be thus minded: and if in anything ye be otherwise minded, God shall reveal even this unto you."

There are so many Black males who have actually ignored the limitations that mainstream society has imposed upon them. There are so many successful Black males who had a dream to achieve greatness, and with that dream, their dream became a vision, and that vision was a part of the aspiration in which they believed in that dream and achieve their greatness, because they refused to allow society to continually be blind towards the Black male and his potential.

Julia, the single Black mother raising her son, regardless to who she actually was, (grandmother, sister, aunt, cousin, or stepmother), did the best that she could to inspire and empower that Black male to be the strong man that he is today. Many single Black mothers want their sons to soar high like eagles. She may not have had a lot to offer, but she offered what little she had to make sure that her son succeeded. The task of raising our sons as single mothers is not easy at all. The single mother who has faith in God has had to reach deep down within her loins and grab a hold to the strength that God has given her as she raises her son.

My eldest son once told me at the age of 18 that he wanted to open up a group home for wayward boys, then he made this little noise with his mouth and winked his eye at me telling me that he was going to start his business before I began mine. I actually laughed and told him that no one would pay him any mind because he was young and a Black male that many would not believe in. Tisk, tisk and shame on me as I was interweaving what society had been teaching our Black males, and that was not to succeed. Then I caught myself and asked him what possessed him to want to start a group home for wayward boys. He said that he realized that what he put me through as a single mother trying to raise Black sons.

Even at a young age, I had unknowingly instilled in him a sense of being successful as a young Black man; he knew the obstacles that he would endure and the challenges that he would face, but he was willing to step out on faith and make it happen. As a single mother, I often lacked the income for my sons or even my daughter to have certain necessities or to be able to participate in certain functions, and even though there was no male figure in the household, my sons had role models such as grandpa and their granddaddy, some of the deacons at the church, coaches and male teachers at the school.

First of all, let me start out by saying that "God created man in His own image, in the image of God, He created him; male and female, He created them. God blessed them..." (Genesis 1;27-28). "God saw everything that He had made, and, behold, and it

44

was very good..." (Genesis 1:31).[73] God's women are not only extraordinary, but they are women that are magnificent and of great significance even if she is a single mother. As the late great Dr. Maya Angelou stated, "she is a Phenomenal Woman." "God chooses ordinary people to do extraordinary things when they honor His will and His way. Dr. Martin Luther King Jr. contended that all cannot be famous because all cannot be well known, but all can be great because all can serve."[74]

Many single Black mothers or any single mother is great because she serves and provide to do the best that she can to raise her child even if her name is never known by the public. I will consistently iterate that Black women have struggled in America since being brought over from Africa on slave ships in 1619. However, because of their struggles, this did not, make them weak. They were women of courage who fought for what they believed in and stood up for what was right, even if it was just her and God and she has to stand alone without man. Many continue to do so today.

There is no woman on this earth that just gives birth to a child, and that includes the mother that is not the biological mother, yet she raises that child. A mother must nurture, protect and cultivate her child as she molds them to be productive in life while also giving that child unconditional love. The Black mother however, has an additional burden bestowed upon her because her children were constantly torn from her loins and inner beings only to be massacred by the harsh evils of life. She not only cries at night for God to guide, protect and direct her child, but she hopes and prays as she consistently constructs a strategy that will assist her in trying to protect her children

---

[73] Scripture quotations taken from the King James Version Bible, the New King James Version Bible, NASB, the NIV Life Application Bible all © 1960, 1962, 1963, 1968, 1971, 1972, 1973, 1975, 1977, 1978, 1984, 1995; New Strong's Concise Concordance & Vine's Concise Dictionary of the Bible © 1997, 1999 by Thomas Nelson, Inc.
[74] Jackson, Jesse L., Sr. (2003). Forward: "Death of Innocence: The Story of the Hate Crime That Changed America." Till-Mobley, Mamie, Benson, Christopher. Published by Random House Publishing Group.

from the hurts, harms and dangers of the world, even if it seems to shield her child from such.

Black women are not only women of courage, but they are women of faith. I was a mother who lost my oldest son, I have aunts, and cousins who have lost their children. I have friends who have lost their children, but for me and many of us, we knew that we could not lash out at a world where many could have cared less about the violent deaths of our child. So, with me, God gave me a platform to be a model for other parents who have lost children, especially their sons.

For me, I never had the opportunity to watch the movie about Emmett Till, because I knew the anger that it would stir up inside of me. But I have collected some of the harsh and inhumane images of what hate could create. Over the years, long before I had children, I would feel the hurt and pain that Mrs. Mamie Till-Mobley felt. It was like I was actually there every time I read something about Emmett. By the time the book, "Death of Innocence: The Story of The Hate Crime That Changed America," was published, it further solidified my empathy for Mrs. Till-Mobley, because I now had sons. All I could think of was the pain that my maternal grandmother endured after losing one of her sons, to the harsh realities of hate, and the injustices of a system that was not designed for people of color or people that were poor.

The Black mother, single or married has always been the foundation of her family and her culture. She had to be the foundation of her family because racism is a strong deeply rooted hate and evil as well as the manipulation of the enemy. The enemy is the one who tries to emotionally break the backs and mindsets of a culture that is already depressed while destroying the peace and harmony that, that culture has already created. I consistently use the images of Emmett Till because his mother, a single Black mother, used her strength and courage to allow the world to see what a deeply rooted hate, that is so embedded within another culture creates for a group of people who did not ask to be hated or treated so cruelly. A death of innocence that is labeled before death is society viewing the Black male as the image of hate and being no more than a side of beef.

Oftentimes, I will sit and hear someone say something that my son once said, or I can be having a conversation with one of my other children and they will mention something to me not realizing that their brother said the same thing years ago, yet they do not know that he said it, nor do I always feel the need to reveal what was said. My son always talked about starting his own business long before he even entered high school having been inspired by his grandfather and an older family friend that he looked up to as his second grandfather. My son would always fuss at me about spending money frivolously which I tried not to do often, but because he was young, I paid him no mind. Now I sit and think, wow, he was right. I watch my youngest son as he too oftentimes repeats much of what his brother used to say, but he does not know that his brother also said the same thing so long ago. He too holds his anger at bay knowing that as a young Black man, railroaded and caught up in the injustices of the justice system, he must suffer in silence as so many of our young men must, if they want to stay alive and survive. They were both a death of innocence that were labeled before death who did not ask for the evils of hate and racism to be bestowed upon them.

A parent who has lost a child is devastating, but a mother, who has carried her child and given birth to that child, or the adopted mother who has nurtured and loved that child will never forget the anguish, the numbness, or the cold still that coursed through her veins when she has lost that child. She will function as she gets through it, but she will never forget because of that bond that she had with her child. A pastor once asked me something shortly after the death of my son. He asked me how was I holding up? I replied that I was functioning. I guess he misinterpreted what I had said because when he brought it up in his sermon that day, he said that I said that I was function-able. I smiled because I was function-able. I smiled because I was getting through it the best way that I could. See, when you lose a loved one, everyone is around consoling you until the homegoing celebration, but once everything is over, everyone goes their separate way and they leave the loved one to suffer and mourn alone.

The reason why I titled this chapter, "A Death of Innocence, That's Labeled Before Birth," is because a Black mother is constantly reminded of the negative images of Emmett Till, those before him and those after him. Long before I had children being in junior high, it was like Emmett was my big brother or perhaps even my father, cousin, uncle or friend. Those negative images constantly rang within my mind reminding me of the horror that I never wanted to happen to my children or anyone else's children. How can one take something as the murder of their child, something that is so evil and make it good?

For the Black mother, she allows her faith to take over. People will ask me how do I tolerate many of the things that I do. Many times, instead of directly answering them, because I know that many will never understand, and because my shoes are not tight on their feet, (meaning that they have not experienced what I have) I will just sit back and smile. Other times I will tell people how God allowed me to take my bitterness and turn it into betterness. This is something that you will hear me say often.

If it were not for God being an intrigue part of my life, I really and truly would not have made it. I, just like so many other Black mothers who have lost a child, I had to reach deep within my being and learn to forgive. Oftentimes, I would read what Dr. King would say about "hate not driving out hate, and how only love can drive out hate." I had to learn how to cry in silence, since I did not cry out loud, releasing the poisons and toxins that were being stored in my body because of the unrecognized or deniable hate, bitterness, despair, anger and anguish that I had harbored for so long. I had to learn how to forgive because as Black mothers, we have to put up with so much. I had to let go and let God. I had to turn a negative into a positive and tell myself that God does not allow things to happen by osmosis. My child was only a loan to me from God, and when God took my baby back, He opened up a door and gave me the platform to give back to others through my writings.

One day, my children were outside playing, and it seemed that something was always happening to my oldest son. On this particular occasion, he had been stung by a bee, but instead of my 2 ½ year old son crying, he brings me the dead bee and said that the bee had hurt him. All I could do was smile and console him as his siblings continued to play. On another occasion, I had to go to the store. I asked one of my neighbors to keep an eye out for my children because I had to walk to the store for groceries. I waited until 8:30 p.m. when my children were asleep. When I came back pushing a shopping cart, I had gotten locked out of the house. I did not know whether my neighbor left, or she had fallen asleep, but I did know that she had my key. I stood in the back of the apartment complex wondering how was I going to get in my home? Had she taken my children with her or what? Why did she not have enough consideration to leave a note on the door, the key under the mat or something?

Well it just so happened that another neighbors brother was visiting and had pulled up and saw me pacing back and forward visibly upset. I couldn't call the police because they would have said that I neglected my children, but I know that I did not because I left them in the care of my neighbor who was 15 years older than I. Well, my neighbors brother noticed that I had left the window of my bedroom slightly opened, and with the boost from a friend of his, he was able to climb on the second floor and get inside to open the window.

Thank God my children were still sleep, now I am really upset because my neighbor had my key and she left my babies alone. As I was putting up the groceries after getting over my initial fear of not knowing whether or not my children were safe or not, I fixed myself a banana split. I then felt something eerily behind me. When I turned around, it was my oldest son Bubba standing behind me smiling, asking me could he have some of my banana split. It had to be at least 11:30 p.m., I was upset that he was awake probably hearing me trying to get in the house, but I couldn't stay upset. We shared my banana split while watching television and fell asleep on the couch.

My neighbor had not returned for a few days. I changed my locks and stopped speaking to her other than to say hello. The point of the story is that my none of my children were born to be hated, abused and misused by a system that hates them because of the color of their skin. Their births, especially the boys, was a death of innocence that labeled them long before they existed. It may not necessary be a death in the natural, but it is a death on trying to eradicate, emasculate, and castrate the Black male in America through the Black mother. The unfortunate and sad part of a death of innocence and our Black males is that there is a problem that exists in America; and it is not difficult to realize that it does exist, the regrettable part is that the problem is generally ignored.

Our past dictates our future and our future dictates our present. During the mid-1800s, a Black mother's concern, single or married, was making sure that the Black males in her life did not get lynched or killed as a result of racism. To get a conceptual understand of how racism and not just southern racism was accounted for, in order to control and oppress those who were thought to be subhuman was, if the head of the household was killed first, whether it be the husband, father, or dominate male figure, most of the oppressor's job was completed. To totally complete their jobs, they also had to kill the oldest male in the family, this way not only would they be able to control the rest of the family with fear, then they knew that the rest of the family would not be any problem.

A death of innocence that is labeled before birth means that the Black male was going to be controlled one way or the other. The stories of lynching's, mutilations, and the inhumane treatments of Blacks were just cautionary tales of those unspoken words that you never forgot. And as Blacks look at what is going on around them today, whether the stories were told to them or not, once they realize the truth, they will find that such tales of realization will never be forgotten. Those stories were reminders and warnings to let you know that you as a Black person had the power over no one or nothing because you were nothing; and being a female or a child did not make you immune or excused from the harsh realities of racism, the fact of the matter was that you were Black and considered as being less than human.

The excruciating ordeals that the Black woman must deal with because of someone else's ignorance and deeply rooted hate, is that those who are the oppressors actually hate themselves and do not even realize it. Since being brought over from Africa, Black people have always been denied, life, liberty and the pursuit of happiness.

51

They have been denied the freedom to move about and the freedom to obtain certain luxuries in life. Today, the denial of life is being Black, for both males and females as they are continually being killed like animals on the street as though someone is going hunting for a sport.

Liberty and the pursuit of happiness for the Black male means that you can get so far just as long as you remember who you are, where you came from and that you are not better that those in mainstream society. The luxuries of life mean that you cannot own a major television network that has been a part of mainstream American for almost 80 years. You have to go out and create your own network and hope that it survives and that it can stay Black owned. It means that you must remember your place and better not stray to far from it. Much of what I am saying is not to sound militant or prejudice, it is to point out the fact that you need to learn cultural history instead of just American history. Even God lets us know in II Timothy 2:15, that we must "Study to show thyself approved unto God, a workman that needeth not to be ashamed, rightly dividing the word of truth." We were always taught to study and find out things for yourself.

So, everything that we as single mothers do, we have to be cognitively aware of what it is that we do because what we do is a reflection of us through our children, no matter what walk of life that we come from. We have to teach our children about the hidden facades that are encased within a system such as institutional racism, which is a subtle reminder that every time there is another Black male incarcerated or killed within our communities it continually becomes a harsh reality that is endured on a daily basis. It is too much energy to consume yourselves with hating and discriminating against someone because of their ignorance and fear. We must learn how to enjoy life, because when it's time to meet our creator, we will find ourselves in a pickle realizing that all of the hate, anger and bitterness that we consumed wasn't all worth it.

Julia, The Single Black Mom Raising her Son

Chapter 2

"Optimism is the faith that leads to achievement. Nothing can be done without hope and confidence." Helen Keller

In the late 1960s, there was a television sitcom called Julia played by actress and singer Diahann Carroll. This show looked at an African American woman, who was a single mother from a non-stereotypical perspective. When you looked at this television sitcom, you saw something different. You saw a single Black mom, raising her young son while also working to better their economic circumstances. For many African Americans of that day it was great to observe a Black person whose roles in the television and film industry depicted a more pleasant side of Black life. Most of the roles of that time were blaxploitation movies that were usually derogative, showing African Americans as servants, and slaves, pimps, prostitutes, drug addicts, poor and criminalistics.

Unfortunately, there were several Blacks who felt that Julia's show and her character was a "depiction of a fatherless Black family and this was not a good depiction of the African American community because mainstream society already viewed them in a negative light." Those Blacks who felt this way was because they had come from a traditional environment that was based on certain morals, values and standards, and Julia's show excluded a Black male lead. Obviously, the show's producer's arguments were that the show was "rendered a safer series which was "less likely to grapple with issues that might upset White viewers."[75]

The television sitcom of Julia stayed on the air for three years, from September 17, 1968 until March 23, 1971. The show was a 30-minute sitcom that aired once a week and was created and written by Hal Kantar. For the African American community this was the beginning of a progress that not only gave hope to the Black community, but Carroll also became the first Black woman to be given a lead role in a sitcom at that time on prime-time television. In Carroll's role, she played as a nurse who worked in Los Angeles and a widowed single Black mother raising her young Black son Corey. Corey did not really know his father as his father, Walter Baker, a USAF pilot, had been shot down in the Vietnam War. In this show, the producers showcased Julia as a beautiful single Black mother.

Today, the television series Julia can be remembered as being a groundbreaking show because the widowed, single Black mother was able to debunk the stereotypical aspects of single Black mothers living in the ghetto, being a lazy, welfare, drug addict prostitute. Her character showed her as being a registered nurse demonstrating that she had the necessary skills and education for the profession. Instead of Julia's character showing her as living in a low- class urban area (or the ghetto) of Los Angles, her

---

[75] Spigel, Lynn; Denise Mann (1992). *Private Screenings: Television and the Female Consumer. Minneapolis, Minnesota: University of Minnesota Press. p. 161. ISBN 0-8166-2052-0.*

character showed her living in a nicer middle-class suburban neighborhood with neighbors who were White. Not all single Black mothers dealt with this type of bitter reality concerning the life and times of the everyday Negro. But she is able to debunk the myth that single Black mothers are a tragedy to society as they blame her for the faults of her community.

In one of the episodes, Julia is being interviewed at a company called Aerospace Industries for a nursing position. Dr. Chegley is the employer who interviews her and is surprised to see that a Black woman like Julia presents herself with respect and confidence. Based on her resume, she is highly educated and has been given some of the highest recommendations from her teachers for the nursing position. Dr. Chegley is not quite sure on whether or not he should hire simply because she is Black. One of the questions that Julia poses to Dr. Chegley was, "Did you expect me to be older or younger?" Astound by the question that she poses to her future employer, she receives the position at the end of the episode because of the education and qualifications that she has which are needed for the position. Situations such as these were not often experienced by Black women in the real world because Black women were often discriminated against because of their skin color, despite having an education and the same qualifications as their White female counterparts.

It was likely, especially during that time and period that many single Black mothers were inspired, motivated and encouraged by this episode because they too wanted to experience the same inspiration that Julia had experienced throughout the series. Julia was a single Black mother who was not on welfare and she had a college education. She was raising six- year old Corey, who was not hanging out in the streets, part of a gang, and who was very smart, curious, and respectful to his mother.

For many in mainstream society, it was much to their dismay that again, a single Black mother could debunk the stereotypes that Julia's character portrayed in her show. Her characters narrative presented two realities: (1) it demonstrated to mainstream society that single Black mothers could be of the middle-class status, and (2) even though the show presented what many felt was unrealistic, it also demonstrated that if one dreams it, then they could achieve it. So, achieving one's goals despite their obstacles is attainable vision of what Julia's world might look like in reality.

Visions such as the one played by the character of Julia basically demonstrated that single Black mothers are more than capable of raising their children despite the obstacles and stereotypes of mainstream society. It may take her a little bit longer than her White counterpart, but it is possible. The single Black mother also teaches her children to do the right thing and make the right choices in life even though there may be times that they stray off course. But then there are those children who grow up in two parent households, who are White children who do not make wise choices for themselves or their futures.

Even though Julia was a single Black mother who lived in a nice middle-class suburban neighborhood with White neighbors, she as well as all single Black mothers trying to ascertain their goals, know that they have to work 200 percent harder than their White counterparts in order to keep stability within their home with their children because of the pressures of financial privation. Like single White mothers, single Black mothers teach their children self-esteem, strong family values, working, respect for their peers and the elderly and racial pride, but racial pride from a historical point of view. In his article, "Restructuring African-American Families In The 1990's" Joseph Hill says

"As they (Black children) get older they are taught racial socialization, unity, support and cooperation among Black people in society and high self-esteem."

In one episode of Julia, Corey is shown cutting oranges so that he can make orange juice for him and his mother. This episode clearly shows that this young man is a very smart and responsible six-year-old. During breakfast Julia tells Corey in a soft tone of voice that he is not to open the door for anyone while she was gone. Showing respect for not only himself but for his mother as well, he says, "Yes ma'am," to his mother. Julia's reply is "Good," "oh I like you mister." In a loving manner, Corey says, "I like me too." With this next statement, Julia is reinforcing the self-esteem, self-worth, and self-love for himself as she says, "That's very important. A man has got to like himself." Corey's reply is, "You know why I like me...cause I like what you like."

Corey is only six years old, yet this conversation not only demonstrates Corey's maturity, but it says a lot about how Julia, the single Black mother is raising her son. Even though Julia's husband has died in the war, she still maintains a successful household as a single parent, especially as a single Black mother. Julia is most definitely confident of her mothering skills, as she makes sure that Corey respects himself while also having a continued respect for his mother.

Like most children who comes from a racist family, they are taught to hate yet Julia does not instill that type of behavior in Corey as he easily makes friends with his neighbor, a White boy named Earl, whom he quickly becomes fast and good friends with. This is also a demonstration that Corey is good with his socialization skills concerning his peers while accepting them with open arms and not being judgmental. In the meanwhile, Corey is receiving good grades in school. So, with Julia's character, she has promoted a sense of hope demonstrating that single-mother hood is not a fixed situation for women, especially the Black woman, and that there is always the possibility of being able to date and get married after having children.

Julia made history in 1968 not only by breaking the colorlines and negative myths and images about single Black mothers, but she influenced the way in which single Black mothers were being portrayed on television in later decades, paving the way for other single Black mothers in reality. The show and Julia's character represented a small, but growing number of single Black mothers who had the ability and the opportunity to access higher education and live comfortable lives such as the character that Julia portrayed in the late 1960's and early 1970's.

Unfortunately, all dreams and fairytales have a happy ending because the actual show was surrounded with controversy. There were those both White and Black, but especially in the African -American community who felt that the show was unrealistic, and that the show's character was a sellout, and that she was playing second fiddle to the White man. Those within the Black community also felt that Julia was not a representation of the majority of Black women. During an interview conducted by Henry Coleman for the Archives of American Television, (March 3rd, 1998) Diahann Carroll asserted: "I'm a Black woman with a White image. I am as close as they can get to having the best of both worlds. The audience can accept me in the same way, and for that reason I don't scare them."

There were many within the Black community that were angry that the show did not put any emphasis on Black culture or focus on her African-American roots; and again, this is why many Blacks in the community felt that the show was a fairy tale because Julia was a minority, a single Black mother who was living a dream by being in a mostly White middle-class world.

There were those liberal White press and young Black militants who referred to Julia's character as being false and distorted. A good example was the episode when Julia speaks to Dr. Chegley on the phone the day before her interview with him at Aerospace Industries. The doctor then tells Julia to be at his office the next morning on time and to look presentable because he was tired of looking at nurses that were ugly. The first stereotype is that nurses are ugly, this is why Julia's character of a Black woman had to be beautiful.

In response to Dr. Chegley's statement, Julia says, "I'll do my best sir." "But has Mr. Colton told you?"

"Told me what?" asks Dr. Chegley.

That "I'm colored," says Julia.

Dr. Chegley then asks Julia, "What color are you?"

"I'm a negro," says Julia.

Dr. Chegley then sarcastically asks Julia, "You've always been a negro or are you just trying to be fashionable?"

Julia then smiles at Dr. Chegley's remark.

"Nine o' clock. Try to be pretty," says Dr. Chegley.

So, in reality, a Black woman such as Julia, must first overcome the racial and stereotypical obstacles of first being Black and then being a woman despite her having an education, and good references. So, despite how well she was educated, her being Black was an obstacle that she had to overcome. Had she been any other Black woman, then she would have not been given the opportunity of being employed at a place like Aerospace Industries because of her race. However, because Julia's character was presented in a white world, Dr. Chegley's character did not demonstrate ignorance and

60

ignored the statement that Julia made about being a negro in addition to validating that she was to see him the next day.

At Carroll's request and just after three seasons, she asked to be released from her contract. She indicated that the controversy from the show had become too intense, and that it almost killed her. She had been hospitalized twice from stress and only weighed 99 pounds. Hal Kanter, the writer and creator of the show, and also a White man, stated during an interview that was conducted by Sam Denoff for the Archives of American Television on the 22nd of May 22nd, 1997, that he had been invited to a NAACP (National Association for the Advancement of Colored People) luncheon along with other writers and producers. The date of this particular luncheon is unknown.

Kanter went on to say that he was inspired by a speech made by a gentleman by the named of Roy Wilkins, who said that he was annoyed with the television industry because they did not have more Blacks that had positive roles. Kanter continued by stating that when he returned home he began writing the pilot script for *Julia*.

The next television show whose character was of a single Black mother was a show called, "That's My Mama," which aired on ABC from September 1974 to December 1975, another 30 minute comedy sitcom. The scene was set in a middle class African American neighborhood located in Washington, D.C. Theresa Merritt was one of the lead characters who played Eloise Curtis. Her deceased husband, Oscar Curtis owned a successful barbershop that he had given to their son, Clifton Curtis played by Clifton Davis, just before he passed away. Her younger child, Tracey who is played by Lynne Moody, is married to a successful accountant and lives with her husband away from home. Clifton lives in the house with Eloise and the barbershop is located next door to the house (a set of double doors separates the barbershop from the living room).

Even though Clifton is in his mid-20's, he has a wild spirit living spontaneously as he enjoys life as a bachelor, however, he also knows that Eloise is mama, the authority figure and what she says goes in her house. She is also the same way with Tracey despite her being married. Although Tracey lives with her husband, when she visits Eloise, her mother still tells her what to do. Clifton and Tracey are both intellectual individuals who first and foremost are respectful to their mother. They show respect for their mother by helping to carry some of her load, such as being helpful around the house. They take her words of wisdom into consideration in every situation that they may encounter. Also, being widowed and a single Black mother, Eloise proves that being an authority figure never stops even when her children have grown into adulthood.

In one of the episodes *"The Witness,"* Tracey has a lecture that she must attend at school. Eloise, being a concerned mother does not want her out alone because of a robbery that took place in the area earlier that morning.

Eloise: "I don't want you going out alone."

Tracey: "I can't miss this class it's my final lecture."

Eloise: "You're not going out alone and that's my final lecture." Clifton then steps in and tries to defend his little sister Tracey.

Clifton: "Mama," "Tracey's a big girl now."

Eloise: "I'm not going out there and I'm even bigger."

Now even though Tracey is married to Leonard, played by Lisle Wilson, a successful businessman, whenever she is visiting at her mother's house, whatever mama said goes, and her mother's rules applies at all times.

In one episode, *"Mama Steps Out,"* Eloise conveys the message that single Black mothers can never be too old to date and enjoy their lives. Just because their spouse

62

may no longer be around does not mean that they have to stop living. In this episode Clifton takes notice of mama getting ready to go out in her best clothes and coming home late. His sister Tracey states that their mother is in love.

Clifton: "What do fifty-year-old people do on a date?"

Tracey: "Probably all they can as quick as they can."

Clifton: "You mean if they can."

Eloise is dating a gentleman by the name of Will Harrington, and of course he too is an older gentleman who has six children. However, the only reason why he is dating Eloise is because he wants someone to marry so that she could help him raise his children. Once Eloise learns that Will only want to marry her to use her so that she can take care of him and his needs as his wife and a stepmother, she kindly not only kicks him out of her house but out of her life as well.

Eloise later mentions to Clifton that she may never get married again. Clifton then asks if she would be giving up men entirely.

Eloise: "Oh no," "I'm still gonna mess around."

Another sitcom that portrayed a single Black mother, as a result of being divorced, was "What's Happening," which aired on ABC from August 5, 1976, to April 28, 1979. Eric Monte was the creator of *Good Times, The Jefferson's, What's Happening and the film Cooley High.* Bud Yorkin was the show's television producer and the man who was behind the sitcoms *All in the Family* and *Sanford and Son* who also presented his newest series, *What's Happening!* This show was geared more toward a teenage audience, and the sitcom was loosely based on the 1975 movie *"Cooley High."* The sitcom was about three best friends who went to high school together and ended up becoming roommates at one point and time while growing up in an area of Los Angeles called Watts. There was the aspiring writer Roger Thomas (Raj), played by Ernest Thomas, then there was the class clown Fredrick/Freddy "Rerun," Stubbs who had gotten his nickname because he kept on having to repeat high school courses that he had flunked, played by Fred Berry, and then there was the painfully shy Dwayne Nelson, played by Haywood Nelson and Raj's bratty little sister Dee who was wise-beyond-her-years, played by Danielle Spencer.

As they navigated their way through school-age life in L.A.'s Watts neighborhood, they also dealt with problems such as girls, bullies, and homework, as they always had a partiality for getting into mischief and trying to find ways of getting rich quick, something that was familiar to any teen. Their stories revolved around them struggling to grow up in a lower-middle class neighborhood while striving to do better in life. Others in the cast included, Raj's divorced mother, Mabel "Mama" Thomas played by Mabel King, a single Black mother who worked as a maid and who had her hands full with working full time while also handling Raj and Dee. Then there was Raj and Dee's dad, Bill Thomas, played by Thalmus Rasulala who was seen occasionally during the first two seasons. Shirley Hemphill played as Shirley Wilson who was the sassy, smart mouth waitress who worked at the local restaurant and the kids' hangout, called Rob's Place.

Mabel King in particular, believed that the show's popularity would offer the perfect opportunity to set some strong examples of Black television characters. She did not like the fact that she was being portrayed as a single Black mother working as a maid. She also felt that the show lacked strong family role models which was so much so on many Black sitcoms, which many Blacks felt was "one of the biggest tragedies on television." Because of her strong opinions and true analogy of such, King departed the show after just one season, because she wanted to see her character evolve.

King envisioned the shows scripts portraying her with a traditional family and achieving success. She at least wanted to be seen as a single Black Mama who was going back to school and perhaps getting a better job to better herself and her children. Unfortunately, the producers and mainstream society were not ready to deal with such an image and it was just not going to be.

In the third and final season, Raj and Rerun graduated high school and eventually move into their own apartment together. By that time, the character of Mama had been dropped and then they began showing Shirley who was now living in the Thomas household filling in for Mama as Dee's guardian. Analytically speaking, there was nothing wrong with King wanting to be a traditional family or being a single Black mother who wanted something more for herself and better for her children, especially her son. The sad and unfortunate part of life is that Black males seem to always be faced with unforeseen obstacles which mainstream seems not to understand or even. We can see this in the play "A Raisin In the Sun." It is as though society purposely sets up minority males, especially Black males for failure by consistently portraying the same negative images of them, especially in mainstream media instead of embellishing the positive of the Black community and their males.

The play, *"A Raisin in the Sun"* written by Loraine Hansberry in 1959 and debuted as a drama film in 1961, begins by portraying a few weeks in the life of the Youngers. The Youngers are an African-American family who are living on the South Side of Chicago which is a lower-class neighborhood, the ghetto, during the 1950s, as they struggle to gain acceptance in a White middle-class society.[76] As the play opens, it tells a story about a poor Black family's struggles, as the family waits to receive an insurance check in the amount of $10,000. This money comes from the late Mr. Walter Younger Sr.'s life insurance policy.[77] Because the family has been economically challenged most of their lives, living from hand to mouth, the family's drama comes into play when each of the adult members in the family has an idea as to how they would like to spend the money.[78] They are counting their chickens before they hatch so to speak.

The matriarch of the family is Mrs. Lena Younger, a 60-year-old mother (played by Claudia McNeil in the film version) whom is called Mama. Mama's dream is to purchase a house that she can call her own which would fulfill a dream that she shared with her husband. Mama's son, Walter Lee Jr., sometimes called "Brother"[79] (played by Sidney Poitier in the film version) unfortunately would rather use the money to blindly invest in a liquor store with his friends. This seems to be a get rich quick scheme or an easier way to make money from Walter Lee's perspective which he feels that by investing the money, this would alleviate some of the burdens of oppression and poverty that the family faces.[80] However, Mama objects to Walter's logic for ethical reasons.[81] After being entrusted by Mama with a large portion of the insurance money, Walter secretly invests it into the liquor store scheme thinking that he will make four times as much as he

[76] James, Rosetta. *CliffsNotes on A Raisin in the Sun.* 10 Jul 2018 </literature/r/a-raisin-in-the-sun/play-summary>.
[77] James, Rosetta. *CliffsNotes on A Raisin in the Sun.* 10 Jul 2018 </literature/r/a-raisin-in-the-sun/play-summary>.
[78] James, Rosetta. *CliffsNotes on A Raisin in the Sun.* 10 Jul 2018 </literature/r/a-raisin-in-the-sun/play-summary>.
[79] James, Rosetta. *CliffsNotes on A Raisin in the Sun.* 10 Jul 2018 </literature/r/a-raisin-in-the-sun/play-summary>.
[80] SparkNotes Editors. "SparkNote on A Raisin in the Sun." SparkNotes LLC. 2002.
http://www.sparknotes.com/lit/raisin/ (accessed July 7, 2018).
[81] James, Rosetta. *CliffsNotes on A Raisin in the Sun.* 10 Jul 2018 </literature/r/a-raisin-in-the-sun/play-summary>.

invested, only to be ripped off by one of his so called friends which tests the spiritual and psychological determination of the family's faith to move forward.[82]

Walter's wife, Ruth, approximately 30, (played by Ruby Dee in the film version) has a close relationship with her mother-in-law and is close with the family.[83] Ruth would be compared to a modern-day Ruth from the Bible. Ruth has more of a laid back and kind personality, she is a woman who "is not aggressive and she just lets life 'happen' to her, however, she is a 'worn-out wife' with a tedious, routine lifestyle."[84] Lacking education and sophistication, Ruth still exhibits remarkable strength, even though at times she may be annoyed with Mama's meddling in her and her husband's business, yet, she does allow her mother-in-law to motivate and influence her.[85]

Finally, Beneatha, (played by Diana Sands in the film version) is Walter's younger sister and Mama's daughter. Because Beneatha is the most educated individual in the Younger family, the rest of the family feels that she can sometimes be obnoxious and self-centered; especially in the earlier scenes, as she freely verbalizes her views in a household that has difficulty understanding her perspectives.[86]

Beneatha wants to use the money so that she can go to medical school. She also wishes that her family members were not so interested in joining the White world, or what I would call matriculating into mainstream society as she wishes them to stay closely connected to their culture as much as possible. Instead, it is Beneatha who is actually trying to find her identity by looking back to the past and to Africa.[87]

---

[82] James, Rosetta. *CliffsNotes on A Raisin in the Sun.* 10 Jul 2018 </literature/r/a-raisin-in-the-sun/play-summary>.
[83] James, Rosetta. *CliffsNotes on A Raisin in the Sun.* 10 Jul 2018 </literature/r/a-raisin-in-the-sun/play-summary>.
[84] James, Rosetta. *CliffsNotes on A Raisin in the Sun.* 10 Jul 2018 </literature/r/a-raisin-in-the-sun/play-summary>.
[85] James, Rosetta. *CliffsNotes on A Raisin in the Sun.* 10 Jul 2018 </literature/r/a-raisin-in-the-sun/play-summary>.
[86] James, Rosetta. *CliffsNotes on A Raisin in the Sun.* 10 Jul 2018 </literature/r/a-raisin-in-the-sun/play-summary>.
[87] SparkNotes Editors. "SparkNote on A Raisin in the Sun." SparkNotes LLC. 2002. http://www.sparknotes.com/lit/raisin/ (accessed July 7, 2018).

As Walter and Beneatha is having a difference of opinion, Mama eventually comes home and announces that she has put a down payment on a house with some of the insurance money for the entire family to enjoy. She believes that having a bigger and brighter dwelling will help the family to alleviate some of the stress, depression and oppression that they have been encountering.[88] For some of the members in the family such as Ruth, she is elated to hear this news because she too dreams of moving out of their current apartment and into a more respectable home that is located outside of the ghetto. The house that Mama has put the down payment on is located in an area of Chicago called Clybourne Park, which is an entirely White neighborhood.[89]

Being no weak-minded woman,[90] Ruth is thinking from a more logical perspective than her husband Walter Lee and agrees with Mama and the idea of her buying a house that they can call their own. She too feels that the family should invest the money towards purchasing a home. However, Ruth also hopes that she and Walter can be able to provide more space and opportunity for their son Travis (played by Steven Perry in the film version) as well.

As the story progresses, the audience sees the Younger family as they clash over their competing dreams. Ruth then discovers that she is pregnant and fears that if she has the child, she will end up putting more of a financial burden on the family. When Walter finds out about Ruth's current situation, he does not respond to her admission that she is considering having an abortion, which was illegal at the time.

---

[88] SparkNotes Editors. "SparkNote on A Raisin in the Sun." SparkNotes LLC. 2002. http://www.sparknotes.com/lit/raisin/ (accessed July 7, 2018).
[89] SparkNotes Editors. "SparkNote on A Raisin in the Sun." SparkNotes LLC. 2002. http://www.sparknotes.com/lit/raisin/ (accessed July 7, 2018).
[90] James, Rosetta. *CliffsNotes on A Raisin in the Sun.* 10 Jul 2018 </literature/r/a-raisin-in-the-sun/play-summary>.

When the Youngers' future neighbors find out that the Youngers are moving in, and that they are Black, then the neighborhood welcoming committee decides to send Mr. Lindner, who states that he is from the Clybourne Park Improvement Association, there to offer the Youngers a reasonable amount of money including their deposit in return for their staying away from an area such as theirs (Whites) in Clybourne Park. To the neighborhood welcoming committee's dismay, the Youngers decide that they will refuse the deal, even after Walter has lost the rest of the money in the sum of $6,500 to his crooked so-called friend Willy Harris, who had persuaded Walter to blindly invest in the liquor store and then runs off with his cash.[91]

In the meanwhile, it is obvious that Walter is visibly upset because he wanted to put the entire $10,000 into he and his friends liquor store venture. A venture that Mama refuses to do for moral and ethical purposes as she exercises wisdom. The family then becomes concerned for their safety due to the heated racism of the time when they hear that the house is in Clybourne Park, again which is an entirely White neighborhood. Mama is not pleading but asks the family for their understanding as she explains to them that it was the only house that the family could afford. So, in order to keep the family together, focused and grounded, Mama feels that she needs to buy the house in order to hold the family unit together.[92]

After receiving the news about Mama putting a down payment on a new house that they can call their own, Ruth regains her pleasure and rejoices, but Walter feels betrayed, because he feels that his dreams are being swept under the table, not logically

[91] SparkNotes Editors. "SparkNote on A Raisin in the Sun." SparkNotes LLC. 2002. http://www.sparknotes.com/lit/raisin/ (accessed July 7, 2018).
[92] SparkNotes Editors. "SparkNote on A Raisin in the Sun." SparkNotes LLC. 2002. http://www.sparknotes.com/lit/raisin/ (accessed July 7, 2018).

realizing that by being a Black man, it is equally as hard to obtain a liquor license as it is to purchase a home. Then Walter tries to make Mama feel guilty by telling her that she has crushed his dreams. He is also saying in not so many words that she does not understand the plight of a Black man and that she has just became the obstacle that has stepped on his neck by not allowing him to excel. He then goes quickly to his bedroom, as Mama remains sitting and worrying about what has become of her son, wondering when will he see the importance of certain things in life instead of trying to get rich quick and easy.[93] One cannot appreciate the finer things in life when they are ill gotten than they could if they put in hard work so that they could appreciate it better.

Mama being the head of the Younger household is a little sensitive concerning her children, yet she stands tall and exudes dignity as she demands that the members of her family not only respect her but respect themselves and take pride in their dreams as well as their culture and family history. Her requirements are simple as with many mothers, and that is to keep the apartment in which they live in neat, clean and polished always. Again, she is a woman who stands firm and stands up for her beliefs as she provides perspective from an older generation.

Mama believes that one must strive to work hard in order to succeed as she also maintains her moral boundaries; she rejects Beneatha's progressive and seemingly un-Christian sentiments about God, as she was not raised that way. She also rejects Ruth's consideration to get an abortion which strongly disappoints her. By the same token, when Walter comes to her with his get rich quick and easy scheme to invest the entire

---

[93] SparkNotes Editors. "SparkNote on A Raisin in the Sun." SparkNotes LLC. 2002. http://www.sparknotes.com/lit/raisin/ (accessed July 7, 2018

$10,000 into the liquor store venture, she also condemns this idea and explains that she will not participate in such un-Christian business.[94]

When the time comes, Mama also feels that Walter has finally "come into his manhood," recognizing that he is now beginning to be proud of his family as well as his cultural background which is more important than having money. For Walter, such events within the play are considered to be a rite of passage. As he continues to grow and mature, Walter himself also realizes that he must endure life's challenges in order to arrive at a more of a maturely developed understanding of the important things in life.[95]

During a conversation that Walter and Ruth are having, it is revealed that they still have love left in their marriage, but the stress that they are enduring is because they have both been oppressed by their circumstances. And being trapped in the ghetto, their jobs, and their environment results in their desire to leave physically, as Walter escapes his mental oppression through alcohol, and lashes out at those he feels are involved in his entrapment.[96]

One of the ways for the family to escape their entrapment, seems to be through a strong reliance on each other. Yet, oftentimes, their circumstances seem so difficult for them that they cannot even rely on each other. However, for both Walter and Ruth, they continue to bicker and verbally fight, as they put their own concerns before each other's and before their marriage.[97]

---

[94] SparkNotes Editors. "SparkNote on A Raisin in the Sun." SparkNotes LLC. 2002. http://www.sparknotes.com/lit/raisin/ (accessed July 7, 2018).
[95] SparkNotes Editors. "SparkNote on A Raisin in the Sun." SparkNotes LLC. 2002. http://www.sparknotes.com/lit/raisin/ (accessed July 7, 2018).
[96] SparkNotes Editors. "SparkNote on A Raisin in the Sun." SparkNotes LLC. 2002. http://www.sparknotes.com/lit/raisin/ (accessed July 7, 2018).
[97] SparkNotes Editors. "SparkNote on A Raisin in the Sun." SparkNotes LLC. 2002. http://www.sparknotes.com/lit/raisin/ (accessed July 7, 2018

The down payment that Mama has made on a house seems to be a big deal for Walter and Beneatha which further reveals Mama's belief that in order to be a happy family then the Youngers will need their own property, space and privacy. Her faith and her dream is a perfect example of the quintessential American dream. This is a dream that a single Black mother desires for her family. Part of Mama's dream is the simple desire for consumer goods, which is owning the house. She believes, just as many did in the post–World War II consumer culture believed, at least to some degree, that having a certain type of ownership that can provide their family happiness which was part of fulfilling the American dream.[98]

Consequently, Mama lives vicariously through her children as they are her life, and as she refers to them as her "harvest." Mama does not have any significant dreams of her own, other than her dreaming of having her own home which is the motivation by her desire of having a better life for her family.[99] Even though Mama only mean to have the best that she can for her family, she has also succumbed to the influential fact of how materialistic things or stuff drives the desires of a society that surrounds her. Still, her desires are somewhat far-reaching, if not unrealistic because for Blacks in America, they were largely left out of the depictions of the American dream, especially during this period. It was only White families who populated the suburban areas, it was only White families who were seen on the television programs and in magazine advertisements. Therefore, Hansberry, through her writings performs a radical act by claiming that the general American dream through mainstream society could not always be attainable for

[98] SparkNotes Editors. "SparkNote on A Raisin in the Sun." SparkNotes LLC. 2002. http://www.sparknotes.com/lit/raisin/ (accessed July 7, 2018).
[99] James, Rosetta. *CliffsNotes on A Raisin in the Sun.* 10 Jul 2018 </literature/r/a-raisin-in-the-sun/play-summary>.

the African American but through hard work and perseverance African-Americans could also benefit.[100]

The fundamental nature of the Youngers' desire to be participants in the American dream, such as with many other minority families, often does come with some hardships which are not easily ascertained. Ruth and Walter's concerns about moving into a predominantly White neighborhood is a reflection of the great tensions that have existed for hundreds of years between races in America. Their concerns are the foreshadows of their future which was a result of their past, and among other developments, such as the arrival of Mr. Lindner, who reveals that the White people of Clybourne Park are just as wary of the Youngers as the Youngers are of White people, this is one of the concerns of the family's experiences from the past. The Younger family, just like any other Black family knows the ghosts of the past concerning the deeply rooted hate of racism and what it has done to Blacks over the years.[101]

In the meantime, Beneatha ends up rejecting her suitor, George Murchison, (played by Louis Gossett Jr. in the film version) whom she believes to be shallow, or what she may have perceived as being weak minded and blind to the problems of race and its issues here in America. Subsequently, she receives a marriage proposal from her Nigerian boyfriend, Joseph Asagai, who wants Beneatha to move forward with her life, get a medical degree and move to Africa with him (Beneatha does not make her choice before the end of the play).[102]

[100] SparkNotes Editors. "SparkNote on A Raisin in the Sun." SparkNotes LLC. 2002. http://www.sparknotes.com/lit/raisin/ (accessed July 7, 2018
[101] SparkNotes Editors. "SparkNote on A Raisin in the Sun." SparkNotes LLC. 2002. http://www.sparknotes.com/lit/raisin/ (accessed July 7, 2018).
[102] SparkNotes Editors. "SparkNote on A Raisin in the Sun." SparkNotes LLC. 2002. http://www.sparknotes.com/lit/raisin/ (accessed July 7, 2018).

Now, even though Ruth has made the announcement of her pregnancy, we can see the power that Mama wields as the matriarch of the Younger family. She is the foundation that is solidly grounded and is at the center of her family's life as she controls many of the interactions of the members in her household.[103]

Walter's view concerning education seems to fall somewhere between Beneatha's view and George's views, while he also seems to care more for his son Travis's education more so than for his younger sister Beneatha's education, mainly because not only is Travis his child but because Beneatha is a woman. These were the ideologies that were not only acceptable in many cultures, but it was also acceptable within the marginalized group of Blacks that existed at the time. This is a marginalization that Black women had to fight then and continue to fight today by being both Black and a female.[104]

For centuries now, there have been many African-Americans who had begun to reject the assimilationist ideals that were being forced upon them, believing that by this time, 1950, mainstream America would always mean White America and that by assimilating into their culture would always mean that they, Blacks would be degrading themselves as a culture in order to fit into White society's perceptions of how Blacks should be and act. For these African-Americans they then sought an independent identity that would allow them to be able to embrace and express their heritage and culture without fear of losing their identity.[105]

---

[103] SparkNotes Editors. "SparkNote on A Raisin in the Sun." SparkNotes LLC. 2002. http://www.sparknotes.com/lit/raisin/ (accessed July 7, 2018).
[104] SparkNotes Editors. "SparkNote on A Raisin in the Sun." SparkNotes LLC. 2002. http://www.sparknotes.com/lit/raisin/ (accessed July 7, 2018).
[105] SparkNotes Editors. "SparkNote on A Raisin in the Sun." SparkNotes LLC. 2002. http://www.sparknotes.com/lit/raisin/ (accessed July 7, 2018).

This particular scene closes with Walter's description to Travis of his materialistic fantasy about the future—Walter longs to be a part of a culture that continually excludes him. He wants to be rich if even if it means getting rich quick and easy. Walter feels that by being rich is the solution to his family's problems as he forces his way into being accepted by mainstream America, which is part of his materialistic fantasy. Most of all, he wants his son to have a better life than he has had. Walter also feels that by being rich then he will be able to provide his son Travis with the education he so deserves that was not always afforded to Blacks. Walter's wish for Travis may seem selfish because he wants so desperately to feel like a man, and he believes that Travis's success would be a reflection on his own success as the man of the house.[106]

The Youngers also understood and realized that they were about to fulfill some of their dreams and by doing so, they were not going to allow racism to be one of the obstacles to get in their way. In this scene you will see Mama carefully packing her plant and when she hears of the incident concerning the neighborhood welcoming committee there is a sense of concern. The maturity in the members of her family demonstrates that she can now be proud of her fortitude as they have helped her to hold onto her dream. She also knows that she will need some motivation and inspiration as a token of the dream's power in order to face the hardships that she and her family will endure in the future as well as being in an all-White neighborhood full of people who are unwilling to accept them because of the color of their skin.[107] Mama has now begun to persevere.

[106] SparkNotes Editors. "SparkNote on A Raisin in the Sun." SparkNotes LLC. 2002. http://www.sparknotes.com/lit/raisin/ (accessed July 7, 2018).
[107] SparkNotes Editors. "SparkNote on A Raisin in the Sun." SparkNotes LLC. 2002. http://www.sparknotes.com/lit/raisin/ (accessed July 7, 2018).

Mama's plant is something that symbolizes her dream for her and her family and having an opportunity to escape from their poverty-stricken life. It also represents a dream for the African-American family showing that they are finally able to have a slice of the pie in American society, which is equality and acceptance from the mainstream culture. Additionally, this episode shows, that the fact that Mama continuously holds onto her dream is just as important as the realization of her dream.[108] Even though this initial act begins in despair, the Youngers begin to regain hope and the motivation to pursue their dreams as their lives continues.[109]

The Youngers eventually move out of their two-bedroom apartment, having the ability to fulfill the family's long-held dream. Even though their future seems uncertain and slightly dangerous, they are hopeful as they keep their faith and are determined to live a better life than the life they lived before. Their firm belief is that they can succeed as long as they stick together as a family with the determination to defer their dreams no longer.[110]

While both of Mama's children may have achieved a sense of happiness in being able to purchase their own house, they still have an incomplete fulfillment of their dreams. Mama also realizes that the fulfillment her dreams in being able to move into her own home has at last become a reality. As the matriarch and oldest member of the family, Mama is that single Black mother who is a testament, from as far back as the 1950 who showed the Black community that they too can have the potential of being

[108] SparkNotes Editors. "SparkNote on A Raisin in the Sun." SparkNotes LLC. 2002. http://www.sparknotes.com/lit/raisin/ (accessed July 7, 2018).
[109] SparkNotes Editors. "SparkNote on A Raisin in the Sun." SparkNotes LLC. 2002. http://www.sparknotes.com/lit/raisin/ (accessed July 7, 2018).
[110] SparkNotes Editors. "SparkNote on A Raisin in the Sun." SparkNotes LLC. 2002. http://www.sparknotes.com/lit/raisin/ (accessed July 7, 2018).

able to achieve their dreams and their goals no matter how old you are, it is never too late.

Since Mama has lived to see a dream fulfilled that both she and her husband shared, she can now be proud of, she now has a peace of mind knowing that her family will succeed at fulfilling all of their dreams if they put their minds together and work together as a team. Remember that in unity, it is team work is that makes the dream work.[111]

The less mature members of the Younger family, appropriately named to demonstrate the shifting emphasis of everyday life from the eldest to youngest have also learned how to have an attitude of gratitude concerning accepting their culture as they matriculate into mainstream society and reach certain midpoints in their lives. Now with a new house, they are well on their way to be able to continue to complete the fulfillment of their dreams. It is Mama's last moment in the apartment as she is shown transporting her plant which shows that although she is happy about moving, she will continue to cherish the memories of the past, whether good or bad, that she has accumulated throughout her life.[112]

In the last and final scene is where Hansberry implies, that the sweetness of having your dreams fulfilled instead of deferred accompanies the sweetness of the dream itself. As Mama is leaving the apartment, she is reveling in the sweetness of having her dream fulfilled. She pauses on her way out to show the respect and appreciation for the hard work that went into her and her late husband's ability to make

---

[111] SparkNotes Editors. "SparkNote on A Raisin in the Sun." SparkNotes LLC. 2002. http://www.sparknotes.com/lit/raisin/ (accessed July 7, 2018).
[112] SparkNotes Editors. "SparkNote on A Raisin in the Sun." SparkNotes LLC. 2002. http://www.sparknotes.com/lit/raisin/ (accessed July 7, 2018).

their dream come true. Her husband lingers in her recollections, and when she says to Ruth a few lines earlier, "Yeah—they something all right, my children," it becomes almost an answered prayer of their unmistakably secure futures.[113]

Money for Mama is only a means to an end; the ability to be able to achieve her and her late husband's dreams are more important to her than the material wealth, and her dream was to own a house with a garden and yard in which her grandson Travis can play.[114] She now has fulfilled her dream, influenced her family to embrace and hold on to their culture and family history and now has a peace of mind.

In "A Raisin In the Sun," Mama is portrayed as being one of the most nurturing characters in the play, as she constantly reminds her son Walter that all she has ever wanted is to make her children happy and provide for them a better life than the one her and her late husband has had. She cares deeply for her son Walter as she does the rest of her family, but by being a single Black mother of a son, she shows her son that she cares by entrusting him with the remaining insurance money. She cares deeply for Ruth as well as Ruth is like a second daughter to her as she consoles her when Walter ignores her. Mama also respects Beneatha's assessment of George Murchison as being arrogant, egotistical and self-centered gentleman by telling her daughter not to waste her time with such a "fool." Mama also demonstrates her love for her grandchild Travis, in addition to hoping that their new house will have a big yard in which he can play, so that he does not have to play in the rough streets of the Chicago ghetto. Mama is also very

[113] SparkNotes Editors. "SparkNote on A Raisin in the Sun." SparkNotes LLC. 2002. http://www.sparknotes.com/lit/raisin/ (accessed July 7, 2018).
[114] SparkNotes Editors. "SparkNote on A Raisin in the Sun." SparkNotes LLC. 2002. http://www.sparknotes.com/lit/raisin/ (accessed July 7, 2018).

fond, of her plant, though in a different way, as it gives her that sense of hope when life seems bleak as she tries to nurture it throughout the play.[115]

So, what were the values and purpose of the Younger family being able to achieve their dreams? The values and purpose of the Younger family being able to achieve their dreams is because their family's forefathers came along during a time when their loved ones, like many Black families, were descendants of slaves. With Mama and her late husband being the closest generation to experience the hardships of sharecropping, they truly know what oppression is. In addition to experiencing the hardships of oppression, poverty and racism, they also heard their grandparents, parents, or other relatives talk about what they endured during the latter part of slavery.

Mama and her husband along with their children were part of a pseudo slavery called Jim Crow and its outright racism. Mama and her family, from generations back up until her present day, also understood that mainstream society did not intend for them or those like them to get ahead, thereby subjecting Blacks to being a part of the deferment. With Mama's inner strength and hope, she felt that if you allow your circumstances to hinder and stop you from achieving those goals then that is something that you would have to contend with as she was not going to allow anyone from hindering her from achieving her goals, and that was to buy her own house.

Because of the hardships that Mama had endured throughout her life, she seemed to be accustomed to to the long suffering thereby enduring such hardships. However, for Mama, the Lindners of the world could not disturb her inner peace, by stealing her joy, for she had previously suffered the death of a baby boy and, more

[115] SparkNotes Editors. "SparkNote on A Raisin in the Sun." SparkNotes LLC. 2002. http://www.sparknotes.com/lit/raisin/ (accessed July 7, 2018).

recently, the death of her husband whom she had been married to many years. Mama's strong faith and deep religious convictions gave her the inner strength, physical courage that she needed psychological in order to rise above life's challenges. Even at the lowest point in her life, she asks God to replenish her diminishing strength and is immediately possessed of a more compassionate perception of Walter Lee's foolishness.[116]

In the play, we see the main characters struggling to deal with the oppressive circumstances that rule their lives that Mama was trying so hard to teach her family how to overcome.[117]

The title of the play, "A Raisin In the Sun" references to a conjecture that Langston Hughes famously presented in one of the poems that he wrote about the dreams that many Blacks felt were unattainable, forgotten or put off. He wondered whether or not those dreams shriveled up "like a raisin in the sun," and "festered like a sore?" In either case, every member of the Younger family had a separate, individual dream—Mama shared a dream with her late husband, which was to own their own house. Beneatha wanted to become a doctor, and Walter wanted to have money so that he could afford the nicer things in life for his family.[118]

Throughout the play, the family struggled to attain their dreams, unfortunately, much of their happiness and depression was directly related to their attainment of, or failure to attain, their dreams. By the end of the play, they understood as they learned that the dream of owning their own house was the most important dream because it

[116] James, Rosetta. *CliffsNotes on A Raisin in the Sun.* 14 Jul 2018 </literature/r/a-raisin-in-the-sun/play-summary>.
[117] SparkNotes Editors. "SparkNote on A Raisin in the Sun." SparkNotes LLC. 2002. http://www.sparknotes.com/lit/raisin/ (accessed July 7, 2018).
[118] SparkNotes Editors. "SparkNote on A Raisin in the Sun." SparkNotes LLC. 2002. http://www.sparknotes.com/lit/raisin/ (accessed July 7, 2018).

meant unity within the family dynamics which was built on a firm foundation.[119] It also

meant that they would have the ability to own something as part of the American dream.

Dream Deferred by Langston Hughes

What happens to a dream deferred?

Does it dry up
Like a raisin in the sun?

Or fester like a sore--
And then run?

Does it stink like rotten meat?
Or crust and sugar over--
like a syrupy sweet?

Maybe it just sags
like a heavy load.

Or does it explode?

In order to ascertain their dreams, Mama knew that her family had to not only

overcome their obstacles, one of which was racism and their need to fight racial

discrimination at any cost such as their forefathers did, but they also needed to

overcome their personal hangups. The character of Mr. Lindner made the theme of

racial discrimination very prominent but subtle which in the plot was an issue that the

Youngers could not avoid. The issue of racism could not be avoided because it was the

plague which was infested within the foundation of America. The governing body or

what I call the neighborhood welcoming committee from the Youngers' new

neighborhood, the Clybourne Park Improvement Association, sent Mr. Lindner to

threaten or mildly persuade them not to move into his or shall I say their all-White

---

[119] SparkNotes Editors. "SparkNote on A Raisin in the Sun." SparkNotes LLC. 2002.
http://www.sparknotes.com/lit/raisin/ (accessed July 7, 2018).

Clybourne Park neighborhood. Mr. Lindner and the people whom he represents can only see the color of the Younger family's skin. Again, this is the sore that has festered and infested America which is the deeply rooted hate called racism.[120]

Lindner's offer to bribe the Youngers is also a subtle threat in order to keep the Younger family from moving which also threatens to tear apart the Younger family and the values for which it stands. The offer is basically saying that it is in their best interest that they take the money. Ultimately, the Youngers respond to this type of discrimination with defiance and strength as they stand firm to overcome the obstacles that they have endured from mainstream society for so long. The play has powerfully demonstrated that the way to deal with racism and discrimination is to stand up to it and confront it head on. As a community, you must reassert one's dignity in the face of adversity rather than allow it to continue.[121]

What was the importance of family for Mama Younger? The importance of family for Mama as well as her children was knowing that had they to unite as a family in order to realize the importance of attaining their dreams. With the buying of their home this would be one less struggle that they would have to endure. Yet, there would be many more struggles both socially and economically that they did have to endure throughout the play, but in the end, they had a home.

Because of Mama's background and the life of struggles that both she and her late husband had endured, she strongly believed in the importance of family, and she tried

[120] SparkNotes Editors. "SparkNote on A Raisin in the Sun." SparkNotes LLC. 2002. http://www.sparknotes.com/lit/raisin/ (accessed July 7, 2018).
[121] SparkNotes Editors. "SparkNote on A Raisin in the Sun." SparkNotes LLC. 2002. http://www.sparknotes.com/lit/raisin/ (accessed July 7, 2018).

to instill this value to each of her family members from the oldest to the youngest as she struggled to keep them together and functioning.[122]

Through it all, both Walter and Beneatha have learned a lesson in all of this. By the end of the play, they now understand the importance of family and cultural values. Walter learns his lesson when he had to deal with the loss of the stolen insurance money that Mama had entrusted him with, as Beneatha denies Walter as a brother for also losing the portion of insurance money that was to go towards her tuition for medical school which demonstrated his immaturity and lack of responsibilities. Even as the family faces such a traumatic experience, they are able to come together to reject Mr. Lindner's racist overtures. Even though they are still strong individually, they are now individuals who function even stronger as a family unit. They also realize that when they begin to put the family and the family's wishes before their own selfish needs, then they are able merge their own individual dreams with the family's all-embracing dream.[123]

Each of the characters in the play *"A Raisin in the Sun"* played a significant part because they all had a dream, yet each of their dreams had gone unfulfilled. Each detail, and theme in the play is pretty much the characteristics of what the single Black mother hopes to achieve while raising her children, especially her sons.

Mama is instilling her children that they should face their problems head on instead of allowing them to fester like a sore or stink like rotten meat. She wants her children to stand firm and not run or allow their dreams to be deferred because of their perception of life's circumstances.

---

[122] SparkNotes Editors. "SparkNote on A Raisin in the Sun." SparkNotes LLC. 2002. http://www.sparknotes.com/lit/raisin/ (accessed July 7, 2018).
[123] SparkNotes Editors. "SparkNote on A Raisin in the Sun." SparkNotes LLC. 2002. http://www.sparknotes.com/lit/raisin/ (accessed July 7, 2018).

The reason why I use "A Raisin In the Sun," as an example is to give many of you a glimpse of what is like being a single Black mother raising sons. Whether it is 1950 or 2018, many of the issues are still the same, only today many our youth have not quite grasped the concept of such values and saliences, nor do they understand the importance of their heritage or culture as a collective view.

The Black male is not privileged, nor is he always afforded the same opportunities as many of his male counterparts in mainstream society. He too is like the mule having to carry the extra burdens of both races. He wants to be accepted in both worlds while also having an opportunity to fulfill his dreams. From the perception of White or mainstream culture, he has to be accepted into a world that does not always want to accept him. From his own culture, he has to prove himself and his manhood, while Mama does what she can by being the glue and foundation that will hold the family together while teaching the importance of family and cultural history.

Mother to Son by Langston Hughes

Well, son, I'll tell you:
Life for me ain't been no crystal stair.

It's had tacks in it,
And splinters,
And boards torn up,
And places with no carpet on the floor --
Bare.

But all the time
I'se been a-climbin' on,
And reachin' landin's,

And turnin' corners,

And sometimes goin' in the dark

Where there ain't been no light.

So boy, don't you turn back.

Don't you set down on the steps

'Cause you finds it's kinder hard.

Don't you fall now --

For I'se still goin', honey,

I'se still climbin',

And life for me ain't been no crystal stair.

Just like so many single Black mothers raising sons and the Black males who are determined to fulfill their dreams, such dreams are often driven by the need to have an abundance of money and materialistic things. But remember, all it takes is a dream. As it reads in Habakkuk 2:2 "Then the LORD replied: "Write down the revelation and make it plain on tablets so that a herald may run with it." Don't defer your dreams because it is a goal that you wish to achieve in life, not just something that you experience while you are sleep.

There are those who uses their dreams as a way of establishing their future goals. By implementing your dreams and making it a vision as you write it down and make it plain, it will give you the motivation that you need in order to achieve your lifelong goals. Proverbs 13:12, says "Hope deferred maketh the heart sick; but when the desire cometh, it is a tree of life." Never postpone your dreams allowing them to become deferred no matter how long it takes for you to achieve them. Keep the faith, hold on to hope and continue to aim for the stars.

Even though the Younger family seems to be alienated from the White middle-class culture, (mainstream society) they too harbor some of the same materialistic dreams as the rest of American society. During the 1950s, there was the stereotypical American dream to have a piece of the pie, and that was to have a nice house with a yard, a big car, and a happy family. The Youngers were just like any other family and they too seemed to want to live this dream. Even though their struggle to attain any resemblance of their dream is dramatically different from the struggles of what a similar (White) suburban family might encounter, the Youngers also understand that they are not a stereotypical middle-class family, they are a lower-class family who lives in the ghetto on the South side of Chicago trying to move up to the east side. They live in a world in which being middle class is also a dream.[124]

The plant that Mama cherishes symbolizes her version of an American dream, because she nurtures and cares for it just as she cares for her family. She tries to make sure that it is well taken care of by giving the plant enough light and water not only to grow it but to flourish it so that it becomes beautiful, just as she attempts to provide for her family with the meager yet consistent financial support. Mama also imagines herself having a garden in the new home that she hopes to someday own so that she can tend to it along with her dream house.[125]

This plant in its small pot acts as a temporary stand-in for the much larger dreams that Mama has. As Mama cares for this plant relentlessly, it exemplifies how she is protecting her dream. Despite her and her families cramped living conditions and the

[124] SparkNotes Editors. "SparkNote on A Raisin in the Sun." SparkNotes LLC. 2002. http://www.sparknotes.com/lit/raisin/ (accessed July 7, 2018).
[125] SparkNotes Editors. "SparkNote on A Raisin in the Sun." SparkNotes LLC. 2002. http://www.sparknotes.com/lit/raisin/ (accessed July 7, 2018).

lifetime of hard work that she and her deceased husband has endured, she maintains her focus on her dream that she and her husband shared, which helps her to persevere. Still, no matter how much Mama works to nurture her plant, the plant remains weak, just like the family's hope to get out of the ghetto, because there is so little light.[126]

Nonetheless, with her age and her still working, it is a bit difficult for Mama to care for her family as much as she wants and to have her family grow as much as she wants. So, for now, her dreams of a house and a better life for her family remains unsubstantiated or shall I say deferred because at the moment, it is so hard for her to see beyond her family's present situation.[127] This is how the single Black mother also feels at times as she too raises her children, especially her sons.

For Beneatha, her dreams differ from Mama's, because in many ways, Beneatha's dreams are self-serving. Her desires are to "express" herself and to become a doctor, so she, Beneatha proves herself to be an early feminist who radically views her role as self-oriented and not family-oriented. During the 1950s, feminism had not fully emerged into the American cultures landscape when Hansberry wrote the play, *A Raisin in the Sun,* and Beneatha seemed like a prototype for the more enthusiastic feministic views of the 1960s and 1970s.[128]

Beneatha not only wants to have a career, which is a far cry from the stereotypical American *Leave it to Beaver* mom June Cleaver. June Cleaver was a stereotypical stay-at-home-mom role model of the 1950s. She was also part of a suburban family who was

---

[126] SparkNotes Editors. "SparkNote on A Raisin in the Sun." SparkNotes LLC. 2002. http://www.sparknotes.com/lit/raisin/ (accessed July 7, 2018).
[127] SparkNotes Editors. "SparkNote on A Raisin in the Sun." SparkNotes LLC. 2002. http://www.sparknotes.com/lit/raisin/ (accessed July 7, 2018).
[128] SparkNotes Editors. "SparkNote on A Raisin in the Sun." SparkNotes LLC. 2002. http://www.sparknotes.com/lit/raisin/ (accessed July 7, 2018).

to attain their American dream, but for Beneatha she desired to find her own identity and pursue an independent career without relying solely on a man.[129] She even indicated to Ruth and Mama that she might not even get married, which was a possibility that astonishes them because it ran counter to their expectations of a what a woman's role was supposed to be during the 1950s.

[129] SparkNotes Editors. "SparkNote on A Raisin in the Sun." SparkNotes LLC. 2002. http://www.sparknotes.com/lit/raisin/ (accessed July 7, 2018).

Claudine and Mr. Welfare Man

Family Structure and the Single Black Mom

This Photo by Unknown Author is licensed under CC BY-NC-ND

Chapter 3

"If you can't fly, then run. If you can't run, then walk. If you can't walk, then crawl, but

by all means, keep moving." Dr. Martin Luther King

The 1974 movie "Claudine," played by legends James Earl Jones and Diahann

Carroll, is about a hard-working single Black mother, who works as a maid for wealthy

White families in upper class White communities in order to make ends meet, while also

receiving welfare, just to make ends meet because Mr. Welfare man only gives her

enough assistance in order to keep her from drowning. She has six children, trying to

maintain her family unit, living in the ghetto, in a slum apartment in Harlem, New York,

while trying to find love the second time around. For many single Black mothers,

especially those who were economically challenged, was inspirational, uplifting and

thought provoking.

Hesitant to fall in love again, Claudine meets James Earl Jones who portrayed

Rupert B. Marshall, called Roop, a seasoned garbage man and Claudine's blue-collar admirer who was charming, and charismatic with all of the sensitivity and seriousness that was needed in order to express the dilemmas that Black men went through during a time when many family units were being torn apart by the welfare system, also known as Mr. Welfare Man. While dating, their relationship becomes complex as the movie illustrates the difficulties that Claudine faced concerning her love life, the welfare office, intrusive social workers and trying to keep her children in line.

Claudine has her doubts concerning her and Roop's relationship because he begins to display some subtle signs of being irresponsible which is not good for her children. In addition, even though Roop is good natured and kind hearted, he is reluctant to become a father, and if he marries Claudine then she will lose her welfare assistance.

Directed by a White man named John Berry, he had the ability to convey certain themes that were particularly relevant to not just single Black mothers, but to Black women, who were also encountering some of the same lower-socioeconomic circumstances during the 1970s. Not only did the movie Claudine provide an excellent sense of humor and entertainment, it also tackled serious social issues with an even hand. The audience views a family that is loving but also struggling with an unfair governmental system that displays several stereotypes and subtle forms of racism while also trying to beat the odds of dysfunction and estrangement. Even Curtis Mayfield wrote songs on the soundtrack that provided an equally social conscious that brought awareness to the economically challenged circumstances of the ghetto which was superb.

Oftentimes, Black women were considered as being "welfare queens" who cheated the system in order to get more welfare money. If Mr. Welfare man finds out that she is working, then she is committing fraud by cheating the government. However, mainstream will usually make the assumption that the single Black mother is lazy as those such as Claudine bust their behinds to earn extra to stretch that $30 a month that Mr. Welfare man is giving her. As many in mainstream society would assume of Claudine is that she was a "welfare queen," or just another lazy single Black mother who is out trying to cheat the government by having a bunch of children in order to get more welfare.

The term "welfare queen" was coined in 1976 during Ronald Reagan's presidential campaign. During his speech, her repetitively told the story of a "Chicago welfare queen" who lived off of taxpayer dollars, she had multiple husbands, aliases, addresses, and Social Security cards. So, in the movie, whenever the social worker came around, Claudine and her children had to hide any appliances or furniture that looked new and given to her by her new suitor. In order to continue receiving welfare payments, it had to appear as though Claudine was not working and not receiving any extra source of income. An example was when the social work, Miss Kabak, played by Elisa Loti, is walking up the stoop, Claudine and her children rush to switch the new iron, kettle, and toaster with their old appliances. Claudine has to appear as though she does not have an outside life and is totally dependent upon Mr. Welfare Man. If Claudine is dating anyone and receives any types of gifts, monetarily or materially from her boyfriend, then her social worker has to deduct any money or the assumed value of gifts from the amount of assistance that Claudine is receiving from welfare.

Claudine is constantly denying Miss Kabak the truth about her situation by lying to Miss. Kabak about being unemployed and single. If Claudine does tell the truth about her relationship about her and Roop and mentions that she is employed, then she puts her sense of financial security in jeopardy and the amount of financial aid that she receives from the welfare would decrease, or even worse, she may no longer be eligible to receive any more financial assistance.

What this movie is doing is addressing that there is a problem in the low economic community and the problem is that there are a great deal of Black men and women encounter who encounter the same problems with Mr. Welfare Man/the government, especially at the time that this movie was released. If an individual is employed and makes a certain amount of money, no matter how minuscule, and fails to report such income to the government then without a doubt. The amount of money that you made would be deducted from your welfare check will be deducted and under many circumstances you may be accused of fraud. Claudine says one of the scenes, "If I don't feed my kids, it's child neglect. If I go out and get a job, and make a little money on the side, then that's cheating. I stay at home and I'm lazy. I can't win."

The societal attitude toward the single Black mother are, if a person tries to work in order to make ends meet and are still unable to put food on the table, and make a better life for themselves then it is considered to be a a strike against them by Mr. Welfare Man. Then societal attitudes are like a double-edged sword, because when a person tries to get ahead in life and the issues arises when a Black man or woman does not try and work then society labels them as "being lazy" or "irresponsible" when it was actually the government/Mr. Welfare Man who essentially backs them into a corner. Another issue that this movie addresses is how out of touch, cold hearted and calloused, uncompassionate and somewhat inconsiderate White middle-class female social workers were with the harsh realities that were faced by single Black mothers. In another scene from the movie shows Miss. Kabak, the social worker dressing fairly well and then informing Claudine that she has a "Mrs." title. Kabak also begins to question Claudine and is adamant about Claudine admitting to receiving help from a man. This demonstrates that Kabak was not in tune with Claudine's struggles or any other single Black mother's struggles. When Kabak goes into Claudine's refrigerator without Claudine's permission and finds what was a 6 pack of beer in addition to the soda pops that Roop has purchased for the family, Kabak then does an approximate deduction of $2.15.

In the meanwhile, Kabak the social worker, keeps a continual tab on the comings and goings of Claudine's visitors. Kabak even goes as far as having someone from the neighborhood to act as an informant letting her know what is going on with Claudine and her family's situation when she is not around. Upon her spying on Claudine, she informs her that a man has been coming to see her. Claudine suspects that the nosy woman from across the street has probably been an insider, or "private eye," sharing details about her life with the social worker. Many in the inner communities can relate to this scene, because in a city such as Harlem, there are a great deal of individuals who are sitting on their stoops gossiping or spying on people's business within the community.

What this movie also addresses are the stereotypical attitudes that society have about single Black mothers and that Black women in the 1970s faced, whether it was being lazy, poor, sexually promiscuous or always scamming the government. During this particular scene, the song "Mr. Welfare Man," begins to play in the background as Kabak eventually finds Roop hiding in a broom closet with the gifts that Claudine and the children were trying to hide. The soundtrack for the movie *Claudine* was written and produced by Curtis Mayfield and sung by Gladys Knight & the Pips. It was the perfect song for the movie and Mr. Mayfield did a superb job. Just by happenstance, the group's album for the movie was titled "Claudine." "On and On" was on of the songs that was played as the movie showed Roop's absence and lack of responsibility.

The song "Welfare Man" spoke truths that were in-depth and had a great deal towards expressing Claudine's situation. Like the song, "On and On," the song Claudine has an upbeat tempo, as the lyrics reflect the life struggles that single Black women in general face as they are stereotyped as being lazy, unfit mothers who do not want work and would rather deal with the heartaches and issues of dealing with Mr. Welfare Man. Mr. Welfare Man is a personified version of how society views of the single Black mother. Societal attitudes are very judgmental when it comes to the single Black mother and the welfare system, while Roop is displayed a representation of not only being Claudine's lover, but a somewhat irresponsible father to his own children. For example, there is a verse in the song that says, *"Holding me back, using your tact, to make me live against my will, (hard sacrifice). If that's how it goes child, I don't know, I can't concede my life's for real. It's like a private eye for the FBI, just as envious as the Klu Klux Klan. Though I'm of pleasant fate it's hard to relate, I'll do the very best I can Ooh, so keep away from me, ooh ooh Mr. Welfare"* (Mayfield, 1974).

In another scene, there are certain camera shots that the cameraperson captures as he or she focuses more on the cinematographer showing the intense emotion between Roop and Claudine, such as when Claudine in bed with Roop or her on the phone scolding her children. Another example is of life on welfare between the Black man and Black woman is when Roop says that he will never leave Claudine and how they both will go down to the welfare office confronting Mr. Welfare Man and how they are going to work everything out as she lovingly pulls Roop's head close to her chest. Then the camera zooms in a shot of Roop's face looking very uneasy. His facial expression is an indication that he is nervous about going down to the welfare office and possibly being labeled as Mr. Welfare Man. Mr. Welfare Man is the label given to the man who is stepping in to take responsibility of a single Black mother and her children. It is also the horrid thought of having the government constantly in your business keeping track of your income and possessions which may feel emasculating not only for Roop, but any Black man.

It can be assumed that Claudine had recurring images that obviously challenged the ideas of the Black male and his masculinity. In Roop's case, it is the idea of marrying Claudine, her having six children and possibly of them making him apply for welfare as well, all of which are frustrating. As Claudine asks Roop if he will be there for her as they work on trying to come up with a solution, he replies "don't try to put me the on welfare, because those people down there at the welfare would cut my balls off and then you'd hate my guts." Afterwards, Claudine states that she puts up with it, meaning the issues that he has. Roop replies that she has to put up with it because she is a woman, and she is the one who has six children. In this case, it is the Black male who needs a scapegoat as he uses the Black woman as an excuse for being irresponsible. It seems pretty troubling that Roop speaks to her as if she chose to raise six children without a man, especially men such as Roop who does not want to take care of their responsibilities. It is not Claudine's fault or many single Black women's fault that many of their children's fathers refuse to play a role in their children's lives or their current living conditions.

Claudine is showing a sense of resistance towards, "Mr. Welfare Man" as she continues her relationship with Roop. The correlation of her romantic relationship with Roop and the verse in the song "Welfare Man" says, "*Oooh, It's a hard sacrifice. No no no no, Lordy. Mr. Welfare, Stay away Mr. Welfare I'm so tired, I'm so tired of trying to prove my equal rights. Though I've made some mistakes for goodness sakes, why should they help mess up my life?"* (Mayfield, 1974)

Despite the obstacles that both Roop and Claudine faces, Roop continues with his attempts to romance Claudine, however, there is this constant worry about keeping her children out of trouble and off the streets. Claudine eventually becomes physically weary as she works to make ends meet, being a single Black mother who society frowns upon, in addition to being emotionally drained from explaining to others, such as the social worker Miss. Kabak that having six children does not make her a bad person. As Claudine begins going out with Roop, her children becomes disrespectful by telling her not to come home pregnant because they don't need more children in the house.

In addition to Claudine's issues with her children, Roop's garbage man friend warns him that if the social worker finds out that he's seeing Claudine on the side then he's going to be the Mr. Welfare Man. Roop then becomes hesitant as he begins to think about the thought of ever being on welfare or even dependent on the government. Yet, the lyrics in the song reflects the single Black mother and her struggles to support her family on one paycheck, in addition to finding a man that will accept her and lifestyle and not burden her about the six children, two marriages, and two almost marriages.

In the movie, Mayfield also wrote a song called "To Be Invisible." This is a reminder of Ralph Ellison's "The Invisible Man's" as he addresses racism in America. However, in this scene, Claudine's youngest son, Francis, played by Eric Jones, would reiterate his desires to become invisible and disappear as not to be a burden on the rest of the family. At one point, he even begins using mini boards to speak and convey what he is feeling to his siblings toward the end of the movie. This type of behavior most likely

96

resulted from his feelings of inadequacy. If you stopped, sat back as you paid close attention to the movie, you will realize that the songs that were being played for each scene, and the words complemented the movie what you would hear in Harlem, especially with the honking cars passing by outside in the street.

Displaying his subtle sense of irresponsibility, another scene in the movie shows that just before his big announce to everyone about his engagement to Claudine he is served a court order documents stating that he has to pay more in child support for his biological children. This results in his wages being garnished in order to pay the difference. Because of this unexpected news, Roop becomes so upset about this news that he disappears for a couple of days, moves out of his apartment, has his home phone turned off and purposely loses contact with everyone. In the meanwhile, Claudine has planned a Father's Day celebration to share the exciting news about her and Roops engagement. Not only does Roop not show up to the party, but he does not show up to work. Charles, played by Lawrence Hilton-Jacobs, who is Claudine's oldest son eventually finds Roop inebriated at a bar and angrily confronts him in front of everyone at the bar. The reason why Charles is angry at Roop is because he left his mother without any explanation.

Another scene in *"Claudine"* is when Roop does not show up to the Father's Day celebration and captures the sights of the times such as clothing, furniture, music and other styles of the 70s. The film is set in Harlem, which is the ghetto and as you can see, it is a neighborhood that is rundown and has worn-down brownstones. It also shows the traffic congestion as Claudine's younger sons are swerving in between cars on a bicycle headed towards Roops apartment. The clothes are inexpensive as Carroll wears her button-down shirts with colorful floral designs, and she appears to have shoulder-length permed or pressed straightened hair. Claudine lives in a four-room apartment which is crowded and there is barely enough room for the children or guests to move around.

There is also a scene in Claudine, where the children are not very respectful towards Roop and when the ice cream man is heard, they immediately forget their being disrespectful and lacking hospitality towards Roop in order to get money from him. Then there is Patrice, played by Yvette Curtis who has to pick up the slack when Charlene, played by Tamu, is not around. Such scenes demonstrates that even the children who are products of single Black mothers understand who they can manipulate as Mr. Welfare Man.

Claudine's apartment has décor that includes a technicolor poster of Jimmy Hendrix, demonstrating that this particular film was set during the 1970s. Having an 18-year-old son such as Charles who is being rebellious and not liking the fact of Roop dating his mother, Claudine has to go out looking for Charles finding him at the W.E.B. DuBois Community Center. On the wall at the center, its décor includes paintings of prominent Black figures such as Harriet Tubman, Malcolm X and Langston Hughes which are historical within the Black community. There are signs that says, "Black Youth 407 Unemployed" and "Jobs, Not Welfare." Such settings are in alignment with the times and events that were occurring during the Black Power movement that took place in the late1960s and early 1970s. The signs of protests which indicates that there is a lack of jobs, fair employment and other opportunities for Blacks in the ghetto to rise above the bowels of their environment which gives viewers a sense of how high the unemployment rate was for Blacks during the 1973-1975 recession, a fact that continues to exist in today.

Let it be assumed that money has deep ties to Roop's masculinity, because it seems that he feels if he cannot bring home the bacon in order to impress and take care of Claudine, then exactly what is his purpose for being in a relationship with her. One example is when Roop's pins up his emotions concerning a letter that he receives from court stating that he is willfully neglecting his children and will be receiving a cut in pay which now leads him to breaking down. The good-humored and sometimes sarcastic Roop is now no longer able to wear a mask which hides his feelings or holds back tears because now he is feeling like he has failed at his manly duties. Men are not supposed to cry and yet you rarely see men who do, let alone Black men. Men are taught not to cry and be tough and don't show any emotions. It is also assumed that the director showed a Black man crying in order to reveal that they too are human beings who aren't immune to pain having feelings as well.

In another scene of Claudine, Charles's, watching his mother struggle with him and his siblings goes as far as getting a vasectomy. His reasoning for doing so as he tells his mother "manhood is not between the legs." Charles, even though going about the situation in the wrong way is letting the audience know that having children does not make you a man, especially if you are a Black man, or a poor man who has children. Charles's initial feeling is that if you are a Black man and you are poor then you can't even take care of the children that you are having, and because you cannot take care of your children then you are doing them more of a disservice than helping them. His feelings were that he did not want to procreate and end up in the same situation as his mother, which was to be in a destitute situation. And because of the way that Charles feels, he also tells Claudine that if she loved him then she would have killed (meaning aborted) him when he was born, like many Black women did back in the days of slavery.

99

Charles being the eldest of Claudine's six children and 18 years old, understood what it was like being abject poverty, he understood rejection, and he understood what it was to the lack a male figure in his life. All of these overwhelming feelings ended up hardening him to the thought of ever wanting to have offspring.

As Claudine's movie is coming to an end, Charles feels that it is his responsibility to be the man of the house and an example to his siblings. He is the one who plays a role in bringing Roop back into Claudine's life after confronting him in a bar. Even though he does not care too much for Roop, he is able to recognize what it is that makes his mother happy, as opposed to blaming Claudine for all the misfortune in her life.

Out of the anger Charles wanted to harm Roop because he felt that Roop disrespected his mother and just used her to satisfy his selfish masculine needs, so Charles engages in a physical fight with him. Shortly after the incident that has occurred at the bar, Rupert eventually shows up and just sits outside parked in front of Claudine's apartment. She happens to look out the window and sees him sitting in his car and goes downstairs to speak with him. Eventually after some time, the couple works things out through their conversation and make up. After all of the obstacles that the couple endures and several hardships, they are still in doubt about marriage and debate on whether or not they should marry because of the financial issues that relates to being on welfare. Eventually the couple decides to move forward and marry.

Roop and Claudine holds the wedding ceremony in her tiny apartment but unfortunately it is eventually interrupted when Charles runs inside of the apartment in the middle of the ceremonies as the police are chasing after him and other revolutionists. Roop and some of the other guests who are attending the wedding, including Claudine and the rest of the children, begins fighting with the police and then runs after Charles, leaving the ceremony and several guests behind as they board the police wagon that Charles had been put on by the police.

The film ends on a cheery note with the entire family, along with Rupert, walking happily hand in hand through the neighborhood. In the movie, Claudine's children each fit the part as a common character within the Black community. For example, Charles was the revolutionary and rebellious son who wanted to challenge White supremacy as he and his peers fight for social justice. Charlene was the fass and promiscuous Black teenage girl from a single parent household, who wanted to get out in the world, explore life and see what it was all about. She was also one who grew up without a father, she drank, partied and became pregnant as a teen. Claudine's middle son had a knack for cutting class, talking about dropping out of school, gambling, and believed that the only people who were seen with money were the pimps and the number runners. In this scenario the writers inserted Roop as being a positive Black male figure who is demonstrating to the young man that there is a better way to make it in life without ending up in jail or dead. He gambles with the young man and those who are gambling with him and takes this seemingly problematic scenario, showing the boy that he is skillful mathematician who needs to stay in school, as he added, subtracted, multiplied and divided what he made and what he loss without having to think about it.

As stated earlier, John Berry was the director of the movie "Claudine," having directed over 30 films during his career, he was very savvy as he worked behind the camera, because he was able to convey his themes in a way that were particularly relevant to Black women who were in a lower-socioeconomic circumstance during the 1970s.

The original screenplay was written by Tina and Lester Pine, as the two were able to also convey much of what actually happened in the Black community. *Claudine* was a film that touched upon a great number of issues that are still prevalent today in the Black community. I think the film showed the backstory behind the so-called "welfare queen," and debunked the notion that Black women are burdens on society. At the time, the negative imagery of single Black mothers, and absent Black fathers, was overwhelming in the media, and I think John Berry emotionally countered these perceptions from a realistic perspective.

Only the Strong Black Woman Survives; Beating the Odds

Chapter 4

"De nigger woman is de mule uh de world so fur as Ah can see." Their Eyes Were

Watching God." -Zora Neale Hurston (1937).

Historically, Black women have always struggled to survive just like their male

counterparts. There have also, and always been poor mothers and single mothers who

have always worked outside the home (Kinser 15; Regales) in order to struggle and

survive to make ends meet. Many poor mothers, mothers of color, and immigrant

mothers are often seen going into the work force ahead of White, middle class mothers

(Kinser) often given the jobs that no one else wants.

There are those within mainstream society who feel that, or shall I say, those who

have societal attitudes about a Black woman's existence as being only a mere test of her

ability to survive. It is a test of her ability to survive because she is constantly subjugated

and expected not to get back up. Throughout the years, since slavery, the Black woman

has continued to be abused, mistreated, harassed and invisible to a society who also

refuses to acknowledge her existence, yet, she stands firm and endure. The Black woman

is one who maintains her strength through virtue by using reasoning to temper her reactions and exercising wisdom to conceal her experiences of suffering, while also presenting herself as one who is capable of weathering many storms and adversities.

It is the institution of slavery that has made it relatively easy to eradicate the Black man's capacity to protect Black women and over a period of time, has allowed White's mistreatment of Black women's minds, and bodies but not her spirits or her soul as she silently accepts such abuses with the persuasive crack or beating of the horse whip.

For the Black woman, she must endure the separation, isolation, and forced assimilation, she must be the saviors, the cooks, and the caretakers of everyone's problems including her own. She must also deal with everyone else's children while trying to make the time to deal with her own children. When looking at the old movies with actresses in them such as Hattie McDaniels, Butterfly McQueen, and Louise Beavers, all whom play as maids and caretakers, in reality, they are the personification of how society view them. It is oftentimes the Black women who takes on or is given the tasks of responsibilities for cleaning up other people's messes or uncomfortable situations, yet, she is not the one who created the problem.

The Black woman is also viewed as a superhero because she endures so much. She is the one who tends to be the person to lean on, whom everyone goes to for everything, yet she is still mistreated and abused. In the 1977 movie "Roots," when the villainous Missy Anne lies on Kizzy and has her sold to another plantation, only for Kizzy to be repeatedly raped producing a son by the slaveholder, this is what the Black woman endures mentally and emotionally. No matter how much she has accomplished in life, she is consistently raped by a society that limits its acceptance of her. This is important because I want my readers to visualize how and why the Black woman is viewed with unshakeable strength. She is the sex object, the Jezebel, the Black Sapphire, the superhero among other things as she operates under the watchful eyes of the public, yet she is also distorted and dehumanized by a culture that fails to understand her, but through it all, only the strong survive.

In other aspects of her life, and for many Black women, there has been and can be violence against her in forms such as domestic abuse, psychological, verbal or social abuse, whether she endures that experience within her culture or outside of her culture, she will encounter not only the abuse, but the racism at some point and time in her life regardless of her age which can be similar to living life in an oven, because it is hot, oppressive, and can be extremely dangerous[130] just like those in society who tries to cause her harm.

The Black woman must also endure the societal attitudes of oppression, racism, and again sexism, and poverty which continues to summon the Black woman, and now the Latino, Asian, and other WOC (Women of Color) back into the White man's home to work for him and his family thereby leaving her own family to fend for themselves. White men and Black women have had an extended history of his ability to influence the Black woman's personal space, knowing of how she comes and how she goes, in addition to her family dynamics (after being raped and giving birth to the boss's child for hundreds of years).

At one point and time the Black mother had to deal with raising her children in "segregated neighborhoods, like the one which the Younger family, in "A Raisin In the Sun," had to endure, until they allowed their dreams not to be deferred anymore. Living

---

[130] Plaue, Ethan. "*The Help* Chapter 1." LitCharts LLC, October 4, 2015. Retrieved July 2, 2018. http://www.litcharts.com/lit/the-help/chapter-1.

in such conditions further solidified the existence of the hypocritical beliefs that segregation was 'separate but equal'—this so called legal doctrine was one that allowed local governments to separate services like education and housing for Blacks and Whites."[131] It was acceptable to work for those in an environment who made you subservient to their needs, but you were not equal because you are viewed as being less than.

George Corley Wallace Jr., the Governor of Alabama was a perfect example of such hypocritical atrocities. Wallace was famous for his ideologies on such pro-segregation which was a personification of his characteristics. In his 1963 Inaugural Address, he let it be known that he stood for "segregation now, segregation tomorrow, and segregation forever," he also stood in the front entrance of the University of Alabama in an attempt to stop the enrollment of Black students. He was just one of many who perpetuated the mistreatment of Blacks, especially the Black woman.

Even though Wallace eventually renounced segregation, the damage that he initially caused had been done and his opinions were the driving forces for others to perpetuate and spew their racial hatred towards minorities because of what he truly felt within his heart. Since the 1901 Constitution was written, it's effectiveness had been predicated upon the disfranchisement of the State's Blacks, and most poor Whites, with the Democratic Party being virtually the only party in Alabama.[132] This is why it is important to know cultural history and not just American history. It is also important to

---

[131] Plaue, Ethan. "*The Help* Chapter 1." LitCharts LLC, October 4, 2015. Retrieved July 2, 2018. http://www.litcharts.com/lit/the-help/chapter-1.
[132] "George Wallace, Segregation Symbol, Dies at 79". New York Times. September 14, 1998.

understand the hypocrisy and the beliefs that segregation was 'separate but equal,' all of which not only Blacks, but all minorities more so had to endure as well.

The "separate but equal" doctrine hypocritically claimed to create equality when in actuality they were really reinforcing institutional racism. Just like in the movie "The Help," the housewives, who are mainstream society, and those who tries to rationalize the exploitation of Blacks, uses this an excuse by convincing themselves that Black people are inferior to White people and do not deserve equal pay.[133] This which we know is not an accurate assumption. Yet, there are times when the Black woman neglects to instill certain boundaries that will convey to mainstream society that there are certain limitations in which she will not put up with as she will no longer shoulder the world's problems by being under a boulder; and that the world should not neglect the fact that she is not to be considered as a mule.

Black women in America have often been regarded as the "mules of the world," which is a negative connotation that stemmed out of slavery. The sad part is that no one wants to bear the burden, or what they think may be a burden of being a Black woman and sharing what she endures; nor do many appreciate Black women, yet society needs her and the services that she provides, such as being a maid or a nanny in order for certain individuals in society to continue to live at a comfort level that has afforded them the life of luxury, that they have had since the first slave ships hit the shores of Jamestown, Virginia in 1619. Societal attitudes and their metaphor of the mule becomes a symbol for the Black female's condition of being victimized by rape and subjected to bondage. The burdens that she endured are not only those imposed upon her by

---

[133] Plaue, Ethan. "*The Help* Chapter 2." LitCharts LLC, October 4, 2015. Retrieved July 2, 2018. http://www.litcharts.com/lit/the-help/chapter-2.

physical labor, but by the stereotypical, sexist attitudes about the Black woman, her femininity and her sexuality. Such a transition is also one that results from the attempts of Black men trying to gain their own selfhood from under the crushing feet of the White man, and, in an effort to assert their authority, these Black men subjugate Black women to the role of being a mule.

Published during the latter part of the Harlem Renaissance, 1937, Zora Neal Hurston's *"Their Eyes Were Watching God,"* was a notably down-to-earth novel of a story concerning a middle aged Mulatto woman, attractive and confident, who returns to Eatonville, Florida, after a long absence and running off with a younger man named Tea Cake.[134] All of her life she had been in search for love, spiritual liberation, physical satisfaction, and a way to challenge the seemingly unchallengeable laws of gender and race that Black women consistently encounter.

Janie explains to her friend Phoeby Watson that her grandmother had raised her after her mother ran off. Nanny is what Janie calls her grandmother, who loves her granddaughter unconditionally and is dedicated to her, but her own life as a slave and her experiences with her own daughter, Janie's mother, has warped her worldview. Nanny's primary desire for Janie is to get her married off as soon as possible to a husband who can provide security, stability and social status for her.

Nanny finds a much older farmer named Logan Killicks and insists that Janie marry him. Janie's marriage to Killicks is so miserable that she met and ran off with Joe Starks (Joey) whom she eventually marries. Janie soon becomes disenchanted with Jody and he tries to shape her into his vision, mostly as an arm piece of trophy, of what a

---

[134] SparkNotes Editors. "SparkNote on Their Eyes Were Watching God." SparkNotes LLC. 2007. http://www.sparknotes.com/lit/eyes/ (accessed June 24, 2018).

mayor's wife should be. On the surface, Janie silently submits to Jody; inside, however, she remains passionate and full of dreams. After Jody dies, Janie marries Tea Cake who is twelve years her junior only nine months later.[135] Janie searches for spiritual fulfillment, love, physical satisfaction, and a way to defy the seemingly undeniable laws of gender and race.

The image of the mule emerges repeatedly in different parts of the contexts throughout the novel, and even though it is written in 1937, the symbolic meaning of the mule remains consistent in its figurative meaning as a symbol of the Black female her constant victimization and her consistent bondage by mainstream society. The image of the mule first appears when Nanny tells Janie that Black women are the mules of the earth. What Nanny meant by this is that Black females are the lowest creatures from the human perspective, and they are constantly used by others. For Nanny, she was all too familiar with the evil atrocities of slavery, because she had been victimized while in bondage. She was very well aware of what could happen to an attractive Black female, and having the unwanted attention of her slave master, because her daughter Leafy was a product of such.

Nanny had to flee the plantation in order to escape the brutal beating that had been promised to her by her mistress. Soon afterward, she had the opportunity to experience the sweet taste of freedom and the excitement of emancipation, as she found a place in Florida where she was able to be independent, live, work, and raise her daughter. Her aspirations for her daughter, she hoped, would be to become a schoolteacher, but unfortunately, her hopes were dashed when Leafy too was raped,

---

[135] SparkNotes Editors. "SparkNote on Their Eyes Were Watching God." SparkNotes LLC. 2007. http://www.sparknotes.com/lit/eyes/ (accessed June 24, 2018).

ironically by the town schoolteacher, a White man, who had abandoned both Leafy and Janie.[136]

Throughout the novel, the mule symbolizes victimization, a theme that appears throughout in various ways. Nanny Crawford's reference to mules, "Honey, de White man is de ruler of everything as fur as Ah been able tuh find out. Maybe it's some place way off in de ocean where de Black man is in power, but we don't know nothin' but what we see...De nigger woman is de mule uh de world so fur as Ah can see."[137] Nanny sees sexual desire as dangerous, not wonderful. She sees it as something that threatens Janie's independence and financial well-being. Her comment about Black women being mules of the world shows that she believes that the *only* way for a Black woman to be independent is through financial security. But given Janie's belief that sexual desire=marriage, Nanny's practical-minded decision for Janie to marry the older, wealthy Logan is bound to be unfulfilling for Janie.[138]

The mule then appears again when one morning Logan Killicks goes to buy a second mule for Janie so that Janie and the mule can both productively plow the fields. Logan's forceful attempt to make Janie work now makes her feel as though she herself is being treated as an animal. After three months, it is obvious that Janie is unhappy with Logan Killicks, because he is a much older man who is most definitely set in his ways, so much so that Janie describes him as an old man who is also unattractive. Nanny, however, is looking out for her granddaughter's best interest as she sees Logan as a

[136] Ash, Megan E. *CliffsNotes on Their Eyes Were Watching God.* 16 Jul 2018 </literature/t/their-eyes-were-watching-god/book-summary>.
[137] Lieberman, Charlotte. *"Their Eyes Were Watching God. Chapter 2. "LithCharts LLC, September 17, 2013. Retrieved June 26, 2018.* http://www.litcharts.com/lit/their-eyes-were-watching-God/chapter 2
[138] *Lieberman, Charlotte. "Their Eyes Were Watching God. Chapter 2. "LithCharts LLC, September 17, 2013. Retrieved June 26, 2018.* http://www.litcharts.com/lit/their-eyes-were-watching-God/chapter 2

security blanket for Janie. He is a hard-working farmer who owns 60 acres of land which he farms successfully and has a comfortable house that was purchased for both he and his deceased wife.

After only a year of being married, Logan then begins to reevaluate his young wife's role as his wife. Logan's only desire was to have a wife who would be hardworking such as he on the farm. Because Janie was not raised to do farm work, Logan then begins to have a lack of respect for Janie, and begins treating her almost like a slave, requiring her to complete everyday tasks. Logan is certain that Janie has been spoiled by both her grandmother and by him. As Logan confronts Janie with his analogy of what a housewife should be, he then compares her to his first wife, who chopped wood for him without making any complaints.[139]

While Logan is looking for ways to make Janie work, Joey as she calls him, a charismatic, confident man with money who did not want Janie for love but as an arm piece, but she thinks that he is the man of her dreams. Immediately after meeting Joe Starks, Janie says with confidence that he "spoke for far horizon." The idea of the horizon is an important symbol for Janie, because it alludes to the idea of possibility, something of which Janie may still imagine, the incomprehensible can still be dreamt about. It should be recognized that the significance that Janie makes is an assessment of Joe before actually getting to really know him; this indicates the impulsive nature of desire (her desires in particular) and her tendency to map ideas about desire onto what

---

[139] Ash, Megan E. *CliffsNotes on Their Eyes Were Watching God.* 16 Jul 2018 </literature/t/their-eyes-were-watching-god/book-summary>.

it means to love and be loved.[140] Basically, such ideologies on the part of Janie makes her seem desperate.

Logan is not really a major part in Janie's story, and yet he plays a significant role in the culture of the South, because he is a Black man who acquired his own wealth. Looking for someone to replace his first wife, Logan informs Nanny that he is interested in her granddaughter Janie. Again, trying to look out for Janie's best interest, it is not until Nanny agrees and allow Logan to marry Janie. Once Janie is informed of this does she realize why Logan paying a visit to the house so often.[141]

Lastly, the mule reappears once again when the townspeople of Eatonville makes fun of Matt Bonner's sad looking pathetic mule and accuses him of mistreating the mule by overworking him and nearly starving the poor animal. This also represents mistreatment and betrayal Janie actually pities the mule and his being subjected to such abusive behavior. She can identify with the mule's subjugated treatment because she too suffers the effects of abuse, just as the mule does. While the mistreatment that Janie endures is primarily emotional, the abuse that the mule experiences is mostly physical. Regardless of the type of mistreatment each faces, the mule exists as a symbol of the abuse that Janie encounters in her marriage to Joe.[142] The townspeople's jokes about Bonner and his mule shows another instance of the human impulse for power and control over others, not unlike that which defines Jody.[143]

---

[140] Lieberman, Charlotte. "*Their Eyes Were Watching God* Chapter 4." LitCharts LLC, September 17, 2013. Retrieved June 26, 2018. http://www.litcharts.com/lit/their-eyes-were-watching-god/chapter-4.

[141] Ash, Megan E. *CliffsNotes on Their Eyes Were Watching God.* 16 Jul 2018 </literature/t/their-eyes-were-watching-god/book-summary>.

[142] SparkNotes Editors. "SparkNote on Their Eyes Were Watching God." SparkNotes LLC. 2007. http://www.sparknotes.com/lit/eyes/ (accessed June 24, 2018).

[143] Ash, Megan E. *CliffsNotes on Their Eyes Were Watching God.* 16 Jul 2018 </literature/t/their-eyes-were-watching-god/book-summary>.

One afternoon, the towns men began to engage themselves in a game of mule-baiting. Naturally, the mule begins fighting back in a defensive reaction, however, the more that the animal resists, the more the men begins teasing Bonner about his mule. Having had enough of the townsmen's cruelties, Janie mumbles her displeasure, which is also overheard by Joe. In an unforeseen act of kindness, Joe purchases the animal for both Janie because of her pity for the mule and for the mule, obviously to save him from the enduring hardships which he is encountering.[144]

From that time on, the mule ends up becoming the towns pet, and living in the front yard of the store roaming about at will, leading a life of ease and freedom. Again, Jody's purchase superficially appears benevolent both to the mule and to Janie, through the response of the townspeople they indecisively elevate Jody to the level of Abraham Lincoln which again reveals that he is also after making a gesture that will emphasize his power. For Joey, it is about power, control of people, position, property, and even money which rules his world. The townspeople's reference to Lincoln relates the issue of individual and their quests for power and control, such as that of Jody, to a larger historical pattern of subjugation, such as the history of American slavery.[145]

Thus, it is ironic when the townspeople connect Jody to Abraham Lincoln as a representative figure of freedom, since Jody is engaged in an effort to get power over them.[146] The mule on the other hand conjures a broader theme of victimization and bondage, and thus can be seen in relation to Janie, herself a victim of Jody's domination

---

[144] Ash, Megan E. *CliffsNotes on Their Eyes Were Watching God.* 16 Jul 2018 </literature/t/their-eyes-were-watching-god/book-summary>.

[145] Ash, Megan E. *CliffsNotes on Their Eyes Were Watching God.* 16 Jul 2018 </literature/t/their-eyes-were-watching-god/book-summary>.

[146] [146] Lieberman, Charlotte. "*Their Eyes Were Watching God* Chapter 6." LitCharts LLC, September 17, 2013. Retrieved June 26, 2018. http://www.litcharts.com/lit/their-eyes-were-watching-god/chapter-6.

and even the Black race. It is not known why Joe has display such an act of consideration for Janie.[147] When Jody purchases the mule to appease Janie's sense of pity for it, the town regards Jody as a savior, and adopts the freed mule as a kind of emblem.[148]

Eventually, the mule dies from old age and the townspeople presents an elaborate mock funeral service before they leave the carcass to buzzards. and, in an effort, to further exert his authority, Jody decides to prohibit Janie's attendance from the mule's funeral – the very mule that she was a catalyst for saving. Joey's act of wielding his power and authority is shown to be completely selfish, despite his rationalization. He cares more that Janie act in ways that promote his own power than about her own feelings or connections to others.[149] Janie's submissive role in her relationship with Jody is emphasized by the fact that her only amusement comes from listening to the conversations of townspeople – Jody deprives her of her own voice, and by expressing pleasure in listening, Janie moves toward the realization of her desire to express her own feelings and thoughts, to be a part of the conversation.[150]

At this moment, Janie shows herself to be aware of her desire for self-expression, though simultaneously aware of the consequences of attempting to achieve it. This state of ambivalence is one that ultimately drives Janie to erupt at Jody later in the novel, which is ultimately important in causing her to realize the importance of finding a voice

---

[147]147 Ash, Megan E. *CliffsNotes on Their Eyes Were Watching God.* 16 Jul 2018 </literature/t/their-eyes-were-watching-god/book-summary>.

[148] Lieberman, Charlotte. "*Their Eyes Were Watching God* Chapter 6." LitCharts LLC, September 17, 2013. Retrieved June 26, 2018. http://www.litcharts.com/lit/their-eyes-were-watching-god/chapter-6.

[149] Lieberman, Charlotte. "*Their Eyes Were Watching God* Chapter 6." LitCharts LLC, September 17, 2013. Retrieved June 26, 2018. http://www.litcharts.com/lit/their-eyes-were-watching-god/chapter-6.

[150] Ash, Megan E. *CliffsNotes on Their Eyes Were Watching God.* 16 Jul 2018 </literature/t/their-eyes-were-watching-god/book-summary>.

for herself.[151] Janie's sympathy for the mule indicates her sense of identification with another victim of subjugation, and she does then speak out.[152]

In Hurston's interval of the mule, the animal being given respite near the end of his life, just as the hard-working men and women who was most likely working as sharecroppers just as hard as "mules" who finally get respited at the end of their working day. As Hurston's central character counterattacks others' attempts to script her character's life based on their own selfish terms. In confronting such challenges that the Black woman endures, Hurston invokes the symbol of the mule to characterize Black women's precarious condition in the United States: she is "worked tuh death," "ruint wid mistreatment," yet strong enough to carry impossible "loads" nobody else wants to "tote."

There are so many Black women, especially single Black mothers who are knocking down the stereotypical pillars that the world wishes to see her in as she has demonstrated that she too can make changes. It is asked, what is a pillar? A pillar is the bridge between HEAVEN and EARTH, the vertical axis which both unites and divides these two realms. It is closely connected to the symbolism of the TREE; it also represents stability, and a broken pillar represents death and mortality.[153]

The Black woman is that bridge between her people and the world as she unites and divides the two realms. She is strong because for the most part, she has silently held it together for hundreds of years. The Black woman's 'strength' often comes with that

[151] Lieberman, Charlotte. "*Their Eyes Were Watching God* Chapter 6." LitCharts LLC, September 17, 2013. Retrieved June 26, 2018. http://www.litcharts.com/lit/their-eyes-were-watching-god/chapter-6
[152] Lieberman, Charlotte. "*Their Eyes Were Watching God* Chapter 6." LitCharts LLC, September 17, 2013. Retrieved June 26, 2018. http://www.litcharts.com/lit/their-eyes-were-watching-god/chapter-6.
[153] www.umich.edu/~umfandsf/symbolismproject/symbolism.html/P/pillar.html

unspoken rule which says that those who are considered as being strong, should not complain. Therefore, those who are considered strong, such as these certain Black women who have been discussed in this book, don't complain. By complaining then this would indicate that someone, somewhere, has become problematic to her.

Societal attitudes imply that Black women are capable of enduring the abuse and whatever else it is that she goes through, since she is strong, and by implying such negative attitudes, they take away her option of allowing herself to be incapable or unwilling to carry extreme burden. So, by removing her ability to complain about her circumstances, society convinces themselves that she is actually happy as she goes on about the daily business of suffrage.

Even though the Black woman is no longer limited to domestic services that she was once subjugated to endure as an employee, she is still, too often treated as the modern-day mammy, and in a sense sometimes respected for her intellect of enduring strength, caring, selflessness, and apparent acceptance of her subservience. There are certain beliefs about the Black woman, she is argumentative, all which began with slavery. Black women were seen as being the opposite of White women, which was the societal attitudes to justify their harsh labor, brutal beatings, and rape. The unfortunate part is that some of those old ideologies have since been embraced by America's societal attitudes and given positive qualities by Blacks themselves.

The Black woman is considered as a mule because of her selflessness such as the mule which is also a way for her to feel better about herself. However, when a Black woman does decide to complain, then she is viewed as being angry, and when a Black woman decides to choose her needs and what is best for her over the needs of others, then she is called selfish. When a Black woman strongly requests to be cared for as she exercises her option to a smoother path that will satisfy her demands, then she is considered as being a sellout. So, with this being said, society often fails to realize that a mule is an animal is that is highly intelligent, refusing to be worked to exhaustion and they are oftentimes wrongfully categorized as being stubborn. This is something that the Black woman also refuses to do.

Today, the Black woman would also be considered as a modern-day superhero compared to her White counterpart whose position is viewed as good and delicate in the normal world. Yet, there are those Black women who are passively aggressive who will often refuse to be truthful enough to express their collective frustrations and individual pain. As with anything else, her silence condones the abuse as it has done for so many years. There are many Black women who are perceived to be a superwoman and yet she is often not offered any support. The Black woman tends to be the one who is expected to carry the load. Instead of being compared to a mule thus being called a "jackass," why is it that a Black woman cannot be compared to something that is beautiful such as a diamond, one that has been cut and polished to near perfection or a rose whose petals are as delicate as satin, silk or velvet, yet its thorns are contrasted by symbolizing defense, loss, and thoughtlessness, as it protects itself from those who has mishandled it? The beauty of a rose actually characterizes the strength of a Black woman as it expresses for her, promise, hope, and new beginnings. Yet, the Black woman is not viewed in the same manner by many in society. Oftentimes it is considered that Black women are treated as expendable and disposable commodities.

Throughout the years since slavery, the Black woman has continued to be abused, mistreated and invisible to a society who also refuses to acknowledge her even more so than her Black male counterpart. She too is a Black woman who is in search for her own identity and visibility in White America. However, there are times when she neglects to instill certain boundaries conveying that there are certain limitations that she will not put up with as she will no longer be under the boulder of the worlds problem and that the world should not neglect the fact that she is not to be considered as a mule.

The term "mule" in comparison to the Black woman relates to the triple downgrading —of race, sex, and class. This is something that Black women are faced with daily, because this is how society views her, and that is being the pillar of strength for her race. Paula Giddings, author of *"When and Where I Enter: The Impact of Black Women on Race and Sex in America,"* states, "In its infancy, was particularly harsh. Physical abuse, dismemberment, and torture were common to an institution that was far from peculiar to its victims" (39). This violent type of enslavement also known as bondage, is a reflection of the pervading fallacy at the time when Blacks were considered as being less than human—at least to the point of being classified alongside mules and other domesticated animals of labor. In fact, they Blacks have been treated so bad that they were even considered to be a less valuable commodity than mules.

There are some Black female authors who view being the mules of the world as having negative connotations while others such as myself, have taken such a derogatory meaning and subsequently given it a positive meaning through the act of Signification, as theorized by Henry Louis Gates. Like their Black male predecessors, Maya Angelou's (in I Know Why the Caged Bird Sings) and Zora Neale Hurston's (in Their Eyes Were Watching God) they break free from the restrictions of language and create a new meaning to be compared to as a mule, as one with strength, character and dignity.[154]

---

[154] Taylor, Stephanie Abigail (2007) The Evolution and Ownership of the Concept of the African-American Woman as "The Mule of the World."

For both Hurston and Angelou, they have passionately conveyed that Black women are basically accountable for their conditions, as they invest in the appearance of invulnerability. They wear masks that hides their smiles as they live their lies, keep up the uplifted appearances, perform superhuman tasks of what is perceived as the inevitable, and take care of everyone else, while sacrificing their own feelings and needs, to the detriment of their own health. While women of other groups may also be caretakers, it is Black women, whose strength has too often meant taking care of other families in addition to, or instead of, their own.

According to Widepikia, a mule is the offspring of a male donkey (jack) and a female horse (mare).[155],[156] Horses and donkeys are different species, with different numbers of chromosomes. Of the two F1 hybrids (first generation hybrids) between these two species, a mule is easier to obtain than a hinny, which is the offspring of a female donkey (jenny) and a male horse (stallion). The size of a mule and work to which it is put depends largely on the breeding of the mule's female parent (dam). Mules are reputed to be more patient showing more patience under the pressure of heavy weight, they are robust having skin that is firmer and less sensitive than that of horses, making them more capable of resisting the sun and rain, in addition to them having a longer life span than horses, and are described as less obstinate and more intelligent than donkeys. They have vigor, strength and the courage of the horse. There are those who work with animals who generally find mules preferable to horses. [157],[158]

---

[155] "Mule Day: A Local Legacy." *americaslibrary.gov. Library of Congress. 2013-12-18.* Retrieved 2018-06-22.
[156] What is a mule?" *The Donkey Sanctuary.*
[157] Jackson, Louise A (2004). *The Mule Men: A History of Stock Packing in the Sierra Nevada.* Missoula, MT: Mountain Press. ISBN 0-87842-499-7.
[158] Mule. *The Encyclopædia Britannica: A Dictionary of Arts, Sciences, and General.* **XVII.** Henry G. Allen and Company. 1888. p. 15.

Just as the mule, Black women are often expected to carry the emotional load of an entire race. It is as though they bear the burdens of having to explain to the world the original sins that were committed in America as though she was the one who committed them. It is the Black woman who is the mule, being patient under pressure, she did not lash out in the frustration of being beat, maimed, mutilated, tortured, lynched, shot down like animals, segregating ourselves from the world as many of her people literally wait for an unexpected death at the end of a barrel of a White man's gun because of his ignorance, fear, hatred, and evil atrocities that he bestows upon her people. It was not the Black woman's choice to shed the blood, sweat and tears that were bestowed upon her own people as they endured the harsh realities of slavery, yet she is expected to carry the burdens, and this is why she is considered as the mule of her people. The Black woman has done none of this, yet it is she that is forced to carry the guilt, rage and privilege of mainstream society and their guilt.

Black women are not only powerful, they are also resilient, because slavery, from a negative perspective, has provided her with that extra quantity of strength that she has had to endure for so long. It seems that the Black woman has been given all the ingredients that she will ever need for overcoming any adversity in this life. The Black female slave had to nurse her child, nurse the masters child, cook, clean, wash, be the midwife, the counselor, the nurturer, and be the help mate of the Black man all while maintaining her sense of self. Time has evolved, and we are now in the 21st century and the Black woman is still EVERYTHING to EVERYONE. While the Black woman is often overwhelmed with carrying everyone else's problems then who does she complain to because it is she who is the backbone of all things in space and time.

"Similar to the mule, Black women do a lot and yet, they are underappreciated. Collins (2008) describes the laboring of mules as "dehumanized objects that blends in with the scenery" (p.45). His definition of a mule links to this portion of the book because it demonstrates the idea that single Black mothers, through societal oppressions, societal attitudes and negative stereotypes, are often ignored and treated as insignificant beings (Ross 2012, pg 4). Again, "Black women are one of the most silenced groups in society as race and gender both amplify and disqualify their voices" (Ross p. 6). Oftentimes, she is also unwilling to express her true feelings to a White woman, being more like Aibileen and saying that everything is fine.[159]

The Black woman has always been viewed from a negative perspective since slavery. It is said that Black mothers are the worse mothers around, and this will be touched upon in a future chapter. Well as a single Black mother, of a daughter and two sons, (one son now deceased) who also knows several single Black mothers, I would like for society to understand that not all looks are alike and that one should never judge a book by its cover. Like any other mother in the world, the Black mother has plans, goals and visions for their lives and the lives of their families just as any other mother does.

The Black mother may have to struggle a lot harder than a mother from mainstream society and work 200% harder than the mother from mainstream society, but there are Black mothers who do not fit the stereotypical profile that many may view her as being. Single Black mothers are women, they are real women and should be viewed and treated as such. The Black woman is just as intellectual as any other woman

---

[159] Plaue, Ethan. "*The Help* Plot Summary." LitCharts LLC, October 4, 2015. Retrieved June 28, 2018. http://www.litcharts.com/lit/the-help/summary.

in her own right. She is one who has struggled to survive despite what she has faced in life and she is the trailblazer of tomorrow.

As a single Black mother, for many of us to tell society how we feel can be quite harsh, however, to show society how we feel would be satisfying enough, as we show you how we can persevere and demonstrate our strengths through our actions. There are several single Black mothers who are the equivalent to Michelle Obama, and many other highly educated minority women, so never believe the hype or what is glamorized by the media from a negative perspective. There are several Black women, and single Black mothers who have beaten the odds through their strength, perseverance, determination and the ability to move forward. Kathy Hughes, Angela Benton, Lisa Stone, Karla Campos and so many other single Black mothers who are entrepreneurs.

Unfortunately, the United States consistently engages in conversations on how low-income single Black mothers are part of society's social problem. This assumption of deficiency is reflected in studies of parenting logics and practices.[160] This is societal attitudes towards single Black mothers. What many scholars and researchers do not understand is that oftentimes, the single Black mother's abilities are underestimated by her sophistication and ability to raise her children despite her low-income status. She acquires a skill that is combined with analytical parenting skills that are not recognized by a wider society.[161] "With some inner-city Black communities like Chicago in shambles, conversations often turn to blaming the stereotypical view of the Black single mother—the Black mother having numerous kids living on welfare. And it is true that

---

[160] Verduzco-Baker, Lynn. Anthropology & Sociology Department, Albion College, 611 E. Porter Street, Albion, MI 49224, USA. Email: lverduzco@albion.edu
[161] Fountain, Resheena (2016) "Black Single Mothers Are More Than Scapegoats." **Updated** Apr 07, 2017 https://www.huffingtonpost.com/rasheena-fountain/black-single-mothers-are. Follow Rasheena Fountain on Twitter: www.twitter.com/rasheenacharee

66% of African American families are single parent families, according the United States Census Bureau Data. However, unwed birth rates have declined for Black and Hispanic women, according to the Center for Disease Control. The choice for single mothers to better themselves through higher education has also increased."[162]

The fact of the matter, is that as I stated earlier, Black mothers, especially single Black mothers have to work twice as hard as those mothers in mainstream "and use (appropriately) different parenting logics than those of mainstream middle-class mothers."[163] Our cultures are not only different, but our parenting logics are truly as different than night and day compared to the White low-income mother. Single Black mothers "demonstrate a logic that follows many of the same premises of middle-class parenting strategies, but they also additionally seek to address obstacles that prevent low-income youth from reaching goals: addiction, drug dealing, pregnancy, and 'the street.'"[164] Much of the Black woman's ideologies are based on her survival skills in life and the environment in which she came. Such logic also leads to strategies that may appear to be economical modifications of middle-class practices, however, analysis of mothers' narratives reveals they are not lacking in originality but are expected to prepare their children on how to avoid the threats of their social context. This particular study enlightens society with a previously misunderstood version of intensive mothering."[165]

---

[162] Fountain, Resheena (2016) "Black Single Mothers Are More Than Scapegoats." **Updated** Apr 07, 2017 https://www.huffingtonpost.com/rasheena-fountain/black-single-mothers-are. Follow Rasheena Fountain on Twitter: www.twitter.com/rasheenacharee

[163] Verduzco-Baker, Lynn. Anthropology & Sociology Department, Albion College, 611 E. Porter Street, Albion, MI 49224, USA. Email: lverduzco@albion.edu

[164] Verduzco-Baker, Lynn. Anthropology & Sociology Department, Albion College, 611 E. Porter Street, Albion, MI 49224, USA. Email: lverduzco@albion.edu

[165] Verduzco-Baker, Lynn. Anthropology & Sociology Department, Albion College, 611 E. Porter Street, Albion, MI 49224, USA. Email: lverduzco@albion.edu

First, let me talk about the Black woman because I am a Black woman, and while many Black women may not agree with me, I can say that the majority of us has overcome. There are those Black women who have used their strengths through writing literature in order to overcome their obstacles. There are these few women who were around during the periods of pre, and post slavery who presented in their writings a variety of salient characteristics. In order for many of you to understand what I am about to say, let me break it down from a sociological point of view. When observing history, we must first observe American literature through history, and through American literature and its history, we must then observe African American literature by African American women.

Through their literature, Black women have expressed themselves concerning the injustices of slavery from the 1600s up until today. However, today the injustices that are encountered by Blacks is not called slavery, because that would be politically incorrect. It is a form of pseudo slavery. Audre Lorde stated, "we as Black women are born into a society of entrenched loathing and contempt for whatever is Black and female. We are strong and enduring. We are also deeply scarred" (Lorde, 8).[166]

Demonstrated in many of these writing, these women dealt with the problems of slavery, religion, education and the family's structure which gives more than an extensive account of the slave and their literary works. It also gives a personal account of their perspectives on such matters. The few strong Black women that I focus on from the perspectives of this chapter includes Lucy Terry, Phyllis Wheatley and Frances Ellen Walker Harper. I focus on them because they were all also mothers. There is a profound

---

[166] Lorde, Audre, (1984). *Sister Outsider: Essays and Speeches.* The Crossing Press. California.

essence of survival against all odds, which is forever present throughout their literary works.

Lucy Terry a woman who fought for what she believed in. In 1785, when a neighboring White family threatened the Princes', and they appealed to the governor and his Council for protection. The Council ordered Guilford's selectmen to defend them. "A persuasive orator, Prince successfully negotiated a land case before the U.S Supreme Court in the 1790s, being the first woman to argue before the High Court.[167] She argued against two of the leading lawyers in the state (one of whom later became the Chief Justice of the Supreme Court of Vermont) and won her case against the false land claims of Colonel Eli Bronson. Samuel Chase, the presiding justice of the Court, said that her argument was better than he had heard from any Vermont lawyer.[168] She also delivered a three-hour address to the board of trustees of Williams College while trying to gain admittance for her son Festus. While she was not successful, her speech was remembered for its eloquence and skill."[169]

Phillis Wheatley, Phillis also spelled Phyllis and Wheatly (c. 1753 – December 5, 1784) was the first published African American female poet.[170],[171] She was born in West Africa, and obviously stolen or shall I say kidnapped and sold into slavery at the age of seven or eight and then transported to North America. Phillis was then purchased by the Wheatley family of Boston, where she was taught how to read and write through a family

---

[167] Wertheimer, Barbara M. (1977). *We Were There: The Story of Working Women in America*. New York, NY: Pantheon Books. pp. 35–36.

[168] Smith, Jessie Carney (1994). *Black firsts: 2,000 Years of Extraordinary Achievement*. Detroit, MI: Gale Research. p. 417

[169] Sheldon, George (1893). *Negro Slavery in Old Deerfield*. Boston, Mass. p. 57.

[170] Henry Louis Gates, *Trials of Phillis Wheatley: America's Second Black Poet and Her Encounters with the Founding Fathers*, Basic Civitas Books, 2010, p. 5.

[171] For example, in the name of the Phyllis Wheatley YWCA in Washington, D.C., where "Phyllis" is etched into the name over its front door (as can be seen in photos and corresponding text for that building's National Register nomination)

who also encouraged her to write and publish her poetry when they saw her talent. Mr. Wheatley and his family gave Phillis an unprecedented education to someone who was not only enslaved but was a female which was very uncommon of a female in any race. By the time Phillis was 12 years old, she was reading Greek and Latin classics in addition to difficult passages from the Bible. By the time she was 14 years old, she wrote her first poem, "To the University of Cambridge, in New England."[172]

The publication of her Poems on Various Subjects, Religious and Moral (1773) brought her fame both in England and the American colonies. Figures such as George Washington praised her work.[173] During Wheatley's visit to England with her master's son, African-American poet Jupiter Hammon praised her work in his own poem. Wheatley was emancipated (set free) shortly after the publication of her book.[174] She married in about 1778. Two of her children died as infants. After her husband was imprisoned for debt in 1784, Wheatley fell into poverty and died of illness, which was an attributing factor from starvation, quickly followed by the death of her surviving infant son. She seldom referred to her own life in her poems. One example of a poem on slavery is "On being brought from Africa to America":[175]

> Twas mercy brought me from my Pagan land,
> Taught my benighted soul to understand
> That there's a God, that there's a Saviour too:
> Once I redemption neither sought nor knew.
> Some view our sable race with scornful eye,
> "Their colour is a diabolic dye."

[172] Brown, Sterling (1937). *Negro Poetry and Drama*. Washington, DC: Westphalia Press. ISBN 1935907549.
[173] Meehan, Adam; Bell, J. L. "Phillis Wheatley · George Washington's Mount Vernon". George Washington's Mount Vernon. Retrieved July 17, 2018.
[174] Hilda L. Smith, *Women's Political and Social Thought: An Anthology*, Indiana University Press, 2000, p. 123
[175] "On Being Brought from Africa to America"

Remember, Christians, Negroes, black as Cain,

May be refin'd, and join th' angelic train.[176]

In 1773 and with the first publication of Wheatley's book *Poems on Various Subjects,* she had "become one the most famous Africans (Americans) on the face of the earth."[177] Voltaire stated in a letter that was written to a friend that Wheatley had proven that Black people could actually write poetry. John Paul Jones had asked a fellow officer if he could deliver some of his personal writings to "Phillis the African favorite of the Nine (muses) and Apollo."[178] She was honored by many of America's founding fathers, including George Washington, who told her that "the style and manner [of your poetry] exhibit a striking proof of your great poetical Talents."[179]

Then we have a woman who was another mother who was one with a great deal of strength and courage. Born in 1825 in Baltimore, Maryland Frances Ellen Watkins Harper was able to attend school as the daughter of free Black parents. After losing her mother at a young age, Harper was raised by an aunt. She also attended a school for African-American children run by her uncle, Reverend William Watkins. Bright and talented, Harper started writing poetry in her youth. She kept on writing while working for a Quaker family after finishing school.[180]

Harper was a leading 19th century African-American poet and writer. Harper was also a devoted activist in the abolitionist and women's rights movements in addition to

---

[176] Wheatley, Phillis (1887). *Poems on Various Subjects, Religious and Moral*. Denver, Colorado: W.H. Lawrence. p. 120.
[177] Gates, *The Trials of Phillis Wheatley*, p. 33.
[178] Gates, *The Trials of Phillis Wheatley*, p. 33.
[179] "George Washington to Phillis Wheatley, February 28, 1776". The George Washington Papers at the Library of Congress, 1741-1799.;
[180] Lewis, Jone Johnson. (2018, June 14). Frances Ellen Watkins Harper. Retrieved from https://www.thoughtco.com/frances-ellen-watkins-harper-3529113

publicly advocating education, and, who continued to work after the Civil War for racial justice through her speeches and publications. Her first poem collection, *Forest Leaves*, was published around 1845 but no copies are now known to exist.[181]. The delivery of her public speech, "Education and the Elevation of the Colored Race," resulted in a two-year lecture tour for the Anti-Slavery Society. Harper later moved to Ohio five years later to teach domestic skills, such as sewing, at Union Seminary. The school was run by leading abolitionist John Brown. Harper became dedicated to the abolitionist cause a few years later after her home state of Maryland passed a fugitive slave law. This law allowed even free blacks, such as Harper, to be arrested and sold into slavery.[182]

In 1854, Harper published *Poems of Miscellaneous Subjects,* which featured on one of her most famous, "Bury Me in a Free Land." She also became an in-demand lecturer on behalf of the abolitionist movement, appearing with the likes of Frederick Douglass, William Garrison, Lucretia Mott and Lucy Stone. Harper made literary history in 1859 with the publication of "Two Offers." With this work, she became the first African-American female writer to publish a short story. The following year, she married Fenton Harper, who had several children from a previous marriage. Harper retreated from public life, choosing to live with her husband and children in Ohio. In 1862, she gave birth to a daughter, Mary.[183]

In 1864, Harper returned to the lecture circuit after the death of her husband. She also produced several long-form poems a short while later, including *Moses: A*

---

[181] Lewis, Jone Johnson. (2018, June 14). Frances Ellen Watkins Harper. Retrieved from https://www.thoughtco.com/frances-ellen-watkins-harper-3529113
[182] Lewis, Jone Johnson. (2018, June 14). Frances Ellen Watkins Harper. Retrieved from https://www.thoughtco.com/frances-ellen-watkins-harper-3529113
[183] Lewis, Jone Johnson. (2018, June 14). Frances Ellen Watkins Harper. Retrieved from https://www.thoughtco.com/frances-ellen-watkins-harper-3529113

Story of the Nile (1869) and *Sketches of Southern Life* (1872), which explored her

experiences during the reconstruction.[184]

Harper published her most famous novel *Iola Leroy* in 1892. Four years later, she

cofounded the National Association of Colored Women with Ida Wells-Barnett, Harriet

Tubman and several others. The organization sought to improve the lives and advance

the rights of African-American women.[185]

By the turn of the century, Harper began to scale down her activities, though she

still worked to support such causes as women's suffrage and such organizations as the

NACW and the Women's Christian Temperance Union. Harper died of heart failure on

February 22, 1911, in Philadelphia, Pennsylvania. She was buried next to her daughter,

Mary, at Eden Cemetery.[186]

Bury Me In A Free Land

By Frances Ellen Watkins Harper

Make me a grave where'er you will,
In a lowly plain, or a lofty hill;
Make it among earth's humblest graves,
But not in a land where men are slaves.

I could not rest if around my grave
I heard the steps of a trembling slave;
His shadow above my silent tomb
Would make it a place of fearful gloom.

I could not rest if I heard the tread
Of a coffle gang to the shambles led,
And the mother's shriek of wild despair
Rise like a curse on the trembling air.

---

[184] Lewis, Jone Johnson. (2018, June 14). Frances Ellen Watkins Harper. Retrieved from
https://www.thoughtco.com/frances-ellen-watkins-harper-3529113
[185] Lewis, Jone Johnson. (2018, June 14). Frances Ellen Watkins Harper. Retrieved from
https://www.thoughtco.com/frances-ellen-watkins-harper-3529113
[186] Lewis, Jone Johnson. (2018, June 14). Frances Ellen Watkins Harper. Retrieved from
https://www.thoughtco.com/frances-ellen-watkins-harper-3529113

I could not sleep if I saw the lash
Drinking her blood at each fearful gash,
And I saw her babes torn from her breast,
Like trembling doves from their parent nest.

I'd shudder and start if I heard the bay
Of bloodhounds seizing their human prey,
And I heard the captive plead in vain
As they bound afresh his galling chain.

If I saw young girls from their mother's arms
Bartered and sold for their youthful charms,
My eye would flash with a mournful flame,
My death-paled cheek grow red with shame.

I would sleep, dear friends, where bloated might
Can rob no man of his dearest right;
My rest shall be calm in any grave
Where none can call his brother a slave.

I ask no monument, proud and high,
To arrest the gaze of the passers-by;
All that my yearning spirit craves,
Is bury me not in a land of slaves.

The Slave Auction- By Frances EW Harper

The sale began—young girls were there,

Defenseless in their wretchedness,

Whose stifled sobs of deep despair

Revealed their anguish and distress.

And mothers stood, with streaming eyes,

And saw their dearest children sold;

Unheeded rose their bitter cries,

While tyrants bartered them for gold.

And woman, with her love and truth—

For these in sable forms may dwell—

Gazed on the husband of her youth,

With anguish none may paint or tell.

And men, whose sole crime was their hue,
The impress of their Maker's hand,
And frail and shrinking children too,
Were gathered in that mournful band.

Ye who have laid your loved to rest,
And wept above their lifeless clay,
Know not the anguish of that breast,
Whose loved are rudely torn away.

Ye may not know how desolate
Are bosoms rudely forced to part,
And how a dull and heavy weight
Will press the life-drops from the heart.

In an obituary, it was stated that W.E.B. DuBois said that it was "for her attempts to forward literature among colored people that Frances Harper deserves to be remembered.... She took her writing soberly and earnestly, she gave her life to it."[187] Her work was largely neglected and forgotten until she was "rediscovered" in the late 20th century.[188] The writings of Frances Watkins Harper were often focused on themes of racial justice, equality, and freedom.[189]

[187] Lewis, Jone Johnson. (2018, June 14). Frances Ellen Watkins Harper. Retrieved from https://www.thoughtco.com/frances-ellen-watkins-harper-3529113
[188] Lewis, Jone Johnson. (2018, June 14). Frances Ellen Watkins Harper. Retrieved from https://www.thoughtco.com/frances-ellen-watkins-harper-3529113
[189] Lewis, Jone Johnson. (2018, June 14). Frances Ellen Watkins Harper. Retrieved from https://www.thoughtco.com/frances-ellen-watkins-harper-3529113

With respect and much preservation, Lucy Terry's "Bar Fight," is the epitome of the need for survival. There is a pattern which flows freely like water. In her poem, Terry addresses, and with strong conviction, the need to remember those whose lives were lost in an ambush. The ambush was an unprovoked raid that was executed by local Indians taking place on the 25th of August 1746.[190] The names of whom I shall not leave out...so brave and bold, his face no more shall we behold."[191] Terry-Prince composed a ballad through her poem, "Bars Fight", about an attack upon two White families by Native Americans on August 25, 1746. Up until it's publication in 1855 more than 100 years after being written, it had been well preserved orally.

Wheatley on the other hand did not quite view slavery as many other slaves did, she actually credited slavery as being positive circumstance to her race. She felt that by being introduced to Christianity afforded her the opportunity to present her works as a "safe" subject for a slave poet who was able to read and write. Expressing such gratitude for her enslavement may have been unexpected to most readers and even other slaves.[192] Wheatley felt that with slaves being in a state of moral or intellectual darkness, their skin color and their original state of ignorance concerning Christian redemption paralleled with their current situations.

Wheatley seems to credit God's "mercy" with her voyage to America, and her education in Christianity, even though both scenarios were actually at the hands of human beings who treated other human beings with such cruel and unjust atrocities. So,

---

[190] Liggins-Hill, Patricia, et. al. (1998). *Call and Response: The Riverside Anthology of African American Literary Traditions.* Houghton Mifflin Company. New York. (191).
[191] Liggins-Hill, Patricia, et. al. (1998). *Call and Response: The Riverside Anthology of African American Literary Traditions.* Houghton Mifflin Company. New York. (191).
[192] Lewis, Jone Johnson. (2017, March 25). Phillis Wheatley's Poems. Retrieved from https://www.thoughtco.com/phillis-wheatleys-poems-3528282

for Wheatley, in turning both to God and her education, she reminds her audience that there is a force more powerful than they are, a force that has acted directly in her life.[193] Wheatley ingeniously distances her reader from those who "view our sable race with scornful eye," those who are predominantly White who can read, and perhaps thus nudging the reader to use an open window of perception from a more critical perspective of slavery or at least a more positive view of those who are slaves.[194] As the audience observes Wheatley's attitude towards slavery in her poetry, it is also important to note that most of Wheatley's poems do not refer to her "condition of servitude" at all. Most are occasional pieces, that are written on the death of some notable or on some special occasion. From my analysis on some of Wheatley's work, after the arrest of her husband and her being subjected to poverty, she and her children starved to death. Few refer directly -- and certainly not this directly -- to her personal story or status. She eloquently presents her condition from the perspective of a mother.

In her poem "The Slave Mother," Harper eloquently illustrates how a mother, during the time of slavery could be subjected to some of the harshest cruelties, as they have their children ripped from their being and sold off to another family with the intentions of never seeing them again. The shriek, the burdened heart and breaking despair as a mother watch helplessly. A slave mother knew all too well what it was like to lose a child, especially a son, even if in the physical form as she grieves.[195] In each of her

---

[193] Lewis, Jone Johnson. (2017, March 25). Phillis Wheatley's Poems. Retrieved from https://www.thoughtco.com/phillis-wheatleys-poems-3528282
[194] Lewis, Jone Johnson. (2017, March 25). Phillis Wheatley's Poems. Retrieved from https://www.thoughtco.com/phillis-wheatleys-poems-3528282
[195] jmj616. "Analyze "The Slave Mother" by Frances E.W. Harper." *eNotes*, 26 Oct. 2010, https://www.enotes.com/homework-help/analyze-slave-mother-by-frances-e-w-harper-212141. Accessed 27 July 2018.

writings, Harper paints a vivid picture of what mainstream society expected of not just the slave mother but women as a collective.

During the late "eighteenth and early nineteenth centuries, the ideology of the Cult of True Womanhood pervaded American culture and enforced the idea that a virtuous woman's civic duty was to nurture her husband and children and to remain within the confines of the home."[196] In Harpers poem, *"Iola Leroy"* she challenges both "the social and cultural norm, often the topic of previous literary works. The protagonist, Iola, works as a nurse, an accountant, and a teacher, and she is an outspoken intellectual." *Iola Leroy* also touches upon the idea that "women should be meek and docile, as dictated by a male-dominated society. Several critics also note that *Iola Leroy* resists the literary convention of the tragic mulatta character that was popular in writings of the 1850s and 1860s. These texts often portrayed miscegenation, or racial mixing, as a catalyst to a female character's demise." *Iola Leroy* explores the nineteenth-century ideology that the degree of blackness of one's skin determined one's social class and civil rights.[197]

As we have observed, with just these three women and their work, we will see that there is common link of survival that has been witnessed and experienced within the works of many women like them. These women used their poetry and stories to focus on the immoral injustices of slavery and their continued struggles against all odds throughout American history. Their writings not only lend a significant outpouring of

---

[196] jmj616. "Analyze "The Slave Mother" by Frances E.W. Harper." *eNotes*, 26 Oct. 2010, https://www.enotes.com/homework-help/analyze-slave-mother-by-frances-e-w-harper-212141. Accessed 27 July 2018.
[197] jmj616. "Analyze "The Slave Mother" by Frances E.W. Harper." *eNotes*, 26 Oct. 2010, https://www.enotes.com/homework-help/analyze-slave-mother-by-frances-e-w-harper-212141. Accessed 27 July 2018.

emotion in the struggle to survive, but it also demonstrates a desire to survive the overwhelming odds. Their writings become an enlightenment not only for other African American women but women across the board where they were able to represent themselves effectively. These writers have expressed to America how Black women have been treated unjust with inequality by attacking those who have oppressed them.

The family dynamics and cultural differences that Africans were accustomed to were satisfactory to those of African descent, yet their cultural customs were viewed as barbaric to Europeans and those who were looking to not only capitalize as a financial gain, but also to establish life in the United States of America. Since Africans were viewed as barbaric and subhuman they were also exploited and used as property during chattel slavery in the United States and forced to participate in things that were contrary to the family's values in which they created for themselves in Africa. Families were separated on plantations. Slave men and women were used as breeder tools to produce children so that those who felt as though they were more superior than the African would be able to continue the institution of slavery.

During slavery, the Black family was not recognized as a legitimate institution and it made White people believe that their idea of family was the epitome of what the Black family should be (Omolade, 1987).[198] This belief created unrealistic norms and an institution of slavery which placed Black families in positions that guaranteed that they would never fit into society's definition of the norms.

---

[198] Omolade, B. (1987). The unbroken circle: A historical and contemporary study of black single mothers and their families. *Wisconsin Women's Law Journal 3, 239-274.*

According to Omolade (1987),[199] the ideology of "Black single motherhood began as a viable family type which Black men and women adapted in response to a system which did not recognize their right to a legal marriage and family" (Omolade, 1987 p. 240).[200] The institution of slavery made the Black family's experience uniquely different in comparison to any other race of families in U.S. History because slavery positioned the Black family outside of the norms. Although many minorities' histories have been rooted in brutality at the hands of White Americans, Black people endured physical and psychological abuse for more than four hundred years (Meltzer, 1993).[201]

As mentioned in the previous section of this book, Black families who had a connection to Africa have had their own family dynamics prior to the institution of slavery and these dynamics were shattered due to the ways in which slavery dissected Black households. During the dissection of the Black household, husbands were sent away while Black women were left behind and often brutally beaten and raped with no one to protect them. The lack of protection from this brutal physical abuse, although involuntary, created a disconnection between many husbands and wives during slavery (Meltzer, 1993).[202]

Statistical research done according to the U.S. Census, as of 2011, there were 4,081,854 homes that were headed by single mothers with children under 18 years of age reporting below the poverty in-comes ("Poverty status in the past 12 months"). That same year, there were 962,887 households that were headed by single fathers and

[199] Omolade, B. (1987). The unbroken circle: A historical and contemporary study of black single mothers and their families. *Wisconsin Women's Law Journal 3, 239-274.*
[200] Omolade, B. (1987). The unbroken circle: A historical and contemporary study of black single mothers and their families. *Wisconsin Women's Law Journal 3, 239-274.*
[201] Meltzer, M. (1993). Slavery: A world history. Chicago: First Da Capo Press.
[202] Meltzer, M. (1993). Slavery: A world history. Chicago: First Da Capo Press.

3,232,308 married couple families with children who self-identified themselves as living below the poverty guidelines.

As demonstrated through statistical research, there were more mothers in poverty than fathers and married-couple families in 2011. In that same year, there were 5,527,790 single mothers who headed homes that received food stamps and 1,197,146 single father homes who received food stamps ("Receipt of food stamps/SNAP in that 12-month period by family type"). Research also demonstrated with the statistics, that poverty affected single mothers the most. It has also been consistently demonstrated that women and mothers experience poverty more than men and fathers ("Related Children in Female Householders as a Proportion of All Related Children, by Poverty Status: 1959 to 2011").[203]

From 1959 to 2011, the U.S. Census had reported that there was an increase in the amount of mother-led homes that identified themselves as living in poverty. In 1959, the poverty rate was only 24.1% for mother-led homes and, shockingly, in 2011 this statistic has climbed to 325. This number is related to the proportion of all households in poverty. In other words, of the families that are in poverty, there are about a quarter of the households that are in poverty that were single mother homes in 1959 and half of those families were single mother homes (or female-headed households) in 2011.[204] This demonstrates that even though there is a significant change it is however an obvious increase. Various reasons that could be explained the increase, are such changes such as divorce rates, increased age of a person getting married, blended family rates, rise of

[204] Related Children in Female Householders as a Proportion of All Related Children, by Poverty Status: 1959 to 2011

living costs, teenage pregnancy rates, and lack of jobs.[205] Regardless of how and why, poverty puts a strain on the economic and physical stability of low-income mothers and their families.

Many in mainstream society are not aware that throughout history, poor mothers have had to experience the harshness of having forced sterilization or face some form of retaliation such as termination from their place of employment, however during the 1960s and 1970s in America, such practices were particularly prevalent among poor women of color (Lawrence).

During the 1960s, the number of women who were on welfare had increased and in response, medical doctors began making decisions regarding poor women's bodies and economic situations (Lawrence). These women were often coerced into signing consent forms for sterilization or they did not understand exactly what was going on. Most of the doctors who were performing such procedures or unethical practices were White males often being facetious for reasons such as racism, or who thought they were helping society by limiting the number of births to poor families, by decreasing the use of Medicaid and other welfare programs (Lawrence). Poor mothers were seen as undeserving of children, and by performing sterilization procedures, it was thought to control a "growing problem" (Lawrence). Poor mothers where physically altered because of their socioeconomic status and race.

More than 50 years ago, there was the go-getting "Great Society" agenda that was to begin the "War on Poverty," which at the time would help to eradicate some of the impoverished conditions that plagued America's society, yet, such conditions continues

---

[205] Centers for Disease Control and Prevention

to plague America's today touching nearly every aspect of American life.[206] However, the deep philosophical divide that was created as a result of the "Great Society" has come to define the nation's harsh politics, especially in the Obama era.[207] On the 50th anniversary of President Lyndon Johnson's declaration of a War on Poverty, Republicans and Democrats are engaged in a battle over whether its 40 government programs have succeeded in lifting people from privation or worsened the situation by trapping the poor in dependency."[208] Some of the most aggressive political debates today's can be traced to the aspirations of the Great Society, and the domestic programs that it spawned during the 1960s, and the doubts that it has raised about the role and reach of Washington. Johnson's years in office saw the greatest expansion of government since FDR's New Deal, and even exceeded the scope of those Depression-era programs. The two parties have been fighting about it ever since.[209]

There was a reason for my bringing up the subject of the "Great Society," which is to bring about awareness that further altered the socioecomical status of the single Black mother's ability to survive. In 1964 President Lyndon B. Johnson "announced the War on Poverty in his 1964 State of the Union address. Four months later, in a commencement speech at the University of Michigan, he put forward a more far-reaching vision, declaring that "we have the opportunity to move not only toward the rich society and the powerful society, but upward to the Great Society.[210] It would ultimately include a raft of initiatives such as Medicare and Medicaid, the first direct federal aid to school districts, the Head Start program, the food stamp program, the

---

[206] Source: Washington Post, "Great Society 50th Anniversary," Jan 8, 2014.
[207] Source: Washington Post, "Great Society 50th Anniversary," Jan 8, 2014.
[208] Source: Washington Post, "Great Society 50th Anniversary," Jan 8, 2014.
[209] Source: Washington Post, "Great Society 50th Anniversary," Jan 8, 2014.
[210] Source: Washington Post, "Great Society 50th Anniversary," Jan 8, 2014.

landmark environmental legislation, the Job Corps program which is to provide
vocational education, the urban renewal programs, national endowments for the arts
and humanities, civil rights legislation, and funding for bilingual education."[211] Today,
many of these programs have been cut or eliminated entirely causing the poor mother,
to further become more independent.

The results of the War on poverty was supposed to reduce the poverty rates while also
building a safety net while poor mothers slowly gained their independence to become
self-sufficient.

- The official US poverty rate was 15% in 2012 (most recent available),
  compared with 19% of the population in 1964 when Pres. Johnson
  delivered his "war" remarks in a State of the Union message.

- The poverty rate would be lower still today, economists say, if not for the
  deep recession that ended in 2009 and from which the US economy is still
  recovering.

- Still, a rise in the overall population means that the number of Americans
  who were poor in 2012--at more than 46 million--was higher than the 36
  million in poverty back when LBJ spoke.

- The rise of safety-net programs, including those championed by Johnson,
  has helped to reduce both overall poverty and the likelihood that a single-
  parent household will be in poverty. Another mitigating factor is rising job
  opportunities for women.

---

[211] Source: Washington Post, "Great Society 50th Anniversary," Jan 8, 2014.

- Yet the number of Americans who live in single-parent households has soared since 1964--and those families are still more likely to be poor than two-parent households are.[212]

When LBJ addressed the result of poverty with programs for both urban and rural poor he was basically saying that he was trying to blend urban and cattle country, which meant that the poverty program itself was a blend of the same: of the needs and desperate desires of the poor in the city ghettos and the poor in obscure rural hollows"-- and that the new program must therefore include provisions not only for the urban slums on which attention was focused but also for rural areas.[213]

By providing such provisions, there are those such as Julia, Eloise, Mabel, Mama Younger and Claudine who have demonstrated that they can as well as other single mothers, especially single Black mothers, who could rise above their circumstances and better themselves for the sake of their children, especially their sons, by overcoming, beating the odds and debunking the historical myths about the single Black mother raising her sons.

---

[212] Source: Christian Science Monitor, "Great Society 50th Anniversary," Jan 8, 2014
[213] Source: Passage of Power, by Robert Caro, p. 544, May 2012.

Myths of the Black Woman

Chapter 5

"If you think that education is expensive, then try ignorance." African Proverb

"Success occurs when your dreams become bigger than your excuses."

Here ye, here ye, comes now in the great country of the United States of America, it has come to our attention that there is a problem in the Black community and it is with all of the Black mothers who are not married. It does not matter if the Black mother with children is a widow, divorced, separated, or her significant other, baby daddy, is incarcerated, all that matters is that the world needs to see that it is the fault of the Black woman because her children need male role models in their lives in order for her children to become productive citizens in the community. That is a myth that needs to be debunked because the Black woman is not the mule of the world who is forced to carry its burdens as society wishes her to do.

Since slavery began, there were always the stereotypical attitudes by many in mainstream society of Black women being mammies, the superwomen of their community, welfare mothers, or as Reagan puts it, "welfare queens," sapphires,

Jezebel's and victims of consensual violence. It is images such as these that has been deeply rooted in the foundation of America's psyche as being a normative behavior of Black women.

There are so many negative stereotypes that are often attached to "poor mothers," and "mothers on welfare" by society because of ignorance. Schein argues that the term *welfare* is not neutral (6), and this can be understood, because the term is not only attached to poor mothers, but when many think of poor mothers, they picture images of mothers of color. There has been an economic analysis that has disproved myths such as: women having babies in order to get more welfare benefits and that they move state-to-state in order to keep or increase their benefits (Schein). This analysis also proved that having babies was not a way to increase governmental benefits or make money, but only a way to stay economically challenged and be poorer (Schein, et al.). Since the signing of a new "Welfare Reform" by former President Clinton's welfare reform this too has disproved such myths.

On August 22, President Clinton signed into law "The Personal Responsibility and Work Opportunity Reconciliation Act of 1996 (P.L. 104-193)," a comprehensive bipartisan welfare reform plan that dramatically change the nation's welfare system into one that requires work in exchange for time-limited assistance. With this being said, there are poor mothers, like those in the characters of "Claudine," or "Mrs. Younger" who also represented many Black women who were often demonized for working and trying to get ahead in life making it seem as though the "good mother" did not have to work (Fumia; Rock). Schein also argues that the poor mother and/or welfare mothers are often associated with the images lazy mothers who are trying to scam the system having no aspirations in bettering her life or the lives of her children. It is truly sad that

143

poor mothers, especially Black mothers are also demonized and stigmatized for using welfare as a crutch in order to make ends meet as she pursues opportunities to further herself in life.

So, if you are a Black mother receiving governmental assistance, then this basically means that you as Black women, have to police the way in which you dress, the way that you speak, and your sexuality with the pressures of being upstanding Black women. Not! Many of you know how to act without being a slut, acting or dressing like one such as many in society wants to assume. Many Black women carry themselves with style and grace, whether economically challenged or not.

We cannot portray ourselves as being the kind of welfare mother who makes the rest of us "look bad." And for other welfare mothers, and you know who you are, you need to learn how to adjust your own behaviors in order to avoid the racist, sexist and classed stereotypes that mainstream may want to put us in as they continue to demonstrate their anti-black view of our world, a world in which they know nothing about, but assume by gathering bits and pieces of what you allow the media to portray and by the way in which you carry yourselves. This is the type of ignorance that creates such stereotypes, or ideas that describes groups of people in an oversimplified and prejudicial way. These types of individuals also lack an open window of perception.

With the contradiction of the "good mother" versus "bad mother" on welfare, such arguments concerning poor mothers are they type of stereotypes that are also applied to Black mothers. Of course, it was the poor mothers who were considered to be the "bad mothers" strictly because they were poor, not because of their behavior towards their children (Fumia; Schein). The mothers who became single or poor due to the death of their spouses or those who were divorced were excused from shame and considered to be worthier of being on welfare and public assistance. Those who became poor and single due to their own choices and behaviors were the ones who tend to experience judgment for utilizing the welfare and public assistance system (280-281). Poor and "bad" mothers such as these have "earned" such stereotypes because of their "poor behavior choices."

Then there is the sexual taboo about Black women by certain groups in mainstream, whose obsessions pertains to the search for sexual stimulation. Their meanings are usually based in a fast-paced market that is culturally driven which has a fear of the unknown. This unknown fear has been so entrenched and grounded in the visceral of one's mind that their concerns of the Black woman and her body is fueled by the myth that their bodies have an evil spell for sexual power over White men or they are viewed as being undesired individuals of inferiority.

Then there is the Jezebel who is the seductive temptress, one who has a certain sex appeal that is undeniable. She is the one who is also fass, (fast) enjoying sex at an early age, and fass girls are considered as being bad girls. Before making this assumption, first think about what was it that caused her to be sexually active at a young age. The media oftentimes show the negative images of the Black woman as being hyper sexually active having animalistic behaviors. She is the whore, unlike the good church girl virgin, or the Happily Married Housewife, or the Good Mother. So, in other words, we have to present ourselves from a certain perspective and to prove that we have self-control over our desires, otherwise we will be judged by many in mainstream as being immoral and promiscuous. For many Black women there are certain expectations which makes us even doubt ourselves even outside of the bedroom. Many of us still have this idea that if we dress in tight clothing or in a certain way then we are a "ho" which can also make us feel ashamed of ourselves even in the most "professional" clothing that clings to our curves.

Then there is the Black Sapphire, who is the evil and manipulative "B" word who will do anything to have her way and get revenge. Last, there is the Aunt Jemima who is the sexless long-suffering nurturer who looks after everyone else's needs never having the time to look after her own needs which often leaves her sad and lonely, suffering in silence. In order to dispel these myths, we must first, learn how to keep our cultural private business to ourselves. I already know that this would not work as I am being sarcastic. But on a more serious note, when it comes to respectability, we as Black women must present ourselves from a certain perspective and not present ourselves in a negative light.

As Black women, we must first learn to trust and understand that there's nothing wrong with our bodies, our identity, or our desires when we understand such with tact. We must also learn how to embrace the skin that we are in as we learn how to love ourselves. For many, even though it will take a long process of healing to recover from generations of sex-shaming messages, this is something that we can also learn to overcome. Just like our White counterparts, we as Black women deserve to owner of our sexual desires and make our own choices about how we express them, not allow another culture to own how we expressed them as they forced us too since slavery.

Again, as a Black woman, many of you also need to care about your appearance. Stop walking around the streets and going shopping in pajamas, boy shorts or looking like who done it and what did it to ya as if you got hit by a truck. It is not an oppressive expectation to want to look good. It is looking good that will help you to overcome some of that oppressiveness. By looking good, you make a positive first impression because you never know what positive opportunities that being well kept may bring, unless you just don't care. As quiet as it is kept, remember this, the common standards of professionalism oftentimes favor most Whites, especially men. This does not mean that you cannot express yourself, but there is a way in which you can do so. Now, in White corporate America, they may want you to get a perm. For those of us that are sisters in unity, you know what I mean. This means that you have to go through the hours-long process of flat ironing your hair each morning. Going to the beauty shop every two weeks, instead of being able to wear braids, twists, dreadlocks, or afros which can put many of us at a disadvantage, because many people don't think those styles look professional. This is why you begin your own business and learn how to support each other.

Then there is this age-old adage that many in mainstream who do not even think twice about the widespread rules that say our hair is inherently unappealing. This is also a rule that has no basis in reality because the way in which you wear your hair has nothing to do with whether or not you can perform your job and perform it well. When you are pressured to make drastic changes to your appearance in order to be valued in spaces such as the workplace, such pressure can take a detrimental toll on you. It is sad that we as Black women have to, again work 200 times as hard to get ahead as we put in more time, more money, and more effort than many of our White counterparts in order for society to take us seriously. In addition, there is this possibility that we can lose our sense of self and our confidence in ourselves by internalizing the belief that the way we look naturally is unappealing. This is also part of brainwashing, and again, learn to embrace the beauty within you by loving yourself.

We also must understand that we do not have to make our hair look like our White counterparts hair to be truly accepted into society if one is willing to accept us by who we are and not how we look, but because of mainstreams professional standards, the media images that are constantly displayed on social media, television, in books and magazines that sends messages that White women with straight hair are far more beautiful than Black women with kinky hair, we again, fall for the hype and matriculate into their dichotomy. It should be your choice of how you wear your hair, not theirs. You must take the initiative to look at yourself in the mirror and recognize the natural beauty of who you are, not as someone views you.

With this now being understood, understand this, there is a false propaganda that faults single Black mothers for any conceivable social ill's that is related to Black America which is deeply rooted in the connection of racism and sexism. Such social ill's is also the perfect outlet for mass marketing propaganda through the media. It is sad that Black America have become accustomed to being continually bombarded with the negative associations that are related to terms such as "ghetto culture," intra-racial violence, lazy, the welfare queen myth, and Black criminality, with the principal perception among these being the fabrication of how disastrous single Black mothers are for an entire race. Such stereotypes are either shallow or sensationalized concerning the Black culture.

Because of the false or sensationalized media images of Black America, our culture is perceived as being a failure, yet the entire truth is withheld because it is not referenced of the influence of how an institution systemically oppressed and discriminated a culture for hundreds of years, as Ralph Elliott says, "like the invisible man. For them, they just conveniently lie. And those who accept such behaviors, oftentimes called "Uncle Tom's," are just as dangerous to their own culture

Now let's talk about Uncle Tom's such as Ben Carson, be upset as you may, but if you are partial to him, then you need to taste the truth. He is not one who should be considered as an authoritarian on the lives of children being raised by Black mothers as his childhood was pretty colored itself. He was raised in a home with an absent father and his family also received government assistance. Although he was gifted with a talent, as stated in his book "Gifted Hands," he too had some deeply rooted issues, especially with his temper, which possibly resulted from the lack of having a father figure in the home and having no stability in his family's living and financial conditions. Yet, Carson's mother, Ms. Sonya Carson, sheds a somewhat different light as a single Black mother and how God brought her through despite her obstacles. Me also being a single Black mother, I admire Mother Carson's strength to rise up and persevere despite her son's views, because a child cannot truly fathom what a mother goes through while raising her children, especially her sons. Here is a poem that Momma Carson said that she used to share with her sons.

Yourself To Blame

by Mayme White Miller

If things go bad for you

And make you a bit ashamed

Often you will find out that

You have yourself to blame.

Swiftly we ran to mischief

And then the bad luck came

Why do we fault others?

We have ourselves to blame.

Whatever happens to us,

Here is what we say

"Had it not been for so-and-so

Things wouldn't have gone that way."

And if you are short of friends,

I'll tell you what to do

Make an examination,

You'll find the faults in you...

You're the captain of your ship,

So agree with the same

If you travel downward

You have yourself to blame.

Ben Carson stated that there are a lot of boys in the "inner cities" who grow up without father figures. Again, can he speak for all inner-city boys? There just may be father figures in the home, but that does not necessarily mean that they are positive father figures. Also, a father figure or role model could be an older brother, an uncle, a cousin, a coach, pastor, or teacher, but Carson feels that, as a result, these inner-city boys, never learned how to respect authority. Sounds like something he claims when he lost his temper numerous times or how he stated, whether true or not, how he tried to hit his mother over the head with a hammer. Why would such negative behaviors be something that you are proud of? It appears as though he is describing himself.

So, the first question is, by being a Black man, whose mother was a single Black mother, why would he encourage others to think negatively about how Black women are raising their children, when he himself was a product of such? The next question is, why would he gender-alize (my word) the figure's sex. It should not matter whether the child's role model is a male or female; this has no irrelevancy when it comes to the gender of an individual who is a positive figure just as long as the child respects their parental influence, because we don't commonly see this being said when it comes to the single White mother and how she runs her households. Calling the kettle black, why would one who has experienced what they condemn display such a double standard?

In reading this book, you have found and will continue to find that there is no secret that Black women are among the most exploited and vulnerable individuals in American. It is the patriarchal contempt for women, especially Black women that is intensified by the racist ideas which are systematized into the fabric of our culture which has destined Black women to experience an exclusive form of misrepresentation. And because of this, Black women will continue to be a frequent "whipping girl" or one who is a mule within a system that prefers men and despises Black identities. I can never reiterate this enough, this is why everyone should learn cultural history, not just European or American history.

Cultural history is a part of American history. So as America began the abolishment of slavery, the racial stereotypes about Black women became more persistent. And because of bureaucratic red tape, political fluff or what I call bs bourgeois, in order to justify the wrongs or to oppose social and political advancement for Blacks, there were those White social scientists, theologians, and journalists who dreamed up justifications for the "natural inferiority" of Blacks and how they felt why

Blacks were subordinate to Whites. This is a myth that can also be dispelled, as "No human race is superior; no religious faith is inferior, and all collective judgments are wrong. Only racists make them" (Elie Wiesel).

For decades, Blacks have been painted as being ignorant, lazy, immoral, and criminal. Blacks were also told and continue to be told that they need to get over being oppressed because slavery ended hundreds of years ago. As we can see today, Blacks still endure what is called a pseudo slavery with mass incarcerations, poverty, economic conditions, lack of employment and the consistent shootings of Blacks by the police. Yes, institutional slavery ended, and the damage was done, but institutional racism still continues within America's system. It is also justified because it is a tradition of beliefs in America that is more acceptable by society than not. So, the ideologies that declare Black women being unable to raise their children properly are the catalysts that stems from this legacy of deceit. And because of such fabrications society can pretty much understand, as they view who is actually responsible for Black oppression, poverty, and the criminalization that has been placed at the feet of Black women. So here we are again with single Black mothers being blamed for the state of Black America, because it is easier to blame the victim than to take responsibility for your own actions, and in this case, America's actions.

More than fifty years ago (1965) blaming the Black mother for the downtrodden plight of Blacks in America became the characteristics of a contentious and exceptionally male-centric report titled, *"The Negro Family: The Case for National Action."* A gentleman by the name of Daniel Patrick "Pat" Moynihan, then the Assistant Secretary of Labor and author of the Moynihan report, was a well-meaning, lifelong liberal. His months-long and blundering of research concluded that Black America was caught in a, quote, "tangle of pathology."

Moynihan, growing up in New York, was also the product of a broken home as his father left when he was 10 years-old. So, like Carson, he too was made an authoritarian of broken homes because he came from a broken home, he believed, as did many Catholic thinkers, that solid families were the basic institutions of social organization. Though Moynihan helped develop LBJ's War on Poverty in 1964, and cheered enactment of a historic Civil Rights Act, also in 1964, he thought that much more had to be done to help Black Americans attain anything resembling socioeconomic equality with Whites. But how could he consider himself as an authoritarian when he was neither a sociologist nor a demographer of Blacks in America when he himself was not Black? Maybe because "in early 1963, he produced a report, titled "One-Third of a Nation," that documented very high percentages of young black men in single-parent families who failed mental and physical tests for the military draft."[214]

Now here is the disease that is part of the festering like rotten meat (Langston Hughes) within the foundation of America. He went on to say that there were high rates of families that were headed by single Black mothers. With the snooping of "Mr. Welfare Man," it makes one wonder why the Black male did not make his presence known often as he too was responsible for the Black woman being the way that she was. Moynihan went on to say that he faulted Black women for the social and economic failure of an entire racial group.

---

[214] Patterson, James T. "*Moynihan and the Single-Parent Family: The 1965 Report and Its Backlash.*" Published by Education Next, Volume 15, No. 2; Spring 2015

The importance of learning cultural history. started his research on January 1, 1965. Consulting scholars and civil rights activists, he also delved into major books concerned with African American history and contemporary race relations. These works, by W. E. B. DuBois, E. Franklin Frazier, Gunnar Myrdal, Kenneth Clark, and others, emphasized that a long history of white racism had savaged African American life.[215] There is one thing that I can agree with concerning Moynihan that mainstream will not learn overnight or within a few months by reading a few books, and that is, today, there is still "the racist virus that festers within the American blood stream still afflicts not just Blacks"[216] but America as a whole as it continues to deny the injustices that are constantly bestowed upon Black America. As long as the majority of mainstream refuses to hold themselves accountable for such atrocities, "Negroes will continue to encounter serious personal prejudice for at least another generation."[217] Second, there has now been four centuries of oftentimes unimaginable mistreatments which continues to "take a toll on the Negro people."[218] Moynihan went on to emphasize that, "The circumstances of the Negro American community in recent years has probably been getting worse, not better" which in many ways still holds true today."[219]

To back up Moynihan's claims, there was data that offered validation "concerning Black poverty, unemployment, crime, juvenile delinquency, narcotics use, and serious

---

[215] Patterson, James T. "*Moynihan and the Single-Parent Family: The 1965 Report and Its Backlash.*" Published by Education Next, Volume 15, No. 2; Spring 2015
[216] Patterson, James T. "*Moynihan and the Single-Parent Family: The 1965 Report and Its Backlash.*" Published by Education Next, Volume 15, No. 2; Spring 2015
[217] Patterson, James T. "*Moynihan and the Single-Parent Family: The 1965 Report and Its Backlash.*" Published by Education Next, Volume 15, No. 2; Spring 2015
[218] Patterson, James T. "*Moynihan and the Single-Parent Family: The 1965 Report and Its Backlash.*" Published by Education Next, Volume 15, No. 2; Spring 2015
[219] Patterson, James T. "*Moynihan and the Single-Parent Family: The 1965 Report and Its Backlash.*" Published by Education Next, Volume 15, No. 2; Spring 2015

educational disadvantages. He maintained that the deep roots of such "crisis" lay in foundation of American slavery. White racism, mass migrations, and the urbanization of the Black population, further disorganized Black families in the 20th century. Moynihan did point out that there were some Negroes who were managing to move into the middle-class environment, however, he focused on documenting what he argued was the deteriorating situation of impoverished Black families in the inner cities: "The family structure of lower class Negroes is highly unstable, and in many urban centers is approaching complete breakdown." This was the "fundamental source of the weakness of the Negro community at the present time."[220]

Even the late President Lyndon Baines Johnson realized and understood that there was a deeply rooted problem within the fabric of America's society by stating to Moynihan, "Freedom is not enough, you do not take a person who, for years, has been hobbled by chains and liberate him, bring him up to the starting line of a race and then say, 'You are free to compete with all the others,' and still justly believe that you have been completely fair. Thus, it is not enough to open the gates of opportunity. All our citizens must have the ability to walk through those gates.... We seek not just freedom but opportunity—not just legal equity but human ability—not just equality as a right and a theory but equality as a fact and as a result."

Even though LBJ did not specifically identify what the government should do, he did promise to take action in order to improve the conditions of Blacks in "education, health care, employment, housing, and especially devise 'social programs better

---

[220] Patterson, James T. "*Moynihan and the Single-Parent Family: The 1965 Report and Its Backlash.*" Published by Education Next, Volume 15, No. 2; Spring 2015

designed to hold families together.'"[221] Because of what LBJ presented, there were Civil rights leaders who hailed Johnson's address. Even Dr. Martin Luther King Jr. declared that, "Never before has a president articulated the depths and dimensions [of the problems] more eloquently and profoundly." Johnson himself later said, and rightly so, that this was his greatest civil-rights speech.[222]

If it were not for bad luck, then Moynihan would not have any luck at all as his work had become so incredibly flawed that even psychologist William Ryan make up the phrase "blaming the victim" and, in 1971, Ryan even went so far to publish *Blaming the Victim*. This book was intended to be a contradiction of the Moynihan Report, which Ryan described as a composition of victim blaming that sustained order in favor of those in power, which is the White male. While Moynihan's Report has greatly shaped many governmental programs, perhaps only the occasional reader or individual who is in the realm of academia is familiar with it. It can be stated that Moynihan's report is a worthwhile piece with rich context that explores the problems arising from his conclusions which can be found in *The Black Family in the Age of Mass Incarceration*, but what can be learned which is something that many White writers will never understand, is that such a subject concerning the Black family at their problems still remains risky for them to highlight. The rise in fatherless families does not just exist among Black families, but all families as a whole, White and Black, and even today, "social science seems unable to develop a national family policy. "We are nowhere near a

---

[221] Patterson, James T. *"Moynihan and the Single-Parent Family: The 1965 Report and Its Backlash."* Published by Education Next, Volume 15, No. 2; Spring 2015
[222] Patterson, James T. *"Moynihan and the Single-Parent Family: The 1965 Report and Its Backlash."* Published by Education Next, Volume 15, No. 2; Spring 2015

general theory of family change," Ryan asserted. "And there we shall leave it, the question still standing: who indeed can tell us what happened to the American family?"

Mainstream individuals such as those who make assumptions on just reading a couple of books, having a couple of friends and getting some support from those whose ideologies parallels with yours need to stop using single Black mothers as your scapegoat to justify why Blacks as a whole have been treated unjust since 1619 and you have still not come up with a positive solution. So, instead of examining the recurring social, economic, and political deprivations that contribute to the "inferior" condition of Black America such as you are is simply absurd.[223]

The rates of Black unemployment haven't changed much isn't after the Civil War, and it has consistently been twice that of Whites for well over fifty years. Sadly, the rates of unemployment for Blacks had gotten "so ridiculous in 2010 that it received an investigation from the United Nations." Even when Blacks do obtain gainful employment, they are still paid less than Asians and Whites across almost all industries of employment according to the Bureau of Labor Statistics. And what is even more factual is that Black women are paid even less than Black men. There are still major wealth gaps in American society due to institutional racism. When it comes to institutional racism and education, even when Black students graduate from college, the graduation rates can only be characterized as embarrassingly racist.

Point being is that race, unfortunately plays a significant role in our society in a way that has always affected the wage and economic opportunities for minorities, especially Blacks. So, with that being said, it is not single Black mothers who are failing

---

[223] Patterson, James T. "*Moynihan and the Single-Parent Family: The 1965 Report and Its Backlash.*" Published by Education Next, Volume 15, No. 2; Spring 2015

their community – it just so happens that institutional racism is this nation's way of life, and there are many in mainstream society who are not only comfortable with this, they will have it no other way. Even within the sexist scheme of how society views single Black mothers that stipulates that a man should be able to control his household, this argument still fails when it is applied to the Black community in this specific way.

It is at no time that Black women have ever orchestrated a movement that would have reject Black men. It was the institution of slavery run by White men with wealth and power that orchestrated such movements. Black men did not set up a system which made them seem invisible, caused them to be incarcerated at massive rates, have poor housing opportunity, limited to no healthcare or high unemployment rates or set them up in a system that was designed to destroy them. Black men didn't magically disappear or ask to be hated. "By 2000, more than 1 million black children had a father in jail or prison—and roughly half of those fathers were living in the same household as their kids when they were locked up." These unique circumstances – and *not* the failings of Black mothers – are associated with the behavioral problems of institutional racism. So, by addressing the way that Blacks are marginalized within America's systematic and racists society is not an excuse to universally pardon Americans who practices such misconduct. Mainstream must accept the fact that they way in which our society think about racial differences does play a significant role in suggesting that single Black women are seriously responsible for the degradation of Black America.

With that also being said, to say that single Black mothers cannot properly raise children is flat out wrong, hurtful, and harmful. Such myths are endured because society's foundation is based on a male-centered and White-dominated culture that continues to remain this nation's preferred default setting. In actuality, it is the single

158

Black mothers who are the unsung pillars of the Black community as she carries the weight of the world upon her back like a mule. Black women not only show strength through many of their characteristics, they show courage. They advocate for brighter futures by fighting for racial equality against what is really destroying Black communities such as white supremacist, capitalist patriarchy and the institutions that sustain it.

Poverty, Sexism, Racism and the Black Woman

Chapter 6

"Challenges make you discover things about yourself that you really never knew."

Cicely Tyson.

Society can speak of sex, racism, politics and poverty, yet, who does such a subject fall upon? The Black woman. She is stigmatized as being promiscuous, lazy, neglectful and one who is satisfied with being on welfare which enhances the economic problems in America. Oftentimes society feels as though the Black mother abuses the system as she accepts such handouts. This is not true, because for many, the system is often used as a crutch until she is strong enough to get on her feet. To be blamed for the conditions of her community is to become a victim and to be a victim of our environment can be psychologically damaging and devastating to all involved.

Many in society as well as the media often views the Black woman from a negative perspective as they degrade, ridicule and blame her for the Black community's problem. The Black mother, just like any other mother who get no support is struggling to survive. There are many Black women who successfully attend college and graduate. She also works while sacrificing herself in order to provide a better life for herself and her children.

Today, just like in the days of yesteryear Black mothers want what is best for their children concerning their safety and security while she is trying to herself. For the Black mother, she also has to teach her children street smarts and the art of survival against a racist institution that is despises them. One of the ways in which the Black woman survives is by often obtaining menial occupations in order to "seek in advancing her children beyond her own occupational achievements" (Thronton-Dill, 191). Being single, divorced or widowed with children is already a task, but when you are dependent on governmental assistance, it is also an excruciating and demeaning ordeal in itself, especially for the Black mother. There are some things that many Black women must endure if she works (like in the movie Claudine), and there are many things that Black mothers endure when they don't work (like Mr. Welfare Man).

The Black woman have always been a target/victim of a cold, cruel and unjust society since the beginning of American history. Part of her being ridiculed and belittled is because society views her negatively, and the way in which they feel she raises her children. She is also often viewed with the concept of being an article, one that is used, abused and discarded. And by having this type of perspective is part of the ignorance that society fails to understand. Society, again, must learn cultural history as they pause and reflect on the events of history in order to progress above and beyond their past. Either we as a society will make our own futures or become victims of our past, never stopping and thinking that you as a society do not respect the morals that the Black woman is a human being.

The racism, sex and poverty concerning the Black woman has been exploited by the media which still prevails it plagues, distorts and deprives the conscious of both races. "Historically, the Black woman has been sequestered and placed in ghettos and poor neighborhoods (Goetz), she is portrayed in the negative images of the poor Black welfare woman who has no direction in life. Yet, her struggle to survive and achieve equally often surpasses that of any other women. The Black woman, unlike her male counterpart, has to sacrifice herself differently, so it is she and she alone, who again, suffers in silence.

The Black woman is often viewed as being animalistically wild "always ready" according to myth. She is always responsive unlike the White woman, and she is an ideal vessel for the discharge of purely genital sex. The body of a female slave was the master's for the taking. Sexual rights over her body also became the privilege of the master's sons, neighbors, plantation overseers, and by any extension to any White man around. Such practices were continued through the mid-1940s in southern states. Black women who became wet nurses, housekeepers, and cooks for White families were often forced to continue and comply to the White man and his sexual desires. When his sons reached sexual maturity, it was acknowledged by the father by stating, "you're ready to start taking the maid home."

Black women have often been considered as being sexually different from White women. They have been thought of as being stronger physical, more passionate, and less subjective to ailments that plague the delicate White woman, and that is no myth. White owners who were interesting in slave breeding were often disappointed and surprised to discover that it was not such a natural inclination among Black women to produce either easily and have healthy babies or not produce easily and still not have healthy babies.

However, this should not have come to any surprise if Black women lived in such atrocious and unhealthy conditions, had poor eating habits and not been given proper medical are because Blacks were considered to be chattel.

Does race really matter in a country where a society is divided by sex and poverty? The genetic make-up of one's ethnical background should not matter concerning a mother's ability to raise her child. Her sexual desires should also not matter when it comes to ability to raise her child as long as it does not impede upon her responsibilities to that child.

Since these have always been strong issues in our society, one cannot speak candidly about race without speaking of sex, and one cannot speak candidly about sex without speaking about poverty, welfare and the Black woman. In modern times, many may say that many Black women acquires the position of a "mistress." If this were the case, then the Black woman would now be viewed as a poor Black woman on welfare who is addicted not only to being dependent on Mr. Welfare Man, but she is addicted to sex as well in order to further supplement her income. She is viewed not only as a loose woman but also as a sex object, one that was created and then perpetuated through the system of slavery, being forced to be the White man's mistress as well as a breeder with the Black man having limited to no possession of her and her body. For the White man, taking advantage of and having sex with several Black women was common practice.

Due to the negative situations that Black women from slavery have endured such as being raped by both the White man, and the welfare system, the media now rapes her as it distorts many of societies racial issues in the Black community. Their focus is of the negative issues within the Black community such as violence and poverty a subject that is often thrusted upon the Black woman. Has anyone ever taken a moment to realize

163

that the Black woman is also a human being and that single mother who is struggling to survive? Has anyone realized that she too desires the nicer things in life concerning life's luxuries? The positives aspects concerning the Black mother is that she does struggle to survive and keeps society out of her business as she presses towards the mark of her goals. This is why much of society's knowledge concerning the Black mother is based upon assumptions. There are many single Black mothers who have successfully attended and completed college, while also working and sacrificing themselves from a positive perspective in order to survive.

As far as the myth of the Black woman and her sexuality, it is assumed that both the Black woman and the Black man have an evil spell for sexual power over the White man and the White woman or they are viewed as harmless and de-sexed underlings of a White culture.[224]

Now let's understand and accept this. In 1865, the Civil War ended, but the hate, racism and narcissistic behaviors from many Whites towards many Blacks did not end. First published in 1892, Ida B. Wells Barnett wrote a series of many in one of her publications titled *"Southern Horrors: Lynch Laws and All Its Phases."* During this time, rape was a common and frequent justification for the racial violence towards Blacks, Natives and other minority cultures, but especially Blacks. In Wells-Barnett's pamphlet she wrote, "To palliate this record ... and excuse some of the most heinous crimes that ever stained the history of a country, the South is shielding itself behind the plausible screen of defending the honor of its women." If truth was to be told, Wells was bold enough as a Black woman to point out a host of Southern newspapers that

---

[224] Day, Beth. *"Sexual Life Between Blacks and Whites: The Roots of Racism."* New York World Publishing; Times Mirror 1972.

defended such "lynch's law" with allegations that referenced to such crimes as being an alleged epidemic of Black-on-White rape.

During this time, there was also an editorial, published by the *Memphis Daily Commercial*, where editors blatantly stated, "The commission of this crime grows more frequent every year," and, "There is no longer a restraint upon the brute passion of the Negro." Wells-Barnett was a tyrant when it came to the injustices that Blacks endured at the hands of Whites with no system of justice. With Blacks always having allegations of Black on White rape, which again was of course a convenient way to kill Blacks with justification. Wells-Barnett would always show, that there were never any substantial reasons to charge the accused. She went on to state, "The world knows that the crime of rape was unknown during four years of Civil War, when the White women of the South were at the mercy of the race which is all at once charged with being a bestial one."

Again, the truth of the matter is that sex is a taboo subject when it comes to a Black man desiring a White woman as the Black woman feels devalued. At one time, the White woman envied Black women because of White men's obvious sexual interaction with them so by the 1960s Black women began to resent White women for the opposite reason, which was Black men's obvious sexual interaction with White women. Now the battleground has shifted.

There even came to a point that during the Civil Rights Movement of the 1960s Black men were pursuing sexual relationships with White women, it was as though the Black man had finally conquered power over the White man as the White woman became one of symbolistic conquest because the White man continually controlled both the Black woman and dominated the Black man. The White man has always had the biggest advantage over Blacks in terms of education, employment, finances, political power and other access to opportunities that make for higher status.[225]

In reality, such accusations that Black men were frequently raping White women were excuses and just covers for the consensual and taboo relationships that took place between White women and Black men since it was the White woman who was supposed to be over the slave when her husband or the overseer was not around. White men could not stomach the idea of a White woman desiring sex with a Negro, thus any physical relationship between a White woman and a Black man. So, by the White man's definition of a White woman desiring to have sex with a Black man was their version and excuse to destroy and control the Black male by using the White woman's desire to be an unwanted assault," writes historian Philip Dray, describing Wells-Barnett's argument in his book "*At the Hands of Persons Unknown: The Lynching of Black America.*" In one instance, found Wells-Barnett, a Black man in Indianola, Mississippi, was lynched for raping the local sheriff's 8-year-old daughter. When Wells-Barnett went to investigate, however, she found something very different. First of all, the sheriff's daughter was more than eighteen years old, and was found by her father in this man's room, who was a servant on the place.

The way in which many feels that making America great again is by first recognizing that she/America has a problem with racism, an issue which has existed since the founding of this country. America's foundation was built on racism which is a deeply rooted infestation that continues to have a brutal history of what we call today domestic violence. This is an ugly episode within the history of our nation that

---

[225] Herton, Calvin C. (1961) Sex and Racism in America. New York: Grove Press

continually goes on being neglected and ignored. "In the last decades of the nineteenth century, the lynching of Black people in the Southern and border states became an institutionalized method used by Whites to terrorize Blacks and maintain White supremacy. In the South, during the period 1880 to 1940, there was deep-seated and all-pervading hatred and fear of the Negro which led White mobs to turn to "lynch law" as a means of social control. Lynchings—open public murders of individuals suspected of crime conceived and carried out more or less spontaneously by a mob—seem to have been an American invention. In *Lynch-Law*, the first scholarly investigation of lynching, written in 1905, author James E. Cutler stated that "lynching is a criminal practice which is peculiar to the United States."[226] This continues today, just in a different form.

The majority of such lynchings were by hanging, shooting, or both. No matter how they were done, there was always this sudden outburst of uncontrolled rage, or that unspeakable brutality that just had to be carried out by an insane mob. And just to name some of the more hideous types of brutal nature, there was the tar and feathers, the burning at the stake, the maiming and dismemberment, and castration, parts of which was oftentimes kept as souvenirs, along with other forms of brutal methods of physical torture. Therefore, lynching became a cruel combination of racism and sadism, which was utilized primarily to sustain a particular type of caste system and control in the South. There were those White people who believed that Blacks could only be controlled by fear, as many seem to feel even today. Today, many of these individuals felt that lynching was seen as the most effective means of control, and this is what they felt made America great.

---

[226] James E. Cutler, *Lynch Law* (New York, 1905), p. 1.

Let us not forget about the race riots that were perpetuated by ignorance, hate and fear. In those decades that immediately preceded World War I, there was a pattern of racial violence that had begun to emerge in which White mob assaults were purposely directed against entire Black communities. Such race riots were the product of a White society who had the desire to maintain its superiority and control over Blacks. The extension of control among many of these Whites is when they would often vent their frustrations in times of distress, by attacking those who were the least able to defend themselves. In these race riots, White mobs would invade Black neighborhoods, beating and killing large numbers of Blacks and destroying any property that Black's had acquired, such as they had in the movie "Rosewood." Many times, Blacks fought back, however, fighting back still left many casualties on both sides, even though the majority of the victims and the dead were Black.

Even though there were several race riots between the periods of 1898 to 1943, I remember as a child reading about the Red Summer of 1919. I can remember this so vividly because the picture that was painted as I read it touched me ever so deeply. This race riot was called "The Red Summer" by James Weldon Johnson, who ushered in that it had been one of the greatest periods of interracial violence that the nation had ever witnessed at that time. During that summer there were twenty-six race riots in such cities as Chicago, Illinois; Washington, D.C.; Elaine, Arkansas; Charleston, South Carolina; Knoxville and Nashville, Tennessee; Longview, Texas; and Omaha, Nebraska. There were more than one hundred Blacks killed in these riots, with thousands more that had been wounded and left homeless. But in the essence of it all, it was a negative experience that Blacks consistently endured and as parents, especially mothers, we as Blacks have always tried to protect our children from the harsh realities of racism.

168

In essence, it is unfortunate that the Black community has been forced into a matriarchal structure because of misfortunes such as hate and racism. The rotting and decomposing infestation of hate and racism has become so out of line with the rest of American society, that it seriously retards the progress of the group as a whole and imposes a crushing burden on the Negro male.[227],[228]

Black women have been perceived by many as emasculating castrators of Black men; so, in order to improve the conditions of Blacks within their community, Black men had to assume "their" position as head of the household. However, as many of these men assumed their position as the head of household, many Black men began viewing Black women as being their co-oppressors, and Black men as well as women, were willing to defer the needs of Black women to (re)invest in Black manhood.[229]

The Black woman has always had to fight for economic independence and social respectability that was waged against her following the sexual subjugation that essentially began as part of the system during slavery. This would also explain how legislation was designed to insure a continued exploitation of Black female slaves and their children who were born into slavery.[230]

The Black woman has always been the target/victim of a cold, cruel and unjust society since the beginning of American history and its institution of slavery. She is always belittled and ridiculed, because society views her negatively and often with the

---

[227] U.S. Department of Labor, (29) The Negro Family: The Case for National Action (Washington, D.C.: Government Printing Office, 1965).

[228] Hickman, M. S. (1989). Feminism: Black women on the edge. *Women and Language, 12*(1), 5. Retrieved from http://libproxy.lib.csusb.edu/login?url=https://search-proquest-com.libproxy.lib.csusb.edu/docview/198818528?accountid=10359

[229] For a more detailed discussion, see Paula Giddings, When and Where I Enter: The Impact of Black Women on Race and Sex in America (New York: Bantam Books, 1984), Chapter 18.

[230] Howard, D. (1986). When and Where I Enter: The Impact of Black Women on Race and Sex in America. *Women & Therapy, 5*(4), 106. Retrieved from http://libproxy.lib.csusb.edu/login?url=https://search-proquest com.libproxy.lib.csusb.edu/docview/216240799?accountid=10359

concept of being an article, to be used, abused, and discarded. Therefore, those who are willing to make a change in society must go back and analyze slavery because slavery bred fear, lust, sexual abuse and the dehumanization of not just Blacks but of minorities as a whole. Because of such atrocities that were endured, this usually leads to the Black woman having self-hatred and very low self-esteem for having such physical and sexual acts forced upon her.

The sex, racism and poverty, as well as the media still prevails to plague, distort and deprive the human conscience of all races. "Historically, the Black woman has been sequestered in ghettos and poor neighborhoods" (Gotez). She is often portrayed in negative images of being the poor Black welfare mother who has no direction in life, yet her struggle to survive and achieve equally, often surpasses that of any other woman in other societies. The Black woman unlike her male counterpart has to sacrifice herself differently, so, it is she, and she alone who suffers silently.

Sex is part of politics, and politics is based on power, and power is based on money. It is a known fact that the White man has more advantages than any other group or race of people in America, while the Black woman has less of an advantage than any other race or gender in America. American society has this false ideology that the Black woman, is one who is powerful, and one who take pleasure in sexual prowess in a racist society. Many will ask the poor single Black welfare woman, "how do you survive?" While the wider society is pretending to be worried about what the Black welfare mother is doing to survive, while they (meaning the wider society) mentally and verbally continue to destroy her.

Welfare is a product of our society, a "product of the poverty that shadows many lives and carries people in and out of homelessness, from low paying jobs, to unemployment to shelters to the street to welfare then back to low paying jobs and eventually, from unemployment and then back to the street" (Marin 54) which then becomes a never-ending cycle. It is not the quantity of what a mother gives a child, but the quality of love and affection that is given.

Emotions dealing with Black women, their sexuality and the way in which society views her can differ from scale to scale, and region to region. We must remember that before the birth of welfare in 1935, the Black woman had to do what she must in order to provide for her children. After the birth of welfare, the Black mother still had to experiment with new and different ways to help herself without government assistance. She still worked as a maid, caretaker, cook and childcare provider. Welfare was not created for the poor Black woman or any minority woman. Once called AFDC (Aid to Dependent Child), the welfare system had been created during the Great Depression to help alleviate some of the burdens of poverty for families with children while also allowing White widowed mothers to maintain their households. In 1934, the average amount that was received from the state's grant was $11 per child per month. In most cases, these funds were administered by the state's juvenile courts.

When FDR's New Deal was placed in stone, such public works programs that were created as a result of this New Deal, they were designed to blatantly discriminate against Blacks, which offered them some of the most menial jobs and paying them oftentimes only half of that which White workers earned. Again, we must remember that Aid to Dependent Children was created primarily for White mothers, who were not expected to work; and those relatively few Black recipients who were fortunate enough to receive assistance, only received smaller stipends with the arguments being that "Blacks needed less assistance to live on than Whites."

With welfare programs specifically excluding a significant number of divorced, deserted, and minority mothers and their children, it happened to be that by 1967, there was a welfare caseload that seemed to be turning the tables. At one point, there had been an eighty-six percent of Whites who were receiving public assistance, now forty-six percent had become nonwhite who were receiving public assistance.

Because Americans have always had pride in themselves as having strong work ethics in addition to having a strong sense of individualism and self-reliance, there are many in mainstream society who believed that those who were not capable of taking care of themselves only had themselves to blame for their own misfortunes. It was during the 19th century when local and state governments, in addition to charities, had established institutions such as poorhouses and orphanages for those who were in destitute as well as those in destitute with families. Many of the conditions in these institutions were so deplorably harsh that only the truly desperate would apply for such governmental assistance. The cash relief that was allocated out to the poor was depended on local property taxes, which were also limited. In addition, not only was there a general prejudice that existed against the poor on relief, but local officials frequently discriminated against those individuals who were applying for aid based on their race, ethnicity, nationality, or religion. This is where single mothers, especially Black mothers, oftentimes found themselves in an unbearable situation. So, if they were bold enough to apply for relief, they were often branded as being morally unfit by those within the community, and if they decided to work, then they were criticized for neglecting their children.

Today, even though much of the American public now views welfare dependency as a Black cultural trait, the welfare system has systematically and historically excluded

Blacks from obtaining such benefits, as it was once exclusively designed for those who were White. Besides its misguided faith in the family wage, the Progressive welfare movement was flawed by the elitism of the privileged, White activist network that led it. As a result, a defining aspect of its welfare vision was the social control of poor immigrant families and the neglect of Black women.

Again, Black mothers, on the other hand, were either limited or simply excluded from benefits that were designed for the more privileged. The first materialist welfare legislation was intended for White mothers only. This is not a repeat but stated facts that need to sink in and marinate. Administrators either failed to establish programs in locations with large Black populations or distributed benefits according to standards that disqualified Black mothers. In reality, administrators neither failed to establish programs in economically impoverished areas nor did they intend to distribute benefits according to standards, no more than the founding fathers of this great country intended to include within the Declaration of Independence, slaves as being recipients of the opportunity of having "Life, Liberty and the Pursuit of Happiness," such as any other human being as slaves were considered as chattel.

As a result of such inconsideration, in 1931 the first national survey of mothers' pensions had been broken down by race and found that only three percent of recipients were Black. The exclusiveness of the mothers' aid programs coincided with the entrenchment of formal racial segregation which was another Progressive reform that was also intended to strengthen social order. The Black woman, as always, had to continue to be docile while also being durable, thereby developing an attitude of humbleness in order to function and survive the cruelty and ignorance that she faced on a daily basis.

Given the levels of public assistance that Black and other minority mothers obtained, there had to be some type of outside income found in order for these mothers to provide for herself and her children. This is what oftentimes led her to obtain jobs such as the one Claudine had in order to provide for her family with necessities such as having a roof over their heads with the utilities paid, food, clothes, and shoes, with this being just the basics. Low-income households can oftentimes fall prey to emotional tensions, and in many cases, for the Black woman, it is said that Black men only have children to prove their manhood. I do not feel that this is a true statement, because in my personal opinion if more fathers, across the board, Black or White, would take the responsibility in helping to raise their children by supporting them financially, socially, and morally, this too would help all mothers, including the Black mothers on or off welfare to be more productive in society and tighten the welfare rolls.

In cases such as these, this gives the Black woman the added incentive to go back to work or school, which would also assist in increasing her self-esteem to be a better role model for her children. While every dollar that the absent father pays will help with their children as well as the mother, the father would also be setting a good example as being a parent. These are also the fathers who would like to see their children succeed and have a better outcome in life. Unfortunately, there are fathers who will not step up to the plate as providers which not very promising, to the single Black mother or her children. Environmental conditions such as these that have been forced upon certain groups of people can, and will, in many cases cause aggression and frustration. The aggression usually comes when a person or group of people have been categorized, labeled, ridiculed, and stereotyped against for so long, that it becomes a major part of their frustration.

In the end, it is evident that people such as myself refuse to remain in such a down trodden predicament, but will uplift themselves from the economic disabilities that has caused them to be there. Obstacles such as these are part of society's conformity, which results from indirect pressure on individuals or certain groups of people to change his or her behavior and thoughts. It is not always color that necessarily play a part in situations such as these, just the fact of being on welfare or poor is enough knowledge in itself that one wants to better their condition. What many in our society do not realize is that many of these single mothers do not want to be blocked from attaining their goals so that they too can be successful. My personal goal in rearing my children was to show them that having an education is the power, which holds the keys to success.

As mentioned earlier, the single Black mother tries to protect her child from being a target of mainstream societies evils while also trying to protect herself from being taken advantage of, by being sexually harassed and being sexually assaulted. There are those in society who looks at the single Black mom as a social ill that plagues the Black community because everything that she does is her fault when her children go astray. "Conservative columnist George Will said on ABC's *This Week* that single mothers present a bigger threat to African Americans than the loss of voting rights.[231] Jimi Izrael, who is a frequent contributor to *NPR*, wrote in his book *The Denzel Principle* that "high rates of Black divorce and single-parent families really reflects less

---

[231] Brown, S. M. (2014, Aug). CDC study shatters myth about black fathers. *The Louisiana Weekly Publishing Co.* Aug 25-Aug 31, 2014. Retrieved from http://libproxy.lib.csusb.edu/login?url=https://search-proquest-com.libproxy.lib.csusb.edu/docview/1559519140?accountid=10359

on Black men and more on Black women and their inability to make good choices."[232]

Now in making such negative statements that deflects away from the Black male and him taking care of his responsibility help the Black community? Why would society reflect more on the single Black mother trying to raise her children while working and going to school demonstrate that she has the inability to make good choices when it is mainstream society who also contradicts themselves by saying that there are more Black deadbeat and absentee fathers in the lives of Black children than there are Whites? The statement that was made by Izrael is contradicting in itself. And what would George Will know about the Black community other than what he, as part of the media glamorizes and report since he does not live in the Black community.

It has also been stated that since 1619 a Black woman's sexuality and her motherhood, has always been viewed by society as being negative. The only thing that a Black woman was good for is being a concubine for the master and breeding good healthy bucks as though she was an animal since she was considered to be chattel and uncivilized. Earlier in the chapter, I spoke about what Moynihan wrote his report in 1965, which supported the stereotypes of the Matriarchs, Sapphires, Aunt Jemima's and Jezebel's which played an intrigued role in ensuring that public discussions concerning single Black mothers would be relentlessly negative. The Black male, regardless to how unbeneficial he was, how lazy, shiftless, demeaning, and criminalistics he may have been according to societies standards was still the primary breadwinner in the Black family's household. It was considered to be immoral if there was not a male figure in the

---

[232] Brown, S. M. (2014, Aug). CDC study shatters myth about black fathers. *The Louisiana Weekly Publishing Co.* Aug 25-Aug 31, 2014. Retrieved from http://libproxy.lib.csusb.edu/login?url=https://search-proquest-com.libproxy.lib.csusb.edu/docview/1559519140?accountid=10359

household, because if not, the children would grow up to be incorrigible delinquents regardless of how society viewed him.

For many within the Black community, it is sad, because we as Blacks often put this pressure on each other as well as ourselves, but in actuality, we know that the ultimate culprit is the hate and racism that exists within the bowls of this country. It is the system of White supremacy in the United States that devalues us just because we are Black. But as a natural result of living with such an oppressive system, we can internalize racism as being a disease that has festered so, that it would take a lot of medication to cure as we continue to hold ourselves to such oppressive standards in order to survive.

Such standards are those that make many Black women think that if they wear a dress, for example, that showed just a little bit of skin, then this would make them a "loose woman," because of what mainstream society has been conditioned to believe instead of understanding that we as Black women should be able to wear whatever we want without the assumptions of being promiscuous. Society must also understand that there is nothing wrong with being a sensual with taste, but there is something wrong with being disrespectful towards us.

Then there are those standards that have some people in mainstream scrutinizing how Black women are supposed to behave when they become a little upset and assert their rights to be respected as a woman and as a human being and not be threated and physically attacked for no reason. For many, it is felt that a Black woman who asserts her god given rights are considered to be ab "uppity" know it all when her rights are violated, then they want to blame her for the mishaps that she endures, as they instead look away from the truth.

For the Black mother and her children, especially her son, it is institutional racism that allows the justice system to be unjust, as it allows the police to target, arrest, assault, and kill people of color without consequences every day, regardless of how unjust they are and how "angry" the victims are. So, the more time that society spends playing the blame game against the Black mother for becoming yet another victim of an unjust system, then less time society has to spend fighting for justice. This is just an example of the direst consequences of racist self-hatred. Morality within the political arena for Blacks subtlety eradicates. So Blacks must motivate themselves, understanding that they have a purpose, and in order to motivate themselves, then Blacks must have the motivation of integrity which makes sense because it says that we want to survive. We want to protect ourselves and each other and at the same time maintain our dignity, instead of being treated as though we are inferior.

So with this being said, oftentimes it is not easy to let go and accept some of these rules, because they are based on racism, yet, we also cannot pretend they do not affect our lives. For many Black women, being nice has not saved them from the hostilities and other mistreatments against them as they are stereotyped as being the Angry Black Woman. There are many, mature Black women who do not display outbursts of anger. So, when society makes such an assumption, it will help those who are less mature in their approach towards how they are treated and viewed as having the Angry Black Woman syndrome, to let their maturity be one of those moments that will help them to realize that they can put forth more efforts to avoid the Angry Black Woman stereotype by demonstrating how very misguided society can be because of ignorance. Demonizing Black women who show anger is not about encouraging them to be kind or level-headed.

It is actually a racist and sexist attempt to disrespect and dismiss Black woman even when their anger is justified.

When issues of being disrespected arises why is it that when Black women become angry, it is seen as being unacceptable by society, but the conditions that created her anger are left to fester?" The Black woman as well as the Latina has a right to be angry, because every day, she faces some form of racism, sexism, and violence that takes a toll on her mental and physical wellbeing. Now, you as mainstream are probably Saying that the Black woman internalizes the way in which she deals with her anger, and it turns into shame, anxiety, or fear. However, understand that when she cannot even stand up for herself without being villainized, then she is forced to suffer silently, and told to be "grateful" for how you're being treated, even when you're treated badly. Again, this is the Black woman being the mules of the world. Just like every other human being, Black women deserve to be treated with dignity. Which is exactly why her anger is displayed when she stands up for her dignity. Being angry does not mean that she is any less deserving of having such respect, and it most definitely does not mean that she deserves to be violated, threatened or attacked with violence. Your anger is a gift.

A respectable Black woman is a strong Black woman, is one who can get through anything without becoming so emotional where she becomes, let's say indignant. A strong Black woman can withstand all hardships with limited support. This can also be somewhat misleading because first of all, the Black woman does need support. She is a human being and the image that she is projecting to the world is not always true to what she is actually feeling inside. Oftentimes, she is a train waiting to wreck. There is that inner fear of sadness, and hopelessness, and even though all of those emotions make perfect sense because again, she is viewed as the mule of the world. She is independent,

179

self-sufficient, and always taking care of others rather than tending to her own needs. However, such pressure only adds to the burdens that the Black woman often carries, as she is already dealing with high rates of violence, poverty, and discrimination. It is virtually impossible to respect and yet dehumanize Black women by characterizing them as superhuman beings who can be treated badly because "they can take being mistreated." Respecting the Black woman means that you are willing to recognize their humanity – and with humanity comes emotion. There are times when she need to cry, go to therapy, or ask for help, and have nothing to be ashamed of. Her emotions are there so that she can take care of herself.

For most of society, there are many of us who learn that education is the key to overcoming the obstacles that get in our way. We are told that we can get out of poverty and rise above our circumstances and the stereotypes that we endure while also giving our families and communities hope if we stay in school, get good grades, and go to college. With this being said, it means that the respectability of being an Educated Black Woman is about even more than just obtaining an education. It is also about the racist and classist ideologies that says that we are more valuable if we live up to the standards of White supremacy. This means that you must carry yourselves in a certain manner. It means that you must dress more appropriately, and dress in clothes of sophistication in order to avoid being stereotyped as "ghetto." It means that if you are an educated Black woman, you will not always be associated to the so-called "hood rats" who twerk, and blame the latter for the discrimination that is bestowed against the Black community.

Understand that even if you get the best possible education – which essentially meant learning to fit in with your White peers in the hopes of accessing the opportunities that their White privilege affords them then you might want to reevaluate that analogy as Michelle Obama is a very educated woman, but many within mainstream society would rather accept a porn star as the first lady of the United States than to accept an educated Black woman. So, no matter how educated or how much money that you have, it will not make you feel more respected because you will never totally fit in, as you continue to deal with the subtle racist offensives every day. In actuality, institutional racism says in that unwritten rule that you will never be able to protect yourself from racism with college degrees or by speaking or dressing such as your White peers, because you are not White. In many ways, mainstream academia is not designed to support Black people, just as welfare was not designed to support Black people, it is just another form of racism when we try to escape it this way. However, on a more positive note about unlearning such lessons, and that is learning that academia is not our only source of power.

Being Black, we have the knowledge and the strength within our own culture and traditions – including the very language and behavior that others call "ghetto." With our creativity and intuition, we have created so much. We have things that many in mainstream often emulate such as what we write, our music, dances, hairstyles, and dress, and food among other things which are traditions, some coming from Africa, that has helped us to share our wisdom, express our joy, and resist oppression. We have birthed influential social justice movements, and built resources to help each other survive, and we have also crafted innovative ways to keep our communities safe. Yes an education can be valuable, but it is not the only way for a Black woman to be successful or respectable. And a Black woman should not have to fit the image of the Educated Black Woman in order for her to be safe.

Welfare to Well Being

Chapter 7

Since the 1960s as Black families began to become part of the welfare rolls, "the welfare state has contributed greatly to the demise of the Black family as a stable institution."[233] As of "2016, the number of live births to unmarried women were 1,569,796. The birth rate for unmarried women were 42.4 births per 1,000 unmarried women aged 15-44, and the percentage of all births to unmarried women were 39.8%.[234] The birthrate today of African Americans having children out of wedlock is no "73%, three times higher that it was prior to the War on Poverty" back in the 1960s during former President Lyndon Baines Johnson's term in office. Analysts feel that those "children who are raised in fatherless homes are far more likely to grow up poor and eventually engage in criminalist behaviors than their peers who are raised in two-parent homes."[235] In earlier chapters, I provided you with how there are several single Black

---

[233] David Horowitz and John Perazzo (2012) *"Government Verses the People: How the Welfare State Has Devastated African Americans."* http://www.fbi.gov/about-us/cjis/ucr/crime-in-the-us.-2010/tables/table-43.
[234] www.cdc.gov
[235] David Horowitz and John Perazzo (2012) *"Government Verses the People: How the Welfare State Has Devastated African Americans."* http://www.fbi.gov/about-us/cjis/ucr/crime-in-the-us.-2010/tables/table-43.

mothers who have raised successful children. I also provided you with statistical information that stated that even those, regardless of ethnicity, are just as likely to grow up and engage in criminalistic activities having two parents in the home as they would having only one parent in the home. Yet, according to data from the National Vital Statistics System and the National Survey of Family Growth shows that nonmarital births and birth rates have declined 7% and 14%, respectively, since peaking in the late 2000s.[236]

Those births that took place to unmarried women totaled 1,605,643 in 2013. About 4 in 10 U.S. births were to unmarried women in each year from 2007 through 2013. Nonmarital birth rates fell in all age groups under 35 since 2007; rates increased for women aged 35 and over. Birth rates were down more for unmarried Black and Hispanic women than for unmarried non-Hispanic White women. Nonmarital births are increasingly likely to occur within cohabiting unions—rising from 41% of recent births in 2002 to 58% in 2006–2010.[237] After increasing between 2002 and 2007, the birth rates for unmarried women were lower in 2012 than in 2007 for all race and Hispanic groups. Hispanic women had the highest nonmarital birth rate in 2012 (73 per 1,000) but also the greatest decline since 2007 (28%, from 102 per 1,000). The rate for Black women declined 11% between 2007 (71 per 1,000) and 2012 (63 per 1,000).[238]

Studies show that in "2010, Blacks (approximately 13% of the U.S. population) accounted for 48.7% of all arrests for homicide, 33.5% of arrests for aggravated assault,

---

[236] Curtin, Sally C. M.A.; Stephanie J. Ventura, M.A.; and Gladys M. Martinez, Ph.D. *Recent Declines in Nonmarital Childbearing in the United States.* NCHS Data Brief No. 162, August 2014.

[237] Curtin, Sally C. M.A.; Stephanie J. Ventura, M.A.; and Gladys M. Martinez, Ph.D. *Recent Declines in Nonmarital Childbearing in the United States.* NCHS Data Brief No. 162, August 2014.

[238] Curtin, Sally C. M.A.; Stephanie J. Ventura, M.A.; and Gladys M. Martinez, Ph.D. *Recent Declines in Nonmarital Childbearing in the United States.* NCHS Data Brief No. 162, August 2014.

and 55% arrests for robbery. Also, as of 2010, the Black poverty rate was 27.4% (about 3 times higher than the White rate), meaning that 11.5 million Blacks in the U.S. were living in poverty. Programs such as HUD, food stamps, medi-caid, and other welfare programs were designed as incentives to help those who are economically challenged but not to be a lifetime dependency. So, the behaviors that are perpetuated as a result of poverty, regardless of ethnicity is actually hindering those who are poor.

Being on welfare does not make a mother a bad person, lazy, or loose, because for some, they use it as a crutch until something better comes along. There are several studies that reveals that welfare-to-work programs do not have many benefits for families, and such programs do little to change the social structures that cause poverty or do little to reduce poverty (Schein, Gueron, and Pauly). There are those within our society who feel that there are women who go out and get pregnant on purpose in order to receive welfare benefits. This is not an accurate fact. However, one must remove the consequences of having a child out of wedlock birth that is correlated to the economic conditions that keeps one in poverty and not view welfare as an incentive but as a crutch that will cause one to sink deeper into the bowel of poverty. "Current welfare policies seem to be designed with an appalling lack of concern for their impact on out-of-wedlock births. Indeed, Medicaid programs in 11 states actually provide infertility treatments to single women on welfare."[239]

There are certain penalties that the single mother receiving benefits must face if she marries someone who is, has income, but their income is limited. These penalties which "are embedded in such welfare programs can be particularly severe if a woman on

---

[239] David Horowitz and John Perazzo (2012) *"Government Verses the People: How the Welfare State Has Devastated African Americans."* http://www.fbi.gov/about-us/cjis/ucr/crime-in-the-us.-2010/tables/table-43.

public assistance weds a man who in a low-paying job. As a FamilyScholars.org report states, "When a couple's income nears the limits prescribed by Medicaid, a few extra dollars in income cause thousands of dollars in benefits to be lost. What all of this means is that the two most important routes out of poverty—marriage and work—are heavily taxed under the current U.S. system."[240]

With this being said, for the government to put families who are receiving assistance in precarious situations that would allow them to foster such behaviors by discouraging marriage, the welfare system actually "encourages surreptitious cohabitation,"[241] where "many low-income parents will cohabit without reporting it to the government so that their benefits won't be cut."[242] These couples "avoid marriage because marriage would result in a substantial loss of income for the family."[243] "In a 2011 study that was conducted jointly by the Institute for American Values' Center for Marriage and Families and the University of Virginia's National Marriage Project the study suggested that "the rise of cohabiting households with children is the largest unrecognized threat to the quality and stability of children's family lives."[244]

---

[240] David Horowitz and John Perazzo (2012) *"Government Verses the People: How the Welfare State Has Devastated African Americans."* http://www.fbi.gov/about-us/cjis/ucr/crime-in-the-us.-2010/tables/table-43. Note: The marriage penalties that are embedded in welfare programs can be particularly severe if a woman on public assistance weds a man who is employed in a low-paying job. Consider the hypothetical case, as outlined in May 2006 by Urban Institute senior fellow Eugene Steuerle, of a single mother with two children who earns $15,000 and enjoys an Earned Income Tax Credit (EITC) benefit of approximately $4,100. If she marries a man earning $10,000, thereby boosting the total household income to $25,000, the EITC benefit, which decreases incrementally for every dollar a married couple earns above a certain level, would drop precipitously to $2,200. Similarly, consider the case (also outlined by Eugene Steuerle in May 2006) of a mother of two children who earns $20,000 and thus qualifies for Medicaid. If she marries someone earning just $6,000, resulting in a combined household income of $26,000, her children's Medicaid benefits are cut off entirely.
[241] David Horowitz and John Perazzo (2012) *"Government Verses the People: How the Welfare State Has Devastated African Americans."* http://www.fbi.gov/about-us/cjis/ucr/crime-in-the.-us.-2010/tables/table-43.
[242] David Horowitz and John Perazzo (2012) *"Government Verses the People: How the Welfare State Has Devastated African Americans."* http://www.fbi.gov/about-us/cjis/ucr/crime-in-the.-us.-2010/tables/table-43.
[243] David Horowitz and John Perazzo (2012) *"Government Verses the People: How the Welfare State Has Devastated African Americans."* http://www.fbi.gov/about-us/cjis/ucr/crime-in-the.-us.-2010/tables/table-43.
[244] David Horowitz and John Perazzo (2012) *"Government Verses the People: How the Welfare State Has Devastated African Americans."* http://www.fbi.gov/about-us/cjis/ucr/crime-in-the.-us.-2010/tables/table-43.

"Researchers also concluded that cohabiting relationships are highly prone to instability, and that children in such homes are consequently less likely to thrive, more likely to be abused, and more prone to suffering "serious emotional problems."[245]

This is one of the main reasons why the welfare system has had such a devastating impact among the Black family. The devastating societal consequences of the breakdown in the family's circumstances cannot be overstated. "Father-absent families—Black and White alike—generally occupy the bottom rung of America's economic ladder."[246] Data obtained from the U.S. Census, showed that "in 2008 the poverty rate for single parents with children was 35.6%; the rate for married couples with children was 6.4%. For White families in particular, the corresponding two-parent and single-parent poverty rates were 21.7% and 3.1%; for Hispanics, the figures were 37.5% and 12.8%; and for Blacks, 35.3% and 6.9%."[247]

According to Robert Rector, the senior research fellow with the Heritage Foundation, he indicates that 'the absence of marriage increases the frequency of child poverty by 700 percent' and with this being said, it constitutes the single most reliable predictor of a self-perpetuating underclass. Articulating a similar theme many years ago, Martin Luther King, Jr. said, "Nothing is so much needed as a secure family life for a people to pull themselves out of poverty."[248]

---

[245] David Horowitz and John Perazzo (2012) *"Government Verses the People: How the Welfare State Has Devastated African Americans."* http://www.fbi.gov/about-us/cjis/ucr/crime-in-the-us.-2010/tables/table-43.
[246] David Horowitz and John Perazzo (2012) *"Government Verses the People: How the Welfare State Has Devastated African Americans."* http://www.fbi.gov/about-us/cjis/ucr/crime-in-the-us.-2010/tables/table-43
[247] David Horowitz and John Perazzo (2012) *"Government Verses the People: How the Welfare State Has Devastated African Americans."* http://www.fbi.gov/about-us/cjis/ucr/crime-in-the-us.-2010/tables/table-43
[248] David Horowitz and John Perazzo (2012) *"Government Verses the People: How the Welfare State Has Devastated African Americans."* http://www.fbi.gov/about-us/cjis/ucr/crime-in-the-us.-2010/tables/table-43

Oftentimes, children who come from single-parent households are usually afflicted not only with their economic circumstance, but they are also overwhelmed with social and psychological, disadvantages. As a Heritage Foundation analysis noted, "youngsters raised by single parents, as compared to those who grow up in intact married homes, are more likely to be physically abused; to be treated for emotional and behavioral disorders; to smoke, drink, and use drugs; to perform poorly in school; to be suspended or expelled from school; to drop of high school; to behave aggressively and violently; to be arrested for a juvenile crime; to serve jail time before age 30; and to go on to experience poverty as adults. However, from my personal experience and viewing additional research, I have also found that there are many children who come from two parent homes where one or both of the parents are not only physically abusive, but they too are alcoholics, abusers of drugs and perform poorly in school in areas such as Kentucky and areas that are economically improvised.

Data that was obtain from the National Fatherhood Initiative, showed that 60% of rapists, 72% of adolescent murderers, and 70% of long-term prison inmates are men who grew up in homes where there was an absent father. With regards to the girls in particular, this same entity suggested that those who were raised by single mothers are more than likely to give birth out-of-wedlock, thereby perpetuating the cycle of poverty for yet another generation.[249] This devastating breakdown concerning the Black family is a reasonably recent occurrence, thereby agreeing precisely with the rise of the welfare state. Throughout the era of slavery and well into the early decades of the twentieth

---

[249] David Horowitz and John Perazzo (2012) *"Government Verses the People: How the Welfare State Has Devastated African Americans."* http://www.fbi.gov/about-us/cjis/ucr/crime-in-the-us.-2010/tables/table-43

century, the majority of Black children grew up in two-parent households."[250] Studies that were conducted during the Post-Civil War revealed that most Black couples that were in their forties had been together for at least twenty years. And in the southern urban areas around 1880, there were nearly three-fourths of black households were husband-or father-present; in southern rural settings, the figure approached 86%. As of 1940, the illegitimacy rate among blacks nationwide was approximately 15%—scarcely one-fifth of the current figure."[251] As late as 1950, Black women were more likely to be married than White women, and only 9% of Black families with children were headed by a single parent.[252]

Now these studies were not conducted by Blacks but by Whites, because if one knew cultural history, they would know that during the Post Civil War, Blacks were slaves and only able to marry if given permission by the slave masters. Additionally, slaves and their families were ripped apart from each other as children were ripped from the loins of their parents. Blacks had what is called the extended kin, meaning that even though they were not related by blood, most of them learned how to look out for one another as though they were family. So, if the father or male mentor was not sold away, lynched, shot or maimed then of course there would be a male figure around. This is why it is so important for Blacks, no matter what ethnicity (African, Haitian, Dominican, Cuban, Afro Latin) you come from to learn cultural history because those in mainstream will put numbers together in a clump and allow the blame to fall upon you.

---

[250] David Horowitz and John Perazzo (2012) *"Government Verses the People: How the Welfare State Has Devastated African Americans."* http://www.fbi.gov/about-us/cjis/ucr/crime-in-the-us.-2010/tables/table-43
[251] David Horowitz and John Perazzo (2012) *"Government Verses the People: How the Welfare State Has Devastated African Americans."* http://www.fbi.gov/about-us/cjis/ucr/crime-in-the-us.-2010/tables/table-43
[252] David Horowitz and John Perazzo (2012) *"Government Verses the People: How the Welfare State Has Devastated African Americans."* http://www.fbi.gov/about-us/cjis/ucr/crime-in-the-us.-2010/tables/table-43

First, one must find the root of the problem, which is, as we can observe, stems from slavery. So, in order to solve the problem, yet, they fail to ask the question, why does poverty or welfare programs exist. These programs may be helpful for some, or even many; but they do not address issues such as how does the welfare mother who is trying to work, provide transportation to get to and from work if her funds are limited? How does she pay for child care if her funds are limited (Schein)? How does she pay rent and purchase the basic necessities if she is terminated from welfare for being employed at a low wage paying job? Welfare programs also does not address the deeply rooted problems such as the causes of poverty or the attempt to try to change society. Such programs are seen more as a contributing factor to the problems of poverty instead of eliminating poverty because they do not demonstrate how poor people can apply to college and obtain gainful employment that will pay a livable wage, later leading to a career.

Next, by eliminating those barriers for those who are economically challenged to education and well-paid jobs this would assist in easing some of the pressures off of the welfare system. How can one obtain an education if they cannot afford an education without getting financial aid and then taking out student loans that they will have to pay back over the course of 30 years? Without a decent education beginning with grammar school, how does one obtain employment that will pay livable wages? And so, because someone cannot afford to survive because they are not paid a decent livable wage, this creates opportunities for poor mothers to end up in the cycle of poverty. Now without a doubt, having a higher education is linked to better paying jobs (United States Census Bureau).

189

While many women may be the least economically advantaged, even after a college education, they will still have the opportunity to make more money than those women who do not have a college education (et al.). Having a higher education and better paying jobs are also linked to better general health, and the opportunities to access better health insurance and other resources that are created to provide more stability ("Social Determinants of Health"). Mothers who are economically challenged will often experience higher rates of health issues and social exclusion which eliminates barriers for them to have better opportunities which would also eliminate many health issues (Albanese).

So, with this being said, "if someone was to blurt out the words "welfare mother" at this moment, then the majority of Americans would immediately, without even thinking, associate an image and draw the conclusion that it is an African-American woman, like Claudine, who lives in some urban ghetto with several kids by several different men." (Susan Douglas, *The Mommy Myth,* pg. 175, 2004). Now even though Susan Douglas was referring to a misperception common in 2004, it is truly unfortunate that this type of stereotype persists in America today. Furthermore, this type of stereotypical attitude has been promulgated by a long history of mis-characterizations of single Black mothers by the media on television, through social media and through magazines and books either as welfare queens or domestic servants. Today, Black mothers are turning those tables around as there has been an obvious shift towards more positive representations of single Black mothers as middle-class, successful, educated women who are living comfortable lives.

Ever since the era of former President Ronald Reagan, the single Black mother has been stigmatized and stereotyped as being a welfare queen. This was mentioned in an earlier chapter. During the 1976 presidential campaign, it was Ronald Regan, who

encouraged the idea and conveying it to mainstream society indicating that the single

Black mother were no more than a "welfare queen." Obviously, this idealist woman, the

Black woman, had become his bogeywoman. She became his bogeywoman because

according to society, a Black person in America is not supposed to be intellectual enough

to commit such White collared crimes as their White counterparts does.

Reagan frequently and repetitiously gave descriptive narratives about this

Chicago woman who drove fancy Cadillacs and lived a life of luxury after swindling the

governments welfare programs out of hundreds of thousands of dollars. She was able to

accomplish such criminalistics activities by using fake names and addresses, using

disguises, and possibly a stolen baby. This version of the story that Reagan used, was

used in order to strengthen the idea that the Black female is an unreasonable nuisance

that is tied to lasciviousness, reflecting that she has a desire to leech whatever it is that

she can from the welfare system rather than doing like any other mainstream mother

which is being at home and attending to her children as a loving parent and contributor

to the future of society. He forgot to mention the White woman that committed the same

crime but was pardoned for her actions. Think about that last statement as I so

sarcastically put it.

The welfare system was a system that was created to provide income assistance

for those in need. This welfare-based program provided families assistance with "food,

housing, health, child welfare, and supplemented income assistance that came under the

rubric of welfare."[253] In the 1960s, there was a War on Poverty that afforded more

---

[253] Braun, Craig, Bauer, Peck, 1996; Orrick, 1995.

"opportunities for gainful employment and state determination of programs."[254] Aid to Families with Dependent Children came out of the Social Security Act of 1935. The Social Security Act was designed for poor White women who were widowed or whose husbands were hurt on the job and unable to work anymore. Welfare was not designed for any woman of color. In actuality, as of 2017, there are still far more Whites in America who are receiving public assistance than any other ethnicity in the United States. So, we can debunk Ronald Reagan's stigmatized and stereotypical myth about the single Black mother being nothing more than a welfare queen because of something that one lady did. Just as the rest of mainstream society, you can all stop clumping all of an ethnicity's flaws because of the faults of one individual.

Over the years, there have been several single Black mothers who have been very self-sufficient. The welfare system is a crutch that is only to hold you up temporarily by barely making it. The system was designed to hinder one's progress instead of enhancing their economic achievements. Back in the late 1980s, early 1990s, California designed a program called GAIN. Greater Avenues for Independence, I belief that is what the acronyms stood for. I know the first two are correct, but for the purposes of this book, the point is that the welfare program tried to create a system that would ostracize Black and poor mothers not realizing that this was all that many needed in order to get off of a system that was a generational curse. All they needed was that little push and the confidence in knowing that they were going to succeed in doing better because failing was not an option.

---

[254] Braun, Craig, Bauer, Peck, 1996; Orrick, 1995.

With this system, it said that you had to find a job, get the job and keep the job even if you did not make enough money to sustain for you and your children. "Using case reduction as a measure of welfare dependence, it reported that welfare dependence had decreased. However, that report did not explain how families were impacted by welfare reform. Nor did it address the extent to which these families were achieving self-sufficiency."[255] Let it so be noted that "leaving welfare is not synonymous with leaving poverty (Meyer & Cancian, 1998).

Many single mothers of color moved from welfare to well-being because they were able to legitimately supplement their welfare income by taking menial jobs such as domesticates, certified nursing assistants and working their way up and cosmetologists where they started their own businesses and were able to get a small business loan that was designed for the single and independent mother of color. Many of these mothers of color went back to school to advance their educational levels so that they could achieve their American Dreams for themselves as well as their children.

Here you have two different researchers, Garfinkel and McLanahan (1987) who have also noted, that there are conservatives who have argued that welfare programs have discouraged fathers and mothers from staying together because it affects the income level of the family. Subsequently, the number of single female households that are economically challenge increases. According to Garfinkel and McLanahan (1987), poverty among single female households exists for three reasons: women earn less, they receive meager resources from welfare, and only 40% of white fathers and 19.5% of

---

[255] Bauer, Jean W., Braun, Bonnie, Olson, Patricia D. "Welfare to Well-Being Framework for Research, Education, and Outreach." The Journal of Consumer Affairs. Vol. 34, No. 1, 2000. 0022-0078/0002-1.1.50/62. © 2000 by The American Council on Consumer Interests.

Black fathers pay child support. To raise children without any other resources is a decision-making process that ends up becoming critical for survival.

Just as welfare policies have discouraged many from marriage and the formation of stability in families, they have also discouraged the development of healthy work ethics.[256] As Heritage Foundation scholar Michael Franc noted in 2012: "[T]he necessity of phasing out [welfare] benefits as incomes rise brings a serious moral hazard. In many cases, economists have calculated, welfare recipients who enter the work force or receive pay raises lose a dollar or more of benefits for each additional dollar they earn. The system makes fools of those who work hard."[257]

In his testimony on Capitol Hill, Rep. Geoff Davis (R-Kentucky) agreed that although federal welfare programs "were designed to alleviate poverty while promoting work," they have collectively had "an unintended side effect of discouraging harder work and higher earnings." "The more benefits the government provides," he said, "the stronger the disincentive to work." Yet another Capitol Hill witness, Rep. Gwen Moore (D-Wisconsin)—herself a former welfare recipient—acknowledged in her oral testimony: "I once had a job and begged my supervisor not to give me a 50-cents-an-hour raise lest I lose Title 20 day care." The same work disincentive came into play when Moore contemplated the health coverage she was receiving through Medicaid. "I would want to work if in fact I didn't risk losing Medicaid," she said.[258] Despite her obstacles, Rep.

---

[256] David Horowitz and John Perazzo (2012) *"Government Verses the People: How the Welfare State Has Devastated African Americans."* http://www.fbi.gov/about-us/cjis/ucr/crime-in-the-us.-2010/tables/table-43
[257] David Horowitz and John Perazzo (2012) *"Government Verses the People: How the Welfare State Has Devastated African Americans."* http://www.fbi.gov/about-us/cjis/ucr/crime-in-the-us.-2010/tables/table-43
[258] David Horowitz and John Perazzo (2012) *"Government Verses the People: How the Welfare State Has Devastated African Americans."* http://www.fbi.gov/about-us/cjis/ucr/crime-in-the-us.-2010/tables/table-43

Moore is prove that single Black mothers can overcome their obstacles as she went from welfare to well-being.

Overcoming Obstacles

Chapter 8

Today the regulations concerning welfare are becoming a little harsh for single
mothers, yet, it is those single Black mothers who are often caught between a rock and a
hard place as they begin looking for funding for educational or professional endeavors
so that they can better their livelihoods for themselves and their families. In some states,
single mothers encounter a barrier when they apply for student aid in any form because
is considered a source of income. They are in jeopardy of losing their HUD low income
housing assistance or are required to pay the market value of rent. Their medical and
cash aid is either limited or discontinued all together making single mothers on welfare
ineligible for funding. There are certain groups such as Raise the Nation who are
working desperately to bring about an awareness to these regulations and change such
regulations that will ensure that single mothers are able to improve their lives as well as
the lives of their children.

African-American women have been stigmatized and stereotyped against for
years. So, as a single Black mother, she is viewed as a mother who is not going to make it
in society and neither is her child. She will end up as a prostitute or drug addict, a

welfare queen, and a societal leech while her child if a girl, will end up just like her, or if a boy will end up a gang banging thug and drug dealer. Now there is the realistic view that many of those single mothers, especially Black mothers have both a conscious and unconscious habit of making negative remarks about Black men and their children's fathers. When you put down the father of your child, doing him the same way that society does, then your child is going to believe their father is an irresponsible person. In a world where people are already looking at Black children as being delinquents, our Black children do not need to hear such statements from their mothers even if the father is no good, because all you are teaching your children is how to be disrespectful."[259]

As the author of this book, and a single Black mother I am here to say, that even as I struggled, I overcame my obstacles. Me, nor my daughter ended up as prostitutes, drug addicts, welfare queen or societal leeches, as society likes to assume, nor did my sons end up as gang banging thugs or pimps being a menace to society, and I have completed four years towards my PhD. My obstacle was the murder of my son and then finances. However, I will not allow this to hinder me, as I took on writing as part of my healing process with this being the eighth book that I have completed. I have had to take menial jobs, but I had a job. I have worked in the healthcare field for eight years and began my own business, a nonprofit organization after the violent death of my son on May 17, 2011. I have never, spoken ill willed about my children's father to them and as adults, I still do not. My daughter has worked in the field of education since she was 16 and she is now in her thirties, and she too has a nonprofit organization. During her

---

[259] Owens, D. E. (1998, May 30). `Single mamahood' is helpful voice of experience. *New Pittsburgh Courier,* City Edition; **A11.** Retrieved from http://libproxy.lib.csusb.edu/login?rl=https://search-proquest-com.libproxy.lib.csusb.edu/docview/367964253?accountid=10359

down times in the educational realm (such as summer vacations), she worked in the healthcare field, went back to school became a Certified Nursing Assistant, she currently holds, two Bachelor's and is raising her children. Neither of my sons became pimps, gang bangers, drug dealers or thugs, and my oldest son was attending the local community college with just a few months to go before completing his remaining courses towards his Associates Degree before his untimely demise. My youngest son is employed and making a way for himself. There are several Black mothers who are overcoming the stereotypes of being labeled as welfare mothers or welfare queens.

So, are those of us who do not fit the image of ghetto mothers considered to be that exception to the rule? Do I, like many Black mothers, personify the image as one who raised her teenaged daughter to have multiple children in order to receive public assistance, or who raised her sons to be juvenile deliquents? Have you ever thought that there are many single Black mothers such as myself who have overcome tremendous obstacles despite the labels that mainstream society has placed on us? There are those in mainstream who hear those labels such as "welfare queen," "ghetto," "lazy," and other derogatory statements and quickly equate it to single Black or Latina mothers. We are those single mothers who have beaten the odds, despite the barriers that have been presented before us, and there are many of us.

It is always said that if you grow up in a fatherless home it would lead to child poverty, delinquency, and school failure.[260] This statement is not always an accurate statement. Did you know that there are more children who are the products of teachers, judges and law enforcer that stay in just as much trouble as the child who has grown up

---

[260] Owens, D. E. (1998, May 30). `Single mamahood' is helpful voice of experience. *New Pittsburgh Courier,* City Edition; **A11.** Retrieved from http://libproxy.lib.csusb.edu/login?url=https://search-proquest-com.libproxy.lib.csusb.edu/docview/367964253?accountid=10359

in a deprived area? Did you know that there are also children who come from two parent homes who also grow up and dabble in criminalistic activities? Yes, single mothers are at a disadvantage when it comes to raising children, especially single Black mother, but never underestimate their abilities of what they can accomplish.

There are several of women who choose to raise their children as a single parent, however, "women who do choose the option of being a single mother should recognize that they need to give their child all the advantages that they can. That should start with putting away all the jealousy, bitterness and anger that you may have toward your children's father and make sure your children are allowed to love both their mother and father. Also, for the Black child, you as the parent must help your child to recognize that they live in a world where all things are not equal, especially for them. There are those who will hate them because of the color of their skin, their gifts and talents and they will be discriminated against. They must also understand the importance of having not only a strong work ethic, but a strong support system and an education. Single mothers– particularly African-American single mothers–have to work harder to make sure their children succeed in the world."[261]

As we look at society as a whole, we will notice that Blacks are still being stereotyped against, especially in the justice system. Blacks are still expected to fail, they still have to work 200% harder than their White counterparts and then there are those individuals such as #45 who openly and blatantly still harbor hate, prejudices, against African-Americans as he racist openly display discriminatory practices, looking at

[261] Owens, D. E. (1998, May 30). `Single mamahood' is helpful voice of experience. *New Pittsburgh Courier,* City Edition; **A11.** Retrieved from http://libproxy.lib.csusb.edu/login?url=https://search-proquest-com.libproxy.lib.csusb.edu/docview/367964253?accountid=10359

minorities, individuals with disabilities and of different religious groups as if they are still inferior. However, it is the single Black mother who has to bear the brunt of such ignorance and thinking twice as much as her White counterpart, because she is still considered to be the mule of the world.

Well for me, as a single Black mother, I, like so many of us Black mothers, will continue to rise above our circumstances, because we cannot dwell on any of the stereotypes that many White people have of against us. We have to continue moving forward and persevere. We have to not only believe in ourselves because, there are those who will not believe in us, but we also have to have a positive attitude with the gratitude that follows. We cannot continue to allow those who have abject thinking and attitudes towards us to view us from a negative perspective but allow our actions to be seen through our accomplishments.

A single Black mother has ninety-nine problems, but an individual of ignorance is definitely not one that she will allow to hinder her progress, besides, that is their own person problem.[262] Here is what many of us as Black mothers think that this gives us the inspiration to move forward. By the late great Dr. Maya Angelou:

STILL I RISE...

BY MAYA ANGELOU

You may write me down in history

With your bitter, twisted lies,

You may trod me in the very dirt

---

[262] Owens, D. E. (1998, May 30). `Single mamahood' is helpful voice of experience. *New Pittsburgh Courier,* City Edition; **A11.** Retrieved from http://libproxy.lib.csusb.edu/login?url=https://search-proquest-com.libproxy.lib.csusb.edu/docview/367964253?accountid=10359

But still, like dust, I'll rise.

Does my sassiness upset you?

Why are you beset with gloom?

'Cause I walk like I've got oil wells

Pumping in my living room.

Just like moons and like suns,

With the certainty of tides,

Just like hopes springing high,

Still I'll rise.

Did you want to see me broken?

Bowed head and lowered eyes?

Shoulders falling down like teardrops,

Weakened by my soulful cries?

Does my haughtiness offend you?

Don't you take it awful hard

'Cause I laugh like I've got gold mines

Diggin' in my own backyard.

You may shoot me with your words,

You may cut me with your eyes,

You may kill me with your hatefulness,

But still, like air, I'll rise.

Does my sexiness upset you?

Does it come as a surprise

That I dance like I've got diamonds

At the meeting of my thighs?

Out of the huts of history's shame

I rise

Up from a past that's rooted in pain

I rise

I'm a black ocean, leaping and wide,

Welling and swelling I bear in the tide.

Leaving behind nights of terror and fear

I rise

Into a daybreak that's wondrously clear

I rise

Bringing the gifts that my ancestors gave,

I am the dream and the hope of the slave.

I rise,

I rise,

I rise.[263]

It is very unfortunate that Black males, have to experience facing a particular kind of racism at an early age, such as my sons did. My oldest son experienced racism before he had the opportunity to attend kindergarten. He then experienced racism and racial profiling at the age of 14 which left him feeling a little bitter and untrusting of those who worked in law enforcement. Luckily, I dated someone in law enforcement at

---

[263] Maya Angelou, "Still I Rise" from *And Still I Rise: A Book of Poems*. Copyright © 1978 by Maya Angelou. Used by permission of Random House, an imprint and division of Penguin Random House LLC. All rights reserved.

the time, had friends in law enforcement and have family in law enforcement and he understood that not all in law enforcement demonstrated the same types of behaviors.

A White coach, whom I will call coach "D" at the junior high school that my son attended, gave him and his friends hope and inspiration. Coach did not see these young men as individuals of color, but as individual that needed a positive male role model who would give them the motivation that they needed to be inspired because he believed in many of these young Black males. My son admired his Physical Education teacher and coach and I had to continually teach my sons that not all White people view all Blacks as being the same. This coach did a lot for my son and some of his friends and all they talked about was coach, his wife and all of the things that they had done for them.

As a matter of speaking, as my children were going up, I always told my them that I do not look at a person because of the color of their skin but I do look at the content of their character. The only when I begin to recognize color, is when ignorance of an individual is revealed and that is with any ethnicity. As a single Black mother, I have taught my children not just Black history, but cultural history so that they could have a conceptual understanding of their surroundings and appreciate who they are and where they have come from as well as those from other cultures. I was also able to "instruct my sons in the art of being a Black man in this society with the help of male family members, mentors and close family friends that were also male. No, I can never raise a man as a man could but I as a mother did the best that I could do in teaching them how to respect a woman and treat her as they would want someone to treat me. Yes, the single Black mother faces many challenges and obstacles, but society should never pigeonhole, stigmatize or stereotype her until they have the opportunity to get to personally know her and the culture in which she comes from.

As long as there are those who uses poor mothers and their economic conditions for their own personal gain to line their pockets and then say that it is the poor mother who chose the condition that she is in letting that excuse be their scapegoat, then those individuals will continue to be ineffective for those mothers in coming up with solutions that will shape public policies and their opinions about Black mothers. They are not concerned about those who are economically challenged but only in financing their own propaganda. They too demonstrate practices in which they discussion race and what they view as being the good mother and those who they consider "welfare queens."

These individuals will continue to demonstrate and repeat such discriminations as they exercise their powers which will continue to perpetuate the belief that the Black mother should be held personally accountable for having children only to bamboozle the system. Therefore, they preclude an image of low-income mothers (the good mother) who actually deserves assistance because they use the system in order to overcome those obstacles that were created not by her, but by a society that is structured to produce and maintain inequality. In other words, as long as there are politicians and others who advocate that only Black women utilizes the system to leech off of the system, instead of going out obtain gainful employment or obtain an education in order to better themselves, it is they who continue the vicious stereotypical cycle of racism and discrimination. It is those politicians and individuals who create the barriers that causes many of these mothers to constantly repeat the cycles that they are in; they also create such barriers with no intentions of improving poor mothers' situations but continually cause the devastation that is within the family. It is the "good mother," and not always the "Black ghetto mother" who goes out and does something to improve her situation. There is a difference regardless of ethnicity. So, as long as there are those few individuals of ignorance who have no open window of perception then nothing will change until they change and acquire some knowledge.

Although there are many young low-income mothers who consider themselves to be good mothers (Kaplan, 1997; Luttrell, 2003), there are those policy makers and those within mainstream society who do not recognize teenagers and women who receives public assistance as being good mothers (Douglas & Michaels, 2004; Hancock, 2004). Instead, these types of individuals suggest (assume) that low-income mothers' only raise their teenagers to have children, so that they too can become dependent upon public assistance. With this being said, such assumptions bring about conversations concerning the welfare queen. So, since society already view Black mothers as being welfare queens, this creates a ready-made image that turns a blind eye to the fact that there are those mothers who actually have a maternal devotion to their children. However, those who have no open window of perception with such societal attitudes would prefer to bring about images of Black mothers as women who have irresponsibly had more children so that they can get more governmental support because they have so little self-control and would prefer to live off the welfare system rather than to go out and get respectable jobs (Edin & Kefalas, 2005; Hancock, 2004; Hays, 2003).

Those mothers who are low income are often to referred to as being the working-class and poor women. So, with that being said, our society has this ideology of motherhood, and low-income mothers suggesting that if they really cared about their children, then why would they bring them into the world knowing that they were impoverished? Why wouldn't they get their affairs in order before having children? Unfortunately, those with such societal attitudes do not realize that because children are born into an economically impoverished situation, there are those mothers who do go

205

out and work hard to complete high school and to attain college degrees, obtain stability, obtain well-paying jobs, and have stable marriages before having children. Yet again, it is felt by society, that if mothers fail to follow such pathways as those that were mentioned then they are therefore, perceived as inherently unfit mothers.

There are several studies that demonstrates that being a low-income mothers is challenging, that does not take rocket science to figure out, yet, the negative perception that is associated with low income mothers does not document the fact that there is a differences between societal attitudes, and beliefs, compared to the actual goals, and practices of low income mothers who are actually succeeding compared with middle-class mothers (Edin & Kefalas, 2005; 1012 *Journal of Family Issues 38(7)* Hays, 1996; Lareau, 2003).

It is not easy being a single mother regardless to what ethnicity you are. Being a single mother means that you have to try and perform the roles of two parents knowing that you are not quite capable of doing so. Whether you are receiving public assistance or working menial jobs in order to get ahead, the single mother is not afforded the luxury of having two incomes and someone to fill in the role of the absent parent. As a single mother you must learn how to reach out to trusted family members and friends to be mentors and realize that you do not have to be alone while raising your child. To be a successful single mother, you will also need to realize that when you make certain decisions, you need to act on them and do not make promises that you cannot keep. Go out and find out about community resources and activities that your children can be involved in and know that there are many programs that have part and full sponsorships available to those individuals who cannot afford to put their children in such programs. There are also certain corporations that will make financial donations that will assist with helping children from economically challenged communities to get into and complete many of such activities. There are also those who will not disclose or recommend certain information to certain groups who are economically challenge so you will need to learn how to do the research for those resources.

Here are some suggestions from me personally that I feel some single mothers should think about as they overcome some of the challenges of being a single mother. Understand that I am not a license physician, nor am a licensed psychiatrist but a single mother who put some of these subjects into practice or learned from other mothers who had put such doctrine into practice. There are many challenges that single mothers face, but as a single mother you will have to learn how to deal with such challenges as you meet the needs and interest of your children. Talk to your children, make it a habit of asking them how their day went, allow them to be open with you. Remember that our children also carry emotional baggage that sometimes become unresolved. By having a positive parent, child relationship, this will also help your child to learn how to resist the pressures that they face by their peers. Another challenge that the single parent must face is, let your child know how much you love them. This does not mean going trying to buy their love by showering them with gifts or going out to buy them shoes that cost $150 that will do nothing to benefit them. This means that they need to know that you love them unconditionally and that no matter what trials and tribulations you as a single mother may face, let your child know this because it is very meaningful for your child.

A challenge that a single mother must take into consideration is knowing how to put certain situations into its proper perspective. Realize what is important and know the difference between a need and a want. There are many single mothers that have to learn how to set realistic boundaries of what your child can do and what they cannot do, and what you can and cannot do. Allow yourself and your children permission to have some me time with each other and let them know that as human beings we can be less than perfect. Learn how to spend daily but quality moments with your children even if they are short and in between homework and chores. Some of this time can be expanded by doing activities together. For me, I would take my children to the park and have picnics with them, take them to the beach, the mall or just go out for walks with them. It was the little insignificant things that you thought were not a big deal that was actually a big deal to your children because later down the road, those are the things that they talk about.

Sometimes we have to leave our children with room for error. They need to understand that respect is earned and allow them to understand that there are logical consequences for any types of misbehavior. Some of the boundaries are letting them know that there are consequences that they will face for staying out after curfew or not cleaning up and doing their chores, these are things that they need to know in advance beginning at an early age. You as a parent must make sure that you follow through with those consequences in order to be respected by your children, because if they see that you are always just talk and no action then how do you expect for your children to trust your loyalty? With every action there is a reaction, you may get results but that does not necessarily mean that they will be the results that you were expecting. There is nothing wrong with tough love and using what you do in a firm and loving way. This is called tough love and It does not have to be displayed in an angry or confrontational manner.

Being the primary provider of the family, it is important that you know what gifts you have. What I mean by this is, how can you supplement your income. Can you clean houses, cut grass, do maintenance work, do you have an education, do you have a vocational trade, do you have experience in other areas of the employment field, what skills or talent do you have that can be converted into income for the family that will make ends meet? If you do not, have any of these gifts or talents then that means that you will need to go out and develop ways in order to generate extra income so that you can handle your finances. You should also be aware of opportunities that will allow you to learn and earn more.

Resourcefulness and exercising wisdom concerning your use of time are very valuable in order for you to be able to provide for your family. Time is a valuable and priceless commodity that should not be wasted. Budgeting is also an essential tool that can be used in order to help you avoid financial problems in the future. This means that every month, you write down the amount of income that you bring in, then subtract that from your rent, your electric, water, gas, trash, phone, cable, etc. Learn how to live within your means and not go overboard by explaining to your children that you live on a budget and that it is very important to teach them to learn how to work together as a team and understand your situation without actually restricting them or preventing them from enjoying life. Let them know that when they are not using the lights, turn them off as it uses and waste energy. Let them know that when the heater is on, do not stand with the door open as they do not live in a barn. Tell them that when they take baths, do not fill up the bathtub to the very top as they are not going swimming. Living a simple life do have its advantages and explaining this to your children will make them understand not only the situation, but how to be responsible adults as well.

As a single mother, we must also learn how to give ourselves boundaries. This means that we must learn how to have some me time for ourselves. This does not mean that if a trust family member or friend is willing to keep your children a couple times a month so that you can go out on a date or spend some time out with the girls that you take advantage of the situation. Another concern that a single mother should understand is this, if you ever consider dating do not bring everyone you date around your children. Since I am a little old fashioned, I knew that if I was dating someone that I knew that I was not going to get serious with, then I knew that this person was someone that you DO NOT take HOME to meet your parents, family or your children. If you have the capability of being a single mother well, and you are a strong and confident woman, then you will realize when you are ready to allow someone to be around your children.

Being a single mother has many challenges that she must face. However, no matter how difficult these challenges may be, it is very important for to have a plan and goal. So, when you realize that you are making progress then you will realize that this will give you the boost that you need to be confident in yourself and help you to feel positive. By doing this, the way in which you feel will also make it easier for you to provide the love, attention and guidance your children need to be successful in life. In addition, by you having an attitude of gratitude, it will help you to also be successful at being a single mother as you see the fruits of your sacrifices as your children grow to be emotionally healthy and loving adults.

The Myths of the Absent Black Father

Chapter 9

For years, there have always been negative statements being made about Black fathers and their absence, which mainstream strongly suggests has become a crisis. One of the statements that is most common among mainstream is, "if Black fathers were not absent in their children's lives then there would not be so much chaos and destruction in the Black community and their children would not grow up to be delinquents. In my personal opinion, I wonder should the same be said about those who are not of color and turn out to be mass murderers and serial killers and yet many of them grew up in the "quote, unquote, perfect family with two parents." However, it is obvious that you cannot mix apples and oranges, because the mass murder and serial killer has the mental deficiency of having that perfect life which caused them to go over the edge, while the children of color are just products of their environment which stemmed from their mistreatment since slavery or due to racism. So, they are survivors. It is something how those who are of color get stigmatized as being the bad guy and yet their crimes aren't as atrocious. Neither are correct in the conduct of their actions, and one is no better than the other, but then there is that thing called privilege. This is where institutional and systemic racism comes in.

Today, the family structure and dynamics are constantly changing with the millennials and the microwavable age, not for just the single Black mothers but for all single mothers as a whole. "Many American women under the age of thirty, regardless of race, will give birth outside of marriage; and, this will be across the Atlantic, to the Pacific. In Iceland, there are 66 percent of children who are born to unmarried women. The heterosexual marriage rates are beginning to fall while the divorce rates are beginning to rise not only in the United States but abroad. Unfortunately, it is Black women and their families who will continuously be seen as dysfunctional, and uncommonly so."[264] The next unfortunate aspect of this matter is that there are those Black sons who did not always have an opportunity to interact with their fathers at some point and time in their lives.

Oftentimes there are those Black children who feel the need to blame their circumstances on their home training, or the lack there of, or even blame their communities' contributions or environment. Whether they were neglected or rejected by an absent father, the child may feel that the fathers absent is also a part of their family's disorganization, which is also a part of the "various assumptions regarding society's perception of deviant behaviors which dominates the discussions regarding Black youth" (Aschenbrenner, 1975). Moral development based on social principles plays a significant part in its cultivation, regardless of culture. There are those who are, adversaries of single Black mothers, and these types of individuals will continually say

---

[264] Brown, S. M. (2014, Aug). CDC study shatters myth about black fathers. *The Louisiana Weekly Publishing Co.* Aug 25-Aug 31, 2014. Retrieved from http://libproxy.lib.csusb.edu/login?url=https://search-proquest-com.libproxy.lib.csusb.edu/docview/1559519140?accountid=10359

that they are doing what is in the Black child's best interest at heart and in mind as they continue to point to the decades of research that indicates that children do best when they are raised in healthy two-parent families. However, according to the Center for Law and Social Policy, the results that they obtained while conducting such research, showed results that related to the offspring of single-parent households which are often oversimplified and exaggerated. As stated earlier in this book, most children who are in single-parent families grow up to be just fine, and it is still unclear how much of the disadvantages to children are caused by poverty or family structure or whether marriage itself makes the difference or the type of people who commonly marry."[265]

So, to demonize the single Black mother and say that they are to blame for the destruction and deterioration of their communities and include the fact that absent Black fathers are also contributing factors is not going to improve the lives of their children. What is will do is make the children of color sit back and observe the negative aspects in which mainstream children behave, those such as the Paris Hilton's and the Britney Spears's. This will also make children of color become aware of the societal attitudes toward them.

In fact, to even conceptualize the ideology that 70 percent of Black children are inheritedly damaged actually stigmatizes them. So, because of societal attitudes, the Black parent must again teach their children how to survive in a world that is so cruel towards them because of the color of their skin while also teaching their children how to keep from being negatively impacted by generations of ignorance, hate, discrimination and misinformation about the way that Black households are ran. Stacia Brown said, "I

---

[265] Brown, S. M. (2014, Aug). CDC study shatters myth about black fathers. *The Louisiana Weekly Publishing Co.* Aug 25-Aug 31, 2014. Retrieved from http://libproxy.lib.csusb.edu/login?url=https://search-proquest-com.libproxy.lib.csusb.edu/docview/1559519140?accountid=10359

don't want my child to feel that the way we live is something that we have to defend to the world."[266] As a single Black mother, I too concur with her statement, because a Black parent should not have to live in a society where we have to subject our children to having to walk on eggshells for fear of reprisal.

Societal attitudes have caused so much havoc and detriment to individuals and groups because of ignorance. With this being said, since those in mainstream society are so concerned about the negative aspects of single Black mothers, then why are they not advocating to assist Black communities in bettering their situations instead of allowing the justice system and the social services department to destroy and dictate how Black children are raised? For those of you who do nothing more than talk a good talk but do not practice what you preach and yet you consistently criticize the unmarried Black mothers, instead of criticizing all single mothers, if you spent as much time putting your money where your mouths are by investing in programs that are beneficial to those in economically challenged areas such as "affordable family planning and reproductive health care, universal access to decent child care, improve the urban school systems, provide higher minimum wage, and contribute to the child's college education, which is something that would not break the banks of average people,"[267] then this world would be a better place for not just the mainstream single mothers but all single mothers.

Societal attitudes concerning the single Black mothers must change. When this comes to pass then the welfare-queen image would be nothing more than a

---

[266] Brown, S. M. (2014, Aug). CDC study shatters myth about black fathers. *The Louisiana Weekly Publishing Co.* Aug 25-Aug 31, 2014. Retrieved from http://libproxy.lib.csusb.edu/login?url=https://search-proquest-com.libproxy.lib.csusb.edu/docview/1559519140?accountid=10359
[267] Brown, S. M. (2014, Aug). CDC study shatters myth about black fathers. *The Louisiana Weekly Publishing Co.* Aug 25-Aug 31, 2014. Retrieved from http://libproxy.lib.csusb.edu/login?url=https://search-proquest-com.libproxy.lib.csusb.edu/docview/1559519140?accountid=10359

misrepresentation and a distraction that was created to impede upon and continue the hatred and racism that has been directed not only towards single Black mothers, but towards Blacks in America as a whole instead of bringing shame to mothers who are trying to do their best to raise their children. Yes, common knowledge tell us that all women on welfare struggle, common knowledge tells us that a single mother working a minimum wage paying job struggles, however, there are more White women who struggle on welfare than Black women, because a Black woman will go out and do domestic work in order to supplement her income, where as many, and not to say that all do, but there are those White women who will literally wait for their fairytale knights in shining armor to come and rescue them. And for those who wait on their Prince Charming to ride in on a big white horse, wake up and realize that is not a Cinderella, or Sleeping Beauty moment, this is reality because your children can't live on fairytales.

Societal attitudes are that single Black mothers go out and have babies to get more government assistance, well let's "also note that birth rates among African American women are lower than ever before in recorded history and that part of the explanation for the high percentage of out-of-wedlock Black babies lies with the fact that fewer Black women are marrying and many of those women are deciding not to have children. Married Black women are also having fewer children."[268]

Now let us talk about the stigma of Black mothers whether single or married. Let's begin with Michelle Obama. Even though Barack and Michelle had been married for decades, a Fox News journalist felt the need to refer to Michelle as being Barack Obama's "baby mama. Not only was this not humorous, it was distasteful and

---

[268] Brown, S. M. (2014, Aug). CDC study shatters myth about black fathers. *The Louisiana Weekly Publishing Co.* Aug 25-Aug 31, 2014. Retrieved from http://libproxy.lib.csusb.edu/login?url=https://search-proquest-com.libproxy.lib.csusb.edu/docview/1559519140?accountid=10359

disrespectful. Had the tables been turned and the same was said of one of a White journalists who was a single mother, then their would be a public uproar as everyone would take to social media to spew on how disrespectful it would be to that individual. Yvette Perry, a married mother of twins, found her swollen fingers uncomfortable in her wedding rings after giving birth. But she wore the rings anyway to avoid being stereotyped as a single Black mother. That did nothing to help her situation as the assumptions from mainstream still poised the negative attitudes."[269]

Societal attitudes are that Blacks should get over the past, because they had nothing to do with what happened to our ancestors, but in actuality, they do. They do because many, and I did not say all, but many, continue to perpetuate the ignorance and hate that feeds into their fear. They are a constant reminder of why Black women are continuously stereotyped and stigmatized, they are that constant reminder that tells Blacks that you hate them. This is constantly experienced by Blacks every day, through the media and in other ways. Many in mainstream are constantly trying to create a sense of genocide among Black America, and it is you in mainstream who are that constant reminder that lets Blacks know that the more that mainstream tries to keep Blacks down, the more that Blacks will continually get back up, thrive and survive by doing above and beyond what mainstream could ever fathom. "When life experiences collide with stereotypes, drawing a distinction can be even tougher, and the burden heavier."[270]

As a single Black mother, I did not let everyone know that I was working on my

---

[269] Brown, S. M. (2014, Aug). CDC study shatters myth about black fathers. *The Louisiana Weekly Publishing Co.* Aug 25-Aug 31, 2014. Retrieved from http://libproxy.lib.csusb.edu/login?url=https://search-proquest-com.libproxy.lib.csusb.edu/docview/1559519140?accountid=10359
[270] Brown, S. M. (2014, Aug). CDC study shatters myth about black fathers. *The Louisiana Weekly Publishing Co.* Aug 25-Aug 31, 2014. Retrieved from http://libproxy.lib.csusb.edu/login?url=https://search-proquest-com.libproxy.lib.csusb.edu/docview/1559519140?accountid=10359

PhD, and outside of this book, and some of my autobiography, I still do not let people know what my accomplishments are, I let them assume, and you know what the old adage is about assuming. Yes, I have had those haters and naysayers who said that I could not do it, or cuss me and tell me that I would never accomplish my goals and my dreams; and yes, I have come across those excruciating moments where being stereotyped against has bothered me, however, I learned early in life that I must push forward despite the obstacles and moved on. Yes, I have had to receive food stamps because the money that I made from my job was not enough to pay rent and buy food. Yes, I receive medical assistance because I, like so many others in America of different ethnicities cannot afford insurance. Those who knew that I was working on my PhD have always told me that I was different, because I was a single Black mother trying to make something of myself. There were several of single Black mothers and fathers that were in my classes throughout my educational endeavors who were trying to better their situations, not just me. We did not have the excuse that we could not overcome our circumstances, we just learned how to overcome them and just overcame them.

Raising children is already a complicated task, regardless to if you married or not, Black, White, Brown, Red, Yellow, Blue or Purple. I learned a long time ago that watching the news was depressing, so I stopped watching the news long before my son passed away. My reasoning for not watching the news is because, every time I turned the television to the news, it was me who lived in the inner cities ghettos, even though I was not physically there. So to see myself in the inner city ghettos, all I would hear was something negative about someone Black, you will hardly hear of something positive or of an accomplishment of greatness by someone Black, because this is how the media glamourizes such issues to keep their ratings elevated. If you stop and take notice,

217

whenever someone who is Black, or Brown commits a crime, the media will say, "An individual of African American descent," or "the individual is described as being a Hispanic male," or "the Assailant is of Asian descent." However, when there is no description of the perp, then there is a great likelihood that the suspect is Caucasian.

You may ask, what does any of this have to do with absent Black fathers. Well it all intertwines together. It is consistently said that Black men are absent from their children's lives. Yet, there are many who write and do research about families of different cultures and are not a part of that culture. In addition, when doing research, have those mainstream researchers stopped to think that not everyone who quote unquote, poses for the camera is being genuine?

The Black woman who stands out is more likely to be stigmatized as being a single mom than any other race. There are several families in both the urban city and in the rural community who practices similar parenting behaviors. They provide their children with stable homes, they provide them with the necessities in life, they discipline their children, and yes, they are caring parents. Yes, there are still a lot of broken homes that have too many fathers not living with their children, especially in the Black community, but there are many homes in other communities where those fathers are absent just as well. So, with this being said, it is high time that those with the negative societal attitudes put away the myth about the absent Black father and lay it to rest. Ragland, who noted that while his own father had faults, being absent wasn't among them.[271]

---

[271] Brown, S. M. (2014, Aug). CDC study shatters myth about black fathers. *The Louisiana Weekly Publishing Co.* Aug 25-Aug 31, 2014. Retrieved from http://libproxy.lib.csusb.edu/login?url=https://search-proquest-com.libproxy.lib.csusb.edu/docview/1559519140?accountid=10359

There was a study conducted in 2012 by the federal government which revealed that there were 15 million children in the United States who lived in households where the fathers were absent. This is an enormous increase compared to a similar study which was conducted in 1960 showing that there were only 11 percent of children living in the United States in households where fathers were absent. However, it has also been proven that Black fathers are just as involved with their children as other dads in similar living conditions – or more so – and this was according to the latest study that was released in July of 2014 by the Centers for Disease Control and Prevention's National Center for Health Statistics in Atlanta.[272]

What the Centers for Disease Control and Prevention (CDC) officials focused on was the roles that fathers in the United States played when it came to parenting their children. Much of the research that was conducted by the CDC's previous research was based on family life, which the agency explored and felt that a child's family life was just as an important as a contributor to public health and the child's development, which focused exclusively on mothers. However, the "latest information that was obtained revealed that the stereotypical gender disparity in this area is not forthcoming and that Black fathers are just as hands-on when it comes to raising their children as fathers are in other cultures. In fact, in its coverage of the study, the Los Angeles Times noted that the results, "defy stereotypes about Black fatherhood," because CDC officials found that African-American fathers are more involved with their children on a daily basis than fathers from any other racial group. CDC's studies further revealed that nearly half of Black fathers who were living apart from their young children said that they played with

[272] Brown, S. M. (2014, Aug). CDC study shatters myth about black fathers. *The Louisiana Weekly Publishing Co.* Aug 25-Aug 31, 2014. Retrieved from http://libproxy.lib.csusb.edu/login?url=https://search-proquest-com.libproxy.lib.csusb.edu/docview/1559519140?accountid=10359

them at several times a week, while 42 percent said that they had fed or dined with their children quite frequently, and another 41 percent said they bathed their children, diapered their children or helped bet their children dressed just as often.[273]

When we think of single Black mothers and absent Black fathers, there are those with the societal attitudes who immediately think "inner city youth." So, when such a statement is made, and by beating around the bush and not being straightforward, you as a society are discreetly targeting minorities by referring to the majority of Black people as being "poor" and "ghetto." In doing this, what you are also saying is that since the single Black mother is to blame for the destruction of her community, you are also saying is that, all her children would need, in order to build their communities back up is their father or a father figure which is enough to destroy a racial group's criminalistic environment. This is not only unjustified, but it is also overgeneralized because it does not include the dynamics that are contributing factors to instances or cycles of hardships that would give an explanation for the reasons why people want to place blame on single Black mothers. To insinuate that the absence of fathers in the Black community causes chaos in Black youth is very misleading, especially when the information that is available is only a superficial connection. If a father's absence within a community is the reason why minority youth commit crimes, then please explain why there are so many mass murderers and serial killers that are not of color?

Even though the majority of violent crimes are perpetuated by men, mass murders in America seems to be dominated by White men. It seems that America produces more serial killers and mass murderers than any other culture or country.

---

[273]Brown, S. M. (2014, Aug). CDC study shatters myth about black fathers. *The Louisiana Weekly Publishing Co.* Aug 25-Aug 31, 2014. Retrieved from http://libproxy.lib.csusb.edu/login?url=https://search-proquest-com.libproxy.lib.csusb.edu/docview/1559519140?accountid=10359

Studies have shown that White men, are more likely to commit mass murders than Black men or any other racial group. Even though there are serial killers in other racial groups, Black's, Asian's, and Hispanic's (of any race) who are also serial killers as well, it is White men who perpetuates the dominating factors. "As of September 4, 2016, the database contained information on 4,743 serial killers and 13,105 victims[274] of serial killers. The statistics in this report are based on the serial killer definition derived by the FBI at its 2005 symposium in San Antonio, TX[275]: The unlawful killing of two or more victims by the same offender(s), in separate events.

When it comes to race and demographics concerning serial killers, the subject is often up for debate. "In the United States, the majority of reported and investigated serial killers are White males, from a lower-to-middle-class background, usually in their late 20s to early 30s." [276],[277] Worldwide, studies have shown that serial killers, with the majority being White, range from the ages of 13-64. A 2014 Radford/FGCU Serial Killer Database annual statistics report indicated that for the decades 1900–2010, the percentage of White serial killers were 52.1% while the percentage of African American serial killers was 40.3%.[278] According to the Encyclopedia of Murder and Violent Crime, it notes that "Compared with assailants who kill but one victim, mass murderers are overwhelmingly likely to be male, [and] are far more likely to be White," and the numbers prove it. According to Wikipedia, there is approximately 75% of recorded

[274] Aamodt, M. G. (2016, September 4). Serial killer statistics. Retrieved September 1, 2018 from http://maamodt.asp.radford.edu/serial killer information center/project description.htm
[275] https://www.fbi.gov/stats-services/publications/serial-murder#two
[276] Scott, Shirley Lynn. "What Makes Serial Killers Tick?". truTV. Archived from the original on July 28, 2010. Retrieved September 1, 2018.
[277] Morton, Robert J. "Serial Murder". Federal Bureau of Investigation. Retrieved September 1, 2018.
[278] Aamodt, Dr. Mike. "Serial Killer Statistics" (PDF). Radford University/FGCU Serial Killer Database. Retrieved September 1, 2018

killings that were rampage killings which were perpetrated by White males, as were 71% of massacres in schools, and 60% of workplace rampages. This is a seriously disproportionate number for the number of White males that make up the general population. It is reasonable to say that White males are highly promoted from a social status and this combined with isolation, desperation, opportunity, and mental illness it has led White men who have gone on rampages to make their pain felt by those around them in a very violent way. So, with this being said, society cannot place the blame on the single Black mother, nor can they hold Black fathers solely responsible for the criminalist behaviors of an entire race when there are those who are not of color who has more issues within their community than the Black race.

There are a number of events or statistics that happen to coincide with each other, but this does not mean that there is a cause and effect relationship. An example that was once used indicates this scenario. During the summer when school is out, there are more drownings of children, while the sales in ice cream increases. Now even though the two factors share a commonality, this does not mean that eating ice cream leads to drowning! This just means that even though both events are independent of each other. It just means two, independent events have an insignificant connection that was established upon the other factors.

People of color are habitually seen as being criminalistic. The school-to-prison pipeline in combination with racial profiling are three examples of factors that have been highly overlooked and which hugely affect Black America and their community in particular. Such issues would still be around whether or not there was a positive male role model were present. With this also being said, there are those individuals who complicate the cause and effect method because they are usually looking for anything which proves what they already know is fact. They want to dispel the facts because they know that historically, they have based their findings on their truths rather than determine and accept the fact that the information retrieved, and research actually says what is factual with a more honest approach.

The last myth about Black fathers being absent from their children's lives is that a child needs a father in order to be raised properly. We can debunk this myth as well. There are several single mothers who have raised their children and their children have turned out quite well. So, to say that a Black child needs a father or father figure in order to be raised correctly is inaccurate. Just as with any child of any ethnicity, the only thing that a child needs in order to ensure they are properly raised is love, nurturing, food, shelter, clothing, more affection, and lessons in how to navigate through a world that can be cruel and harsh towards them. So, it is not about the gender of the parent who raises that child, it is about how effectively that adult can be in shaping the growing mind of that child. When it comes to single Black mothers and Black males, society cannot begin to fathom how much disgust, discrimination, racism and White male supremacy distorts societies views of Black women.

Regardless of the political platform, there are those politicians who promotes and exploits what they view as being "traditional family values." However, their views do not deviate significantly from the overall social morals of this country that supports the idea of hetero-normative, male-headed households. Their views further suggests that Black women are considered to be incapable of appropriately raising children without a male figures presence which therefore this would erase the "non-traditional" households while also reinforcing the societal attitudes that are toxic attitudes about Black women in particular and the inferiority of women in general. So, with this being, there are those

223

individuals with their abject ignorance who actually believe that if a certain group of people come from "certain" backgrounds, and are raised in "certain" environments, then these types of people will always get "certain" results. This in itself is not only untrue but wishful thinking. So the moral of the story is that no matter who your parents are, whether successful and rich, Black or White, who are remarkable when it comes to providing their children with the best opportunities – their children are still going to ultimately make their own decisions in their life choices. Sometimes there are those people who have a good upbringing, yet they make poor decisions.

Black Males, Black Crimes, Black Education, Black Employment Rates and Blacks the Media

Chapter 10

Even though the final charges that were brought against the Baltimore police officers who were involved in the death of Freddie Gray have been dropped, as with so many more cases against Blacks and people of color, there is a historical story which demonstrates that Blacks in America are being treated disproportionately due to institutional racism. Blacks are also unfairly targeted by predominantly White police officers and a racist criminal justice system in the United States which continues to dominate a system which is created to build barriers which causes many Black people to fail. The medical examiner deemed Gray's death as a homicide which resulted from the injuries that he sustained while in police custody.

It is sad to say that Blacks are overrepresented when it comes to the criminal justice system in terms of arrests, convictions and street crimes, yet they only represent 13% of the population. With this being said, this still does not justify the police brutality against men such as Freddie Gray, Walter Scott, Eric Garner and so many others. And because racism was built on the foundation of this country, Blacks will continue to be victims of violent encounters with the police as there are many cops who are racists. Just because they wear a uniform does not mean that their jobs cause them to be immune to their opinions.

It seems as though "the criminal justice system hopelessly rigged against Black men, which is leading to a disproportionate amount of them ending up in prison.[279] This question emerged repeatedly in 2013, when a Florida jury acquitted neighborhood watchman George Zimmerman of the murder of Trayvon Martin. Zimmerman shot Martin after trailing him around a gated community because he viewed the Black teen, who wasn't involved in any wrongdoing, as suspicious.[280]

Whether Black males are victims, perpetrators or simply just going about their everyday lives, you will find civil rights activists that will consistently say that Blacks do not get a fair shake in the United States legal system which is a true statement. Black males are more likely to receive harsher sentences for their crimes, which includes the death penalty than males in other cultures. Black males are imprisoned at six times the rate than that of White males, according to the Washington Post. And nearly 1 in 12 Black men age 25-54 are incarcerated, compared to 1 in 60 nonblack men, with 1 in 200 Black women being incarcerated compared to the 1 in 500 nonblack women according to the New York Times.[281]

As you may observe, in a number of the nation's largest cities, there are more Black males who are likely to be treated as criminals, guilty until proven innocent, stopped and frisked by the police without reason than any other group, which is often

[279] Nittle, Nadra Kareem. (2018, June 13). African American Men and the Criminal Justice System. Retrieved from https://www.thoughtco.com/african-american-men-criminal-justice-system-2834814
[280] Nittle, Nadra Kareem. (2018, June 13). African American Men and the Criminal Justice System. Retrieved from https://www.thoughtco.com/african-american-men-criminal-justice-system-2834814
[281] Nittle, Nadra Kareem. (2018, June 13). African American Men and the Criminal Justice System. Retrieved from https://www.thoughtco.com/african-american-men-criminal-justice-system-2834814

based on the fact that the individual looked suspicious. The statistics below, compiled largely by ThinkProgress, further illuminate the experiences of African American males in the criminal justice system.[282]

How many of you remember Jared Scott Fogel, also known as "the Subway Guy," and is an American former spokesperson for Subway restaurant? Well he is also a convicted child molester who was sentenced 5-10 years in Federal Prison. Yet, Bernard Noble who is a 49-year-old father of seven, is serving more than 13 years behind bars in Jackson Parish Correctional Center in Jonesboro, Louisiana. You ask what is his crime? His crime is being caught with the equivalent of two joints' worth of marijuana in 2010. Currently, he has no chance of parole, and the state Board of Pardons and Parole has rejected Noble's petition for clemency in May 2015 simply because he hasn't served 10 or more years in prison yet, which that state's law requires that inmates to have been in the custody of the Department of Corrections for a minimum of 10 years before they will consider an inmate's application for clemency.[283] Yet, Fogal gets sentenced 5-12 years in a Federal Prison for child rape. Now do you not see something wrong with this picture?

It is extremely sad that "we live in a world where people who are living in disadvantaged environments face challenges and situations that seem to never turn out as they do for people in more privileged and un-challenged neighborhoods."[284] The discrepancies in the punishments that Black and White offenders receive can even be found among minors. Are Black youth at risks for failure by a justice system that is

[282] Nittle, Nadra Kareem. (2018, June 13). African American Men and the Criminal Justice System. Retrieved from https://www.thoughtco.com/african-american-men-criminal-justice-system-2834814

[283] Ferner, Matt. "This Man Is Serving More Than 13 Years In Prison Over Two Joints' Worth Of Marijuana," Politics: 08/14/2015 12:01 am ET **Updated** Sep 09, 2015

[284] Ferner, Matt. "This Man Is Serving More Than 13 Years In Prison Over Two Joints' Worth Of Marijuana," Politics: 08/14/2015 12:01 am ET **Updated** Sep 09, 2015

unjust based upon institutional racism? Yes. According to the National Council On Crime and Delinquency, there are more Black youth who are referred to juvenile court than White youth. Black youth are more likely to be incarcerated or end up in an adult court or prison more so than White youth. Blacks make up roughly 30 percent of juvenile arrests and referrals to juvenile court as well as 37 percent of incarcerated juveniles, 35 percent of juveniles sent to criminal court and 58 percent of juveniles sent to adult prisons.[285]

The term "school to prison pipeline" was created to illustrate how the criminal justice system sets the Black male up for failure by paving a pathway to prison for Blacks when they are still very young. The Sentencing Project has found that Black males who were born in 2001 have a 32 percent chance of being incarcerated at some point in their lives. In contrast, white males born that year have only a six percent chance of winding up in prison.[286]

Is there a disparity between Black and White drug users? Yes. While Blacks in the United States make up only 13 percent of the population, drug users who are Black, comprise 34 percent of individuals arrested for drug offenses and more than half (53 percent) of individuals are imprisoned for drug-related offenses, according to the American Bar Association. In other words, if you are Black and a drug user, you are four times more likely to end up in prison than that your White counterpart who is also a drug user. There is a difference in the way in which the criminal justice system treats Black drug offenders and White drug offenders which became especially clear when

---

[285] Nittle, Nadra Kareem. (2018, June 13). African American Men and the Criminal Justice System. Retrieved from https://www.thoughtco.com/african-american-men-criminal-justice-system-2834814
[286] Nittle, Nadra Kareem. (2018, June 13). African American Men and the Criminal Justice System. Retrieved from https://www.thoughtco.com/african-american-men-criminal-justice-system-2834814

sentencing laws required that crack-cocaine users were to receive much harsher penalties than those who were powder-cocaine users. The reason being is because, in the 1980s at the height of its popularity, crack-cocaine was most popular among Blacks in the inner communities, while powder-cocaine was most popular among Whites. In 2010, Congress passed the Fair Sentencing Act, which was supposed to help erase some of the sentencing disparities that were related to cocaine.[287]

In 2013, there were a quarter of young Black males who stated that they had at some point in their lives been mistreated by the police. Gallup interviewed approximately 4,400 adults during the periods of June 13 to July 5, 2013, for its Minority Rights and Relations poll concerning police interactions with those in economically challenged area and racial profiling. What Gallup found is that 24 percent of Black men who were between the ages of 18 and 34 felt they had been mistreated by the police during the month of these interviews. Meanwhile, there were 22 percent of Blacks from the ages of 35 to 54 felt the same way with 11 percent of Black males older than age 55 who agreed.[288] These numbers are significant given that many people have absolutely no dealings with police in a month-long period. The fact that these young Black men who were polled had contact with police and roughly a quarter of them felt that they had been mistreated by the authorities during their encounters indicated that racial profiling remains a serious issue for African Americans.[289]

---

[287] Nittle, Nadra Kareem. (2018, June 13). African American Men and the Criminal Justice System. Retrieved from https://www.thoughtco.com/african-american-men-criminal-justice-system-2834814
[288] Nittle, Nadra Kareem. (2018, June 13). African American Men and the Criminal Justice System. Retrieved from https://www.thoughtco.com/african-american-men-criminal-justice-system-2834814
[289] Nittle, Nadra Kareem. (2018, June 13). African American Men and the Criminal Justice System. Retrieved from https://www.thoughtco.com/african-american-men-criminal-justice-system-2834814

When it comes to race and the death penalty, this is another area where Blacks are disproportionally represented. There are a number of studies that have shown that an individual's race influences the likelihood on whether or not that defendant will receive the death penalty. "In Harris County, Texas, for example, the District Attorney's Office was more than three times as likely to pursue the death penalty against Black defendants than against their White counterparts, according to an analysis that was released in 2013 by University of Maryland criminology professor Ray Paternoster. Upon doing research, it is also a known factor that the justice system is bias regarding the race of victims in death penalty cases. While Blacks and Whites suffer from homicides at about the same rate, the New York Times reports that 80 percent of those executed had murdered White people. Such statistics make it easy to understand why African Americans in particular feel that they are not treated fairly by the authorities or in the courts.[290]

For decades now there has been attention drawn toward certain policies regarding the crisis of Black males which has focused on a variety of areas in which Black males have suffered disproportionately from social ills because of societal attitudes. This have included everything from education, housing, employment, and health care, just to name a few. Perhaps in no other area, though, have these problems been displayed as prominently as in the realm of crime and the criminal justice system.[291]

---

[290] Nittle, Nadra Kareem. (2018, June 13). African American Men and the Criminal Justice System. Retrieved from https://www.thoughtco.com/african-american-men-criminal-justice-system-2834814

[291] Mauer, Marc. (1999) The Crisis of the Young African American Male and the Criminal Justice System. Prepared for U.S. Commission on Civil Right

In the areas of criminal justice and institutional racism, which is also considered as systematic discrimination, Blacks as a whole have been seriously affected "in this area with two significant regards. The first issue is that Blacks are more likely to be victimized by crime than any other groups. This creates a set of individual and community problems which impedes upon other areas of productive activity. Second, the dramatic rates at which African American males have endured, demonstrates that there has been some form of criminal justice supervision which has also created a complex set of consequences which affects not only individual victims and offenders, but their families and their communities as well.[292]

There is a wealth of statistical information which indicates what a walk through almost any urban courthouse or state prison, and this is displayed quite graphically. If you are a courtroom observer in any large or urban city such as New York, Chicago, Detroit, Atlanta, Los Angeles or any other major city you will witness an unequivocally large amount of Black and Brown faces that will be sitting at the defense table or shackled together on the bus transporting prisoners from the jail for court hearings. In the prison visiting rooms, there are mothers, wives, and girlfriends who have traveled often for several hours by bus or car waiting to see their loved ones in stuffy and noisy visiting room with very little privacy.[293]

The living conditions behind prison walls can be atrocious and have never been pleasant nor have they been comfortable, yet, a harsher political climate now threatens to undo many of the reforms that had been achieved through litigation and political

---

[292] Mauer, Marc. (1999) The Crisis of the Young African American Male and the Criminal Justice System. Prepared for U.S. Commission on Civil Right
[293] Mauer, Marc. (1999) The Crisis of the Young African American Male and the Criminal Justice System. Prepared for U.S. Commission on Civil Right

advocacy over the past several decades. Congressional action in 1994 prohibited inmates from receiving Pell grants in order for them to continue higher education studies, while other states have passed their own legislation denying inmates access to various forms of recreation or cultural activities. Much of this legislation has not only been just mean-spirited but it has been counterproductive as well, by limiting prisoners' access to the acquisition of skills that might be used constructively upon their return to the community.[294] By further implementing such harsh conditions this now disproportionately affect African American males and other minorities due to their overwhelming numbers within the criminal justice system. The state of these disproportions can be seen in the following:

• 49% of prison inmates nationally are African American, compared to their 13% share of the overall population.[295]

• Nearly one in three (32%) Black males in the age group 20-29 is under some form of criminal justice supervision on any given day -- either in prison or jail, or on probation or parole.[296]

• As of 1995, one in fourteen (7%) adult Black males was incarcerated in prison or jail on any given day, representing a doubling of this rate from 1985. The 1995 figure for White males was 1%.

• A Black male born in 1991 has a 29% chance of spending time in prison at some point in his life. The figure for Hispanics, is 16% and for White males is 4%.

---

[294] Mauer, Marc. (1999) The Crisis of the Young African American Male and the Criminal Justice System. Prepared for U.S. Commission on Civil Right
[295] Unless otherwise specified, all data on prison and jail populations throughout is taken from various reports of the Bureau of Justice Statistics.
[296] Marc Mauer and Tracy Huling, "Young Black Americans and the Criminal Justice System: Five Years Later," The Sentencing Project, October 1995.

Demographically, while African American males have been the group who are most severely affected within the criminal justice system, there are also other minorities who have been disproportionately affected as well. Hispanics between the periods of 1990-96 constituted 17% of the prison population nationally, compared to their 10% share of the total population. The number of Hispanic inmates increased by more than half in the period. Women, and particularly minority women, while incarcerated in smaller numbers than men, have also experienced dramatic growth in recent years. The number of women in the prison system increased by 418% from 1980 to 1995, compared to a rise of 236% for men. Black women are now incarcerated at a rate seven times that of White women.[297]

There are 283,000 Hispanics[298] in federal and state prisons and local jails, making up slightly over 15% of the inmate population.[299]
• Nearly 1 in 3 (32%) persons held in federal prisons is Hispanic.[300]
• As of 2001, 4% of Hispanic males in their twenties and early thirties were in prison or jail as compared to 1.8% of white males.[301]
• Hispanics are the fastest growing group being imprisoned, increasing from 10.9% of all State and Federal inmates in 1985 to 15.6% in 2001.[302],[303]

Historically, the criminal justice system has served as the main point to much of societies racism. Institutional racism, which stems from slavery, has had a long legacy of "practices such as the convict leasing system, extra-judicial lynchings, and police

[297] Beck, A.J., Karberg, J.C. & Harrison, P.M. "Prison and Jail Inmates at Midyear 2001," April 2002. Washington, DC: Bureau of Justice Statistics.
[298] The term "Hispanics" refers to persons who may be of any race.
[299] Beck, A.J., Karberg, J.C. & Harrison, P.M. "Prison and Jail Inmates at Midyear 2001," April 2002. Washington, DC: Bureau of Justice Statistics.
[300] Federal Bureau of Prisons Population Count; June 2003
[301] Ibid.
[302] Harrison, P.M. & Beck, A.J. "Prisoners in 2001," July 2002. Washington, DC: Bureau of Justice Statistics.
[303] Mumola, C.J. & Beck, A.J. "Prisoners in 1996," June 1997. Washington, DC: Bureau of Justice Statistics.

brutality all which have shaped the history of African Americans and the criminal justice system."[304] However, it has been more than thirty years, and there has been some significant changes that have occurred in some aspects of the justice system. Some of those changes have been that in many jurisdictions minorities have moved into positions of leadership within law enforcement, the courts, and corrections systems. Supreme Court decisions have placed restrictions on such practices as prosecutorial bias in jury selection. Despite these constructive changes, though, racial disproportions have worsened over this period of time, and institutional racism still exists as it will take decades to be restructured.[305]

As we assess the extent to which racial bias within the criminal justice system has contributed to such disparities, society must realize that there is an abundance of mixed research evidence. The burden of the death penalty provides the most compelling evidence for ongoing racial disparity. If you look back on cases that I mentioned in chapter one, examples of those who were falsely accused of crimes, electrocuted or lynched only to find more than 60 and 70 years later were done out of ignorance, hate, and systematic discrimination are just a few examples of what is being stated here.[306]

There has been a series of studies demonstrating that, control for a wide range of variables, which is the race of both the victim and offender, both which has a significant impact on the determination of a sentence of death as opposed to life in prison. David Baldus and colleagues, for example, found that murder defendants charged with killing

---

[304] Mauer, Marc. (1999) The Crisis of the Young African American Male and the Criminal Justice System. Prepared for U.S. Commission on Civil Right
[305] Mauer, Marc. (1999) The Crisis of the Young African American Male and the Criminal Justice System. Prepared for U.S. Commission on Civil Right
[306] Mauer, Marc. (1999) The Crisis of the Young African American Male and the Criminal Justice System. Prepared for U.S. Commission on Civil Right

Whites would face a 4.3 times greater chance of receiving death than those charged with killing Blacks.[307]

Again, the foundation concerning the crisis of African American males and the criminal justice system extends as far back as does the nation's history. Unfortunately, despite admirable progress in reducing racial bias in many areas of society during the past several decades, there is still an overrepresentation of Black males that are still in the justice system which demonstrates that this crisis has clearly worsened. While the situation is of urgency to find out why such a crisis exits, there is some reason for cautious optimism. There is now a support system for change within the criminal justice policies and programs which has been growing in recent years and continues to grow.[308]

With the introduction of drug courts, prison-based treatment programs, and community policing, these are just some of the suggestions that some of the public and policymakers support as they continue to look for problem-solving responses to individual and community crises. In addition, many communities are now engaging in locally-based programs that provides support to young people. These programs include mentoring programs, recreational activities, life skills and personal skills development. The challenge for the community at large is being able to engage them in a broad discussion of the mix of family, community, and government initiatives that can begin to reverse a cycle that has been set in motion in recent years.[309]

---

[307] David C. Baldus, Charles Pulaski, and George Woodworth, "Comparative Review of Death Sentences: An Empirical Study of the Georgia Experience," Journal of Criminal Law and Criminology 74 (fall 1983): 661-753
[308] Mauer, Marc. (1999) The Crisis of the Young African American Male and the Criminal Justice System. Prepared for U.S. Commission on Civil Right
[309] Mauer, Marc. (1999) The Crisis of the Young African American Male and the Criminal Justice System. Prepared for U.S. Commission on Civil Right

According to the US Census Bureau in 2017 there was an "estimated

47,411,470 African Americans in the United States meaning that 14.6% of the total

American population of 325.7 Million is Black. This includes those who identify as

'Black Only' and as 'Black in combination with another race'. The '*Black* Only' category

by itself totaled 43.5 million African Americans **or** 13.4% of the total population."[310]

Below you will find various tables from over the past few decades that shows the

population of Blacks in America. When viewing these charts, take note of the brief

history and the institution of slavery, up until today concerning how the crisis of the

African American male and the criminal justice system extends as far back as does the

nation's history. Remember, America was built on the foundation of racism, and

institutional discrimination.

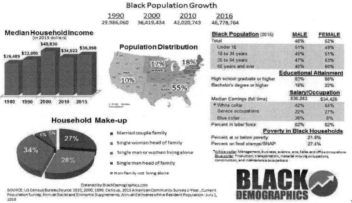

---

[310] Created by BlackDemographics.com: Source: US Census Bureau Source: 2010, 2000, 1990 Census, 2015 American Community Survey 1-Year, Current Population Survey Annual Social and Economic Supplements, Annual Estimates of the Resident Population: July 1, 2016.
[311] Created by BlackDemographics.com: Source: US Census Bureau Source: 2010, 2000, 1990 Census, 2015 American Community Survey 1-Year, Current Population Survey Annual Social and Economic Supplements, Annual Estimates of the Resident Population: July 1, 2016.

African American Population Growth

Black Population from Year 1790 - 2012
(includes free and slave) source: US Census Bureau
BlackDemographics.com

Year	Black Pop	% of US	Free		Slave	
1790	757,208	19.3%	59,52	8%	697,681	92%
1800	1,002,037	18.9%	108,435	11%	893,602	89%
1810	1,377,808	19.0%	186,446	14%	1,191,362	87%
1820	1,771,656	18.4%	233,634	13%	1,538,022	87%
1830	2,328,642	18.1%	319,599	14%	2,009,043	86%
1840	2,873,648	16.8%	386,293	13%	2,487,355	87%
1850	3,638,808	15.7%	434,495	12%	3,204,313	88%
1860	4,441,830	14.1%	488,070	11%	3,953,760	89%
1870	4,880,009	12.7%	Slavery ended (1865)			
1880	6,580,793	13.1%				
1890	7,488,676	11.9%				
1900	8,833,994	11.6%				
1910	9,827,763	10.7%				
1920	10,463,131	9.9%	Harlem Renaissance(1920s)			
1930	11,891,143	9.7%				
1940	12,865,518	9.8%	World War II (1941- 45)			
1950	15,042,286	10.0%				
1960	18,871,831	10.5%	Civil Rights Movement (1954-68)			
1970	22,580,289	11.1%				
1980	26,495,025	11.7%				
1990	29,986,060	12.1%	Los Angeles Riots (1992)			
2000	*36,419,434	12.9%				
2010	*42,020,743	13.6%	Barack Obama (2008 - Present)			
2012	*44,456,009	14.2%				

*Black or African American alone or in combination
with another race. This was not recorded prior to the 2000 census.

[312]

When Africans were kidnapped from Africa in 1619 and brought over to the New World, it was estimated that out of the 10-12 million Africans who survived the long journey that were brought to the New World as slaves, there were approximately 500,000-700,000 of them who were brought to came to the United States. Out of these

---

[312] Source: The Trans-Atlantic Slave Trade Database http://slavevoyages.org,
Wikipedia http://en.wikipedia.org/wiki/Atlantic_slave_trade, BBC http://news.bbc.co.uk/2/hi/africa/6445941.stm

numbers, there were only about 4.4%-5.4% of all the Africans who were shipped to the Americas. The majority of the other Africans, which were about 35%, were sent to Brazil and the remainder were sent to places such as South America and the Caribbean colonies. The largest ports of entry for American slaves were Baltimore, Savannah, Charleston and New Orleans. According to the first United States census count 92% of the 757,208 African Americans were slaves. The last census count during slavery in 1860 counted 4,441,830 African Americans of which 89% were slaves. By the turn of the century (1900) the Black population grew to more than 8 million and more than doubled every 50-year period since reaching 42 million by 2010.[313]

EDUCATION

In 2013 there were approximately 48% of Black men that were 25 and older who attended college. Even though half of them did not complete a degree in comparison to the 58% of all men who attended college, it was just under half who did not have a degree.

EDUCATIONAL ATTAINMENT (25 & up)

	Black Men	All Men
Less than high school diploma	18%	14%
High school graduate (or GED)	35%	28%
Some college, no degree	24%	21%
Associates degree	7%	7%
Bachelor's degree or higher	17%	30%
Attended College	48%	58%

---

[313] Source: The Trans-Atlantic Slave Trade Database http://slavevoyages.org,
Wikipedia http://en.wikipedia.org/wiki/Atlantic_slave_trade, BBC http://news.bbc.co.uk/2/hi/africa/6445941.stm

There is most definitely a large disparity between Black men and 'all men' in America and those who have a Bachelor's degree. Statistics show that there are only 17% of Black men in America who have a Bachelor's degree compared to 30% of 'all men.' Secondly, another disparity is the number of Black men who finished high school but did not pursue higher education, which was 35% compared to 28% of 'all men.' Also, observe the percent of Black men who have an Associate's degree, which is only (7%) which is equal to that of 'all men' (7%) in America. The charts also indicate that only 18% of Black men over 25 did not complete high school. This is still higher than the percent for men of all races and ethnic groups together.

EMPLOYMENT

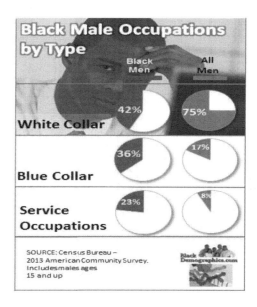

When it comes to African American males ages 16 to 64 studies showed that they had a lower participation rate in the labor force (67%) compared to 'all males' (80%). Labor force participation refers to the percent of men who were either working or looking for work. Males not in the labor force include those who may be full time students, disabled, and others who are not looking or gave up looking for employment for other reasons.

EARNINGS & EMPLOYMENT

	Black Men	All Men
Ages 16 to 64		
Percent who are in the labor force	67%	80%
Percent who are unemployed	11.2%	7.3%
Below poverty level	26%	15%
Ages 16 and up		
Median earnings for 2013	$37,290	$48,099
Worked full-time, year-round	37%	48%
Earnings NOT from full time work	23%	23%
No earnings all year	40%	30%
Occupation type		
White collar	42%	75%
Blue collar	36%	17%
Service occupations	23%	8%

Out of all of the 37% of African American males who worked full time all year in 2013, they had a median earning of $37,290 compared to $48,099 for 'all men.' Of the Black males who were ages 16 to 64 years, it was reported that 40% had no earnings in 2013 which was higher than the 30% with no earnings of 'all men' in the same age group. Also, there was a larger percentage of Black males 16 to 64 were unemployed than for 'all men' (11.2% compared to 7.3%) and were living below the poverty level (26%) than 'all men' (15%).

Compared to 'all men' that were in the United States, it was the Black men who worked that were much less likely to work in occupations that may have been considered as white-collar jobs and it was Black males who were much more likely to hold blue collar or service jobs. There were only 42% of Black men who were working that held white collar jobs compared to 75% of 'all men.' For the purpose of the above table, white collar occupations included but are not limited to jobs in management, business, computers, office, legal, education, and so forth.

African American Employment

Black Unemployment Rate: July 2018: 6.6%

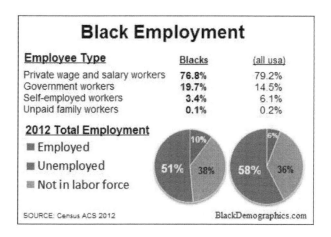

There are those studies which indicates that there are more than 20% of the Black population who are working that are over 16 years and are employees of the federal, state, or local government which is just over 5 percentage points higher than the national average. On the other hand, there is a much smaller percentage of African Americans who are self-employed which is (3.6%) which is also less than the national average of 6.2%.

Occupations of African Americans

No matter what obstacles that Black women have faced, it seems that it is Black women who have made some of the greatest strides recently. Studies show that in 2011 33% of Employed Black women have positions in management or professional occupations compared to 23% of employed Black men. As a matter of fact, it is 64% of working Black women who holds "white collar" occupations compared to the 50% of African American men, with thirty six percent of employed Black males holding position in the line of "blue collar" workers compared to the 8% of Black Women.

OCCUPATION OF AFRICAN AMERICANS

All civilian employed population 16 years and over	Blacks	(all usa)
Management, business, science, and arts occupations	28.1%	36.1%
Service occupations	25.7%	18.3%
Sales and office occupations	25.9%	24.5%
Natural resources, construction, and maintenance occupations	5.3%	9.0%
Production, transportation, and material moving occupations	15.0%	12.2%
Male civilian employed population 16 years and over		
Management, business, science, and arts occupations	22.6%	32.8%
Service occupations	22.8%	15.2%
Sales and office occupations	18.9%	17.5%
Natural resources, construction, and maintenance occupations	10.9%	16.4%
Production, transportation, and material moving occupations	24.7%	18.1%
Female civilian employed population 16 years and over		
Management, business, science, and arts occupations	32.6%	39.6%
Service occupations	28.1%	21.7%
Sales and office occupations	31.8%	32.1%
Natural resources, construction, and maintenance occupations	0.6%	0.9%
Production, transportation, and material moving occupations	6.9%	5.7%

SOURCE: 2012 U.S. Census Bureau Statistics ACS

BlackDemographics.com

The charts that are show above categorizes the African American workforce by industry. As you may observe, Blacks are again overrepresented in government jobs such as education, social assistance, and public administration. African Americans also have a large presence in the health care industry which is expected to see substantial job growth for the foreseeable future.

African Americans by Industry	Black	All
Educational services, and health care and social assistance	29.5%	23.2%
Retail trade	11.5%	11.6%
Arts, entertainment, and recreation, and accommodation and food services	9.6%	9.6%
Professional, scientific, and management, and administrative and waste management services	9.1%	10.9%
Manufacturing	8.5%	10.5%
Public administration	7.2%	4.9%
Transportation and warehousing, and utilities	7.1%	4.9%
Finance and insurance, and real estate and rental and leasing	5.9%	6.6%
Other services (except public administration)	4.3%	5.0%
Construction	2.9%	6.2%
Information	2.0%	2.1%
Wholesale trade	1.7%	2.6%
Agriculture, forestry, fishing and hunting, and mining	0.6%	2.0%

SOURCE: 2012 U.S. Census Bureau ACS   TABLE: BlackDemographics.com

"Among the major race and ethnicity groups, Hispanics continued to have the highest labor force participation rate (68.5 percent) in 2008, while the participation rate for blacks was the lowest (63.7 percent). The participation rates for whites (66.3 percent) and Asians (67.0 percent) were roughly midway between the rates for blacks and Hispanics, continuing a long-term pattern." (Shandira Pavelcik)

Years	White	Hispanic	Asian	Black
2000	67%	68%	67%	65%
2010	66%	68%	67%	64%

SOURCE: 2010 U.S. Bureau of Labor Statistics

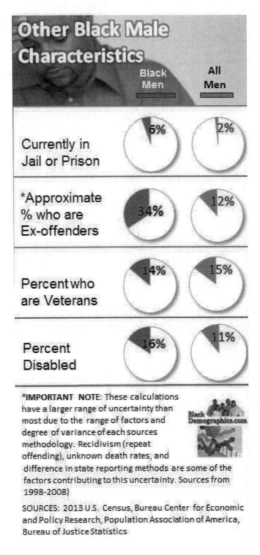

Other Black Male Characteristics

	Black Men	All Men
Currently in Jail or Prison	6%	2%
*Approximate % who are Ex-offenders	34%	12%
Percent who are Veterans	14%	15%
Percent Disabled	16%	11%

*IMPORTANT NOTE: These calculations have a larger range of uncertainty than most due to the range of factors and degree of variance of each sources methodology. Recidivism (repeat offending), unknown death rates, and difference in state reporting methods are some of the factors contributing to this uncertainty. Sources from 1998-2008)

SOURCES: 2013 U.S. Census, Bureau Center for Economic and Policy Research, Population Association of America, Bureau of Justice Statistics

OTHER CHARACTERISTICS

There are approximately 6% of working-age (18-64yrs old) Black males who are currently incarcerated either in state or federal prison, or in a county or municipal jail.

These numbers are three times higher than the 2% of 'all men' who are in the same age group. What is even more disturbing is that there are approximately 34%* of all of the Black males that are of working-age who are not incarcerated are exoffenders compared to 12% of 'all men' who are. This means Black males have at one point and time in their lives been convicted of a felony. This data coincides with the increased absence of Black males that are in the labor force because ex-offenders are prevented from obtaining a large percentage of occupations either by law and are often legally discriminated against by private employers. Even though Blacks have an unemployment rate that is almost double than that of the overall population, remember that the Black workforce is just as diverse. Because the federal government was one of the first to integrate, African Americans have been over represented in that sector.

OTHER CHARACTERISTICS

Ages 18 to 64	Black Men	All Men
In Jail or Prison	6%	2%
*Approximate % who are Ex-offenders	34%	12%
Percent who are Veterans	14%	15%
Disabled	16%	11%

SOURCES: Center for Economic and Policy Research, Population Association of America, Bureau of Justice Statistics, U.S. Census Bureau

Further studies indicate that at least fourteen percent of working-age Black men are veterans of U.S. military which is just slightly lower than all male veterans (15%). There is an even larger percentage of working age Black men who are considered to be disabled (16%) compared to 'all men' (11%).

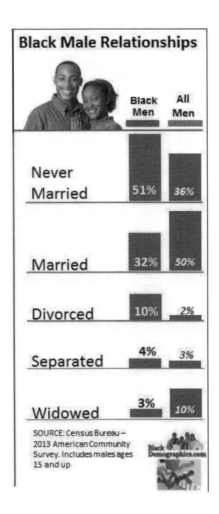

Black Male Relationships

	Black Men	All Men
Never Married	51%	36%
Married	32%	50%
Divorced	10%	2%
Separated	4%	3%
Widowed	3%	10%

SOURCE: Census Bureau – 2013 American Community Survey. Includes males ages 15 and up

Black Demographics.com

The U.S Census Bureau released a report in 2012 that studied the history of marriage in the United States. While doing research, they discovered that there were some startling statistics when they calculated marriage by race. What the studies found were that African Americans that were age 35 and older were more likely to be married than their White counterparts from approximately 1890 until sometime around the

1960s. Not only did they exchange places during the 60s but in 1980 the number of those Blacks that were NEVER married began a staggering climb from about 10% to more than 25% by the year 2010 while the percentage for White women remained under 10% and just over 10% for White men. One of these studies also illustrates how closely the marriage graph for Black men aligns with the incarceration numbers which also experienced an abnormal climb beginning in 1980. Even though this does not prove a definite connection, it does indicate that the marriage rates and incarceration rates are related due to the assumption that men in prison are less likely to marry.

RELATIONSHIPS

Black men and marriages today are just about the opposite as it was years ago. The percentages of Black men who are married and those who have never been married are almost the exact opposite of those percentages for 'all men' in the United States. Even though there are approximately 51% of Black men who have NEVER been married compared to the 50% of 'all men' are currently married. There are only 32% of Black men who are currently married while only 36% of 'all men' in America have NEVER been married. Black men are also slightly more likely to be separated from their spouses (4%) compared to all men at 3%. In addition, Black men are much less likely to outlive their wives and therefore are less likely to be widowed (3%) compared to 10% of 'all men.' Black men are more likely to be married than Black women. As a matter of fact, there are approximately 364,000 more Black men who are married than there are Black women even though Black women are 51% of the Black population. Even though the vast majority of Black men (86%) are married to Black women, there is an even larger percent (94%) of Black women are married to Black men.

Marriage in Black America

In the United States, marriages have been part of a declining institution, and such a decline has been even more evident in the Black community. In 2016 there were only 29% of African Americans that were married compared to the 48% of all Americans. Half or at least 50% of African Americans have never been married compared to 33% of all Americans.

Once you observe all of the available data, we can see that even though there are fewer Black women who are "now married," there are even more Black women than there are Black men who have been married at least once. This is because there is a higher percentage of Black women who are divorced and widowed than there are men. Additionally, in 2016 those numbers fell just under half or 48% where Black women had never been married which is up from 44% in 2008 and 42.7% in 2005.

Marital Status

15yrs & older	African Americans			All USA
	All	Men	Women	
Married	**29%**	32%	26%	48%
Divorced	**12%**	10%	13%	11%
Separated	**4%**	3%	4%	4%
Widowed	**6%**	3%	8%	6%
Never married	**50%**	52%	48%	34%

Source: U.S. Census Bureau, 2016 American Community Survey 1-Year Estimates

Note: figures are rounded and therefore may not total 100%

BlackDemographics.com

There is also this assumption that there is a large percentage of Black men who marry outside of their culture, like to White women. This also alludes to the fact that this is one of the main causes of lower marriage rates among Black women. Such information however is only partially true. While there are those Black men who do marry White women at twice rate that Black women marry White men, studies show that in 2017 there were only 15% percent of the Black men who were married to non-Black women which is up from 11% in 2010. There are approximately three-fifths of those non-Black women were White. So, with this being said, there is evidence that there is an increase of Black men who are "marrying out" of their racial demographic. As a matter of fact, the Pew Research Center released a report finding that there are 25% of Black male newlyweds who in 2013 were married non-Black women compared to 12% of Black women who went and "married out" to non-Black men. Nonetheless, Asian women and Native American women still have higher rates of interracial marriage. Black women were the least likely to marry non-Black men at only 7% in 2017, and only 4/% were married to White men.

Black Marriage in 2017

among non-Hispanic African Americans age 15 and up

Who Black men married

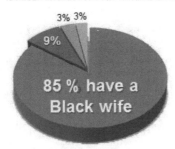

3% 3%
9%
85 % have a Black wife

- Black spouse
- White spouse
- Hispanic spouse
- Other

NOTE: There are 479,617 more married Black men than married Black women

NOTE: White" refers to Non-Hispanic White alone, "Black" to Non-Hispanic Black alone, and "Other" to Non-Hispanic Other alone or any race combination.

Who Black women married

2% 1%
4%
93% have a Black husband

BLACK DEMOGRAPHICS

BlackDemographics.com

Source: U.S. Census Bureau, Current Population Survey, 2017 Annual Social and Economic Supplement

Black Interracial Marriage

How many Black men and women have 'married out'? (2017)

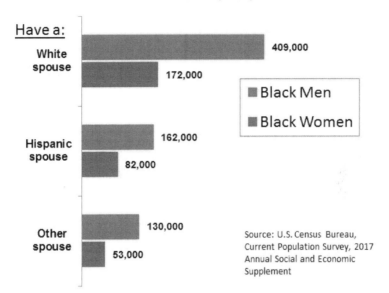

Have a:

White spouse
- 409,000
- 172,000

■ Black Men
■ Black Women

Hispanic spouse
- 162,000
- 82,000

Other spouse
- 130,000
- 53,000

Source: U.S. Census Bureau, Current Population Survey, 2017 Annual Social and Economic Supplement

BLACK DEMOGRAPHICS

BlackDemographics.com

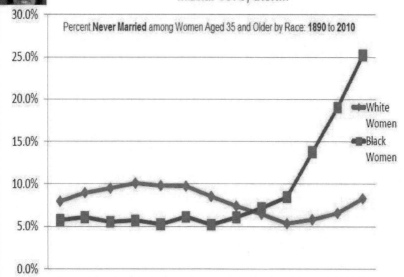

Black Women More Likely to be Married than White Women

...Until 1970, then...

Percent **Never Married** among Women Aged 35 and Older by Race: **1890** to **2010**

Legend:
- White Women
- Black Women

X-axis: 1890 1900 1910 1920 1930 1940 1950 1960 1970 1980 1990 2000 2010

Y-axis: 0.0% 5.0% 10.0% 15.0% 20.0% 25.0% 30.0%

Heading reformatted and posted by **BlackDemographics.com**

Source: U.S. Decennial Census (1890-2000); American Community Survey (2010). For more information on the ACS, see http://www.census.gov/acs

Chart created by: United States Census Bureau

Black Men More Likely to be Married than White Men

...Until 1960. Then...

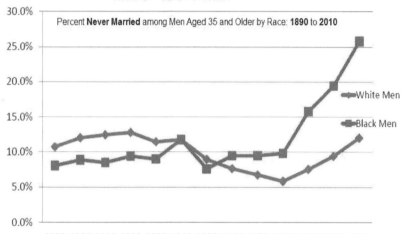

Percent **Never Married** among Men Aged 35 and Older by Race: **1890** to **2010**

White Men

Black Men

30.0%
25.0%
20.0%
15.0%
10.0%
5.0%
0.0%

1890 1900 1910 1920 1930 1940 1950 1960 1970 1980 1990 2000 2010

Heading reformatted and posted by **BlackDemographics.com**

Source: U.S. Decennial Census (1890-2000); American Community Survey (2010). For more information on the ACS, see http://www.census.gov/acs

United States Census Bureau

Chart created by:

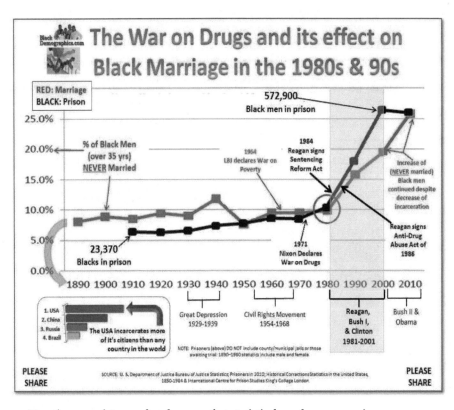

The War on Drugs and its effect on Black Marriage in the 1980s & 90s

Many in our society are already aware that statistical numbers concerning a disproportionate number of Blacks that are incarceration, are not only as a result of systemic racism, but also a result of the shortcomings within the Black community or rather the community's environment. There are those who are quick to say that Black people commit more crimes than White people. The truth of the matter is that the media glamorizes the negative aspect of those within the Black community more expeditiously than they report on crimes within the White community, even if those within the White community are also economically challenged.

With this being said, by making such assumptions, these statements are used to justify a belief that Blacks as a whole have a natural propensity to be criminalist, or that Blacks create a "culture of violence," and use their economic conditions to blame for problems that Black people in America face. Again, while Blacks make up more or less 13% of the United States population, and White's make up 64%, it is Blacks who make up more than 40% of the prison population, while Whites make up only 39% of the prison population. Understand this, even though there are approximately five times as many more Whites than there are Blacks in this country, it is Blacks and Whites who are just about equal in numbers pertaining to the incarceration rates. One must also understand that the fact that Blacks are incarcerated at five times the rate as Whites, does not mean that Blacks have committed five times as many crimes. Here are some of the reasons why:

(1) If a Black person and a White person each commit the same crime, the Black person is more likely to be arrested and sentenced for that crime than the White person, and if the White person is arrested and sentenced, the White person will not receive as harsh of a punishment than the Black person. Much of this is due in part to the fact that Black people as well as their communities are more heavily policed than the White communities.

(2) It is a known fact that Blacks, more often than White, often live in dense urban areas. Such urban areas are more likely to be heavily policed than the suburban or rural areas where it is not as concentrated with Blacks. When you have people, who live in close proximity to one another, then this gives the police the ability to be able

and monitor more people more often. In areas that are more heavily populated by the policed, and the people who are committing the crimes are usually caught more frequently. This could help explain why, for example, when Blacks and White smoke marijuana at similar rates, it is always likely that Blacks are at 3.7 times the rate more likely to be arrested for marijuana possession. (The discrepancy could also be driven by overt racism, more frequent illegal searches of Blacks, or an increased willingness to let non-Blacks off with a warning.)

(3) Facts are that when Blacks are arrested for a crime, then they are convicted a lot more often than Whites are arrested for the same crime. Blacks are also often given harsher punishments.

(4) Remember, having an arrest and a charge does not always lead to a conviction. Also understand that a charge may be dismissed, or a defendant may be declared as not guilty at trial. So, whether or not the arrestee is convicted, this is often determined by whether or not the defendant can afford a reputable attorney. It is sad that the communication of poverty and the trials outcomes often helps explain why. For example, while Black defendants only represent approximately 35% of drug arrests, which is approximately 46% it is the percentage of those Blacks who are actually convicted of drug crimes. (This discrepancy could also be due to racial bias on the part of judges and jurors.)

(5) When Blacks are convicted of a crime, they are more likely to be sentenced to incarceration or a harsher punishment compared to Whites who are convicted of the same crime.

(6) When a person is convicted of a crime, a judge frequently has the discretion in determining whether or not the defendant will be incarcerated or given a less severe punishment. This can be anywhere from probation, to community service, or fines. There was one study that found, that in a particular region where Blacks were incarcerated for convicted felonies, of which the offenses were at 51% of the time, Whites who were convicted of felonies were often incarcerated at 38% of the time. This same study was also used as an empirical approach to determine whether or not race, was confounded with any other factors that were a key to determining if this was the main factor in judges' decisions to incarcerate.

With the incarceration rates standing as they are, Whites being arrested less frequently and given less harsher punishments than Blacks, how far have Blacks progressed? In 1940, there were 60 percent of Black women who were employed as domestic servants; by the late 1990s, the number had gone down to 2.2 percent, while there were now 60 percent of Black women who held white- collar jobs.[314] With ignorance, discrimination and racism, it was in 1958, where 44 percent of Whites said that if a Black family were to move into their neighborhood becoming their neighbor,

---

[314] Thernstrom, Abigail and Stephan Thernstrom. (March 1, 1998) "Black Progress: How Far We've Come, and How Far We Have to Go."

then they would move; as of the late 1990s, that figure became 1 percent.[315] Then in 1964, the year the great Civil Rights Act was passed, there were only 18 percent of Whites who claimed to have had a friend who was actually Black; by the late 1990s, that percentage went up to 86, while there were 87 percent of Blacks who said that they had White friends.[316] Now when speaking about Black males and the incarceration rates, Black women as domesticates as they transition to white-collar positions to Whites being Blacks neighbors, let's talk about Black homeownership.

Even though progress is slow in coming for those in the African American community, yet there is still much progress needed. The issues concerning race and race relations is a version that has essentially been suppressed for more than a half century. The good news is that more than 40 percent of Blacks now consider themselves as being members of the middle class, while homeownership for Blacks have declined to levels that has not seen since before passage of the Fair Housing Act of 1968.[317] According to the Urban Institute report, it showed that "in the three decades after the Fair Housing Act passed, Black homeownership rates in America had risen by nearly six percentage points. But from 2000 to 2015, that gain was more than erased as the Black homeownership rate dropped to roughly 41%. By contrast, the homeownership rate among White Americans is about 71%.[318] For years, it has been virtually difficult for Blacks to qualify for a home loan through traditional banks due to institutional racism

<hr>

[315] Thernstrom, Abigail and Stephan Thernstrom. (March 1, 1998) "Black Progress: How Far We've Come, and How Far We Have to Go."
[316] Thernstrom, Abigail and Stephan Thernstrom. (March 1, 1998) "Black Progress: How Far We've Come, and How Far We Have to Go."
[317] Rodney Brooks, **Next Avenue** Contributor (May 10, 2017) "Declining Black Homeownership Has Big Retirement Implications"
[318] Rodney Brooks, **Next Avenue** Contributor (May 10, 2017) "Declining Black Homeownership Has Big Retirement Implications"

and because of this, it "amplifies a concern that in the last 15 years, Black homeownership rates have declined to levels not seen since the 1960s, when private race-based discrimination was legal," says the Urban Institute report.[319]

Whenever there is a crisis in our country, it is the poor and minority cultures which suffer. In the case of homeownership, it is the Black community which gets hit the hardest by the housing crisis than other groups. "In general, African Americans bought homes at the peak of the bubble at higher rates that Whites and were often offered costly subprime loans, even when they qualified for prime loans with lower interest rates. Also, Black families did not benefit as much as White families, overall, from the post 9/11 recovery."[320]

It appears that the racial wealth gap between Blacks and Whites in this country has hit an all-time high as the median net worth of White households is now 20 times that of Black households.[321] Some wonder why this is. It could be a possibility that in reality we cannot "eliminate the lingering effects of slavery and Jim Crow, or change an individual or groups stereotypes, which is one area where Blacks may be inadvertently contributing to the racial wealth gap: When most Blacks buy homes, it seems as though Blacks hurt themselves economically.[322] While home ownership has always been an important conduit in creating a solid White middle class, it has not necessarily done the same for many Black homeowners, because Blacks and Whites buy homes in very different neighborhoods and Blacks often pay more for homes.[323] Research has shown that homes

---

[319] Rodney Brooks, **Next Avenue** Contributor (May 10, 2017) "Declining Black Homeownership Has Big Retirement Implications"
[320] Rodney Brooks, **Next Avenue** Contributor (May 10, 2017) "Declining Black Homeownership Has Big Retirement Implications"
[321] Contributor Dorothy Brown, (Dec 10, 2012) "How Home Ownership Keeps Blacks Poorer Than Whites."
[322] Contributor Dorothy Brown, (Dec 10, 2012) "How Home Ownership Keeps Blacks Poorer Than Whites."
[323] Contributor Dorothy Brown, (Dec 10, 2012) "How Home Ownership Keeps Blacks Poorer Than Whites."

that are purchased in majority Black neighborhoods do not appreciate as much as homes in overwhelmingly White neighborhoods. This appreciation gap usually begins whenever a neighborhood is more than 10% Black, and it increases right along with the percentage of Black homeowners. Yet it is felt that most Blacks perfer to live in majority minority or mixed neighborhoods, while most Whites prefer to live in overwhelmingly White neighborhoods.[324]

Both race and class go hand in hand and if you think that there is no correlation, then you may be incorrect. In a 2001 Brookings Institution study, it showed that "wealthy minority neighborhoods had less home value per dollar of income than wealthy White neighborhoods." This same study also concluded that "poor white neighborhoods had more home value per income than poor minority neighborhoods."[325] The Brookings study was based on a comparison of home values to homeowner incomes in the nation's 100 largest metropolitan areas, and found that even when homeowners had similar incomes, Black-owned homes were valued at 18% less than White-owned homes. The 100 metropolitan areas were home to 58% of all Whites and 63% of all Blacks in the country.[326]

Because of racial barriers and discriminatory practices, it is sad to say that many "working class Black Americans struggle to obtain affordable housing. The percentage of Black homeowners decreased between 2005 and 2012 from 46% to 42.5% which is just about a 1 percent difference than what the Urban Institute study showed. Many of these

[324] Contributor Dorothy Brown, (Dec 10, 2012) "How Home Ownership Keeps Blacks Poorer Than Whites."
[325] Contributor Dorothy Brown, (Dec 10, 2012) "How Home Ownership Keeps Blacks Poorer Than Whites."
[326] Contributor Dorothy Brown, (Dec 10, 2012) "How Home Ownership Keeps Blacks Poorer Than Whites."

losses can be attributed to the housing crisis where so many Americans lost their houses to foreclosure. This also means more than half of all African Americans rent."[327]

Many in our society that are renters are also struggling. Facts are that "59.2% of renters spend more than 30% of their income on rent. "This is an increase from 53% in 2005. This is important an important factor because it is recommended that a house should pay no more than thirty percent of a households' income for housing costs. For those who are homeowners, the percentage of households that are spending more than 30% of their income on housing increased from 40% to 43.9% during the same time period. Although this is lower than it is for renters it is still higher than the national average of 33.9%. So, by having to use so much of our income for housing makes it much more difficult for African Americans to make ends meet, especially since Blacks have also experienced a large increase in median gross rent from $686 in 2005 to $820 per month in 2012 in some areas of the United States while area such as Southern California are more than doubled than the prices above. Also, the median value of homes owned by African Americans decreased from $126,000 in 2011 to $122,200 in 2012.

HOUSING IN LOS ANGELES COUNTY

Property Value

$537,900 ± $4,937 2016 MEDIAN

$497,200 ± $2,638 2015 MEDIAN

"In 2016, the median property value in Los Angeles County, CA grew to $537,900 from the previous year's value of $497,200. The data below displays, first, the property

---

[327] Contributor Dorothy Brown, (Dec 10, 2012) "How Home Ownership Keeps Blacks Poorer Than Whites."

values in Los Angeles County, CA compared to other geographies and, second, owner-occupied housing units distributed between a series of property value buckets compared to the national averages for each bucket. In Los Angeles County, CA the largest share of households has a property value in the $500k-$750k range, with the average range of property taxes being $3,000 plus. **Rent vs. Own**, in 2016 there were 44.6% of those in Los Angeles County, CA who owned their homes. As you see, that was a decline compared to 45.1% in 2015. This percentage of owner-occupation is lower than the national average of 63.1%. This chart shows the ownership percentage in Los Angeles County, CA compared to its parent geographies.[328],[329]

The median home price in California reached a new peak in May 2018, exceeding $600,000 for the first time ever. In a new report from the California Association of Realtors, it found that Statewide, the median home price was $600,860 in May 2018. This topped the previous high of $594,530 which notched 11 years ago during the pre-Great Recession real estate bubble, according to the data released on Tuesday June 19, 2018.[330] The increase was largely driven by high costs in the Bay Area, where the median price sat above $1 million for the second month straight. In San Francisco, buyers paid an average of 18 percent over the asking price. But in Southern California prices lag behind the rest of the state, CAR said.[331] Though the median home price in Orange County were well above the statewide figure, at $818,000, in Los Angeles County it was

---

[328] https://datausa.io/profile/geo/**los-angeles-county**-ca

[329] The **American Community Survey (ACS)** is conducted by the US Census and sent to a portion of the population every year. Data USA does not contain the entire ACS dataset but instead relevant topics to the curated profile pages of the site. As of the 2014 (most recent) ACS release there are 1 year and 5-year estimates. Previously there was also a 3-year estimate which has now been discontinued.

[330] MARTIN, ERIKA (JUNE 20, 2018) "Median Home Price in California Tops $600,000 for 1st Time." https://**ktla.com**/2018/06/20/**median**-home-price-in-california-tops-$600,000-for-1st-time.

[331] MARTIN, ERIKA (JUNE 20, 2018) "Median Home Price in California Tops $600,000 for 1st Time." https://**ktla.com**/2018/06/20/**median**-home-price-in-california-tops-$600,000-for-1st-time.

slightly lower, at $528,540. Despite this, sales across the region were down by 5.8 percent compared to last year. San Bernardino County — where the median home price was comparatively lower at $289,900 — was the only county in Southern California to see an increase. Home prices in Southern California are still on the rise, though not as markedly as in the Bay.[332] The growth rate was in the double digits in both San Bernardino and Los Angeles counties, but in the single digits elsewhere across the Southland. Still, there remains a shortage of homes priced under $200,000 on the market. The number of houses available in that range dropped by 28.7 percent over the last year, and the number priced between 200,000 and $300,000 declined 13 percent.[333] This is one reason why it is difficult for African Americans to own homes especially in certain areas.

Black Housing Statistics

HOUSING TENURE	Black	all races
Owner-occupied housing units	42.5%	63.9%
Renter-occupied housing units	57.5%	36.1%
UNITS IN STRUCTURE		
1-unit, detached or attached	55.6%	68.8%
2 to 4 units	13.0%	7.9%
5 or more units	27.5%	17.3%
Mobile home, boat, RV, van, etc.	4.0%	6.0%
MONTHLY OWNER COSTS AS A % OF HOUSEHOLD INCOME		
Less than 30 percent	56.1%	66.1%
30 percent or more	43.9%	33.9%
OWNER CHARACTERISTICS		
Median home value	$122,200	$171,900
Median selected monthly costs with/ mortgage	$1,327	$1,460
GROSS RENT AS A PERCENTAGE OF HOUSEHOLD INCOME		
Less than 30 percent	40.8%	48.0%
30 percent or more	59.2%	52.0%
GROSS RENT		
Median gross rent	$820	$884

SOURCE: U.S. Census 2012 American Community Survey

BlackDemographics.com

[332] MARTIN, ERIKA (JUNE 20, 2018) "Median Home Price in California Tops $600,000 for 1st Time." https://ktla.com/2018/06/20/median-home-price-in-california-tops-$600,000-for-1st-time.
[333] MARTIN, ERIKA (JUNE 20, 2018) "Median Home Price in California Tops $600,000 for 1st Time." https://ktla.com/2018/06/20/median-home-price-in-california-tops-$600,000-for-1st-time.

States with High Black Home Ownership

Percent of Black owner-occupied housing units

TOP 10	Bottom 10
Mississippi 55.6%	Arizona 33.5%
South Carolina 53.4%	Washington 33.2%
Alabama 52.7%	Massachusetts 32.7%
Delaware 52.7%	Nevada 32.2%
Maryland 52.2%	Oregon 31.3%
Virginia 50.0%	Iowa 30.8%
Louisiana 49.2%	Rhode Island 30.7%
Georgia 48.5%	New York 30.0%
North Carolina 47.8%	Wisconsin 28.3%
Florida 46.9%	Minnesota 24.3%

Source: US Census 2011 ACS
Includes Black and Black in combination with other race(s)

BlackDemographics.com

As you can see according to the above statistical data, California is not included. However, such facts are rarely reported by mainstream media, so it is still societal attitudes by mainstream which assumes that many Blacks still live in ghettos, often in high-rise public housing projects, with a continuation of crime and still receiving a welfare check which is seen as the Blacks main source of income. Such stereotypes tend to cross racial lines. Within their own culture, there are many Blacks who are even more inclined than Whites to exaggerate the extent to which African Americans are still trapped in inner-city poverty, which in some case are correct. "In a 1991 Gallup poll, there were approximately one-fifth of all Whites who thought that Blacks were still trapped in inner-city poverty, yet almost half of Black respondents, said that at least three out of four African Americans were impoverished urban residents. And yet, in reality, Blacks who considered themselves to be middle class outnumber those with incomes below the poverty line by a wide margin.[334]

It can be stated that more than fifty years ago most Blacks were most defiantly trapped in a cycle of poverty, even though many of them did not live in inner cities.[335] "When Gunnar Myrdal published 'An American Dilemma' in 1944, many Blacks lived in the South and on the land as laborers and sharecroppers. (Only one in eight owned the land on which he worked.) A small 5 percent of Black men nationally were engaged in nonmanual, white-collar work of any kind; yet, the vast majority of Black males still held ill-paid, insecure, manual jobs—jobs that few Whites would take. As previously stated, back then, there were six out of ten African-American women who worked as household servants who, driven by economic desperation, often worked 12-hour days for pathetically low wages. Segregation in the South and discrimination in the North created a sheltered market for some Black businesses (those such as funeral homes, beauty parlors, and the like) that served in the Black community who were barred from patronizing "White" establishments. But the number was minuscule."[336]

After the Stock Market Crash of 1929 followed by the Great Depression, it was during the FDR era, that brought about many changes mostly for poor Whites, however, Blacks also reaped some of the benefits. During the 1940s, there was a deep

---

[334] Thernstrom, Abigail and Stephan Thernstrom. (March 1, 1998) "Black Progress: How Far We've Come, and How Far We Have to Go."
[335] Thernstrom, Abigail and Stephan Thernstrom. (March 1, 1998) "Black Progress: How Far We've Come, and How Far We Have to Go."
[336] Thernstrom, Abigail and Stephan Thernstrom. (March 1, 1998) "Black Progress: How Far We've Come, and How Far We Have to Go."

demographic and economic change, which was accompanied by a marked shift in some

of the Whites racial attitudes towards Blacks which started Blacks down the road to

more opportunities and much greater equality. The New Deal legislation, which was one

such opportunity, "set minimum wages for being paid, which was more secure, and a

certain set of hours which eliminated the incentive of southern employers to hire low-

wage Black workers, which put a damper on further industrial development in the

region. In addition, the trend towards a more modern agriculture, such as the invention

of the cotton gin, and a diminished demand for American cotton coupled with a in the

face of international competition which were all combined began to displace Blacks from

the land."[337]

Because of such consequences that caused Blacks to be displaced workers, there

became a shortage of workers in northern manufacturing plants that followed the

outbreak of World War II. Southern Blacks who were in search of employment began

boarding trains and buses in a Great Migration that lasted throughout the mid-1960s.

Many Blacks found what they were looking for, the wages were so strikingly high that in

1953 the average income for a Black family in the North was almost twice that of those

who remained in the South. And through much of the 1950s those wages continued to

rise steadily, and the unemployment rates were low.[338]

By the time the 1960s rolled around, there were only one out of seven Black men

who still labored on the land, or shall I say, worked as sharecroppers, and almost a

quarter of other Black men were working in white-collar positions or in skilled manual

---

[337] Thernstrom, Abigail and Stephan Thernstrom. (March 1, 1998) "Black Progress: How Far We've Come, and How Far We Have to Go."
[338] Thernstrom, Abigail and Stephan Thernstrom. (March 1, 1998) "Black Progress: How Far We've Come, and How Far We Have to Go."

occupations. Then there were another 24 percent who had semiskilled factory jobs that meant that their membership in the stable working class gave them a sense of security, while a larger proportion of Black women who did work as servants their jobs had been cut in half. So even those who did not move up into higher-ranking jobs were doing much better than the sharecropper in the south.[339]

The 1960s brought a sense of hope and a ray of sunshine into the lives of many Blacks, because a decade later, the gains were even more striking. Ironically, from 1940 to 1970, Black men had cut the income gap by about a third, and by the 1970s they were earning (on average) approximately 60 percent of what White men brought home. The advancement of Black women was even more impressive. Black life expectancy went up dramatically, as did Black homeownership rates. Black college enrollment also rose by 1970 to about 10 percent of the total, three times the prewar figure.[340]

During the following years these trends continued to rise, even though they were at a more leisurely pace. For instance, in the 1990s, there were more than 30 percent of Black men and nearly 60 percent of Black women who held white-collar jobs. Whereas in 1970 there were only 2.2 percent of American physicians who were Black, by 1990s this figure became 4.5 percent. Yet, while the portion of Black families who had middle-class incomes rose by almost 40 percentage points between 1940 and 1970, by the late 1990s, it had only inched up another 10 points since then.[341] Now when it comes to the

---

[339] Thernstrom, Abigail and Stephan Thernstrom. (March 1, 1998) "Black Progress: How Far We've Come, and How Far We Have to Go."
[340] Thernstrom, Abigail and Stephan Thernstrom. (March 1, 1998) "Black Progress: How Far We've Come, and How Far We Have to Go."
[341] Thernstrom, Abigail and Stephan Thernstrom. (March 1, 1998) "Black Progress: How Far We've Come, and How Far We Have to Go."

issues of employment, education and affirmative action let's see who benefitted, and if is a help or a hinderance.

There has been a swift change concerning the status of "Blacks for several decades followed by a definite slowdown that begins just when affirmative action policies get their start: that story certainly seems to suggest that racial preferences have enjoyed an inflated reputation. "There's one simple reason to support affirmative action," an op-ed writer in the New York Times argued in 1995. "It works." That is the voice of conventional wisdom.[342] There are some gains that have most likely been attributed to the "race-conscious educational and employment policies. The number of Black college and university professors have more than doubled between 1970 and 1990; the number of physicians tripled; the number of engineers almost quadrupled; and the number of attorneys increased more than six-fold. Those numbers undoubtedly do reflect the fact that the nation's professional schools changed their admissions criteria for Black applicants, accepting and often providing financial aid to African-American students whose academic records were much weaker than those of many White and Asian-American applicants whom these schools were turning down. Preferences "worked" for these beneficiaries, in that they were given seats in the classroom that they would not have won in the absence of racial double standards."[343]

Unfortunately, such professionals only make up a small fraction of the total Black middle class. And their numbers would have grown without preferences, the historical record strongly suggests. In addition, the greatest economic gains for African Americans

---

[342] Thernstrom, Abigail and Stephan Thernstrom. (March 1, 1998) "Black Progress: How Far We've Come, and How Far We Have to Go."
[343] Thernstrom, Abigail and Stephan Thernstrom. (March 1, 1998) "Black Progress: How Far We've Come, and How Far We Have to Go."

since the early 1960s were in the years 1965 to 1975 and occurred mainly in the South, as economists John J. Donahue III and James Heckman have found. In fact, Donahue and Heckman discovered "virtually no improvement" in the wages of Black men relative to those of White men outside of the South over the entire period from 1963 to 1987, and southern gains, they concluded, were mainly due to the powerful antidiscrimination provisions in the 1964 Civil Rights Act."[344]

Employment and affirmative action policies basically said that minorities and female owned companies must be given an opportunity to benefit from such policies since at least 30 percent of Black families were still living in poverty. By the end of the 1990s it had been found that many of these programs were often fraudulent, with White contractors offering minority firms a certain percent of the profits with no obligation to do any of the work. "Alternatively, set-asides enrich those with the right connections. In Richmond, Virginia, for instance, the main effect of the ordinance was a marriage of political convenience—a working alliance between the economically privileged of both races. The white business elite signed on to a piece-of-the-pie for blacks in order to polish its image as socially conscious and secure support for the downtown revitalization it wanted. Black politicians used the bargain to suggest their own importance to low-income constituents for whom the set-asides actually did little. Neither cared whether the policy in fact provided real economic benefits—which it didn't."[345]

It is often wondered why has the engine of advancement been stalled? Well it seems as though when affirmative action was enacted decades ago, their policies were

---

[344] Thernstrom, Abigail and Stephan Thernstrom. (March 1, 1998) "Black Progress: How Far We've Come, and How Far We Have to Go."
[345] Thernstrom, Abigail and Stephan Thernstrom. (March 1, 1998) "Black Progress: How Far We've Come, and How Far We Have to Go."

instituted to assist with the poverty rate which has basically remained the same. Even though there were many Blacks who had benefited from affirmative action by numerous other measures, there was still that small but significant percentage of Black families who still live below the poverty line, even today. Even today, the unemployment rates for Blacks remains about twice that of Whites. Racial preferences and persistent inequality still holds precedence in America, even though having more than a quarter-century of affirmative action has done little more of nothing whatever to close the unemployment gap.[346]

Persistent inequality, discrimination, and segregation is obviously a serious matter still today in this country, "and if discrimination were the primary problem, then race-conscious remedies might be appropriate. But while White racism was central to the story in 1964, today the picture becomes much more complicated.[347] Today, Blacks and Whites now have the opportunities to graduate almost at the same rate from high school and are almost equally likely to attend college, yet, on average they are not equally educated.[348]

"The National Assessment of Educational Progress (NAEP) is the nation's report card on what American students attending elementary and secondary schools know. Those tests show that African-American students, on average, are alarmingly far behind Whites in math, science, reading, and writing. For instance, there are many Black students who get towards the end of their high school career are almost four years

---

[346] Thernstrom, Abigail and Stephan Thernstrom. (March 1, 1998) "Black Progress: How Far We've Come, and How Far We Have to Go."
[347] Thernstrom, Abigail and Stephan Thernstrom. (March 1, 1998) "Black Progress: How Far We've Come, and How Far We Have to Go."
[348] Thernstrom, Abigail and Stephan Thernstrom. (March 1, 1998) "Black Progress: How Far We've Come, and How Far We Have to Go."

behind White students in reading; the gap is comparable in other subjects. A study of 26- to 33-year-old men who held full-time jobs in 1991 thus found that when education was measured by years of school completed, Blacks earned 19 percent less than comparably educated Whites. But when word knowledge, paragraph comprehension, arithmetical reasoning, and mathematical knowledge became the yardstick, the results were reversed. Black men earned 9 percent more than White men with the same education—that is, the same performance on basic tests.[349] NAEP math tests, for example, revealed that only 22 percent of African-American high school seniors but 58 percent of their White classmates were numerate enough for such firms to consider hiring them. And in reading, 47 percent of Whites in 1992 but just 18 percent of African Americans could handle the printed word well enough to be employable in a modern automobile plant. Murnane and Levy found a clear impact on income. Not years spent in school, but strong skills made for high long-term earnings."[350]

"In 1971, the average African-American 17-year-old could read no better than the typical White child who was six years younger. The racial gap in math in 1973 was 4.3 years; in science it was 4.7 years in 1970. By the late 1980s, however, the picture was notably brighter. Black students in their final year of high school were only 2.5 years behind Whites in both reading and math and 2.1 years behind on tests of writing skills." Today, the educational outcomes and the money spent towards education is still a separate but unequal issue. There are still large amounts of Black students who are not performing as well as White students. Even with affirmative action, black progress came

[349] Thernstrom, Abigail and Stephan Thernstrom. (March 1, 1998) "Black Progress: How Far We've Come, and How Far We Have to Go."
[350] Thernstrom, Abigail and Stephan Thernstrom. (March 1, 1998) "Black Progress: How Far We've Come, and How Far We Have to Go."

to a halt, and serious backsliding began. Between 1988 and 1994, the racial gap in reading grew from 2.5 to 3.9 years; between 1990 and 1994, the racial gap in math increased from 2.5 to 3.4 years. In both science and writing, the racial gap has widened by a full year.[351]

The educational system in American is rampant with problems, beginning with the huge differences between White students and students of color. It has been more than 60 years since Brown vs. Board of Education (1954), yet the school systems in the United States are still separate and unequal. There are those who indicate that by the year "2022, the number of Hispanic students in public elementary and secondary schools is projected to grow 33 percent from the 2011 numbers."[352] The number of multi-racial students are also expected to grow 44 percent. As the percentage of White students in our educational system begins to shrinks and the percentage of students of color begins to grow, then the U.S. will be left with an education system that does not serve the majority of its children properly, and with this being said, then the gaps America's educational system will prove to be especially problematic.[353] In addition to the problematic educational systems, there are other factors to consider which are contributing influences to the disparities in education. Such factors include lower wealth, lower health, lower parental education levels, more dealings with the justice

---

[351] Thernstrom, Abigail and Stephan Thernstrom. (March 1, 1998) "Black Progress: How Far We've Come, and How Far We Have to Go."
[352] Cook, Lindsey (January 28, 2015; U.S. News & World Report). U.S. Education: Still Separate and Unequal, The data show schools are still separate and unequal.
[353] Cook, Lindsey (January 28, 2015; U.S. News & World Report). U.S. Education: Still Separate and Unequal, The data show schools are still separate and unequal.

system and other circumstances which creates a perfect barrier that leaves Blacks without the same educational opportunities as Whites.[354]

While there is no obvious explanation on what the cause is for this disturbing turnaround, we do know that the early advantages that Blacks were achieving during the 1960s and 1970s undoubtedly had a lot to do with the growth of the Black middle class, however, the Black middle class did not suddenly begin to shrink in the late 1980s. The poverty rate, especially in the Black community, was not dropping significantly when educational progress was occurring, nor was it on the increase when the racial gap began once again to widen. Even with the large increase in out-of-wedlock births and the sharp and steady decline in the proportion of Black children growing up with two parents, this still does not explain the fluctuating educational performance of Black children. It had been one established that children who are raised in single-parent families do less well in school than others, even when all other variables, including income, are controlled. Yet, this is also a myth that can be debunked as there are children who are raised in single parent households that will do just as well as children who grow up in two parent households. However, there is that disintegration of the Black nuclear family which was presciently noted by Daniel Patrick Moynihan as early as 1965 that there was and occurrence that was rapidly growing in the period in which Black scores were rising, so it cannot be invoked as the main explanation as to why scores began to fall many years later."[355]

---

[354] Cook, Lindsey (January 28, 2015; U.S. News & World Report). U.S. Education: Still Separate and Unequal, The data show schools are still separate and unequal.
[355] Thernstrom, Abigail and Stephan Thernstrom. (March 1, 1998) "Black Progress: How Far We've Come, and How Far We Have to Go."

The questions that we should ask is, "why is there such a decline in Black children's educational performances? Is it because of the increased violence and disorder of inner-city lives that had come along with the introduction of crack cocaine and the drug-related gang wars in the mid-1980s which could have most likely had something to do with the reversal of Black educational progress? Chaos in the streets and within schools can always affect a child's learning abilities inside and outside the classroom.[356] Many in mainstream also do not realize that school shootings in the inner-city schools and drive by shootings among the gangs occurred long before such shootings that occur today. The only reason why it was not common is because it occurred in the inner-city schools and did not affect those who were in mainstream society, so it was not a concern. Also remember this, many of those children were from two parent homes or did have interactions with their fathers or a male role model. Yet, as just stated, the chaos and commotion, environmental upheaval, the crack epidemic, possible homelessness are all just some factors that plays in a child's learning ability.

Why are Black and students of color the ones who are the most academically disadvantaged? Why is there such a deficiency for their education in a country that is supposed to be so great? These students just like their White counterparts are hit hardest and they are the ones who are most in need of education. "Yet in the name of racial sensitivity, advocates for minority students too often dismiss both common academic standards and standardized tests as culturally biased and judgmental. Such advocates have plenty of company."[357] Such tests can be abolished—or standards

---

[356] Thernstrom, Abigail and Stephan Thernstrom. (March 1, 1998) "Black Progress: How Far We've Come, and How Far We Have to Go."
[357] Thernstrom, Abigail and Stephan Thernstrom. (March 1, 1998) "Black Progress: How Far We've Come, and How Far We Have to Go."

lowered—but once the disparity in cognitive skills becomes less evident, it is harder to correct."[358] "Closing that skills gap is obviously the first task if black advancement is to continue at its once-fast pace. On the map of racial progress, education is the name of almost every road. Raise the level of black educational performance, and the gap in college graduation rates, in attendance at selective professional schools, and in earnings is likely to close as well. Moreover, with educational parity, the whole issue of racial preferences disappears."[359]

Even though the progress of Blacks in America has, over the past half-century has been impressive, yet exercising wisdom and having basic common knowledge seems to be very conflicting nevertheless. And yet the nation has many miles to go on the road to true racial equality. Today, racism, discrimination and prejudice are not just distant memories as it is alive and well today. For many who are not awake (aware) or who refuse to accept this fact view racism, discrimination and prejudice as an illusion, the sort of fantasy to which intellectuals are particularly prone because it does not affect them. Is racial equality a hopeless task, or an unattainable ideal? Thurgood Marshall had once envisioned that there be an end to all school segregation within five years of the Supreme Court's decision in Brown v. Board of Education. Today, there are still many Blacks in particularly, who are still discouraged. In 1997 the Gallup poll found that there was a sharp decline in optimism since 1980; only 33 percent of Blacks (versus 58

---

[358] Thernstrom, Abigail and Stephan Thernstrom. (March 1, 1998) "Black Progress: How Far We've Come, and How Far We Have to Go."
[359] Thernstrom, Abigail and Stephan Thernstrom. (March 1, 1998) "Black Progress: How Far We've Come, and How Far We Have to Go."

percent of Whites) thought both the quality of life for Blacks and race relations had gotten better.[360]

As of August 8, 2018, polls that had been taken says that the majority feels that race relations has gotten worse under Trump. This statement is an accurate assumption. One year after Trump said that there were "some very fine people on both sides" of the violent protest in Charlottesville, Virginia, there were 55 percent of voters who felt that the race relations had gotten worse while 18 percent stated that race relations have remained the same. 51 percent Whites, 79 percent Blacks and 60 percent of Hispanics thought that race relations had gotten worse. [361] The 1950s and 1960s dealt with the Civil Rights Movement where Blacks in America were fighting to obtain equal rights in a country for which they lived in. With this being said, if race relations have gotten worse under Trump, what do you think the chances are of Blacks and other minorities getting a decent education in America? There are still those stereotypical ideologies that Blacks students cannot achieve their educational goals. They are still being dismayed by many educators, such as they were in the 1940s, 50s, and 60s that they should pursue other opportunities other than in the fields that they wish to achieve. For those of you who have seen the movie "Hidden Figures," remember many of those Black men and women were told the same thing, yet they continued to move forward and pursue their dreams. Black children are often told that they have behavioral problems and that they will grow up to be delinquent criminals or become involved in criminalistic behaviors.

---

[360] Thernstrom, Abigail and Stephan Thernstrom. (March 1, 1998) "Black Progress: How Far We've Come, and How Far We Have to Go."
[361] Steven Shepard (August 8, 2018; Politico) "Poll: Majority says race relations have gotten worse under Trump."

It is not a teacher's job to judge a student period, especially based on a child's skin color. Even though this is the new millennium, there is still a deeply rooted stubbornness when it comes to racial achievement and that gap being closed. It is sad to say that schools today just as they were over 50 years ago are still just as segregated. So, when it comes to affirmative action, there are many who have stated that affirmative action did not work. As a matter of fact, affirmative action did work for some, mostly White women. For many women, not necessarily of color, they have benefitted quite well from affirmative action. Today, there are more women who have been able to obtain higher education and given opportunities in the workforce more than ever before, due to the affirmative action policies. Even though primarily White women benefitted immensely from affirmative action, they are now also some of the fiercest opponents towards affirmative action.[362]

When it came to the affirmative action policies originally, the subject of gender was actually a blind spot in the original document. "Sex discrimination protections were not included when affirmative action policy was initially institutionalized in the 1960s. The National Labor Relations Act in 1935 just happened to be one of the first federal documents to use the term "affirmative action" in order to correct the unfair labor practices. While the Public Works Administration temporarily followed racially proportional hiring practices (which were dismantled at the end of World War II), it was not until President John F. Kennedy issued an executive order in 1961 that required that affirmative action was to counter employment discrimination among federal

---

[362] Thernstrom, Abigail and Stephan Thernstrom. (March 1, 1998) "Black Progress: How Far We've Come, and How Far We Have to Go."

contractors, which specifically gave attention to race, and this is what made affirmative action institutionalized."[363]

"When it came to affirmative action, in some ways, the narrow focus that was on 'race' and 'color' was the excuse and the government's response to the demands of the burgeoning Civil Rights Movement that brought racial discrimination to the front and center in America."[364] So, while we are on the subject, over the years those who have benefited the most, which were mostly White women, have become some of affirmative action's most dispassionate opponents. According to the 2014 Cooperative Congressional Election Study, there were nearly 70 percent of the 20,694 self-identified non-Hispanic White women who surveyed that they were either somewhat or strongly opposed affirmative action. White women have also been the primary plaintiffs in the major Supreme Court affirmative action cases, with the exception of the first — *Regents of the University of California v. Bakke* in 1978 — that was brought to the courts by a White man.[365] Yes it is a widespread assumption that even Justice Antonin Scalia brought to the fore during oral arguments for the *Fisher* case. He asserted that affirmative action hurts African-American students by putting them in elite institutions they are not prepared for. Study after study shows there's simply no evidence for the claim.[366]

---

[363] Massie, Victoria M. (Vox. June 23, 2016) "White women benefit most from affirmative action — and are among its fiercest opponents."

[364] Massie, Victoria M. (Vox. June 23, 2016) "White women benefit most from affirmative action — and are among its fiercest opponents."

[365] Massie, Victoria M. (Vox. June 23, 2016) "White women benefit most from affirmative action — and are among its fiercest opponents."

[366] Thernstrom, Abigail and Stephan Thernstrom. (March 1, 1998) "Black Progress: How Far We've Come, and How Far We Have to Go."

When we observe the actual effects of affirmative action bans we also observe that this suggests the ideology that it is based on a false dichotomy. Since California passed Prop 209 in 1996 barring racial considerations for college admissions at public universities, UC Berkeley have witnessed a significant drop in the number of Black students, from 8 percent pre–Prop 209 to an average of 3.6 percent of the freshman class from 2006 to 2010.[367]

Understand that this drop is not necessarily tied to students of color who are underqualified. Rather, it is tied to the 58 percent of Black students who were admitted from 2006 to 2010 and rejected Berkeley's offer of admission. Alumni, administrators, and current students noted that the possible reason could be that Blacks student have a feeling of isolation, or because the school lacks other students of color, at UC's flagship campus — an ironic consequence of the affirmative action ban.[368]

Asian-American applicants decided that they too would challenge the colorblind meritocracy myth. According to a sociological study in 2009, it was found that White applicants were three times more likely to be admitted to selective schools than Asian applicants with the exact same academic record. And a 2013 survey found that White adults in California deemphasize the importance of test scores when Asian Americans, whose average test scores are higher than White students, are considered. Furthermore, existing race-neutral admissions policies like legacy admissions show that taking race out of the equation does not make admissions processes any more just.[369]

---

[367] Massie, Victoria M. (Vox. June 23, 2016) "White women benefit most from affirmative action — and are among its fiercest opponents."

[368] Massie, Victoria M. (Vox. June 23, 2016) "White women benefit most from affirmative action — and are among its fiercest opponents."

[369] Massie, Victoria M. (Vox. June 23, 2016) "White women benefit most from affirmative action — and are among its fiercest opponents."

Historically, the majority of college campuses has been predominantly White. 84 percent of college students in the US were White in 1976 compared with only 60 percent in 2012 — which makes it far more likely that the beneficiaries of legacy admissions practices are White applicants. There are those White women, like Fisher, who stand as a testament to affirmative action's success. The sad part is that, the dismantling of affirmative action is launched at people of color, but it also affects White women, and the willingness to erase them from the story is part of the problem.[370]

There is a reason why affirmative action is needed today, especially for Blacks and many other individuals of color. One of the main reasons why affirmative action is needed today is because "Trump's Justice Department has decided to launch a project to identify and then sue universities that they deem to have affirmative action policies that discriminate against whites in admissions. The department, as this story reports, is looking for outside attorneys to participate because staffers who handle education issues did not want to do it "out of concerns it was contrary to the office's long-running approach to civil rights in education opportunities."[371] The Justice Department plans a new project to sue universities over affirmative action policies. Even though affirmative action in the college admissions process for African Americans has been losing support in the United States for some time, with the supposed "colorblind" methods of admissions, which is gaining ground in the courts, there are powerful arguments for why the practice is still needed."[372]

---

[370] Massie, Victoria M. (Vox. June 23, 2016) "White women benefit most from affirmative action — and are among its fiercest opponents."
[371] Strauss, Valerie (August 2, 2017; The Washington Post) "Actually, we still need affirmative action for African Americans in college admissions. Here's why."
[372] Strauss, Valerie (August 2, 2017; The Washington Post) "Actually, we still need affirmative action for African Americans in college admissions. Here's why."

Race and color matters when it comes to the educational system in America, especially when it comes to college admissions. It was written in 2014 by Richard Rothstein, a research associate at the Economic Policy Institute, a nonprofit created in 1986 to broaden the discussion about economic policy to include the interests of low- and middle-income workers. He is also a fellow at the Thurgood Marshall Institute of the NAACP Legal Defense Fund, and the author of books including "Grading Education: Getting Accountability Right, and "Class and Schools: Using Social, Economic and Educational Reform to Close the Black-White Achievement Gap." His newest book is "The Color of Law: A Forgotten History of How Our Government Segregated America." He was a national education writer for the New York Times as well.[373]

There are those who fail to realize that, in Abigail Fisher's case, there were only five of the 47 students who were admitted with lower grades and test scores than Abigail's that were minority, while the other 42 were White. Forget about the fact that there were 168 Black and Latin students with grades that were just as good as or better than Fisher's who were also denied entry into the university that year. In the case of Fisher's, she felt that playing the race card is what gets America's attention. It was obvious that she did not do the research. "But there is another, even more fundamental, drawback with this debate: Its core premise is deeply flawed. The debate's underlying assumption is that statistical measures — GPAs, SATs, ACTs, and AP test scores — are the most objective, and hence useful, gauge of an applicant's merit. Clearly, or so the thinking goes, a well-off applicant with near-perfect SAT scores and a 4.3 GPA (adjusted

[373] Strauss, Valerie (August 2, 2017; The Washington Post) "Actually, we still need affirmative action for African Americans in college admissions. Here's why."

with extra points from AP courses that are common in affluent schools and rare in low-income schools) is more qualified than an inner-city student with lower numbers. So, the debate rages about whether universities should admit "less qualified" applicants, on the basis of criteria designed to help offset historical inequities."[374]

Now when we talk about historical inequalities, let talk about students who are in low-income communities. These students have to deal with the every day responsibilities that students who are well off cannot even begin to fathom. Students who are low-income coming from economically challenged areas, they often make their way, despite the obstacles that they endure, through under-resourced schools that have large classes which are taught by overstressed teachers. They are constantly reminded regularly of their academic "limitations" as they are evaluated relentlessly on mind-numbing tests. And for those economically challenged students who do overcome such enormous obstacles have to literally claw their way into a top college. "They encounter upper-crust classmates questioning whether they belong, as evidenced by the recent "Affirmative Dissatisfaction" controversy at Harvard."[375]

Yet on the dimensions of tenacity and grit, as well as personal accomplishment, these students run circles around many "highly qualified" upper-crust applicants. And, in fact, research by former university presidents William Bowen and Derek Bok on the outcomes of affirmative action programs found that minority students admitted to

---

[374] Strauss, Valerie (August 2, 2017; The Washington Post) "Actually, we still need affirmative action for African Americans in college admissions. Here's why."
[375] Strauss, Valerie (August 2, 2017; The Washington Post) "Actually, we still need affirmative action for African Americans in college admissions. Here's why."

selective universities did as well or better than their White counterparts on a number of outcomes — and opened doors for generations after them.[376]

So the next time someone brings up the subject of affirmative action, one must critically think broadly about how many in mainstream evaluate the merits and potential of our youth and how race and segregation plays a significant role in the educational system. Think about how different the outcomes could be for the school years of all children, both rich and poor; think about how it would be if the educational system were aligned with lives of the students and what they endure on a daily basis, instead of tailoring to the needs of Princeton statisticians. If we take just some of these issues into account, then this society just might begin to make progress after decades of failed education reform that would allow many students to graduating as they make their way in the world as adults. [377]

In 2014, Richard Rothstein wrote, "Chief Justice John G. Roberts Jr. says that 'the way to stop discrimination on the basis of race is to stop discriminating on the basis of race.' In university admissions, this means becoming "colorblind," taking no affirmative action to favor African Americans. Apparently intimidated by Roberts's Supreme Court plurality, many university officials, liberals, and civil rights advocates have exchanged their former support of affirmative action for policies that appear closer to Roberts's. In effect, these newer plans say that the way to stop discrimination on the basis of race is to pretend colorblindness but devise subterfuges to favor African

---

[376] Strauss, Valerie (August 2, 2017; The Washington Post) "Actually, we still need affirmative action for African Americans in college admissions. Here's why."
[377] Strauss, Valerie (August 2, 2017; The Washington Post) "Actually, we still need affirmative action for African Americans in college admissions. Here's why."

Americans. One approach is to favor low-income students regardless of race. Another adopts the Supreme Court's embrace of diversity as educationally beneficial, prompting universities to enroll disadvantaged minority students for this purpose while making no obvious attempt to remedy historic wrongs. Some persuade themselves that these are the best possible policies.[378]

It seems that "in recent years, Justice Ruth Bader Ginsburg has been one of the few leading public figures, on or off the Court, unabashedly willing to challenge Roberts's colorblindness. In a case decided in April 2015, she gained a new ally in Justice Sonia Sotomayor for an uncompromising defense of affirmative action. Instead of "winks, nods, and disguises," Ginsburg has called for race-conscious policy to offset the still-enduring effects of slavery and the subsequent unconstitutional exploitation of its descendants under Jim Crow. "Only an ostrich could regard the supposedly neutral alternatives as race unconscious," Ginsburg has said, and only a contorted legal mind "could conclude that an admissions plan designed to produce racial diversity is not race conscious." Sotomayor recently added (mocking Roberts's aphorism) that "the way to stop discrimination on the basis of race is to speak openly and candidly on the subject of race, and to apply the Constitution with eyes open to the unfortunate effects of centuries of racial discrimination."[379]

"In contrast to this plea, Cashin's previous book, "The Failures of Integration," was an impassioned call for housing policy that would finally incorporate Black families into American society. It was anything but colorblind. "Indirect approaches are no

---

[378] Strauss, Valerie (August 2, 2017; The Washington Post) "Actually, we still need affirmative action for African Americans in college admissions. Here's why."
[379] Strauss, Valerie (August 2, 2017; The Washington Post) "Actually, we still need affirmative action for African Americans in college admissions. Here's why."

substitute for a frontal attack on what is ailing us as a nation," she wrote, concluding that "the rest of society should stop fearing us [Blacks] and ordering themselves in a way that is designed to avoid us where we exist in numbers. America created slavery, Jim Crow, and the Black ghetto. America has shaped stereotypes grounded in fear of black people. ... America has to get beyond fear of black people and fear of difference to begin to order itself in a way that is consistent with its ideals." Convinced that race-based affirmative action is politically dead, Cashin seeks an alternative more palatable to white opponents. She concludes that race-based affirmative action gives unfair advantage to middle-class African Americans who don't need it, while low-income youth of all races do."[380]

It is sad but true that Black and Latin students are seriously underrepresented from an academic perspective. It was found that 16% of the nation's public-school students are Black, but only 9% of those students are enrolled in gifted and talented programs. Additionally, there are at least a quarter of high schools with the highest percentage of Black and Latin students where their schools do not offer Algebra II and it is a third of those schools that do not offer chemistry. So, when looking at these figures, it does not take a rocket scientist to see that these numbers do not add up.[381]

Another sad factor is that students of color are often disproportionately subjected to disciplinary actions in school. They are most often suspended or even expelled from school. And for those students who spend time in detention throughout the educational experiences, it causes them to fall further behind in their classwork and classroom time.

---

[380] Strauss, Valerie (August 2, 2017; The Washington Post) "Actually, we still need affirmative action for African Americans in college admissions. Here's why."
[381] Johns, David J. (2016) "Disrupting Implicit Racial Bias and Other Forms of Discrimination to Improve Access, Achievement, and Wellness for Students of Color." and The U.S. Department of Education Civil Rights Data Collection (2016).

Black students only represent 18% of the students that are enrolled in preschool however, there are 48% of preschool students who receive more than one out-of-school suspension. Studies also show that Blacks and minority students from kindergarten through high school are four times more likely to be suspended from school and twice as likely to be expelled than their White counterparts.[382]

Studies further reveal that Black males are approximately three times more likely (20%) to receive suspension from school than White males (6%), while Black girls are six times more likely (12%) to receive a suspension from school than While girls (2%). The study that was conducted by David J. Johns indicates that "the solution should be to end excessive discipline measures against students of color. And by solving some of these matters, Zero tolerance policies should be banned, schools should discourage suspensions and expulsions (especially for more subjective infractions such as willful defiance), schools should invest in counselors and professional development for teachers and leaders on how to best implement discipline, including the use of restorative justice, which creates a safe space for the accused and the affected to make amends amicably. Schools should also adopt trauma-informed approaches to school discipline such as 'What's wrong?' Instead of 'What's wrong with you?'[383]

When it comes to a Black or minority student and their ability to learn, societal attitudes should be so negative as the students "learning and development abilities are impaired by explicit and implicit biases, as well as overt racism. The stress of racial

---

[382] Johns, David J. (2016) "Disrupting Implicit Racial Bias and Other Forms of Discrimination to Improve Access, Achievement, and Wellness for Students of Color." and The U.S. Department of Education Civil Rights Data Collection (2016).
[383] Johns, David J. (2016) "Disrupting Implicit Racial Bias and Other Forms of Discrimination to Improve Access, Achievement, and Wellness for Students of Color." and The U.S. Department of Education Civil Rights Data Collection (2016).

discrimination also plays a big part in the child's learning ability that would explain the gaps in the Black and Latin students' performances compared to the performances of their White counterparts. Researchers found that the physiological response to two sources of race-based stressors leads the body to pump out more stress hormones in Black and Latin students:

- Perceived Discrimination: The perception that you will be treated differently or unfairly because of your race, or the color of your skin.
- Stereotype Threat: The stress of confirming negative expectations about your racial or ethnic group.
- The biological reaction to race-based stress is compounded by the psychological response to discrimination or the coping mechanisms that students of color develop to lessen the distress.
- Over time children develop strategies to reduce the racial stressors; however, these strategies have consequences for academic success.
- Students might cope by devaluing the importance of tests or deciding that doing well in school is not a part of their identity, which then affects academic performance.[384]

"We can't assume that every blocked opportunity leads someone retreating. In fact, I think the narrative and the arc around Black education is often finding

---

[384] Johns, David J. (2016) "Disrupting Implicit Racial Bias and Other Forms of Discrimination to Improve Access, Achievement, and Wellness for Students of Color." and The U.S. Department of Education Civil Rights Data Collection (2016).

success in spite of barriers." L 'Heureux Lewis-McCoy, associate professor of

sociology and Black Studies at the City College of New York.[385]

"Even today the motion picture has not quite outgrown its immaturity. It still uses talented Negro players to fit into the ~d stereotypes of the loving Mammy and comic servant..."

-Edith J. R. Isaacs *in "Theater Arts, "August 1942*

With the incarceration rates of Blacks, especially our Black males and the educational disadvantages that Blacks and other minorities endure, lets now focus on Blacks in the media. I cannot reiterate enough about how the media glamorizes the glitz and glamour of the negative aspects of Blacks and the Black community. When speaking about crimes in the Black community, the media use the most incriminating photos to demonize and discredit victims of color, yet, they display the positive photos of suspects and victims who are White. When we look at those last few mass murderers, all whom were White, they are personified by the media as being the good kid that would never harm a fly, so it is obvious that they have a mental illness. Yet those such as Chris Dorner are portrayed as an angry Black man who hates all Whites despite what he endured concerning his job and racism. The media also perpetuates an unequal representation which also affects how Blacks are perceived and the societal attitudes that many in mainstream has towards Blacks.

It has been a long time coming but during the 20th Century, there have several minorities who have made momentous advances towards their independence and equality in American society by achieving their American Dream. Again, because of the

---

[385] Johns, David J. (2016) "Disrupting Implicit Racial Bias and Other Forms of Discrimination to Improve Access, Achievement, and Wellness for Students of Color." and The U.S. Department of Education Civil Rights Data Collection (2016).

backlashes of slavery, oppression, the setbacks and suppressing of the Jim Crow era of segregation in the South that many minorities have endured, Blacks as well as other minorities still overcame. Blacks now have the ability to vote, own their own land and use some of the same public facilities as Whites. Such advances are part of who we as Blacks are in Americans, yet it seems as though Blacks still have not fully penetrated the collective whole of American society. Despite the achievements and the political rights and power that minorities have obtained over the years, there are those with the White supremacist ideologies and racist beliefs that were indoctrinated into the American psyche who still have the societal attitudes of negativity who can only be helped with prayer. Then there are those, because they choose to change and have begun to have an open window of perception who have just recently began to reverse such negative societal attitudes, slowly but surely. Sad but true, such negative ideologies have been ingrained in the mindset of Americans since the beginning of slavery.[386]

Such unethical ideologies are no longer the blatant practices that were once upheld by the law and celebrated with the atrocities of Blacks being beaten, tortured such as being tarred and feathered, mutilated, or lynched, but instead it is the subtle practice that is the "crown jewel" of the entertainment industry such as in the media and film industries. For such entities, mainstream may "not see the confederate flags that used to fly in parks during Sunday picnics or on days where Whites would take their children out of school just to see a lynching, nor will mainstream see the outward signs that relegated people colored to separate facilities, but what we do now see is minorities

---

[386] Horton, Yurii, Price, Raagen, and Brown, Eric "Blacks and the Media: Portrayal of Minorities in the Film, Media and Entertainment Industries." (Poverty & Prejudice: Media and Race; June 1, 1999)

who are casted on film with the negative images of being criminals, drug addicts, and undesirable leeches to "White upper-class" America. It is the Paramount Pictures, NBC's, ABC's and Universal Studios of the world who are the propagators of the negative stereotypes and unavoidable stigmas that many thought were once left behind; it is the negative stigmas of those who have been shackled for hundreds of years believing that the woes (chains) of segregation had been broken. Unfortunately, such ideologies are beginning to resurface in our sitcoms, newscasts and in big screen movies.[387]

As many people of color know and few in mainstream fell to realize is that historically, the portrayal of minorities in film and television has been less than ideal. Whether the roles of minorities are the negative images where minorities appear in disparaging roles or do not appear at all, minorities have always been the victims of an industry that relies on the old ideologies that are going to appeal to the "majority" at the expense of the insignificant minority.[388] Unfortunately, minorities cannot place all of the blame on White males who run the industry, because there are a small number of Blacks who are in the entertainment business who perpetuate such stereotypes as well. "Even though they defend their actions as an 'insiders look' into the life of a certain minority group, they are just as guilty of some of the same offenses that opponents have accused the media, film and entertainment industries of being guilty of.[389]

[387] Horton, Yurii, Price, Raagen, and Brown, Eric "Blacks and the Media: Portrayal of Minorities in the Film, Media and Entertainment Industries." (Poverty & Prejudice: Media and Race; June 1, 1999)
[388] Horton, Yurii, Price, Raagen, and Brown, Eric "Blacks and the Media: Portrayal of Minorities in the Film, Media and Entertainment Industries." (Poverty & Prejudice: Media and Race; June 1, 1999)
[389] Horton, Yurii, Price, Raagen, and Brown, Eric "Blacks and the Media: Portrayal of Minorities in the Film, Media and Entertainment Industries." (Poverty & Prejudice: Media and Race; June 1, 1999)

As Blacks, we cannot and should not contribute to the crude cycles that many in mainstream lack the ability to recognize when it comes to the unconscious racism of the media, film and entertainment industries. Instead, we as a Black community, need to begin by breaking such cycles and formulate a new industry that is more representative of the harsh realities that are perpetuated American society towards Blacks and other minorities today. In an earlier chapter of this book, I spoke of Oscar Micheaux, who was a Black man, an author, film director, and independent producer of more than 44 films. Even though his company, The Lincoln Motion Picture Company was short lived, it was one of the first movie company that was owned and controlled by Black filmmakers as he had become one of the most successful Black filmmakers of the first half of the 20th century.[390],[391]

You will continually hear me speak about how in 1619 slaves were being kidnapped from Africa and brought over to America to serve as lifetime indentured servants/slaves for generations upon generations. What is even more disturbing, and disgusting is that Blacks, whether from the Motherland or from the Americas have consistently been treated as second-class citizens since the inception of this country. They have been subjected to the evils and cruelties of a deeply rooted hate that this country was built upon. Blacks have never been treated as completely equal to Whites, and in many ways, they still are not completely treated as completely equal to Whites. There have always been the negative stereotypes of Blacks as being criminalistic, obtuse, lazy, dumb, foolish, cowardly, submissive, irresponsible, childish, violent, sub-human,

---

[390] The Lincoln Motion Picture Company, a First for Black Cinema. African American Registry. May 24, 2005. Retrieved September 8, 2018.
[391] Moos, Dan (2005) Outside America: Race, Ethnicity and the Role of the American West in National Belonging. University Press of New England. p. 53. Retrieved September 8, 2018.

and animal-like, and as such, societal attitudes continue to run rampant concerning these negative stereotypes. Such degrading stereotypes have not only been reinforced and enhanced by the negative portrayal of Blacks in the media, but they too are continually perpetuated today.[392]

Black characters have appeared in American films since the beginning of the industry in 1888. Unfortunately, Blacks were not even hired to portray themselves as Blacks in the early works of the film industry. Instead, White actors and actresses were hired to portray the characters of Blacks while in "blackface."[393] This is not surprising. So, by refusing to hire Black actors to portray themselves as Black characters, Whites always decided to portray Black characters in blackface as demeaning stereotypical characters who were always being created as Blacks who were presented in an unfavorable light.

When having a closed window of perception, think of societal attitudes, Blacks being negative, and then think of the original movie that was made in 1915 "Birth Of A Nation," by D.W. Griffith. In addition, then think about how Blacks were purposely portrayed in films with negative stereotypes that was reinforced by White supremacy concerning Blacks, and in many ways, this still happens today. This has had a tremendous effect on our society's view of Blacks since motion pictures. Such negativity has also had more of an impact on society and their attitudes towards Blacks than any other entertainment medium since 1888 (Sampson 1977; 1).[394]

---

[392] Horton, Yurii, Price, Raagen, and Brown, Eric "Blacks and the Media: Portrayal of Minorities in the Film, Media and Entertainment Industries." (Poverty & Prejudice: Media and Race; June 1, 1999)
[393] (http:/www.moderntimes.com/palace/black/open.htm).
[394] Horton, Yurii, Price, Raagen, and Brown, Eric "Blacks and the Media: Portrayal of Minorities in the Film, Media and Entertainment Industries." (Poverty & Prejudice: Media and Race; June 1, 1999)

Of course, for years, the media has always seemed to have set the tone for the morals, values, and images of American culture. There are those individuals who have yet to encounter Blacks or many other minorities, yet, because of ignorance and a deeply rooted fear that has been instilled within them based on a foundation of hate, these individuals believe that such degrading stereotypes of Blacks and other minorities are actually based on reality and not fiction. Think about all of the old school westerns and how they have portrayed, Native Americans, Asian Americans as well as African Americans, look at some of the characters that these individuals were portrayed as. It seems as though individuals such as these, and because of their ignorance, believed everything that were portrayed about minorities, especially about Blacks and because of such, they based their determination by what they saw and continue to see on television. It seems that after over a century, one-hundred and thirty years, since the making of movies, such atrocious stereotypes continue to plague Blacks and other minorities today, and until such negative images of Blacks and other minorities are extinguished from the media, it is sad to say that Blacks will always be regarded as second-class citizens and as other minorities will feel the effects of the negative stereotypes within the media as well.[395]

Even though, I have mentioned Oscar Micheaux in chapter 2, and spoke about him being a product of a single mother after his father's absence, I felt that it would be important to mention him and the history of African Americans in the media. There are many who often pay tribute to Micheaux as being the father of Black filmmakers. However, William D. Foster, also known as Bill Foster, began producing films just about

---

[395] Horton, Yurii, Price, Raagen, and Brown, Eric "Blacks and the Media: Portrayal of Minorities in the Film, Media and Entertainment Industries." (Poverty & Prejudice: Media and Race; June 1, 1999)

a decade earlier than Micheaux. Foster was a pioneering African-American film producer who was a very influential figure in the history of the Black film industry during the early 20th century, along with others such as Micheaux. Foster laid the groundwork for the modern Black film industry today.[396]

It was in 1910, Foster, who was a sports writer for the *Chicago Defender*, when he formed the Foster Photoplay Company, which was the first independent African-American film company. Even though many, especially today are not familiar with Foster's work, he was not a complete stranger to show business and the film industry. He was an actor, writer and worked under the stage name of Juli Jones. Foster also worked as a press agent for vaudeville stars such as Bert Williams and George Walker.[397]

Foster had a vision for the African-American community to do something that would be shed light from a positive perspective. Foster wanted his people to portray themselves as they wanted to be seen, and not as someone else depicted them. He was influenced by the Black theater community and wanted to break the racial stereotyping of Blacks in film.

The first film that Foster produced and directed was *"The Railroad Porter,"* which was released in 1912, and it is credited as being the world's first film with an entirely Black cast. The film is also credited with being the first to have a Black newsreel, featuring images of a YMCA parade. Foster's company then produced four more films that were silent shorts.[398] This film paid homage to the Keystone comic chases, while attempting to address the widespread and disparaging stereotypes of Blacks in the film

---

[396] "African American Cinema – Race movies." Film Reference.
[397] Mark A. Reid, *Redefining Black Film*. Berkeley and Los Angeles: University of California Press, 1993, p. 7.
[398] Gaines, Jane M. *Fire and Desire: Mixed-Race Movies in the Silent Era*. Chicago: University of Chicago Press, 2001, p. 95.

industry.[399] The types of films that were being portrayed by Whites in the film industry for Blacks were called "Race Films."

Similar to Blaxploitation movies, "Race film" was a designation that was applied to films that were produced for African-American audiences, between the years of 1910 and 1950. There were not too many of these films that survived because of the poor quality of production. Needless to say, that in the last 40 years, historians have painstakingly pieced together a thriving community of practice, and the contributions that have been made by Blacks of which is greatly indebted to many Whites.

Unfortunately, race films then became blaxploitation movies. Even though many of the roles that Blacks played in seemed to have been viewed as being more positive, they still portrayed Blacks as being docile slaves, loyal servants, mammies, caretakers, cooks, maids, butlers, yes men and women, later followed by uneducated, ghetto, welfare families who were caught up in a cycle of drugs and other criminalistic behaviors. Foster's films themselves, they drew upon the ability to uplift a movement, by telling a story. One example was in his film of a Pullman Porter (*The Railroad Porter*, 1913), it was about an esteemed position in the African-American community.[400]

However, there were those movies such as D.W. Griffith's "*Birth of a Nation*" (1915) which galvanized African-American writers, thinkers, and filmmakers. And even though the film, a box office record-breaker, this film was also very racist, as it depicted Blacks as being rapists during the Civil War and the Ku Klux Klan as heroes. Even though this movie was widely protested by the African-American community, Griffith's

---

[399] The Railroad Porter at IMDb
[400] See Allyson Nadia Field, "The Ambitions of William Foster: Entrepreneurial Filmmaking at the Limits of Uplift Cinema," in, by Barbara Lupack, Routledge Advances in Film Studies (New York: Routledge, 2016), 53–71.

"Birth of a Nation" sparked a number of filmic responses — most obviously *Birth of a Race* (1918), which was a famously troubled production that was conceived as a direct response to Griffith's film — but also, indirectly, a number of other thinkers and filmmakers.[401] The movie *"Birth of a Nation"* helped to give "a shared (though certainly not unified) purpose to a growing number of production companies that saw themselves as recuperating African-Americans' onscreen image, even as they were determined to turn a profit. Among these were the Lincoln Motion Picture Company (founded 1916), and — most famous of all race film companies — the Micheaux Film Corporation, founded in 1918 by author and filmmaker Oscar Micheaux."[402]

Moreover, race films only rarely received meaningful attention from the "mainstream" press. The widespread segregation of the motion-picture industry also meant that many funding channels, exhibition venues, and business opportunities were closed to African-American filmmakers. "Unequal development is a major factor in the construction and development of Black cinema," writes Clyde R. Taylor: "as much of an invisible hand in the making of the movie as any force of capitalism functioning silently in the marketplace."[403]

Even though Blacks have had many challenges in the film industry, race films have articulated narratives of the African-American community and an identity that moved audiences then, just as they continue to resonate with audiences now. In the films that survive, such as Micheaux's *Within Our Gates*, African-American life in the

---

[401] *George P. Johnson, Elizabeth Dixon, and Adelaide Tusler, George P. Johnson: Collector of Negro Film History (interview), Tape, July 11, 1967, http://oralhistory.library.ucla.edu/Browse.do?descCvPk=27283.*
[402] *George P. Johnson, Elizabeth Dixon, and Adelaide Tusler, George P. Johnson: Collector of Negro Film History (interview), Tape, July 11, 1967, http://oralhistory.library.ucla.edu/Browse.do?descCvPk=27283.*
[403] Clyde R. Taylor, "Black Silence and the Politics of Representation," in, ed. Pearl Bowser et al. (Bloomington: Indiana University Press, 2001

early part of the 20th century emerges as complex, contested, and fully realized. Rather than the "pickaninnies" and watermelons that populate films designed for White audiences, we see African-American characters deeply engaged in the political and intellectual life of the day, debating racial uplift and waging philanthropic campaigns even as they wrestle with the romantic torments typical of melodramas of the period. Before "race films," Blacks were viewed as being nothing more than "shufflin, shiny-faced, head-scratchin' simpletons whose eyes bugged out eyes as they leaned on brooms and spoke bad English," however, after the introduction of "race films," Blacks were depicted with more dignity and respect.[404]

Such portrayals of the Black community began to be shown in a more positive light as their films addressed some social concerns of the community. As you can see, this was done in order for Blacks and the Black community to ensure that they would have more positive roles as they tried to stop reinforcing the negative stereotypes about them through film, they had to do this by making their own movies.[405]

It is sad and unfortunate that there are still far too many movies, films and shows that portray minorities in negative ways and too few shows that deals with the reality of life. Even though there has been progress made in the way in which minorities are portrayed on television, we as a society still have a long way to go. What must be done is that the entertainment industry must be made aware of how it must illustrate the importance of the social responsibility that each and every member of American society

---

[404] http://www.moderntimes.com/palace/black/introduction.htm
[405] http://www.moderntimes.com/palace/black/introduction.htm

must come together in unity to ensure that television portrays minorities accurately and without bias.[406]

In the new wave and age of technology today, television has become an integral part of our society, which means that it is very imperative that the wrong ideas and values do not go across the airwaves and into the homes of unsuspecting young children. According to a report named *Reality in Television,* "Studies have shown that television teaches stereotypical attitudes and preconceptions about people and lifestyles that they would have no contact with outside of watching the way these people are shown by television." Unfortunately, in a time where children spends much of their time, now more than ever, watching television unsupervised, it is now the television who becomes the teacher.[407]

I must say that once such stereotypes and misconceptions have become ingrained in the psyche of our children here in American, then they become self-perpetuating. They do not have the ability to combat the effects of such a phenomenon, and what we have now done could essentially create an environment that is every bit as hostile as Jim Crow America and the segregated South. Given the fact that such remedies are extremes, but not without hope, and without changes in the media there is that plausibility that there could be such a disaster.[408]

Minorities today, more specifically African-Americans and Latino-Americans seems to still be the casualty of a media that perpetuates social stereotypes and ethnic

---

[406] Horton, Yurii, Price, Raagen, and Brown, Eric "Blacks and the Media: Portrayal of Minorities in the Film, Media and Entertainment Industries." (Poverty & Prejudice: Media and Race; June 1, 1999)
[407] Horton, Yurii, Price, Raagen, and Brown, Eric "Blacks and the Media: Portrayal of Minorities in the Film, Media and Entertainment Industries." (Poverty & Prejudice: Media and Race; June 1, 1999)
[408] Horton, Yurii, Price, Raagen, and Brown, Eric "Blacks and the Media: Portrayal of Minorities in the Film, Media and Entertainment Industries." (Poverty & Prejudice: Media and Race; June 1, 1999)

homogeneity. Movies, films, social media, television, books and magazines, and the news are all guilty of what most people would consider to be racist beliefs and acts. Despite the progress that has been made within the entertainment and media industry over the past few decades, these should be lessons learned of reforms that should produce results that are significantly more substantial than those that we have witnessed. It is only when we as a society have accomplished as such will our status as Blacks and as second-class citizens begin to evaporate.

In addition, I would also like to briefly touch on these factors about women in the media. Today there are more Black women in the media than ever working behind the scenes on television programs as writers, producers, and as directors. They are bringing out from the shadows the positive images that single Black mothers in real life are actually achieving unlike what societal attitudes wishes to display. Oprah Winfrey, although not a single Black mother, but she is a Black woman, was the first who entered into broadcasting and became a success. There were not many Black women who were involved in the behind the scenes or in front of the camera. During an interview with TV Week publication Winfrey said "...Had there not been a Civil Rights Movement, I would never have been able to be in broadcasting. I got my first job in broadcasting, unquestionably, with no doubt, because I was Black, and I was female."

At the age of 19, Oprah was hired as an anchor at a local TV station in Nashville, Tennessee. Oprah ended up moving to Chicago years later Oprah where she hosted "The Oprah Winfrey Show." Oprah had the opportunity to run her show from behind the scenes, as a producer and a writer, and in front of the camera as a host. It was her name and her face that inspired even more Black women to step out on faith, step up to the plate and get involved in the media industry. What was most important, is that Oprah became a role model not only for Black women, single women, but all women. There were more Black women who preferred to be single mothers, raise their children and also be successful without being in a relationship with their children's fathers. In today's society there are more Black women who are successful in obtaining white collar jobs, living in upper-class neighborhoods, and having more money to buy the things that they want. They now have the ability to turn an illusion of middle to upper class equality, self-determination and democratic ideals for single Black mothers into a reality. There are those single Black mothers who followed the money from product placement in television shows. They are able to now portray themselves from a more realistic perspective even though the media industry still have a long ways to go.

As with anything pertaining to Blacks, and other minorities and their societal advancements, American is still in a disarray. The plight of Black men still holds the highest incarceration rates (Coy, 2012), as they are reflected negatively in all forms of media, and, many of them have the lowest success rates in academics, and some their decision-making paths needs reviewing. It is stated that there are various reports regarding Black men and their issues that represents the conditions within the Black community. Crimes such as drug activity, gun violence, and mass incarceration plague the Black urban communities and represent the struggles that most Black men face on a daily basis as adults (Patton, 2012). This may be true for some Black and Latin males within the urban communities but it is does not have validation for all minorities within urban communities as they struggle to survive, pressing towards the mark of a higher calling, which is to better their condition.

According to Coy (2012), "the United States has the highest incarceration rate than any other country in the world. Now why is this? And with that being said, why are

300

those that are incarcerated primarily those of color? There are approximately 2.3 million people behind bars, mostly those of color. Coy (2012) states, that the statistics of agencies that are assigned to report the actual numbers do not know incorporate figures regarding incarcerated inmates. In addition, many of these numbers are either not reported or are skewed. It is sad to say that even today, there are more "people are in U.S. prisons than in the country's active duty military" (Coy, 2012). The exclusion of correct information regarding the penal system's inmates has a tremendous impact on the statistics regarding the inability of Black men to hold and maintain employment or higher education.

Also, according to Coy (2012), the current reports or surveys of many households exclude those households where family members are inmates. The reported figures for employment/population are bad enough, considering that their ages may range from 16 to 24, which is at 33% for Blacks as of August 2012 compared to 52% for Whites who were in the same age group. The numbers, skewed for both groups give an impression that is much better than it really is, yet these numbers do not account for those Black men who are actually incarcerated (Coy, 2012), on parole or probation. Therefore, with this being said, the prison system affects a Black men's ability to become academically fit for society. According to Hing (2014), race and disability plays a vital role in the school-to-prison pipeline.

Because race plays a vital role in the school-to-prison pipeline, there are several inequities that are affecting the lives of Black men, which include the biases within the American school system which places them at a great disadvantage creating an avenue that leads toward the penal system. In other words, the system is actually designed to create barriers to cause many minorities to fail. Such schools that are within

301

economically challenged areas, the inner-cities or the ghetto are not provided with the accurate tools that are needed in order for these children to succeed. As I go left just a little, if you think about the economic conditions of impoverished areas, don't you notice that there are more fast food restaurants and junk food places than there are grocery stores? Just an observation. So with all of this being said, without any type of behavioral intervention for students who are at risk or who are in trouble, or who miss school, or who have difficulty grasping certain educational concepts, or because there is a cultural difference in the teaching style of the teacher which disallows the minority student to grasp certain educational concepts, then many Black students move from school into the criminal justice system (Hing, 2014).

According to Hing (2014), during the 2011 school year, there were more than 3 million public school students who were suspended, with an additional 100,000 students who were expelled which were overwhelmingly Black. Warde (2008) found that most Black men who complete their bachelor's degrees have a worldview that is instilled in them concerning the importance of education. This is also not necessarily a worldview but a traditional view that is taught to most minorities, especially Blacks as it stemmed out of slavery. Remember, many Whites felt that as long as they kept Blacks in abject ignorance, then they would be able to control them. So, Whites made it a law that Blacks were not allowed to read or write and anyone caught teaching them would be severely punished if not killed. So, somewhat refute Warde's statement, it is not that it is a worldview ideology concerning the importance of having an education, it is an ideology that was instilled in Black individuals such as myself that stemmed from the atrocious cruelties of slavery.

302

As Hing (2014) reported, "according to the Department of Education, Black students' suspensions or expulsions happens at more than three times the rate of White students. With the exception of American Indians, no other racial group has had to experience the racial discipline or punishment so disproportionately. The U.S. Secretary of Education warned schools about the school-to-prison pipeline, stating, "Too many students are unnecessarily removed from schools through suspensions, expulsions, and other exclusionary discipline practices" (Hing, 2014). With this being said, let me use an example. My five-year-old granddaughter was being bullied, however, she did not know how to deal with her situation and was not comfortable telling an adult as she was always reprimanded by her teacher. So, instead of informing the teacher of her being bullied, she began acting out, instead of the teacher asking her what was wrong and dealing with the situation she gave this five-year-old child a referral and sent her to the principal's office who then recommended suspension. Before suspending my granddaughter, the principal decided to contact my daughter. My daughter, being an educator herself, asked my granddaughter what was the problem and told her to use her words instead of acting out. My granddaughter explained the situation and realized that it was the fault of the teacher as my granddaughter was not the only child in her class that was experiencing such disparages. With this being said, had my daughter, being in the field of education since she was 16 beginning as a cafeteria worker, not gotten to the root of the problem, the possibility of my granddaughter being suspended would have been another statistic for the negative individuals in mainstream to use against another Black individual. Currently, my granddaughter is being home schooled.

Now what about other Black and minority students who suffer similar situations beginning in preschool and do not have a support system such as my granddaughter who could articulate to both the child and the educator on how they can resolve such issues. Then there is that likelihood of the student dropping out of school, which in many cases increases the likelihood that some of them will end up in prisons (Hing, 2014). Hing (2014), however, states that there is a holistic approach that can be shared between the family and the community which helps to address such issues that children face before entering schools.

Once mainstream educators become aware of the external issues realizing that they may be the problem as the unconsciously display their inward biases and prejudices that many of these students have to deal with as the educator also understands the academic challenges that these students endure, then they will also realize that these academic challenges that are needed will help to curb at-risk behaviors that leads many of these students to prison, which means that an intervention must take place.

Even though the problems in academic achievement among Black male exist, there are several reports that also reveal that there are more Black males in prisons versus Black males that were enrolled in post-secondary education. In 2000 there were 829,000 Blacks in prison compared to 717,491; and in 2001 at 842,00 in prison compared to 712,724 enrolled in college. However, from 2002 through 2010, the numbers reversed with somewhat of an increase of those men enrolled in college compared to the number of Black men in prison[409].

According to Cook (2012), in summarizing a 2007 report from the *Washington Post (2011)*, there were more Black males who experienced being incarceration than

---

[409] BJS 2014, National Prisoner Statistic Program, Federal Justice Statistic Program 2010, National Corrections Reporting Program 2010, Survey of Inmates in State and Local Correctional Facilities 2010, and National Inmate Survey, 2010

those who experienced the opportunity of receiving a higher education. Such reports are the type of reports that misinform the public regarding Blacks and other minorities in the educational and the penal system today. Yet, there are those with the societal attitude that would rather remain talking about the negative aspects within the inner-city communities than trying to bring about change. So, for the Black male, being at risk for prison or involved in criminal activity presents the outcome of behavior that allows room for growth which begins at the earlier stages in their educational development. Within the family structure and family functioning, there is this belief system that propagates beyond the internal and external factors, while Black males may develop negative or positive ways of coping that extend beyond childhood.

To Be Young, Gifted and Black, So Don't Give Up On Your Dreams

Chapter 11

Oftentimes it is wondered why the term single Black mother is synonymous with the racial overtones and negative stereotypical myths of her being an abusive, drug addicted prostitute and welfare queen who only sees her children as an opportunity to obtain subsidized governmental assistance. As mentioned in an earlier chapter, during the 1970s and the Reagan era, the Black mother was also seen as one who only raised her children in the inner-city ghettos around the drugs and violence which creates Black on Black crimes. Society fails to realize that there is also White on White crime, and Brown on Brown crime just like there is Black on Black crime, the only reason why mainstream speaks more about Black on Black crime is because the media glamourizes Black on Black crime than any other culture in the nation. With it being assumed that because the Black woman is the cause for the deterioration of her community, then her daughters will follow in her footsteps while her sons, having no father figure, grows up to be a thug, or a drug dealing pimp or a wanna be a rapper or gang banger. This is one reason why Black mothers are viewed to be the worst mothers in existence.

Another thing that society fails to realize is that there are many young Blacks who are gifted, yet they are marginalized and pigeonholed into one category which depicts a negative connotation of all Blacks. For many Blacks, it is the evolution that embodies the frustrations that Blacks, especially Black males have while trying to cope in a racially unjust and economic system that promises them an advancement but oftentimes defers them from achieving many of their goals because of the color of their skin.

In the play, "A Raisin In the Sun," Walter Lee's sister, Beneatha, was an example of one who was a young, gifted, and intellectual Black woman who aspired to participate fully in the American culture. She as well as Asagai, demonstrated the Africanist intellect as she strived to remember her African roots. Asagai, was also a gifted, and intellectual Black man who aspired to participate fully in his African culture as he shared it with his American Black culture.

Lorraine Hansberry was a talented young gifted and Black woman who also aspired to participate in the American culture while also trying to connect with her African culture. Her upbringing was that of a middle-class Black family with activist foundations. She was the "granddaughter of a slave and the niece of a prominent African-American professor."[410] Hansberry grew up with a profound awareness of her culture concerning African-American history and the ongoing struggle for civil rights. In 1938 Hansberry's family moved to an all-White neighborhood in Chicago. Having to deal with discrimination and racism, the family suffered violent attacks from their White neighbors, who had signed a restrictive covenant to exclude Black families from their community.

---

[410] Jumper, Alexandra, "*A Raisin in the Sun*." LitCharts LLC, October 17, 2013. Retrieved July 30, 2018. https://www.litcharts.com/lit/a-raisin-in-the-sun.

Hansberry's family was determined to fight a good fight against racism by exercising their rights for "life, liberty, and the pursuit of happiness" as they fought the covenant all the way to the Supreme Court, which ruled in favor of the Hansberry's in 1940. Hansberry then attended the University of Wisconsin for several years before dropping out and moving to New York in 1950 to pursue writing and social activism. Hansberry's best-known work was, *A Raisin in the Sun*, which premiered in 1959, making her the first African-American female playwright to have a play produced on Broadway. She died suddenly of pancreatic cancer at 34, in 1965.[411]

For those of you who do not know about Jim Crow Laws, they were statutes and ordinances that were established between 1874 and 1975 to separate the White and Black races in the American South. More than 50 years after the Civil War, especially in the 1920s and 30s, the discriminatory "Jim Crow" laws in the South prompted many African Americans to relocate to Northern cities, as they looked to the North as a land of opportunity. This movement was called the Great Migration. Nonetheless, while the North did not have such laws demanding policies of segregation be followed, such discriminatory practices also persisted also in the North, which led to the segregation of housing, education, and employment. So, in 1949 the United States Congress passed the National Housing Act which was to address the substandard housing conditions thereby providing adequate and more integrated housing options for minorities. In 1954 the Supreme Court ruled in *Brown v. Board of Education* also stated that school segregation was unconstitutional.[412] Even though such discriminatory practices existed,

---

[411] Jumper, Alexandra. "*A Raisin in the Sun*." LitCharts LLC, October 17, 2013. Retrieved July 30, 2018. https://www.litcharts.com/lit/a-raisin-in-the-sun.
[412] Jumper, Alexandra. "*A Raisin in the Sun*." LitCharts LLC, October 17, 2013. Retrieved July 30, 2018. https://www.litcharts.com/lit/a-raisin-in-the-sun.

it did not stop those such as Hansberry from pursuing their dreams and sharing their story through their craft. Young, gifted and Black.

In 1969 Nina Simone performed a song in memory of her late friend Lorraine Hansberry titled, "To Be Young, Gifted and Black." Even though the song was written in the late 1960s and not during the Harlem Renaissance, it carried many of the same themes as those themes from the Harlem Renaissance. What this song demonstrated, and continues to demonstrate today to mainstream society, is that there are Blacks who are young, gifted and Black. It says to a wider society, "hey, White America, guess what, I have talent also, I may be young and Black, but understand, we are not all alike." In her song, Simone is celebrating all of the "billions" of Black youth who have untapped talent or what one may call, an individual with unbound talent, as she tells them not to back down from their gifts and talents or give up on their dreams. She continues to say that "there's a world out there that is waiting for [them]" and that their "quest[s]" has only just begun.

As the song represents a certain theme of the Harlem Renaissance it shows in this song a sense of pride. Simone even states that, "we can all be proud to say to be young gifted and Black." Even though this song was written in the 1960s, when Blacks were still being oppressed, and still fighting for equal rights, this song illustrated an intense passion and pride in the Black culture. Even today, it also shows the theme of identification concerning race.[413] Simone uses the collective "we" in this song, thereby showing a strong connection to her race, while celebrating the happiness of being Black and gifted.

---

[413] Jumper, Alexandra. "*A Raisin in the Sun*." LitCharts LLC, October 17, 2013. Retrieved July 30, 2018. https://www.litcharts.com/lit/a-raisin-in-the-sun.

To demonstrate being young, gifted and Black, *"Mother to Son"* was also a project that Hansberry worked on which was originally titled as a play called, *The Crystal Stair*, which was a name that, like *A Raisin in the Sun*, comes from a Langston Hughes poem. The poem, which is one that I have used earlier in this book, called "Mother to Son," speaks to the hardships that many African-American families have faced: "Well, son, I'll tell you: / Life for me ain't been no crystal stair / . . . But all the time / I'se been a-climbin' on."[414] It demonstrates how the mother speaks specifically to her son as she deals with the turmoil, trials and tribulations concerning slavery, the ripping apart of families and the lynching of friends and loved ones. Even during a time of endured hardships, many slaves were also young, gifted, and of course Black in their own right.

To be young, gifted and Black is to be like the Black women and men who are unknown, or who mainstream takes forever learning about, such as those in "Hidden Figures" who were mostly physicists and mathematicians. These were mostly Black women, who were also Black mothers. For those who were part of the "Hidden Figures" era during World War II, it was the Jim Crow laws that hindered their growth but did not break their spirits and deter them from moving forward and succeeding.

Something that society has refused to accept is that there is a double standard when it comes to the issue of segregation, discrimination and racism and making America great again, as it focuses on just certain groups while leaving many groups at bay. History, consistently repeating itself has demonstrated this time and time again since after the Civil War. Right after WWII, there was a concern globally about the "Cold War" between the United States and the Soviet Union which at that time had intensified

---

[414] Jumper, Alexandra. "*A Raisin in the Sun.*" LitCharts LLC, October 17, 2013. Retrieved July 30, 2018. https://www.litcharts.com/lit/a-raisin-in-the-sun.

as people began making bomb shelters in order to protect themselves just in case Russia dropped a nuclear bomb.[415] "Yet as the United States dedicated itself to fighting the spread of Communist oppression around the world, there were many Black Americans, including many at the National Advisory Committee for Aeronautics (the NACA) who wondered why at the same time the United States perpetuated the oppression of African-Americans on its own soil.[416] Being young, gifted and Black did not afford one the same opportunities and privileges as those of mainstream society, yet even today, many in mainstream still turns a blind eye to the cruelties of the disease that plagues this country called racism.

To be young, gifted and Black meant that for decades, children who were viewed or identified as being gifted was based particularly by race which was usually the White race. If you were a youth of color, regardless of how gifted you were, this meant that you were in the percentile that was going to be underrepresented in programs that were designed for gifted youth who were White students. The real reasons for such underrepresentation is actually not poorly understood by those of color, it is poorly understood by those within mainstream society who refuse to acknowledge that America has a problem with racism and discrimination as they set themselves on a pedestal for being superior compared to other races.

For decades, not just Black students but minority students as a whole had been told that they were not intellectual enough to further their educational aspirations or pursue certain careers and always directed towards those positions that many in

---

[415] Jumper, Alexandra. "*A Raisin in the Sun*." LitCharts LLC, October 17, 2013. Retrieved July 30, 2018. https://www.litcharts.com/lit/a-raisin-in-the-sun.
[416] Jumper, Alexandra. "*A Raisin in the Sun*." LitCharts LLC, October 17, 2013. Retrieved July 30, 2018. https://www.litcharts.com/lit/a-raisin-in-the-sun.

mainstream refused to take. In 1939, there was an experiment that was conducted called the "Clark Doll Experiment." This was an experiment that was conducted by Dr Kenneth Clark and his wife Dr. Mamie Phipps Clark, both whom were Black psychologist. What they did was they asked Black children to choose between a Black doll and a White doll. The study was conducted in order view children's attitudes towards race. The dolls that were used in this experiment were the same except for their skin color, however, most of the children thought that the White dolls were nicer.

The Clark's were known for their doll experiments during the 1940s and "testified as expert witnesses in the Briggs v. Elliott (1952), which was one of five cases combined into the Brown v. Board of Education (1954). Because of the work that they had previously conducted over the years, the Clarks' work contributed to the ruling of the U.S. Supreme Court in which it determined that *de jure racial segregation* in public education was unconstitutional. Chief Justice Earl Warren wrote in the *Brown v. Board of Education* opinion, "To separate them from others of similar age and qualifications solely because of their race generates a feeling of inferiority as to their status in the community that may affect their hearts and minds in a way unlikely to ever be undone."[417] Again, with such a landmark decision, to be young, gifted and Black, did not deter many Blacks from moving forward and dismissing the logic that they were incapable of obtaining their goals by living out their dreams.

This 1954 landmark decision in Brown v. Board of Education and the Clark's doll experiment helped in persuading the American Supreme Court that "separate but equal" schools for Blacks and Whites were anything but equal in practice and therefore was

---

[417] Ludy T. Benjamin, Jr. *A Brief History of Modern Psychology*, pp.193-195. Blackwell Publishing (2007). ISBN 978-1-4051-3205-3

against the law. It was the beginning of the end of Jim Crow. During this experiment, it was unfortunate that because Black children had experienced such cruelties based on their skin color, they felt that the Black doll was the bad one. In 1950 44% said the White doll looked like them! In past tests, however, many children would refuse to pick either doll or just start crying and run away.[418]

In one of the studies that the Clark's conducted was the testing of 300 children in different parts of the country. Kenneth found that Black children who went to segregated schools, or those who were separated by race, were more likely to pick the White doll as being the nicer one. In the test that he conducted in 1950 that was used for *Brown v Board*, he asked 16 black children in Clarendon County, South Carolina, the same question that he asked the 300 children. Of these 16 children, there were 63% who said that the White doll was the nicer one and preferred to play with the White doll.

While conducting this same experiment, Clark also asked children to color a picture of themselves in order to identify themselves based on the color of their skin. Many of the children chose a color that was a shade lighter than themselves.[419] Sad to say but "these findings exposed internalized racism in African-American children, self-hatred that was more acute among children attending segregated schools. This research also paved the way for an increase in psychological research into areas of self-esteem and self-concept."[420] Such internalization cannot be reiterated enough to mainstream society of the affects that racism has upon minorities, especially Blacks.

---

[418] Dweck, Carol S. (2009). *Prejudice: How It Develops and How It Can Be Undone*. Switzerland: Karger. doi:10.1159/000242351
[419] Clark, Kenneth; Mamie Clark (1950). "The Negro child in the American social order". *The Journal of Negro Education*. **19** (3): 341–350. JSTOR 2966491.
[420] O'Connell, Agnes (January 1, 1990). *Women in Psychology*. Greenwood Publishing Group.

It was in 2005, when filmmaker, Kiri Davis repeated the experiment as the Clarks in Harlem as part of her short but excellent film, "A Girl Like Me." During her experiment, and despite the changes that had occurred in some parts of society over the decades, Davis found the same results as did the Drs. Clark had found while conducting their studies of the late 1930s and early 1940s. In the original experiment(s), the majority of the children choose the White dolls. When Davis repeated the experiment, there were 15 out of 21 children who also choose the White dolls over the Black dolls. "In an alternative interpretation of the Clark doll experiments, Robin Bernstein has recently argued that the children's rejection of the Black dolls could be understood not as victimization or an expression of internalized racism but instead as resistance against violent play involving Black dolls, which was a common practice when the Clarks conducted their tests.[421]

However, being a Black woman, and mother of two sons, I would only partially agree with Bernstein, except for the fact that as Black children usually encounter issues with self-hate and low self-esteem at an early age, whether directly or indirectly (indirectly because they have observed the hatred of racism) is because of their experience as a victim of racism and violence. For Davis, even though her experiment was not a huge sample size, the truth of the matter was that society had changed, but really had not changed, and for those who are minority, it is not shocking to still see how easily many of these children could choose the White doll compared to the Black doll. Look at how society socially treats Blacks today with the same practices of institutional racism.

---

[421] Robin Bernstein, _Racial Innocence: Performing American Childhood from Slavery to Civil Rights,_ (New York: New York University Press, 2011), 235-242.

In 2009 after Obama became President, the Clark experiment was again conducted on "Good Morning America" in which ABC conducted the test. It was asked of 19 Black children from Norfolk, Virginia the same questions that were asked since 1939. It is hard to compare their numbers because they allowed "both" and "neither" as an answer. They also asked the last question first, making it far easier to answer: 88% of these children said that the Black doll looked most like them. ABC then added an additional question as well: "Which doll is pretty?" The boys said both, but 47% of the Black girls said the that the White doll was the pretty one.[422]

To be young, gifted and Black means that society consistently instills the negative ideologies in minority children that being White is the superior race and that minority children lack the capacity to think in the same manner or beyond that of their White counterparts; and that in order to compete and surpass such a myth, all minority children, but especially Black children have to work 200 times as hard just to be close to their counterparts in intellect. It has been constantly demonstrated that no one race is more superior to another race as God created us all in His image. Additionally, it has also been demonstrated that there are those who are just as intellectual if not more than many of their Caucasian peers.

The doll test for many minority children and the end results of each similar study that has been conducted over the years are proof that such debilitating factors of racism can be mentally and psychologically overwhelming for any individual, especially a child. Because of such psychological and adverse effects that racism has on Blacks either because their skin color, their environment, their social status or their economic

---

[422] Clark, Kenneth; Mamie Clark (1950). "The Negro child in the American social order". *The Journal of Negro Education*. **19** (3): 341–350. JSTOR 2966491

conditions, the resources that are provided for Blacks and other minorities for mental health are limited. At one point, Mamie Clark found that there were insufficient psychological services[423] for minority children and that society's segregation was the cause for gang warfare, poverty, and low academic performance of minorities children.[424]

---

[423] Butler, Stephen. "Mamie Katherine Phipps Clark (1917–1983)". The Encyclopedia of Arkansas History & Culture. Retrieved 2014-04-24.
[424] O'Connell, Agnes (January 1, 1990). *Women in Psychology*. Greenwood Publishing Group.

Bibliography

Angelou, Maya. I Know Why the Caged Bird Sings. New York: Bantam, 1993.

Arnesburg, Liliane K. "Death as a Metaphor of Self in I Know Why the Caged Bird Sings." CLA Journal 20.2 (1976): 273-291.

Baker, Narviar Cathcart, and Joseph Hill. "Restructuring African-American Families in the 1990s." *Journal of Black Studies* Sept. 1996: 77-93

Benesch, Klaus. "Oral Narrative and Literary Text: Afro-American Folklore in Their Eyes Were Watching God." Callaloo 36 (1988): 627-35.

Block, Alex Ben. "Oprah On The Record." *Television Week*. Chicago. 19 APR 2004. S6-12

Boehmer, Elleke. Colonial & Postcolonial Literature. New York: Oxford UP, 1995.

Bolden, Tonya. Tell All the Children Our Story: Memories and Mementoes of Being Young and Black in America. New York: Henry A. Abrams, 2002.

Brodsky, A. E. (2000). The role of religion in the lives of resilient, urban, African American, single mothers. *Journal of Community Psychology, 28,* 199–219.

Brodsky, A. E., & DeVet, K. A. (2000). "You have to be real strong": Parenting goals and strategies of resilient, urban, African American, single mothers. *Journal of Prevention and Intervention in the Community, 20,* 159–178.

Carby, Hazel V. Reconstructing Womanhood. New York: Oxford UP, 1987

Carson, J. E. (2004). *Life histories of successful Black males reared in absent father families* (Unpublished doctoral dissertation). The University of Toledo, Toledo, OH.

317

Cherlin, A. J. (2006). On single mothers "doing" family. *Journal of Marriage and Family, 68,* 800–803.

Clarke, Deborah. "'The Porch Couldn't Talk for Looking': Voice and Vision in Their Eyes are Watching God." African American Review 35.4 (2001): 599-613.

Cosby, Biba and Alvin F. Poussant. "Unwed father." *Michigan Citizen,* 30.9 (19 Jan 2008)

Creswell, J. W. (2007). *Qualitative inquiry & research design choosing among five approaches* (2nd ed.). Thousand Oaks, CA: Sage.

DeBell, M. (2008). Children living without their fathers: Population estimates and indicators of educational well-being. *Social Indicators Research, 87,* 427–443. doi:10.1007?s11205-007-9149-8

Deborah Roempke Graefe and Daniel T. Lichter. " Marriage Among Unwed Mothers: Whites, Blacks, and Hispanics Compared," *Perspectives on Sexual and Reproductive Health* 34.6 (Nov/Dec 2002) 286-293

Douglass, Frederick. Narrative of the Life of Frederick Douglass, an American Slave, Written by Himself. Gates. 387-452.

Douglas, Susan J., and Meredith W. Michaels. "The War Against Welfare Mothers." *The Idealization of Motherhood and How It has Undermined All Women: The Mommy Myth.* New York: Free Press, 2004. 173-202.

Ferguson, Sally Ann. "Folkloric Men and Female Growth in Their Eyes Were Watching God." Black American Literature Forum 21.1/2 (1987): 185-197. Gates, Henry Louis Jr. The Norton Anthology of African American Literature, 2nd ed. New York: Norton, 2004.

Gates, Henry Louis Jr. The Signifying Monkey. New York: Oxford UP, 1988.

Giddings, Paula. When and Where I Enter: The Impact of Black Women on Race and Sex in America. New York: Perennial, 2001.

Giorgi, A. (2008). Concerning a serious misunderstanding of the essence of the phenomenological method in psychology. *Journal of Phenomenological Psychology, 39,* 33–58.

Green, B. L., Furrer, C., & McAllister, C. (2007). How do relationships support parenting? Effects of attachment style and social support on parenting behavior in an at-risk population. *American Journal of Community Psychology, 40,* 96–108. doi:10.1007/s10464-007-9127-y

Haleman, D. L. (2004). Great expectations: Single mothers in higher education. *International Journal of Qualitative Studies in Education, 17,* 769–784. doi:10.1080/0951839042000256448

Hill, Lee Alan. "Mission Possible." Television Week. Chicago. 19 APR 2004. S2

Hill, Shirley A. "Class, Race, and Gender: Dimensions Of Child Rearing In African-American Families." *Journal of Black Studies* 31.4 (Mar 2007): 494-508

Hilton, J. M., & Desrochers, S. (2000). The influence of economic strain, coping with roles, and parental control on the parenting of custodial single mothers and custodial single fathers. *Journal of Divorce & Remarriage, 33,* 55–76.

Holland, R. (2009). Perceptions of mate selection for marriage among African American, college-educated, single mothers. *Journal of Counseling & Development, 87,* 170–178.

Hooks, Bell. *Where We Stand: Class Matter.* New York. Great Britain: Routledge. 2000

Hurston, Zora Neale. "Characteristics of Negro Expression." Gates. 1041-53.

Hurston, Zora Neale. Their Eyes Were Watching God. New York: HarperCollins, 1998.

Jackson, A. P., & Scheines, R. (2005). Single mothers' self-efficacy, parenting in the home environment, and children's development in a two-wave study. *Social Work Research, 29,* 7–20.

Jackson, Aurora P. "Black, Single, Working Mothers in Poverty: Preference for Employment, Well-being, and Perceptions of Preschool-Aged Children." Social Work. Vol. 28: January 1993: 26-33.

Johnson, R. B. (1997). Examining the validity structure of qualitative research. *Education, 118,* 282–292.

Johnson-Garner, M. Y., & Meyers, S. A. (2003). What factors contribute to the resilience of African-American children within kinship care? *Child & Youth Care Forum, 32,* 255–269.

Jones, D. J., Zalot, A. Z., Foster, S. E., Sterrett, E., & Chester, C. (2007). A review of childrearing in African American single mother families: The relevance of a co-parenting framework. *Journal of Child and Family Studies, 16,* 671–683. doi:10.1007/s10826-006-9115-0

Kent, George E. "Maya Angelou's I Know Why the Caged Bird Sings and Black Autobiographical Tradition." Kansas Quarterly 3 (1975): 72-8. Mule of the World 29

King, Sigrid. "Naming and Power in Zora Neale Hurston's Their Eyes Were Watching God." Black American Literature Forum 24.4 (1990): 683-96.
Marin, Peter. "Virginia's Trap." Mother Jones. July/Aug. 1992: 54-59.

Kotchick, B. A., Dorsey, S., & Heller, L. (2005). Predictors of parenting among African American single mothers: Personal and contextual factors. *Journal of Marriage and Family, 67,* 448–460.

Ledford, E. M. (2010). *Young black single mothers and the parenting problematic: The church as model of family and as educator* (Doctoral dissertation). Available from ProQuest Dissertations and Theses database. (UMI No. 3395082)

Lichter, S; Amundson, Daniel. *Center for Media and Public Affairs,* Don't Blink: Hispanics in Television Entertainment. April, 1996.

Lichter, S; Amundson, Daniel. *Center for Media and Public Affairs,* Distorted Reality: Hispanic Characters in TV Entertainment. June, 1997.

Lincoln, Y. S., & Guba, E. G. (1985). *Naturalistic inquiry.* Beverly Hills, CA: Sage.

McAdoo (Ed.), *Black children* (pp. 175–189). Thousand Oaks, CA: Sage.

Maxwell, J. A. (2005). *Qualitative research design: An interactive approach.* Thousand Oaks, CA: Sage.

Meisenhelder, Susan. "False Gods and Black Goddesses in Naylor's Mama Day and Hurston's Their Eyes Were Watching God." Callaloo 23.4 (2000). 1440-8.

Miles, M. B., & Huberman, A. M. (1994). *Qualitative data analysis: An expanded sourcebook* (2nd ed.). Thousand Oaks, CA: Sage.

Millner, Denene. "Black Women in Hollywood: Diahann Carroll." *Essence Magazine* (Mar 2009)

Morrissette, P. (1999). Phenomenological data analysis: A proposed model for counselors. *Guidance and Counseling, 15,* 2–7.

Moustakas, C. (1994). *Phenomenological research methods*. Thousand Oaks, CA: Sage.
"Mule." 1998. American Donkey and Mule Society. 9 Feb 2007.
<http://www.kyhorsepark.com/imh/bw/mule.html> "Mule." OED Online 2nd Ed.
1989. Oxford English Dictionary. 9 Feb 2007. <oed.com>

Naylor, Gloria. "A Question of Language." 75 Thematic Readings: An Anthology. New
York: McGraw-Hill, 2003. 22-5.

Noble, Peter. The Negro in Films Kennikat Press: New York. 1969 { 1948]
Rhines, Jesse Algeron. Black Film White Money Rutgers University Press: New Jersey.
1996

Olson, Laura Katz. "What Ever Happened to June Cleaver?" The Fifties Mom Turns
Eighty." *Race, Gender& Class* Jan 2003:129+

Onwuegbuzie, A. J. (2003). Expanding the framework of internal and external validity
in quantitative research. *Research in the Schools, 10,* 71–90.

Onwuegbuzie, A. J., & Leech, N. L. (2007). Validity and quantitative research: An
oxymoron? *Quality & Quantity: International Journal of Methodology, 14,* 233–249.

Osborne, J. W. (1990). Some basic existential–phenomenological research methodology
for counsellors. *Canadian Journal of Counselling, 24,* 79–91.

Social Eugenics and Welfare Policy." *Race, Gender, and Class* 10:1 (31 Jan 2003) **11+**

Richardson, G. E. (2002). The metatheory of resilience and resiliency. *Journal of
Clinical Psychology, 58,* 307–321.

Rivers, S. W., & Rivers, F. A. (2002). Sankofa Shule spells success for African American children. In H. P.

Rochon, Michael J. "Conference to Provide Insight On Motherhood," *The Philadelphia Tribune* 114.13 (24 Apr 1998): 1

Rowe, D. M. (2007). Marriage and fathering: Raising our children within the context of family and community. *The Black Scholar, 37,* 18–22.

Sampson, Henry T. Blacks in Black and White: A source Book on Black Films The Scarecrow Press, Inc.: Metuchen, New Jersey. 1977

Smith, Sidonie Ann. "The Song of a Caged Bird: Maya Angelou's Quest after Self-Acceptance." The Southern Humanities Review (1973): 365-75.

Spradley, J. P. (1979). *The ethnographic interview.* San Diego, CA: Harcourt.

Terdiman, Richard. Discourse/Counter-Discourse: The Theory and Practice of Symbolic Resistance in Nineteenth-Century France. Ithaca: Cornell UP, 1985.

Thornton-Dill, Bonnie. "The Means to Put My Children Through: Child-Rearing Goals and Strategies among Black Female Domestic Servants." Socialization. 1980: 191-200. Truth, Sojourner. "Ar'n't I a Woman." Gates. 246-9.

Turner, H. A. (2007). The significance of employment for chronic stress and psychological distress among rural single mothers. *American Journal of Community Psychology, 40,* 181–193. doi:10.1007/s10464-007-9141-0

Van Kaam, A. (1959). Phenomenal analysis. Exemplified by a study of the experiences of "really feeling understood." *Journal of Individual Psychology, 15,* 66–72.

Van Kaam, A. (1966). *Existential foundations of psychology*. Lanham, MD: University Press of America

Walker, Alice. In Search of Our Mother's Gardens. New York: Harcourt, 1983.
Walker, Pierre A. "Racial protest, identity, words, and form in Maya Angelou's I Know Why the Caged Bird Sings." College Literature 22.3 (1995). 91-101.

Wall, Cheryl A. "Mules and Men and Women: Zora Neale Hurston's Strategies of Narration and Visions of Female Empowerment." Black American Literature Forum 23.4 (1989): 661-80.

Warde, B. (2008). Staying the course: Narratives of African American males who have completed a baccalaureate degree. *Journal of African American Studies, 12,* 59–72. doi: 10.1007/s12111-007-9031-4

Washington, Booker T. Up From Slavery. Gates. 572-602.

Welter, Barbara. "The Cult of True Womanhood: 1820-1860." American Quarterly 18.2 (1966): 151-74.

Wilson, A. D., & Henriksen, R. C. (2012). The lived experience of Black collegiate males with absent fathers: Another generation. *Journal of Professional Counseling: Practice, Theory, & Research, 39,* 29–39.

Wilson, A. D., & Henriksen, R. C. (2013). Moral development and the phenomenon of absent fathers. In B. J. Irby, G. Brown, & R. Lara-Alecio (Eds.), *Handbook of educational theories.* Charlotte, NC: Information Age.

Woody, D., & Woody, D. J. (2007). The significance of social support on parenting among a group of single, low-income, African American mothers. *Journal of Human Behavior in the Social Environment, 15,* 183–198. doi:10.1300/J137v15n02_11

Made in the USA
Columbia, SC
30 July 2023

20925299R00178